The Sound of Tuning Out

SHANE W. O'HAIRE

Copyright © 2024 by Shane W. O'Haire

All rights reserved.

No portion of this book may be reproduced in any form without written permission from the publisher or author, except as permitted by U.S. copyright law.

To A.K., you may not have written this book, but you are the reason it exists.

PART ONE

Caleb Bodkin
Jul 16

My phone pings, I check the home screen to find a notification from LIV: **Full_Metal_Jake** has a new story.

This can't be. My brother cannot be posting this. My finger hovers over Jake's profile picture for a few seconds before I click on it to view his new LIV story. It begins to load and I realize I'm shaking.

There is nothing scary about the story. I've seen it before. Jake took this video about two years ago when he was fifteen and the five black hairs on his chin had made their debut, or as he called them, his "beard." I made fun of him for two weeks until he gave up and shaved it. It was the summer I graduated from Berkeley, and I was staying with my parents until September, when my MBA program was scheduled to start that fall. With a lot of time on my hands, tormenting my little brother was my favorite thing to do.

The mundane nature of the video makes it so eerie to watch now. The story shows Jake sitting in his room wearing his Iron Maiden T-shirt, holding his favorite guitar, the Blue Burst Dean ML 1981. I don't know much about guitars, or any musical instruments, but Jake would talk my ear off about a topic I wasn't remotely interested in until I became an expert. Jake is playing the solo from a song by Pantera, his favorite band. The short video ends there.

I miss him...

He is not away on vacation with his friends like he was planning to do this summer.

Jake's been dead for three days now.

A tiny part of me is thankful, though, because the story doesn't show him sitting in our garage where he died. I can't bear to look in its direction. The garage was Jake's den. He spent most of his time there, either practicing for an upcoming show with his band, or creating content for his YouTube channel.

Local YouTuber Dies at Family Home Unexpectedly, the local papers wrote.

Was it really unexpected? I mean, what did we really expect when we agreed to watching him do that silly stunt over and over again?!

Still, the sight of this story is disturbing, sad, and sickening.

I take a screenshot and text Emily:

"Did you do this?"

Three minutes later, my phone vibrates with a response:

"I thought it was you, or Andy," Emily texts back. "Who do you think it is?" She continues nonstop "And wtf! Why'd you think it was me?"

She is so quick with her texting.

I understand why she might be offended that I think she's the person who stole Jake's account, but honestly, she's the bigger asshole here because I'm distressed and not thinking straight. I don't respond.

Emily is Jake's girlfriend. In my defense, she is my number one suspect because she is the typical attention-hungry teen girl, social-media addict, the human form of everything annoying about Gen Z, and therefore an excellent candidate upon whom to take out all my anger. She is annoying enough, privileged enough, and present enough.

Then again, maybe this identity thief is someone from Jake's high school, a friend, an acquaintance, or a secret admirer. Especially since LIV is mostly popular among teens and college kids.

I go next door to Jake's room to check his phone; I punch in his birthday and go to LIV; he's signed out of his account.

Weird ... but I'll worry about that some other time.

Who else is sick or stupid enough to hack into a dead guy's LIV account? Someone who thinks invading Jake's privacy after he ceased to exist is a good idea, a cute, fun tribute, or a comforting act.

It's none of the above!

"Thanks for posting this tribute. He was so talented," one of Jake's classmates messages me.

That's it! I am not going to sit back and let everyone think I am this irresponsible, irrational, and inconsiderate asshole.

As I walk back to my room, I press on the three dots in the right corner and choose "Report."

"Why are you reporting this post?" LIV asks. A list of options follows the question, none of which includes, "Someone is stealing my dead brother's identity," so I choose "False information."

However, reporting this content is not nearly enough. This intruder must be denied any digital identity. So, I decide to follow it up with a "Request to Remove Account of Deceased User" and a complaint email to the LIV customer service team in which I ask them to stop the activity on Jake's account, investigate the matter further, and take the necessary steps to prevent any similar future actions by inconsiderate jerks.

The heartbreak of admitting that my little brother is no longer an active member of the online community and will remain inactive forever makes my chest feel too tight and leaves me fighting for breath. In this moment, I realize that the reality of my loss is starting to seep through my daily routine. It's hard to admit it to myself, and then to put it in writing is like admitting my defeat in this battle against my own grief.

How am I supposed to carry my tone? Emotional? Matter-of-fact? Like he is just another lost account; it's business as usual?

Life doesn't go on the way we think it will after we lose someone we love and care about deeply. We take a detour, thinking that one day we are going to end up back on the main road. But the truth is that we unlock a new area on the map, and things never go back to the way they were.

I hit "send" on my phone, and then I lie awake on my old bed, thinking about the reality of the situation, tears blurring my vision. This simple process of reporting the story magnified my anguish. I can hardly breathe. This much stress is not good for someone in my condition, and it just occurred to me that I haven't taken my supplements today. I have to do it because my parents don't have the strength to deal with my fragility at the moment.

I can already guess what the response from the LIV customer service team is gonna sound like. "We are sorry for your loss … we apologize for the inconvenience and for failing to protect your dead brother's privacy … we will take the necessary action…" Probably some investigation into who did it and whose failure it was.

Nothing that will make me feel better.

Because nothing is going to bring Jake back.

More sympathy, pity, regret … all immediate triggers for my sorrow.

I need a break to mourn my loss and a break from mourning. So, I drift into restless sleep.

The Hills Inquirer

Local YouTuber Dies at Family Home Unexpectedly

By EVA MARTIN Jul 14, 2024

Red Hills resident and guitarist from the metal band Unreleased, Jacob Bodkin, died on July 13; the cause is believed to be a stunt gone wrong. He was seventeen.

The authorities in King County responded to a call by Jessica Bartlett, the Bodkins' neighbor, who found Jacob unresponsive in the family home's garage.

"I walked to the Bodkins' house to complain about the noise. I could hear the music louder than usual. Just like before the Bodkins rebuilt their soundproof garage," Mrs. Bartlett told the Hills Inquirer.

"I kept knocking with no answer. I couldn't ignore the noise because I had the ladies from my book club over, and the noise was very distracting." Jessica continued.

The door to the garage was unlocked, so after knocking for several minutes with no answer, Jessica said that she had to go in to speak to Jacob. To her shock, she found him on the floor, in a pool of blood, with his head and shoulders under a stack of Marshall amplifiers and speakers, weighing more than 150 pounds altogether.

Lt. Walter Crouse of the King County Sheriff's Office confirmed on Saturday that the body was with the medical examiner to determine an exact cause of death.

THE SOUND OF TUNING OUT

Jacob was the host of the YouTube Channel "The Dean." The name comes from "the Dean from Hell," Dimebag Darrell's guitar; Dimebag is the guitarist from the iconic metal band Pantera. Jacob used this channel to talk about guitar playing techniques and sounds, upgrades and fixes, covers of his favorite songs, and to promote songs by his band Unreleased.

A distinctive feature of Jacob's channel was his closing stunt, inspired by a live performance by Eddie Van Halen in 1982. The act required Jacob to run up a stack of fake amplifiers designed to look like a towering wall and then kick it to gain momentum for a somersault while carrying his guitar. The southern wall of the Bodkins' garage was covered with fake amps, with only three real amplifiers placed at the far-left end of the stack. The real amplifiers were used to create "the Brown Sound," the warm and powerful guitar sound he talked about frequently in his videos.

The initial investigation analysis suggests that when Bodkin was performing the stunt for the last time, he accidentally kicked the real stack of amps, which landed on him, killing him.

In a heartfelt post, the Bodkin family shared the devastating news on social media. "It is with great sadness that we inform everyone that Jake Bodkin passed away yesterday," read a statement on the band's LIV page.

Brett Howe

Jul 12 (Four days earlier)

www.strengthcircle.com

Online Support Group: Parents of Troubled Teens/Addiction & Recovery

> *If you or someone you care about is dealing with prescription drug abuse, this community is here for you. Share your experiences, find support, and connect with others who are facing similar challenges. You don't have to face addiction alone. Ask questions, offer advice, tell your story, and find hope for recovery right here.*

750 Members   **2,045 Posts**   **3 Online**

Thank you all for your messages of support and your replies to my last post. I decided it was worth it to go to the conference, and I was glad I did because I got to meet really interesting people in the industry. Right until three hours ago at least, when I came back to an empty house.

Yes, Donna is missing … again.

I don't know what to do.

About two weeks ago, I registered to attend the Innovation in Finance conference in Seattle scheduled for July 11 and 12. For convenience, I decided to spend the night at the hotel where the conference was taking place. It was a nice change to skip the stress of bad traffic so early in the day.

You know from my previous post how I was hesitant to leave Donna alone for that long, but this conference was important for my career progression. As a guy in my late forties with not many connections or roots in the Seattle area, the best way to find a job is through networking, and this event was a great networking opportunity. I've exchanged my business card with so many leading professionals; I'm hoping it will lead to a better-paying job to support my mentally ill daughter. Her treatment programs are not cheap, and neither are the shrink's bills.

I have spoken about the improvement I've seen lately in Donna's behavior in this group. It is slow indeed, but I'll take whatever comes my way. She has changed therapists and psychologists frequently over the past four or five years. Only six months ago, I finally found the one therapist who agreed to work with her and whom I could afford.

As she has just turned nineteen, I do hope that she can regain some sense of herself and some joy for the future. She struggles with low self-esteem, severe anxiety, panic attacks, depression, and CPTSD (complex post-traumatic stress disorder). The journey has been long, and she still has a long way to go (we still have a long way to go). Until recently, I could not talk with her without triggering her aggressive side.

Fellow parents, how do you help someone you can't talk with? How do you develop or heal your relationship?

About three months ago, she received a stellate ganglion block (SGB). SGB involves injecting the right side of the neck around the main nerve that controls the sympathetic nervous system with a local anesthetic. The purpose is to tame the hyperactive responses to dangerous or stressful situations, which can be heightened in a person with CPTSD. The effect of this treatment is supposed to last for six months on average. A friend of mine had recommended it. He said that his brother-in-law served in the army, and those injections have helped him to deal with the stress and physical pain. The SGB did lower her reactivity. She has been calmer recently, and I can talk without her becoming quickly agitated. That has been wonderful because I can actually connect with her, and I am grateful for that.

I am not sure what happened next. She's been distant lately. Yesterday morning, she said she needed fresh air and that she wanted to go for a walk near the playground. She loves that place. Sometimes, if the park is empty, she sits on the swings and listens to music.

It is 10 p.m. now. I'm getting worried. It is not the first time Donna has left the house for a couple of days. I am guessing she will be back later tonight. I just hope she's not using again.

It's been four months since I joined this support group, and you guys have been amazing. Unfortunately, my work schedule may restrict my ability to join in-person meetings, but this online group proved to be just as effective.

If you have any ideas or success stories to share, please do so! I need your help.

Caleb Bodkin

Jul 16

It feels like I've been asleep for a whole day. My body aches, and my head feels heavy. I try to lift my neck, but I have no power to do so. I can't even move my hand to reach out for my phone. I am aware of my surroundings, but am unable to move. It's suffocating.

The room is dark. My vision is blurry, but the most unsettling thought is that I can feel someone in the room with me.

I can't look around, but I hear shuffling, and I can see the shadow of someone standing right next to the foot of the bed.

I can't speak. I can't scream. I can't even breathe.

Suddenly, the shadow creeps up closer; I can see their shape and silhouette. I want to jump, but I can't.

I can't see their features either, only a dark shadow, an outline.

The shadow continues to lurk closer to me, almost touching my hand. It is muttering something, but I can't understand it.

The gibberish grows louder, and I try to scream, cough, or make any noise, and I can only manage a muffled moan. The shape moves to sit on my chest. Finally, it moves closer to my ear and says something...

Hush? Push? Watch?

I'm not sure.

I wake up, gasping for air.

It's okay. I am used to this by now. Hypnagogic hallucinations, like sleep paralysis, are one of the symptoms of hypokalemic periodic paralysis (HPP). However, after all these years, they still freak me out because they feel so real every time. They also happen more frequently during stressful times and when I forget to take my potassium supplements.

Speaking of which, did I take my supplements today?

When I am fully awake, I quickly scan the room.

There is no one around. The room is bright, with the afternoon sun shining directly through the window onto my desk, where a picture of Jake and I at the Grand Canyon has been sitting for the past ten years. In that photo, I am fourteen; Jake is eight. I am wearing my God of War tee, which I still have. Jake is wearing his Spider-Man hat, which he lost that same day. I am smiling at my mother behind the camera's lens, and Jake is sticking his tongue out, utterly clueless as to where life will take us.

I notice the glow of my phone silently ringing. It's Andrew, Jake's best friend and bassist from his band.

"Hey, are you okay?" Andrew asks.

"Yeah, I'm fine. Just nodded off for a bit," I tell him, half aware of what is happening. The sobriety in Andrew's tone brings me back to reality. He does not sound like his usual self, upbeat and loud. It's odd.

"Did LIV get back to you about Jake's profile?" Andrew asks.

"I'm not sure, maybe, why? Is the story still up?"

A pause. "I figured you must have had some answers by now because someone posted a new video." Andrew's impatience is evident in his tone.

I check LIV again. The new story is just another video of Jake playing another metal cover.

I notice that his profile picture has turned pale, with faint colors and a gray tint. Also, there is a small pink-reddish dot on the corner.

THE SOUND OF TUNING OUT

Fueled by anger, sadness, and genuine perplexity, I move on to check my email to find LIV's customer service team response.

Dear Caleb,

We extend our condolences and appreciate your patience and understanding throughout this process.

We regret to inform you that the Request to Remove Account of Deceased User cannot be processed since the user (the deceased) subscribed to our Epilogue service while they were still with us. Epilogue is a new feature that lets you connect with your loved ones from beyond the grave by sharing memories, milestones, previous posts, anniversaries, and even new content.

An epilogue is the final chapter at the end of a story that often wraps up all the loose ends by speaking without restrictions. The user can pre-record all new content with the intention of releasing it based on a set date or triggers from the LIV community. This service aims to keep one's memory alive through one's digital footprint and gives a chance for followers to remember them the way they wish to be remembered. Followers can view content by the Phantom users (the deceased users who had subscribed to the Epilogue service). The user may choose to save new material or share their most cherished memories, which they hope to keep even after their passing.

Once notified of a user's death, LIV will automatically run the new feature per the agreed-upon terms and conditions (charges apply). The user's account will be switched to the Phantom status, characterized by the faded color scheme and the Amaranth dot, denoting the immortality of the user's memory.

We hope this feature will help you and your family throughout the grieving process. We also ask that you respect the wishes of the deceased user.

May they rest in peace.

Please click here if you are interested in learning more about this feature.

Thank you,

LIV Support Team

As I read the email, my phone is pinging non-stop with new messages and DMs from everyone. When I hit the icon for the Messages app, I see at least forty new messages from Emily alone. It makes sense now; she must be going crazy trying to find out what is going on.

"Wtf?" says the last of Emily's texts. I don't bother to scroll up.

I take a screenshot of the email from LIV and send it to Emily and Andrew.

"This is insane!" Emily texts back two or three minutes later.

Turns out it wasn't Emily after all. She's harmless, however annoying.

All these messages and calls were draining my battery while I was asleep.

Three dots appear, indicating that Emily is typing a message. Then, my phone dies.

Thankfully.

Brett Howe
Jul 16

www.strengthcircle.com

Online Support Group: Parents of Troubled Teens/Addiction & Recovery

> *If you or someone you care about is dealing with prescription drug abuse, this community is here for you. Share your experiences, find support, and connect with others who are facing similar challenges. You don't have to face addiction alone. Ask questions, offer advice, tell your story, and find hope for recovery right here.*

750 Members   2,049 Posts   2 Online

Yesterday, I officially reported Donna as missing at the Red Hills Police Department. She has not been home for five days now. I'm worried sick!

I don't think the police are taking my case seriously because of Donna's troubled past; the frequency of similar reports under my name in the last three years since we moved to this town is not helping my case.

I can't blame them. Even I expect Donna to show up any day now asking for money.

I called Christine (for those of you who don't live in the region or who just joined the online group, she is the leader of our support group in the

Seattle Area). She suggested I continue with this journal to keep track of my emotions, actions, and perception of Donna's motives and state of mind. Christine had been a teenage runaway herself. That's why she knows how to help parents understand kids. She says the little princess I once saw in Donna is still there; I just have to reach out and stay in touch. I try to follow her advice as much as possible, but even Christine thinks that Donna is a lot of work.

Christine recommended that I share a happy memory with everyone here to stay positive and offer a glimmer of hope. I must take my mind off the dark possibilities that scare me beyond comprehension.

Donna was only three the first time she went on a toddler ride at a carnival. She loved anything on wheels. So I sat her in a tiny police car, buckled her in, turned around, and stood at the railing to watch.

I'll never forget the joy and delight in her face and voice. To her, she was driving a real police car, and if she had been any happier, I'm sure she would have exploded. I stood there as a grown man surrounded by other parents, doing my best not to cry. Anastasia was, as always, filming Donna and waving at her. Anastasia always got so excited, like a little kid, when Donna showed any signs of interest in anything. I think that's why Donna was so attached to her mother. They shared this bond that I could never establish. I don't know whether it was a girl thing or because of my long working hours.

"We are both on a journey of discovery, which is so exciting!" Anastasia once told me.

"She is discovering the world, and I am discovering who my daughter is." Anastasia had this thirst for adventure and thrill, and I guess she wanted to pass on her passion to Donna.

Things were good back then. Very simple.

Donna has not always been trouble; she used to be the sweetest little girl. She loved Minnie Mouse, tea parties, and anything fast.

THE SOUND OF TUNING OUT

I can't help but think that I failed miserably as a father. Yet, I don't know what else to do. I have dedicated my life to being her father, but she clearly can't see that.

And now, I am sitting here trying not to lose my mind as I wonder what she has been up to for the past five days!

But above all, I miss my daughter. What if she leaves me for good this time?

Caleb Bodkin
Jul 16

No, I have never heard of Epilogue before.

I also can't believe Jake signed up for it without saying anything. This sounds like the kind of idea Jake and I would bring up during dinner to toy with Dad's short temper. I think it's definitely out of character for Jake to keep this a secret. He never mentioned signing up for this service to anyone. Not even his band! And it is not the sort of thing you absentmindedly agree to without giving it a second thought, like a casual click to answer the YouTube surveys that pop up every now and then. He actually went out of his way to subscribe and even paid almost $100 for it!

My phone has been charging for almost ten minutes, so I try to turn it back on. When the screen lights up, I find that Emily has already shared the screenshot from my email to her online accounts. Plural!

As expected, mourning Jake's death is more of an attention-grabbing tool for her. I text Emily:

"WTF Em! I didn't wanna share this email with the entire world! My phone is about to explode rn!"

Emily: "I'm Jake's gf! My followers are expecting updates constantly."

Caleb: "Wow ... how convenient."

Emily: "Excuse me! How dare you!"

Messages and calls come from my friends, family, neighbors, Jake's friends, etc.

"Did you do this?" ... "I don't understand." ... "Is this legal?"

I can't keep up with all the messages, so I decide to post a clarification. I post a screenshot of the email received from LIV's customer service team with the following caption:

"Many of you have been asking about Jake's recent LIV stories. I have not posted any of these stories, nor do I have access to his account. As said in the email, this is a new service by LIV. I don't personally agree with this, but according to the email, Jake has signed up for it, and I must respect his decision. The post was automatically uploaded after the hype about the rumored Pantera reunion. Thanks for your concern."

Liked by V.Pittman79 and 438 others

View all 256 Comments:

Dave STX Wtf!

X_Aud_X cool, RIP Jake

KevinZZ_94 didn't know they had this service ... RIP

Stephie_Ida5 I received their promotional email apparently, they randomly selected accounts across the country

Katy_Lee02 me too! I signed up!

Bad_gator76 what a talented kid ... what a shame

Bridget.Kelly4 that's creepy ... JMO

Emily.Illingworth I am so heartbroken ... Jake was the love of my life

Madd_one_07 @ Emily.Illingworth I would LOL at this if I hadn't just lost a very close friend of mine

Child_of_hell_02 @ Emily.Illingworth I thought you guys had broken up

Aye-1989 what a sad way to go. I couldn't believe my ears when I heard of the accident! RIP

Brett_Howe1971 So sorry for your loss. RIP

NAT_GTNG sign me up!

Polka.Dudz.22 they shoulda named it digital deathbed

Olivia_Ortiz03 I got the promo email as well! But I never signed up. Too freaked out!

Maywarren_ I thought it was a scam! I got the email too!

Avedemutis_33 Is that even legal?

Maggie_day_1 Looks like it! Yeesh! I got goosebumps

Ade-Priz22 no one saw this coming! Praying for the family

Hellz_Bellz_Astrong not to sound insensitive but that stunt did not look safe at all RIP

Jessica Bartlett 395 RIP, Jake. You were a talented kid. Prayers to your family

Load more comments

#1 Why You?

I have a story to tell, but it's one I never share.

First, I want you to ask yourself, if you were to write a book about your life, where would the first chapter start? Today? Last year? Five years ago? How can anyone make such a big decision? Trying to determine what matters and what doesn't in one's life. Do you have a defining moment that changed the course of your life?

That moment for me was the first time I saw your face after you found out everything I'd done. I saw fear, confusion, and dread in your eyes. It made me think of prey looking into the eyes of predators.

Oddly enough, it made me think of a time I was filling out a form on an online dating website, and one of the questions was, "Describe yourself in one word." I had the strongest urge to type "Addict" and be completely honest about who I am, what I look like, my hobbies, and the challenges I struggle with daily. But we all know that online dating websites are not the typical space for honesty. Nearly nothing you find online is true.

I could be anyone. Literally anyone … Eventually, I was wise enough to cancel that dating profile because, yes, most of what you find online is meaningless junk, and people lie about who they truly are all the time. But … in my case, the truth goes beyond stupid lies about looks, money, and whatnot. It can be very dangerous.

I am writing this to you because I know you are looking for answers. And those answers are in my fucked-up history. So here are some fragments of my deepest secrets. I decided to write these messages to you of all the people, although I can count the times I've spoken to you on the one hand. These messages come from my intense passion, a place I keep deep inside. It is so powerful it triggers my mind so often, more than I'd like it to. In these messages, you'll read the sacrifices, the extreme lengths I'd gone to, and the pain I endured over the years. So the least I can do is use them to justify myself and my actions.

Since I was just a child, I knew I had this evil power. It made me feel alive when everyone treated me like a ghost.

Nobody listened. No one cared to understand.

I am writing these messages in blood that is not my own. The scars of suffering are etched, along with the tragic climax of the end of my empty existence.

Brett Howe

Jul 17

www.strengthcircle.com

Online Support Group: Parents of Troubled Teens/Addiction & Recovery

> *If you or someone you care about is dealing with prescription drug abuse, this community is here for you. Share your experiences, find support, and connect with others who are facing similar challenges. You don't have to face addiction alone. Ask questions, offer advice, tell your story, and find hope for recovery right here.*

752 Members   **2,052 Posts**   **6 Online**

What though the radiance which was once so bright,
Be now forever taken from my sight,
Though nothing can bring back the hour
Of splendour in the grass, of glory in the flower;
We will grieve not, rather find
Strength in what remains behind.

    I found this note in her room. It's a poem by William Wordsworth. Donna loves poetry. Please share your thoughts on this, any idea what she is trying to tell me? responses are appreciated!

Earlier this summer, we were discussing enrolling her in a poetry course. On one rare occasion when we had a proper conversation, she told me she was fascinated by literature and poetry. I was excited about the idea because I knew she needed to connect with others and meet people her age who shared her interests, which sounded like a solid plan.

I fantasized about her becoming a successful teacher, writer, or editor one day. I dreamed about her coming home and telling me about this guy she had been dating with whom she wanted to start a life on her own, that she would bring him over for Thanksgiving.

At this point, I just hope she is going to be here for Thanksgiving.

One thought that terrifies me is this could be her goodbye note. Am I ever going to see her again? I sometimes stop to turn and look for her. I get the feeling that I'm being watched. Maybe she's watching me from a distance. Perhaps she misses me? Or she needs money?

Yesterday, I left $50 on the kitchen counter for her in case she came home while I was at work.

A couple of months ago, I confronted her about stealing $100 from me. She said she needed a new pair of sneakers, but I knew she was lying. I don't mind her stealing money from me as long as I have a sign that she's okay. I'm used to it.

I need to make sure that my baby is well. Then, whatever struggle she is going through right now, she can get over it and come home to me. Maybe this time, she will realize that living on her own is not as fun as it sounds without the education and the job to support you. I am also worried about her medication. She has a very specific schedule. The doctors are very careful about her dosage to ensure the medication will not interfere with her body development because she started taking antidepressants at a very young age. She was only eleven when she started taking them.

I have no way of finding out where my daughter is. She doesn't answer when I call. I have the Find My Phone feature set up without her knowing for cases like these, but I guess she must have figured it out.

Donna has no presence on any social media platform, and I think she made that choice mainly to avoid people and, sadly, me. I have texted her several times since she went missing. I pleaded with her to come home to take her meds. I know that promising unconditional support for any and all ideas without providing necessary boundaries or guidance, can worsen the situation. Especially when your child is an addict. And I agree with what a lot of you have been telling me about "effective parenting" and "balancing support with appropriate interventions," but I can't help it. This morning I sent her a text promising she can do whatever she wants if she comes home. I know this does not qualify as good parenting, but if she leaves me for good, there will be no parenting to be done!

This is a desperate attempt at salvaging whatever is left of our relationship.

Caleb Bodkin
Jul 17

I'm sitting in the living room, staring beyond the glass double door that leads to our backyard. I step outside on this hot summer day and try to breathe in some fresh air. I inhale a few deep breaths and take in the smell of every past lazy summer spent with my brother at this house, the freshly-cut grass from the Bartletts' lawn, the wet earth after the rain, the sweet and spicy smell of the rhodies that invade most of the front yards in the neighborhood, and a faint trace of someone's breakfast, probably the Howes'.

I take my time before exhaling. I want to keep all the memories trapped in for as long as I can. To hold on to what feels like the last time I'm gonna smell this cocktail of refreshing scents from my childhood years. Every cell in my body is fighting to stay in memory lane and refuses to turn around the corner to face reality.

Our family moved to Red Hills Ridge when I was four. They considered other eastside neighborhoods, but the fresh mountain air, the beautiful surrounding area with all the trails and parks, were worth the extra twenty-minute commute my parents had to deal with, especially for my mother, a runner and a winter sports enthusiast. My dad also enjoys the scenic commute on I-90 on his way to work to Mercer Island.

THE SOUND OF TUNING OUT

I start to walk toward the forest that extends beyond our backyard. Before I go any further, I stop and call out to Fenrir to follow me. It feels like my Blue Nose Pitbull is essential for my existence these days. After a few seconds, he comes out of the house, trotting toward me. I look down at his beautiful brindle coat and remember the first time I laid my eyes on him as a three-month-old puppy. Mom gave him to me as a gift for my twelfth birthday. When I left for college almost six years later, I was so heartbroken for leaving him behind.

"Fen has been acting up since you've left. Chewing on your stuff in your room constantly," Mom told me once in one of our weekly phone calls during my first semester at Berkeley. "It is a sign that he misses you," she said.

I lean in and hug him, giving the hairs between his ears a ruffle. "Let's clear our heads ... how about a walk?" I say to the hairs on his head as I kiss him.

We walk without direction for about twenty minutes in the woods. I see myself as a character in one of my open-world video games. I have just finished a chapter that unlocked a new area to advance in the storyline. In the gaming world, you can choose to make as much of that story as you want. You can either stick to the original storyline or unpack more and more by doing side quests and missions. For this part of my life, I choose to do the minimum.

I notice that my breath is becoming shorter and heavier, so I decide it would be reckless to do any physical activity before having breakfast or taking any supplements. When I make it back to the backyard, I feel so tired, I crash on the first lawn chair I see.

Fenrir sits beside me, chewing on something. He looks sad and seems unenthusiastic

I check my phone. The news about LIV launching a new service has picked up, and the topic is trending on social media. More accounts are being switched to the new "Phantom Status" as LIV calls its dead users. I read an article and head back inside to have breakfast.

I see my mom sitting at the kitchen counter, staring at her phone, watching one of Jake's videos, crying her eyes out. I remember the notification from this morning on my homepage:

"**Diane Bodkin from your contacts is now on LIV.**" Mom was on LIV now! I automatically grabbed my phone and was prompted to text Jake that our mom was on social media.

"Mom, are you okay?" I ask her.

She doesn't answer. I don't think she heard me.

The doorbell rings. It is Jessica Bartlett. Jake had a nickname for her: "The Bitch." Nothing fancy, he just hated her because she had caused a lot of trouble for him over the years. She constantly complained about the noise from Jake's practice, so my dad had to soundproof the garage, which wasn't good enough because "There's a difference between soundproofing and sound-absorbing, so the panels and foams are not enough to stop the noise from spreading." As she put it, "You have to build a room within the garage."

All residents are members of the Red Hills Residential Homeowners Association, which approves design plans, sets standards for upkeep, fence height, and other "good neighbor" rules, and coordinates community and neighborhood events. So every time Jessica Bartlett complained, my parents succumbed to her outrageous demands. One time, she brought full-fledged plans, including a list of vendors in the area. She thought she was helping Mom "tackle a shared problem." My parents ended up paying close to $5,000 to shut her up.

When Jake's band was accepted into the lineup for the Rockverse Festival in 2023, he gained a lot of followers. He'd text me stuff like, "Check this out! I got 500 followers but the bitch ain't one!"

When I open the door for Jessica, she hugs me and pats my back. She has a basket of baked goods with her, which smells so good that I almost feel guilty for how I used to speak about her with Jake.

"Caleb, why don't you make your mom and me some tea?"

"Sure," I say, hating that I'll have to join them for at least the next half hour as I prepare my breakfast. When Jessica enters the kitchen, she sees Mom sitting on one of the chairs, crying and watching videos of Jake. She is lost in Jake's digital footprint, stalking his LIV account, new posts, old posts, reels, etc.

Jessica hugs my mom. When she sits on the chair across from her, I can see Jessica's eyes are teary and her cheeks are flushed.

"I've always warned him about that stunt. I should have been firm when I said no ... We spent so much on that garage for his channel. We wanted to support him..." Mom says. She's not a fan of the metal/rock genre, nor does she have the same appreciation my father has for Eddie Van Halen's amp wall run. She starts to cry again. Jessica gets up and takes my mom in a long embrace.

I place a cup of tea in front of Jessica and return to the kitchen to fix myself a potassium-rich smoothie. I double the ingredients and make a glass for my mom. I can't remember the last time I saw her eat something.

"Here you go. Maybe you should take a break." I place the glass on a coaster on the kitchen counter where my mom is sitting. She looks unfazed like she can't see me or the drink.

"I'm fine," Mom says. She blinks and regards me with an intense look, "Why did Jake subscribe to this Epilogue service?" she asks and I sense a hint of anger in her tone, as if I'm withholding information from her. It takes me a moment to realize that she is talking to me.

"I don't know. I've been thinking about the same thing since I saw the first video. I've asked Lauren about it, too. But you know Lauren, she never really talks to me about anything," Jessica says. Lauren is her daughter; she studies in Boston and barely visits.

"What did Andrew say? They were so close; Jake must have said something to him," Mom asks.

"He doesn't know either." I pause and then continue, "Where's Dad?"

"Upstairs. He was awake when I left the room," Mom says with a deep sigh that echoes her frustration. Her features change, and she looks angry rather than sad. "I have nothing to say to him. I have nothing to say to anybody." Finally, she turns to Jessica. "I can't help but blame him for encouraging that dangerous behavior! I've spoken about this many times before, but they made fun of me and called me paranoid. I told Jake that this silly move was unnecessary for his show. I thought he might slip, fall, and hurt himself but not die! I never thought his life was in danger!" Mom says as she has a sudden emotional outburst and breaks down in tears.

"Nobody saw that coming, dear," Jessica says. "Besides, men process grief in a totally different way. When Gary's mother passed, he took off for a few days and stayed out of town, completely shut off from the rest of the world."

I bet Gary Bartlett was getting the comfort he needed in the arms of his girlfriend. She must know that Mr. Bartlett has a girlfriend! I know that much and don't even live with the guy. At least three different kids from my high school had spotted him with another woman at bars in Seattle and Bellevue.

I get up and join Fenrir, who's sitting by the glass doors in the living room. He's resting his head on the floor, ears pulled back, eyebrows upturned; he looks exhausted and withdrawn.

I check Jake's YouTube channel. My eye catches Jessica Bartlett's name; she joined his channel and left a comment on his last video:

THE SOUND OF TUNING OUT

"RIP, Jake. You were a talented kid. Prayers to your family."

I cover my face with my hands and weep. I don't know why, but I send Jake a text:

"You have 10,586 followers, and the bitch is one."

And then I see Jake's sneakers in Fenrir's mouth. He's chewing on them. I didn't know it was possible, but my heart breaks even more.

Brett Howe

Jul 18

www.strengthcircle.com

Online Support Group: Parents of Troubled Teens/Addiction & Recovery

> *If you or someone you care about is dealing with prescription drug abuse, this community is here for you. Share your experiences, find support, and connect with others who are facing similar challenges. You don't have to face addiction alone. Ask questions, offer advice, tell your story, and find hope for recovery right here.*

753 Members   **2,058 Posts**   **5 Online**

This is the longest she's been away from home. She's never done this before. I am so worried about her. She has been gone for more than a week now. The police are still treating it like a runaway kid case. Again, I don't blame them, considering Donna's history, but I cannot help but worry like crazy about my daughter.

When I went to the station today to check for any updates, one police officer had the audacity to look me in the eye and say to my face, "Relax, Mr. Howe; she will turn up soon. She always does."

I could see pity in everyone's eyes.

"I would like to know what steps the police are taking to find my daughter," I said, sounding more furious than I wanted to show. I don't want them to think I'm being hostile toward them. Over the years, I've learned that being on good terms with the authorities goes a long way. Last summer, Donna went missing for a day. The police eventually found her in an abandoned house in the neighborhood, high, barely awake. I had to pay the owners' $500 for the damage she caused when she broke in. It could have been worse, but the police officer was very sympathetic toward us.

Some outsiders who have no clue how difficult it is to raise a troublesome teenager may sympathize with Donna. Not the police, though. They have witnessed firsthand how Donna can be violent, even dangerous sometimes.

I have to forgive her. I have to support her. After all, she grew up without her mother, and I had to be both figures to her. So whenever she acts in a way that she shouldn't, I have to assume Anastasia's role and spoil our little princess.

The police have their hands full with Jake Bodkin's death. I understand that the accident is complicated and bizarre. The boy died in their garage while performing one of those crazy challenges. Things like that don't happen in a neighborhood like Red Hills Ridge. This is a very quiet and peaceful suburban community.

Jake's death has made Donna's recurring disappearance even less significant. So I will have to push from my end to ensure everyone is still doing their job and not being distracted by this tragedy. I do feel for his family, and I sympathize with them a great deal, especially since he was around Donna's age. But I have a responsibility toward my daughter.

Caleb Bodkin

Jul 18

It's been five days. Five long, agonizing days since the accident. Somehow, they feel like months.

I look back at last week and feel like a different person. I see a clueless, unsuspecting idiot going about his day, thinking that everything is going to go the way he planned.

Last Tuesday, I had three prospective tenants look at my studio apartment. I was planning on subletting it for the remainder of the lease contract, due to end the following December. After receiving the offer for the new job in Seattle, I was trying to tie up all the loose ends before leaving Berkeley. My plan was to surprise my family on August 15 when I went to celebrate my mother's birthday and tell them the good news. I was excited to move to my favorite city, closer to my hometown and far away from my ex-girlfriend.

Around noon, I was about to grab something to eat with a friend when my phone rang. It was my dad. He was frantic. I couldn't understand what he was saying at the beginning. He kept on screaming Jake's name.

"It fell on him! There is blood everywhere! Come home now!" he shouted.

"Dad, I don't understand what is happening. Calm down!" I tried to stay calm.

"Your brother is dead! Come home now!" he said.

"What are you talking about! What is going on!"

I kept yelling at the phone. "Dad!"

I tried to call him back, but he didn't pick up.

"Is everything okay?" my friend Derrick asked.

I didn't answer, I was too busy trying Mom.

"Caleb, hey, are you okay?" Derrick held my elbow and turned me to face him, looking into my eyes "What the hell is going on?"

I stopped for a second that seemed to last too long. Time seemed to stop as the words sank in. My heart pounded in my chest, and a cold wave of shock washed over me.

"He said..." I tried to breathe but I forgot how to. "Jake is dead." I remember feeling dizzy as the words fled my mouth "I have to go ... right now." I was shaking.

I don't remember much of the next five to six hours, only fragments of useless details.

I remember Derrick sitting me down on the couch...

I remember staring helplessly at the cheap black fabric as I cradled my head between my fists.

Tears were running down my cheeks, as my world was falling apart before my eyes, and as I sat helplessly watching...

I remember Derrick fumbling with his phone, telling me about the next available flight, ordering me an Uber, walking me to the car, "His flight takes off in less than two hours, please hurry up, Southwest Airlines," Derrick told the driver.

All my senses were telling me to shut down, escape this sudden, awful reality by simply giving in and collapsing right then and there on my apartment floor. Except for that spark of hope, the unreasonable, stupid glimmer of delusion that I had mistaken for hope. It kept me going, dragging me to my parents' porch.

Maybe this is all just a misunderstanding? I was saying to myself.

I didn't think to bring anything, but thankfully my phone and wallet happened to be on me.

I made it to Oakland Airport thirty minutes after my dad had called. It took a while until I boarded the flight to Seattle-Tacoma.

By the time I was at my parents' front door, the sun had already set. The bright orange of the sunset sky darkened the silhouettes of buildings, trees, and cars in the neighborhood. I remember thinking about how eerie our house looked and how empty the whole town seemed.

It had rained the night before. My parents' steps were muddy. It looked like so many people had come in and out. The door was unlocked. No one was home; I went to the garage.

"CRIME SCENE, DO NOT ENTER" ran the yellow ribbon. I saw the garage in a total mess of mud and blood.

The scene around me told a very messy story. The air in the room felt stuffy. I felt like I was in a daze. My mind was struggling to process the scene before me. Jake's stack of expensive amps was gone; in its place was a pool of blood and fragments of broken pieces. The window at the back of the room leading to the backyard was open; it had rained earlier in the afternoon, and the stream of rain coming through it soaked everything beneath the window, boxes, an old surfboard, shoes, all sorts of things. Jake's collection of guitars sat neatly across the opposite wall as if belonging to a different room from a quieter time.

As I looked at the empty spot where the amps had fallen, I was digesting my dad's words almost six hours later. "Those things are too heavy," Dad had said earlier. At first, I hadn't understood what he was referring to. The shock from the scene took its toll on my body. I dragged myself to the steps of our next-door neighbor.

Nobody was home at the Howes', so I went to the Bartletts'.

"Mr. Bartlett, what happened to Jake?" My question came through my sobs and unsteady breath. "Where is everyone?"

"I'm sorry. There's been a terrible accident. You should go to the hospital." He, too, seemed shaken up and nervous. "I'll take you. I don't think you should be driving." Fenrir came and jumped on me. "I'm supposed to take care of the dog; everyone is at the hospital."

I could hear my sobs as if they were coming from somewhere else. I grabbed the railing desperate for balance and sat on the stairs, resting my elbows on my knees as I wept, snot and tears racing out of me, landing on the stairs between my legs. I clutched my chest, trying to ease the tightness. Fen came to my side, gently trying to rest his head on my lap. Mr. Bartlett sat beside me, unfazed by the wet stairs, and patted my back. "I'm so sorry, Caleb. I can't imagine what this must be like," he said.

My senses were heightened, my adrenaline surged, and I was high on shock. Yet, I felt like a ragdoll, a puppet without a visible puppeteer. I wanted to lash out, desperate to return to my real world. This felt like a mistake, an alternate reality, a nightmare.

Mr. Bartlett then drove me to the hospital where my parents and his wife were.

When I entered the emergency room's waiting area, I saw my mom sitting in one of the ugly orange plastic chairs, crying. Jessica Bartlett was holding her hand, her face a mask of anguish. Jessica saw me first and nudged my mom. When Mom saw me, we exchanged a look of horror as we both acknowledged the weight of this new reality, pulling us down the dark depths of this black hole. Just the two of us. It lasted only for a split second before we both completely broke down.

My mom hugged me and cried on my shoulder. She didn't say anything intelligible; she was wailing. It felt like the world had suddenly gone silent. I couldn't move. Amid all the sadness of the situation, my mind could still recognize this moment as one that would change my life forever.

A few horrible minutes passed by. I was sitting on one of the chairs, cradling my head, my thoughts spinning in confusion. A hand touched my shoulder. "Your father's blood pressure was acting up after seeing Jake," Jessica said. "They're tending to him. The nurse told us a few moments ago that he's stable, but they need to keep an eye on him tonight."

My dad was released from the hospital twenty-four hours after being admitted. I kept checking on both of my parents the first two days I was back home. They were in no shape to handle any funeral arrangements, which meant I had to.

The next day, I went to the funeral home to see Jake.

"His upper body got the full impact," the funeral home director said. "We cleaned his face, but there's still work to be done."

Jake's entire body was under the white cover except for his left hand.

"In case you want to hold his hand. We know this is a very difficult time for you," she told me as we entered the cold, sterile room where they kept his body.

I nodded, keeping my gaze fixed on the metal table.

She removed the sheet.

They'd done some stitching around the eyes; from his mouth to his nose, his face was black and blue. Although his face was sort of squashed, a better word for it, it was still him.

I asked to be alone with him for five minutes. I didn't do anything. I didn't speak to his corpse. I wasn't even trying to silence the thoughts in my head. They seemed to stop completely. I went there for a reason I still can't figure out. I stayed for almost fifteen minutes. I stared at the empty vessel that had carried my brother for the past seventeen years. I was not ready to let go.

THE SOUND OF TUNING OUT

I remember thinking to myself how quiet the room was. It was so weird. Jake's constant chattering defined his character and the energy around him. He was always going on about guitars, bands, sound effects, and band logos, so he seemed unaware of his surroundings. This information came in handy on certain occasions, like the time when I wanted to impress Ria Johnston with my knowledge about metal bands. I'm not a fan of the genre per se, but I'll admit, the info Jake stored in my subconscious with his constant blabbering proved useful that night at the bar when I was introduced to Ria. Not that it mattered much, since three weeks later, I ended things with her after realizing that she was kind of a psycho.

Super random, I know; why would that pop into my head when I saw Jake's body?

My convo with Jake plays in my head; I called him the next morning after I met Ria at the bar to tell him about what happened and to jokingly thank him for oversharing useless info.

"Oh really! What happened to 'Jake, I stopped listening about ten minutes ago,' asshole?!" he said, because I often teased him when he took too long explaining something.

I hear the funeral home director talking on the phone in the other room and tapping away on her keyboard, which brings me back to this very moment.

That's the sound of death, distant shuffling in the background, reminding me that life still exists anywhere but here.

I am staring into the white sheet that covers Jake's body. The hand is out for me to hold. I decide to go for it, and I grab it. When I wrap my fingers around his palm, it feels so cold and stiff.

I am so absorbed in the moment when I feel a familiar feeling of a squeeze around my hand. It doesn't register at first; it is too normal, safe, and mundane, but then I realize this is impossible! Fear washes over my whole body like ice-cold water splashed on my face. I try to snatch my hand out of Jake's grip, which feels more like a claw, but I can't. He is clinging to me; I can't even move my hand away. Blood stains the sheets around his head; a circular dent in the white surface of the sheet is forming, indicating that the corpse is taking a deep breath. He is trying to pull my hand toward his head; I try to resist. I am trying to call for help!

Do they have cameras in here?! Can someone see this?

He reaches for me with his other hand, drawing me closer to his head. The sheet is sliding off his face. I am screaming, but nothing is coming out. I jerk my body away from his in a sudden motion, and I start falling. The ground feels like air, and I fall so fast into a hole. Darkness envelopes everything until I can see nothing.

When I open my eyes, I find myself in my room. It is 4:38 a.m.

I haven't been sleeping well lately, nor have I been able to keep up with the timing of my medication. Between the funeral arrangements, helping my parents out, and dealing with my distress, I'm neglecting my meds and even skipping some doses.

THE SOUND OF TUNING OUT

I go down to grab a glass of water. When I get to the bottom of the stairs, I see my mom sitting in the living room, looking at old photos of Jake. She's choosing the ones that will go in the memorial slideshow for the funeral.

"This was when we took you and your cousins to the indoor playground outside Las Vegas. Do you remember?"

"Yes, but I don't think Jake remembered that day. He was what, three? Four?"

"Three years and eight months. I asked him once; he said he vaguely remembers the freaky rabbit," Mom says.

"He lied."

We both laugh.

That trip was so much fun. It is one of my favorite memories.

I hold my mom's head close to my chest, and we both cry for a while. A dark thought creeps into my head that my loss has not only made a very beautiful part of my life sad to remember but also irrelevant to my future.

#2 Why Now?

You are invited to this extraordinary journey. I have dropped all the weight of my life, and I am free at last. I've been carrying my stress, guilt, and shame everywhere.

I am exhausted.

This baggage of personal conflicts consumed my patience, my appetite for life, and my soul. I go to bed hoping not to wake up, because it seems easier than dealing with this sickness. I thought I was still fooling everyone around me by living in a dark world of self-isolation and depression. I destroyed my closest relationships and caused severe pain and damage to everyone around me. Over the years, I've lost a lot of money, got bailed out, stayed clean for a few months, relapsed, and got caught again. Unfortunately, it has only gotten worse. Occasionally, addiction can be stopped (for a short while at least), but even then the cleanup of the mess left behind and the mental anguish it leaves continues.

I feel like a ghost of my former self. I want to be normal. At this point though, I sound like a hypocrite when I make the claim that I am nothing but an addict. I've been struggling with addiction for most of my life now. So my "normal self" is pretty much this damaged, good-for-nothing, isolated individual. But the fact remains that I am in an awful place.

Such moments of clarity do not last for long, though, when your mind starts to ask for more of that addictive rush, just like when your body is pestering you for another dose. Suddenly, it makes sense why you're doing what you've been doing. Somehow, something that's clearly so damaging is okay to keep doing. There is no going back. There is no point in going anywhere, either.

    I am done ... I am taking a trip down the road to redemption starting today. If this life isn't good enough. If this relationship isn't meaningful enough ... If they aren't enough ... Then what is ... The answer is nothing ... I now know for sure. So why now? Because all my life, I've felt like a ghost, and now I am ready to cross over. I am nothing.

Brett Howe
July 20

www.strengthcircle.com

Online Support Group: Parents of Troubled Teens/Addiction & Recovery

> *If you or someone you care about is dealing with prescription drug abuse, this community is here for you. Share your experiences, find support, and connect with others who are facing similar challenges. You don't have to face addiction alone. Ask questions, offer advice, tell your story, and find hope for recovery right here.*

755 Members   **2,061 Posts**   **2 Online**

I cried uncontrollably at Jake Bodkin's funeral. I didn't really know him all that well. It was so embarrassing. I certainly did not want to attract attention at a funeral. In the beginning, I was fine. Even as I walked in and greeted the Bodkins ... but when they brought in the coffin, I couldn't control my tears. Surely, I was not the only one crying there; his sudden death touched many in the community.

I don't know what came over me. I just couldn't imagine that such a tragedy could happen to someone Donna's age. Jake was a year younger than Donna. She was not there with me, which made things even worse.

THE SOUND OF TUNING OUT

I saw Jake frequently, on his way to school, at the local grocery store where Donna worked for a couple of weeks (she couldn't keep a job, or any commitment for that matter, any longer). I think I spoke to him less than ten times. I was never close with the Bodkins or anyone in the neighborhood; I barely had time for the social pleasantries between my job and my commitment to Donna.

I am comfortably an introvert. Have been all my life. But I kept to myself for the most part while living in Red Hills, paying my respects when needed and staying out of trouble, since Donna had caused enough for the both of us. I didn't want to burden anyone with my problems.

That's why I chose this online group. Not just for convenience but also because I know you cannot be reading this entry unless you have voluntarily looked for it, either because you are in a similar situation or because you have been.

I cried, not for myself, but because of the grief and sorrow his family was going through. Seeing his father and cousins carry his casket was one of the most heartbreaking things I have ever witnessed. I thought about this young boy who would never come back and his life that had been cut short. I felt a sense of loss and grief that was almost too much to bear.

I miss Donna so much. I want to hold her and keep her safe from everything and everyone else.

Caleb Bodkin

Jul 20

It's a beautiful July day. The scenery of the green lawn and flowers of the churchyard is picturesque. With everyone bustling about and getting things in order, you'd think it's someone's wedding. The sound of children playing, birds singing, and distant traffic reminds us that the reel doesn't stop for us, our family, tragedies, and suffering. It just means we were missing out, taking a break, zoning out into your diversion off the course.

A parade of mourners dressed in black, with the soundtrack of my parents, aunts, neighbors, teachers, and friends, crying tells a tragic story. Everyone feels the connection to the occasion; there's no denying the weight of this heartbreak on the whole community. Everyone in attendance is putting themselves in Jake's or my parents' shoes. No one is doing a good job of keeping it together. Even Mr. Howe, our neighbor, breaks down in tears. I didn't know he liked Jake or knew him all that well. He's a nice guy and mostly keeps to himself. I know he has a troubled kid who's been in and out of rehab many times; she's around Jake's age, but we never had the chance to interact with her. I bet he's standing there imagining himself in our shoes and weeping for the loss, which might just as easily be his someday.

Once at the burial site, my father, uncle, and cousins carry the coffin to the grave, place it on wooden struts, and position the lowering straps through the handles.

I was not encouraged to be amongst the pallbearers. "What if you get an attack?" my uncle said. He was right. Different reasons trigger those attacks, and one of those triggers is extremely stressful situations, like say, your young brother's funeral. Also, I didn't have anything to eat all day. I've no appetite for anything.

The pallbearers lift the coffin by the straps, allowing the wooden struts to be removed. And then, the coffin is lowered into the grave. My mom is overcome with grief. It looks like she's going to faint.

The moment when Jake goes underground is intense and painful. I don't just see sadness on people's faces. The finality of placing someone you'd loved all these years six feet under broke down any façade of composure. I see shock, surrender, sympathy, and vulnerability.

Nevertheless, in a way, this reunion has the sweet taste of homecoming. Whenever I recognize an old face from a better time—when our family was whole—a wave of gratitude washes over me. Finally, I understand how funerals came about and why people showed up.

My brother's funeral is a sad one. There's none of those side conversations that typically make these occasions seem more like a social obligation. Everyone in attendance is genuinely struggling with their loss.

I receive guests with my parents for an hour or so. I see my parents' friends whose kid I was close with briefly one summer when we were both ten and with whom I haven't spoken since. I see my old high school teachers, who taught Jake the same subjects six years later. I even see my ex-girlfriend from the ninth grade, who has put on a little weight and is still very cute.

And then, I let myself take a break outside. I stare into the beautiful landscape when Takuya comes outside with a glass of water for me.

"Thanks, Tak," I say. He sits down next to me.

Takuya's dad, Ren, is Japanese. Ren lived in Japan until he was twenty-five. He met my aunt during one of her trips to Japan. Their love story took off because of their shared passion for the outdoors and her fascination with Japanese culture. Tak is four years older than I am. The last time I saw him was a year ago, on his wedding day at a vineyard in California.

"How you holding up?" he asks.

"I'm not okay," I say.

Tak lowers his gaze. "Yeah. It's tough."

We sit in silence for a long minute, then I speak. "I was playing Call of Duty with him just a few nights ago."

Tak's frown grows deeper, and a tear escapes the corner of his eye. "I'm sorry. This is harder than I imagined." There's a long silence. Each one of us is lost in our own thoughts, summoning once-beautiful memories that morph into melancholy in the shadow of our grief "Wow... I haven't played video games in so long..." Tak finally says.

Memories from 2015 of Tak and I playing Skyrim come rushing to me at that moment. As a child and during my early teen years, we visited my grandmother during vacations. Pat, my oldest cousin, let us play Skyrim on his Xbox 360. My grandmother was cool and would let us move it to my aunt's old room and play all night. I was fifteen, and Jake was nine; he would try so hard to stay awake with the older, "cooler" kids but would eventually fall asleep by eleven.

I still see Tak every once in a while if he is in town or if I end up in his neck of the woods during family vacations, holidays, weddings, or funerals. We aren't that close anymore, but we've stayed in touch on all digital platforms. So I know details about his everyday life, like where he gets his coffee every morning or where he goes to work out five days a week. I haven't lost touch with him in that sense, but do I really know this grown-up in front of me?

A few hours passed; it's past midnight. Tak, Pat, Eve, and I sit in my parents' living room with the TV on. They're showing reruns of an old sitcom. We stare staring into the screen but don't actually watch.

Fenrir is restless, sitting beside the glass doors, staring into the woods. Finally, Eve decides to break the silence.

"I've always loved your family's living room," she says. "When we were kids, we used to sit here and eat while the adults ate in the dining room, and I loved the glass doors that led to the backyard and the beautiful views. It was so different from my parents' Brooklyn walk-up apartment."

Eve is twenty-two and studying to become a nutritionist at Penn State. She is definitely more Bowman than any of the cousins; last year, my mom invited her to the Annual Bowman Trip, an honor none of the cousins had previously experienced.

"We are house-hunting now, and I want a similar view with the baby on the way. Also, Rusty, our Lab, needs his space. So, it's not that difficult to get good value for your money down in Texas," Pat says. He is the eldest of all the cousins, so his mature way of steering the conversation into something closer to reality is almost natural.

"Three days ago, I said goodbye to Jake at the funeral home. I held his stiff, cold hand. It didn't feel real," I interrupt their conversation. Silence follows. "I still felt something. I don't know how to describe it." My voice breaks. "I don't know where to go next when I need to see him." I don't want the conversation to shift to other topics.

Eve moves closer and gives me a hug, her tears starting to soak my shirt. I briefly catch Pat giving Tak an awkward look.

"I guess it's not so bad having this Epilogue stuff after all," Pat says.

Brett Howe

Aug 23

www.strengthcircle.com

Online Support Group: Parents of Troubled Teens/Addiction & Recovery

> *If you or someone you care about is dealing with prescription drug abuse, this community is here for you. Share your experiences, find support, and connect with others who are facing similar challenges. You don't have to face addiction alone. Ask questions, offer advice, tell your story, and find hope for recovery right here.*

768 Members   **2,102 Posts**   **3 Online**

I want to start this entry by thanking all members here for their endless support and love. It has been a great help.

I have some updates on Donna's whereabouts from the police. Someone from the small grocery shop where she worked last year said they saw her heading toward the hiking trails.

When I showed the poem I found in Donna's room to the police, they suggested that Donna had either run away or killed herself. I don't know where they got that from! There is nothing about the poem that suggests ending one's life! I looked up the meaning on several websites, but none indicated that!

"Maybe she ran off with that boyfriend of hers," one of the officers said. I told him that Donna doesn't have a boyfriend.

"Well, some witnesses from town saw them together a couple of times in the past month or so."

It was so hard for me to control my temper at that moment. I mean, I am expected to trust the police to find my daughter while they casually dismiss my concerns because of the town's gossip. Of course, these rumors have no truth to them! I would have known. Donna wouldn't be able to hide such a thing from me.

I stormed out of the station after making a scene because, in all honesty, I don't think they are doing their job. Although the police have been taking Donna's disappearance a little more seriously since Jake Bodkin's funeral, they had no right to jump the gun and make such assumptions with no solid proof.

I put out missing person posters everywhere around town and wherever I could online.

I don't think I can make it without Donna. She is my purpose in life.

Please, God, keep her safe. I won't ask for anything else ever!

Caleb Bodkin
Aug 23

My alarm clock interrupts a bizarre yet sad dream. It is more like a subconscious remake of a once-happy memory I had to abandon for a while with my recently extremely busy schedule.

In my dream, Jake and I are both ten, and we have both of our heads under the water, trying to see who lasts longer. We are in Uncle Eric's pool. From underneath the water's surface, I can make out the shapes of adults, my parents, my uncle and aunt, their friends, and their kids. I am holding Jake's hand. I pull him up with me as I try to resurface. When my head pierces the surface of the water in a swift, smooth move, I find myself alone.

No one is around.

I see a dark shape floating in the distance. I swim to it. As I reach out and grab it, I become aware that I am standing on the ground, and I see a shadow of something falling over my head. It is Jake's amp stack. I look down at the thing in my hand and realize that it is Jake's Seahawks hat.

I've been looking for that hat everywhere. I asked my parents, his friends, and even at his school. It's been driving me crazy. I guess I just wanted to have it for its sentimental value, one last piece of him to hold on to. It carries all the memories of nights in my parents' living room, watching Seahawks games, teasing my dad, and calling him an outsider because he's originally from California and still has a soft spot for the 49ers. All the fights, the yelling at the TV, the crazy gatherings we had. I just needed that hat.

I hit the snooze button, dreading being awake in a world where my brother is dead. Before my mind starts taking me to dark places, I get up and start getting ready for work. It's been a good distraction. Although I only started last week, I haven't been dwelling on Jake's memories as much. The first week was mainly all training courses, orientation, networking events, etc. It was hectic.

This new beginning is much needed. I have met new people who know nothing about Jake or me after spending the last few weeks in my hometown, where everyone knows us and has nothing to talk to us about but the tragedy of losing Jake.

I check my phone before getting ready to shower. I see a text from Andrew.

"WTF! CALL ME WHEN U SEE THIS!"

Right then, I realize there are seventeen missed calls, including eight from my dad. So I call him back immediately.

"Caleb, what the hell is that about? Do you understand it?" Dad blurts out the second he picks up.

"What are you talking about?" I say.

"Jake's new story! Go check it now!" he says impatiently.

I keep him on the line while I go to LIV and press on Jake's profile picture to view his story. The story was posted 15 minutes ago.

The frame shows our $5,000 garage, the fake amp wall, and the stack of real amps in the near corner where he usually sits and plays or starts his episode on YouTube. There is another stack of real amps and speakers, the heavy-duty stuff he uses for big gigs like the Rockverse Fest or some other big venues where his band had played. That big stack is in the far-left-hand corner of the frame. He doesn't use these amps for his daily practice. They stand in the back to blend in with the fake amps on the wall.

Jake has a special stand for his phone when he shoots these episodes. That's why the frame captures everything.

"Domination" by Pantera is playing in the background. It's weird because usually, he edits it into the opening scene; he never actually plays it while recording. "Domination" is his theme song for The Dean episodes on YouTube. It looks like he is about to record a new session. I can't tell what he's doing because he's standing too close to the screen. Only his hair and his right shoulder are visible. We are past the thirty-second mark, where Jake usually stops the song and starts talking about his topic for the day. Jake is still hovering at the same angle, shuffling in the same spot.

"It looks like this video was filmed by accident. What's the big deal?" I ask Dad.

Then Jake moves to sit on his chair, the usual spot where he talks to his followers.

He's looking down at his guitar; his head movements are unstable, like he's dizzy. He starts playing terribly. It sounds like fumbling around, out of tune, out of key, making random noises. "What's the point of this video? And what's wrong with his hair?" Dad doesn't answer.

Jake's hair looks dark and wet. He looks up; his face is covered in blood, trickling from the middle section of his head between his forehead and crown.

"What is he doing!" I ask Dad over the speaker

"I don't get it! Nobody seems to get it! I even asked Andrew," Dad says. "Is it a joke? Or a prank? Glenn is calling me back! I gotta take this!" Dad says before he hangs up.

I continue watching the weird video. I check the length of the video, ten minutes, which is the time limit allowed through Epilogue.

Drool starts to dribble down on his guitar. At the 3:52 mark, when he usually does the wall run stunt, this zombified version of my brother stands up and looks at the screen, eyes twitching rapidly, hands shaking. He clumsily drags his guitar with him to the wall, and I know what is about to happen, but I don't want to see it. I can't do anything to stop it from happening. I want to pause because I don't want the scene to end. I already know the sad ending. The heavy bass is playing, and heavy breathing with it. It is probably an instrumental sound effect, but I have never paid attention to it before. I have heard this song a thousand times, yet I don't think I've ever heard it like that. In the background, I can hear a screeching sound, like metal being dragged across the floor, and the sound of an exhale. This is the outro to the song. It sounds so intense at that moment, like every effect is heightened to add to the tragic factor.

The ending begins. Jake runs toward the wall and drops his guitar with a high clank that still manages to make a noise through the loud music. No wonder Jessica Bartlett went nuts that day. He runs on the wall clumsily. When he lands on the floor, he steps on something that twists beneath his foot; it looks like an old shoe box. He falls on the ground just beneath the stack of real amps, which contains one fake speaker at the bottom, topped with a real amp head, an EVH amplifier cabinet, and the speaker. The total height of the stack is six feet two inches, and the total weight is more than one hundred and fifty pounds combined. The wall of fake amps, made of wood panels balanced by a diagonal stand in the backside, is still bouncing back and forth due to the strong shove that Jake gave seconds ago when he ran across it. Jake shows no resistance and no awareness of what is happening. He is on the floor. The fake wall rocks back and forth, bringing a long, big surfboard to fall on top of the amp head, and the whole fragile structure collapses on Jake's upper body.

I can see his arms making a final twitch. Life is crawling out of his damaged body. I watch as the last flicker of light slowly dims, like a wick

THE SOUND OF TUNING OUT

smothered by the candle's wax, and the fire changes into smoke, soon the smell and shape of which will be only a faint memory.

The song ends, and another begins.

The hum and the buzz from his broken guitar continue until the video ends.

#3 Who's Responsible?

Do I blame my family for my problems? Yes, indeed...

Whether by choice or due to unruly circumstances, they were never there for me.

My grandma was the only person ever who loved me unconditionally. Although I can count the times I saw her on my hands, usually during the holidays, she was the only source of light in my dark world. She came from Russia to visit my mother and spend time with me whenever possible. My father never really liked or hated her; he simply disregarded her as if she were a piece of furniture. He treated her like she could not comprehend even the simplest human interaction. Just because she couldn't speak English, to him, she was incapable. She did not like him at all. I don't recall seeing them talking ever. He never really cared enough to try. He didn't even try to learn my mother's native tongue.

Granny would set aside a sliver of her low income every month to be able to see us on Christmas, her only child and grandkid. My mother told me that she had a brother too, but he'd died many years ago.

The older I got, the more I learned about this cruel world we live in, and the more I appreciated my granny. She was like an angel or like one of those fairies in the stories she used to read to me.

She was in her eighties, living off her retirement pension payment in a small town where she had lived in central Russia. What she made in a month wouldn't get us through the week here. Still, she'd save enough to afford the ticket, which was too expensive even for my parents. Not that we had much to show for it, but we were definitely in a better financial position than my grandma.

My parents never bothered with any Christmas traditions, so I knew Santa was not real, and I'd tell the kids at school to spoil the fun for them. But I'd feel so excited whenever my granny could make it on any given Christmas. She was like the real Santa, giving me Christmas presents like used books (fairy tales and Russian folk tales) and candies like Mishka Kosolapy (clumsy bear). But the most important gift of all was the Christmas spirit. We'd spend the whole day cooking deviled eggs, Olivier Salad, and meat pots, preparing for Christmas Eve dinner. My father would complain about the strong aroma, and storm out early in the afternoon. Sometimes, he'd skip the whole holiday, and my mother would lock herself in her room. I really didn't care since my granny was there. Then, my babushka and I would wrap random small items with candy wrappers and create Christmas tree ornaments. I loved that ritual so much it became our own little thing. Ironically enough, they didn't celebrate Christmas where she came from, but she did all of that just for me ... and that was one of the sweetest things anyone has ever done for me.

She kept in touch over the years. Every once in a while, she'd call my mother, talk, then fight, and eventually, my mother would hand her over to me. The warmth and sweetness I heard in her tone sounded better than any word in my language. I longed to be with her all the time. We could sit and have tea, and I could listen to her fairy tales all day long. I would rummage through the Russian vocabulary I had learned over the years and match them to the pictures in those books to try and understand what she was telling me.

I remember my mother promising that she'd pay for me to take Russian lessons so I could communicate with her and Granny. Then she promised to teach me herself.

But like every promise in that household, they were piled up in a corner, among the other broken things.

PART TWO

The Metropolitan Daily

The Afterlife in the Digital Age

By Sophia Riggs
Sep 8, 2024

When Jacob Bodkin, the guitarist of the tribute metal band Unreleased, died in his family home garage this summer, his death was ruled an accident, a stunt gone awry. Then his "Phantom," a term recently standardized thanks to LIV (Instagram's trendier counterpart), came back to haunt us and prove that Jake's death was anything but accidental. This incident has led LIV's users, mostly Gen Z, to praise the app even further. But they shouldn't be so quick to judge. Like anything else, this coin has two sides.

More than a few people questioned whether Epilogue, a feature that allows deceased users to post stories on their LIV accounts, might be upsetting to the recipient. Similar existing cloud-based systems by other tech companies such as Inactivity Alert by Yahoo and Inactive Account Manager by Google, allow users to manage their accounts and data in the event of prolonged inactivity or if they pass away. Although no platform has allowed interactive user activity involving dead users, we expect competitors, including Instagram, Snapchat, and TikTok, to chime in.

THE SOUND OF TUNING OUT

LIV, a popular social networking app among Gen Z since 2020, focuses on some of this generation's most important topics such as positivity, mental health, and sustainability. Unlike Instagram, LIV removes filters to encourage genuine self-expression, prompts collaborative action among communities through shared narratives with "Collab Sesh" and prioritizes environmental sustainability as it uses efficient coding that caters for minimal CPU usage, restricts background tasks to when the device is charging, and offers energy conservation tips to its users. All these features have driven the young crowd toward this platform as they consider it their home, a safe zone that speaks their language. It all makes sense since the creators behind this app are Gen Zers themselves.

Just last winter, the app released a new feature called "Positive Vibes" which offers daily notifications to support users' mental health, and before that, it released the "Safe Zone" feature which combats targeted bullying by incorporating content moderation tailored to user identity. And let's not forget the "Appreciation Glow," which reminds users to post something they are grateful for once a month. But Epilogue feels like a bold leap toward an unknown territory. So why tap into the grimmest of all topics like death?

First, a little background about Epilogue: the idea came to Adrian Lawson two years ago. Lawson's late wife, Monica Massey, a then-rising influencer whose account started getting attention and growing interest from followers on the platform, died during a tragic ski accident when Mrs. Lawson was thirty-one years old. Mr. Lawson was working as a senior product manager at LIV.

"I wanted to keep her memory alive, and I know that she'd be happy to know that my idea had actually pulled through," Lawson said.

Mr. Lawson continued, "If I die, my family will come and search the internet and find all kinds of things about me. With Epilogue, I'm saving everyone the trouble of stumbling upon unpleasant or irrelevant material. Now, I'm giving people the tool to create their legacy. You are entitled to a legacy no matter who you are.

"The idea was an instant hit at the office. I focused on selling it as a treasure box of the person's outlook on life, what they thought mattered the most at the end of the day, rather than a last message kind of thing." Lawson explained, "To that end, nobody should be able to decide how you will be remembered.

"We all exist as digital entities and unlike our organic forms, our virtual existence is not limited to a place or a time. As Pericles said, 'What you leave behind is not what is engraved in stone monuments, but what is woven into the lives of others.'"

While some families cherish recordings of their dead loved ones, others think it's disturbing.

Jake Bodkin was one of the early subscribers to Epilogue, LIV's latest addition to its vast range of features and services. It is one of the few paid services offered by the platform. Jake's account was switched to its current Phantom status once the band's page released a statement about his untimely death. His contacts (or "Phans" since Jake was recognized as a Phantom user) started to see his stories according to certain triggers defined by Jake upon subscription.

A month ago, Jake's account was triggered to share a disturbing Phantom story. The video in question documents the last few minutes of Jake's life. It proves that Jake had suffered serious injuries to the head before the stack of heavy amplifiers (weighing approximately one hundred and fifty pounds) fell on his head. Initially, it was believed that the stunt that ends The Dean's episodes had gone wrong. However, the footage has led the police to reopen the investigation, casting doubt on the original ruling.

"Over the weeks since Jake's death, I grew fond of my brother's stories from beyond the grave. My main goal right now is to obtain all these videos that Jake has been creating in his final days to understand the circumstances around his death more clearly," said Caleb Bodkin, Jake's older brother. "We are certain that he met with foul play," he continued.

Jake's Phantom account on LIV has seen an exponential growth in popularity over the past few weeks because of this mystery. His Phantom stories are among the most viewed videos on multiple social media platforms. This prompted the users to call him the Black Dahlia of the digital age since he gained great popularity after his death. Users are sharing Jake's stories on other platforms such as Instagram, TikTok and X. His "Phans" are hoping that one of his unreleased stories will reveal more details about his death. The investigation has become a kind of whodunnit. Many theories are being considered.

Most popular theories among the online community point toward suicide.

"Who needs a suicide note if you have Epilogue?" one user commented.

"Why would anyone commit suicide that way? What happened to classics like jumping off a bridge or into Snoqualmie waterfalls, or good old gun to the head ... Jake was killed!" another user from the opposing team commented.

Simultaneously, true-crime fanatics or amateur internet sleuths, most notably, the CrimeBC Online forum members look at Jake's videos and digital life as irresistible material as they work together in a crowdsourced model inviting contributors from all over the world to investigate unsolved crimes.

One of the most active users on CrimeBC is Patricia Oona Williams, a.k.a. "Trish_ona_mish." Patricia told TMD, "I honestly love Epilogue; it is a brilliant idea that fits our digital age. It is a great source for me to satisfy my obsession with Jake's life. In one way, I am always thinking of new hashtags to promote a new story by Jake's Phantom. I mean, it was heartbreaking to watch his brother pleading with his Phans. So I want to help in every possible way. And we all want answers!"

Jake's case is one of many cases on CrimeBC that Patricia follows, although his is the only one related to Phantom stories or the Epilogue feature so far.

"I'm expecting some major bombshells to drop in the years to come. We're gonna see more killers confessing to their crimes, more victims coming forward with messages from beyond the grave, and who knows, maybe even some long-sought justice being served," Ms. Williams continued. "You know who would be obsessed with this service? Jack the Ripper and the Zodiac Killer. I'm not even kidding!"

"It is like a morbid version of reality TV. We follow many of these accounts, knowing that the owners are, in fact, dead and that whatever they are talking about has come to an end. When I saw Jake's dedication of 'Hollow' to DD, in my head I was like, 'Spoiler alert! This ends sooner than you think, buddy!'" a Phan commented to TMD.

"As a metalhead, I find Jake's the most interesting Phantom channel so far! The gore, the odd circumstances around his death, and the metal soundtrack!" said Julie Threston, thirty-three, a bartender based in Detroit.

Jake's Phantom content contains music covers of his favorite songs, but a recent video suggesting a secret love affair piqued the interest in Jake's personal life. This video was released almost two days after the video of Jake's death, prompting the internet community to think that the same trigger was responsible for the release of both videos and toward the possibility that the mysterious DD was a suspect in a possible crime.

"I love you. I am so happy to have had the chance to get to know you. I never told you this while I was alive … in case this video comes out sooner than I think … yikes! Anyways! When I tell you in person, I will delete this video … I don't wanna be lame AND dead; Maybe LIV will go out of business twenty, thirty, hell, even fifty years from now, haha, who knows?! So this might all go down the drain." This was a recorded message by Jake Bodkin to a person he referred to as DD or Deedee.

The family of Jake Bodkin has entered a legal battle with LIV Inc., the mother company of LIV, to obtain Jake's digital assets.

"My son's death was not an accident. This much is very clear to everyone; we need the content because it might contain evidence," Diane Bodkin, Jake's mother, said.

"This service could become tricky if not used properly," Edwin Hawkins said. He represents the Bodkin family in their legal case against LIV. The nature of Epilogue and similar services also raises larger concerns about one's digital assets.

The privacy settings are agreed upon with the account owner once they subscribe. You can ask to make your account public entirely or keep some stories private while allowing public access to others. The user also accepts that their Phantom channel will be used for advertising should they gain considerable following marked by the threshold of 500K followers.

With the boom in Jake's channels on LIV, YouTube and Instagram, is the immediate family entitled to the proceeds from the advertising associated with the accounts?

Adrian Lawson urged people to go over the terms and conditions and decide for themselves whether they want to be present in the lives of their loved ones after their own demise. The users give LIV their consent to use their material, which can be historical or new.

In order to switch the account from the regular to the Phantom status, you need to provide a copy of the death certificate, an obituary, or a news article as evidence. Once LIV confirms the user's death, it will automatically sign them out from all devices. Moreover, Phantom stories cannot be accessed except by a handful of LIV employees. "These are just a few examples of LIV's efforts at protecting the user's privacy," Lawson said. Algorithms will work their magic and provide this material on specific dates (time frame chosen by the user) or triggers in the platform. For example, Bodkin's debut as a Phantom, which showed an old cover of the guitar solo from "Floods" by Pantera, showed up because of the buzz around the upcoming Pantera tour.

For a one-time fee of $95.99, users can upload material to their Epilogue depository. The service lasts for up to five years. "It is simply the timeframe that our servers allow us to keep up with the number of users that we currently have without facing any technical issues. We are working on making this period longer," Mr. Lawson added.

LIV's R&D team selected accounts randomly to send promotional material for this service. "We didn't want to make a big fuss before testing the outcome on a small figure. As a result, the promotional email was sent to only 30% of the accounts in LIV's user database. The launch of the first Phantom stories from those who opted to use this feature was due this July," Lawson said.

The feature is available globally, so expect to see an increasing number of accounts with the faded color scheme and the Amaranth dot. Amaranth is a summer flower known as the unfading flower. It signifies immortality in reference to the flowers that generally do not wither and retain bright reddish tones of color, even when dead.

"I began thinking about my own death after losing my brother. I want to legally arrange my accounts, property, and personal information, to save my family any hassle when I'm gone," Caleb Bodkin said. But instead of turning to the usual estate planning methods, Bodkin is taking the time to review his digital footprint and the terms and conditions of his social media accounts.

"Talk to your lawyer about your valuable digital assets, if you have any, and who should be in charge when you die," said Edwin Hawkins.

"Otherwise, you're putting those who love you the most in a difficult position because they have to go to court to get access to your digital life."

This leads us to the question, what are we looking to achieve by promoting this service to the younger generation? It is hard to imagine that adults in their sixties and seventies will be considering Epilogue.

As of August 2024, approximately 64% of global Instagram users were under the age of forty. In comparison, 69% of TikTok users and 74% of LIV users fell into the same age bracket, with LIV having the largest proportion of younger users among these platforms.

Have corporations taken data monetization too far as they try to monetize death?

Caleb Bodkin

Sep 9

Of course I know who the mysterious DD is!

It's Donna Darko, as in Donna Howe.

After Jake's bloody video became viral, we were all convinced that his death was not accidental. So, I was trying to figure out ways to find Jake's recorded videos for Epilogue. I decided to invade his privacy and learn more about my brother in his final days.

I saw nothing out of the ordinary in his camera roll. So I moved to his messages. His conversation with Donna was pinned to the top, which means it was the most important convo to Jake. Their first text was back in January. Their conversation did not seem random or meaningless. The more I read the exchange of messages, the clearer it became that Jake had feelings for Donna Howe. As serious as it can be for a seventeen-year-old. It wasn't only flirting, some of the conversations were very deep. Also, they were texting daily. I did not understand a lot of the things they talked about and the references they used. It's like they had their own language. The most important thing

I kept thinking, Donna Darko! WTF? Why? I don't know much about Donna except what Jake used to tell me. So many kids bullied her and made up horrible rumors about her. I don't remember her lasting more than a year at Red Hills High.

I remember Jake telling me how kids started calling her Donna Darko because she once submitted a very disturbing poetry assignment, and the teacher thought Donna was suicidal. She called her father, and they suggested counseling. I believe she did go to the school therapist, or that's what I heard, at least.

It didn't stop there. One time, she submitted a short story to the school paper about a murder that was never discovered. Again, Kayla, the girl in charge of the school paper, reported her to the principal because she was "concerned." I don't think Kayla was really concerned; I remember telling Jake that day that Kayla was a bully in her own way. Donna didn't talk to anyone; she didn't go to any parties and didn't try to impress boys by wearing makeup or trendy clothes.

All of that could pass as part of the life of a high school student, except that everyone knew about Donna's mental problems and drug abuse. Donna's journey at Red Hills High concluded with one crazy incident that marked the finale of that saga. One day, some kids from her class chased her and sprayed her face with pepper spray. The point was to prove that one of her eyes was fake, referencing the creepy rabbit from Donnie Darko. It was a nasty rumor and a worse joke. Two kids were expelled, and another was suspended because of that incident; Donna dropped out. I think what happened that day messed her up even more because shortly after, I heard that she tried to commit suicide. Last I heard, her dad sent her away to some camp or rehab facility.

I was never a bully, and neither were my friends. I always steered away from anything weird. I had enough on my plate, with my condition and all. I was diagnosed with hypokalemic periodic paralysis when I was sixteen. It's a rare disorder characterized by muscle weakness or paralysis when there is a fall in potassium levels in the blood. I've been dealing with the symptoms since childhood. As a kid, any illness that caused fever meant I needed several weeks to recover. Occasionally, I would just fall flat on my face as I was racing my friends. Up to the ninth grade, I wasn't committed to taking my meds on time. I didn't understand how important it was. As I grew older, I vowed to be responsible about my medication and dietary restrictions in order to lead a normal life. And I did. With enormous support from my mother (who is a health freak, by the way), I managed to enjoy the little things that fall under the "normal life" template.

I saw some recent pictures of Donna which she had sent to Jake just a few months ago. I guess she's kind of cute. She showed a new side of her to Jake. This mysterious unpredictable girl whose history and the town's gossip had made her into some sort of a dark mystery, has suddenly opened up to him, out of everyone else. She let him in on her secrets and insecurities. She showed him how misjudged and misunderstood she'd been. After I read the texts, I called Andrew.

"What did he see in her?" I asked Andrew.

"I don't know, I teased him about it when he first told me, but he didn't take it well, and I was like whatever, dude ... none of my business," he said.

"What was she like? Did you hang out at all?" I asked him.

"We hung out a couple of times; she loved those woods. I remember her taking us to this weird, shady spot once, and I freaked out. I even shared my live location with Nick and told him, 'Just in case Donna decides to go Darko on Jake and me,'" he said.

"Was she weird though?" I asked Andrew.

"Frankly, no. But she wasn't interesting either. I thought she was kinda boring. Still, I can't just get over her crazy past," he said.

"I know. She goes missing around the same time Jake dies under mysterious circumstances. It doesn't sound right," I said.

"Did you tell the police?"

"Yes, I plan to."

THE SOUND OF TUNING OUT

JAKE "THE DEAN" DEATH VIDEO! Unreleased guitarist! The following content may contain suicide or self-harm topics. Viewer discretion is advised.

Learn more

I understand and wish to proceed

35,876,327 views August 27

Jennifer Reese

This case scares me. It's something out of a nightmare! Why is he acting so weird?! I hope that Jake has found peace and that the case closes soon. RIP Jake

TR_xx253

He's on something for sure...

Hopper58

They should use this video for an ad to warn kids against drugs

Thatonepitbull

The creepiest part to me is that we don't know who, if anyone, had done this to him. AND if not for this video, we would have never found out about the criminal. Again, IF there was ANY!

Chriss156

Does not look like suicide to me

Kate Dibiase

When I first saw this video going viral, I thought it was fake, but now I am obsessed! I heard that a Netflix documentary is in the works, btw. But if you need to learn more about Jake's story, go to www.crimebc.com/idiedazombie; this is a direct link to the page dedicated to his case. It really clarifies a lot of things. This is basically the Wikipedia of murder stories, and what's cool about this website is that sleuths have their corner, and they can build the case together. They record the information similar to what a blockchain does. It is difficult or impossible to change the info because once confirmed, it goes into the Black Box (which you need to pay for). Exactly like a classic blockchain, each verified thread in the chain contains information. Every time a new piece of news or evidence is added to the Black Box, which contains only verified data, that info is added to every participant's ledger. Check it out!

XTaila21

OMG! I love those guys; they actually solved Lydia Silverstone's case by providing evidence that the stills taken from the surveillance security cam had been tampered with, and it led the authorities to the real killer. It says under Jake's thread that he must have been attacked before doing the stunt for the last time. Whoever hit him on the head wanted to kill him, of course, but didn't know that Jake was still alive. They left him there, assuming his family would find him dead on the floor later. I can only imagine the killer's relief when the death was ruled accidental.

Jessica Yang

I tried to visit the link it wouldn't let me view the Black Box

Kate Dibiase

You can view the current conversation threads and participate with confirmed data (you must provide the source), but you must pay for a subscription to view the Box.

Hugo Perez

Did the police reopen the investigation?

Dragz Johnson

Yes! I saw his family's press conference yesterday. Heartbreaking.

Nixie2036

Great talent. I actually liked some of their original stuff. RIP

Angus88SOL

Only last week, if you typed the words 'Jake Bodkin' and 'Unreleased' you'd get info about the band, but now Google completes the sentence with 'unreleased death footage.'

Nixie2036

You're right. I just tried it! Any idea why they chose that name for their band?

Angus88SOL

Because their original tracks sounded a lot like Black Sabbath, Pantera and Slayer, so people might mistake their material for unreleased demos by those legends.

Kayla_Tron

He was going to die anyways after that blow, no chance of survival…

View more comments

Brett Howe

Sep 10

www.strengthcircle.com

Online Support Group: Parents of Troubled Teens/Addiction & Recovery

> *If you or someone you care about is dealing with prescription drug abuse, this community is here for you. Share your experiences, find support, and connect with others who are facing similar challenges. You don't have to face addiction alone. Ask questions, offer advice, tell your story, and find hope for recovery right here.*

781 Members   **2,142 Posts**   **8 Online**

I'm taking matters into my own hands. I'm organizing a search for Donna.

I've been going out on my own and looking for my daughter in places where I think she might have gone. I checked some nearby towns and motels and even spoke to some local teens who claimed to be good friends with my daughter. I can see why Donna never really clicked with anyone here. Everyone Donna's age is very rude and selfish. I can see how my mentally unstable teenage daughter suffers a great deal here. It's heartbreaking.

Is this an issue with this generation as a whole, or just in this town? Of course, not all kids here are like that, but the few I've spoken to recently are so hostile. I went to the grocery store where Donna was last spotted and where she worked briefly last summer. The girl who works there was extremely unpleasant.

The police spoke to Donna's therapist. He said that Donna did not have any suicidal tendencies.

"Her last meeting with her therapist was two weeks before her disappearance. Anything could tip a troubled teen like Donna toward the worst in a matter of two weeks, but still, this is good news," the police officer said.

"Any news is good news at this point," I told him.

@muminhell thanks for your comments. Yes, I know exactly what you're talking about. I have to say that over the years, her odd behavior has caused some people to spread nasty rumors about me as a father, being abusive, and things of that sort. Over the years, family and friends have questioned my parenting capabilities throwing all sorts of useless advice at me left right and center. Even her therapist in Seattle has, on multiple occasions, asked about our relationship in a way that made me feel she was hinting at abuse. Of course, none of that has any truth to it. I have dedicated my life to raising my kid the proper way. That's why I chose to stay single all these years. I needed to focus on her needs first. It is so frustrating that she doesn't see it this way.

Following up on the claim that Donna was seeing a boy from around here, the police said they were looking into any connection that may lead them to her whereabouts. Donna has never really dated a guy steadily. As steady as it can be for an eighteen-year-old with mental issues. Aside from casual hookups and flings in an attempt to piss me off or to tell me that she's free to do whatever she wants or to make a statement about being completely independent.

But in reality, Donna had bigger issues to deal with. Dating was not on her mind. I would have loved for her to meet a nice boy with whom she could sneak around and have teenage fun like any normal girl. But I'm not going to lie to myself. Donna's emotional energy was focused on the negative rather than the positive.

On a good day, Donna would throw fits of rage. She would physically attack me, leave the house for hours, and then come home tired and hungry, or someone would report her odd behavior, and I'd have to pick her up at the station.

On bad days, however, I'd have to confront the worst demon of all: emotional numbness, where she would be completely depleted of any feelings, and I'd start wondering if she was still alive. She would retreat to her room for days, refusing to eat or speak.

She has told everyone that she hates me. So when she turned eighteen, I never expected to see her again. But she stayed; I know she stayed because she needed the money and a roof over her head.

At this point, I'm desperate, and I'll gladly accept her terms, no matter how cruel.

Caleb Bodkin
Sep 12

Every weekend since my move to Seattle and Jake's passing, I've been visiting my parents. Last weekend I went to the Howes' and asked about Donna. I needed to find out more about Jake and Donna's relationship.

"Mr. Howe, did Donna ever mention Jake to you? You know, Donna and Jake had been texting for a while before he died. It seems like they liked each other. They even texted after she went missing."

"How do you know that?" he asked. A look of concern mixed with something else passed over his face, maybe fear?

"Jake's phone."

"To tell you the truth, I don't really know. She never mentioned anything about Jake to me. But, you know, she was not the most talkative type." He paused for a few seconds. "How are your parents holding up?"

"I mean, they were miserable before they saw the bloody video of Jake. Now, they're going crazy. Honestly, I'm going crazy. I don't know what to do."

"Yeah, I know. That video is something out of a horror movie," Brett said.

"So, you follow my brother?"

"Not really. I'm too old to be among his followers." He lit a cigarette. "I am overwhelmed with worry for my baby girl, and now you're telling me she was somehow involved with your brother. And she goes missing around the same time ... I'm trying to wait for updates from the police without over-analyzing the situation."

I feel sorry for the guy. He must be so worried about Donna, and the news about her involvement with Jake didn't help. I told him that the police are reopening Jake's case after the horrible video on his LIV account because they don't think it was accidental anymore.

"I don't mean to sound insensitive or anything, but you know, this worries me a lot," he said.

"May I ask why?"

"You know, the police are not taking Donna's case seriously. They aren't making an effort to find Donna. They're certain that she ran away. And I've told them it doesn't make sense because she was never away for that long, she has nowhere to go, and it's dangerous to be gone without her meds for two months now. First, they were distracted by your brother's tragedy, and I'm sorry about that, truly. But honestly, reopening your brother's case will kill any effort at finding Donna." He stopped trying to hide the agitation in his voice.

I soften my tone because I don't want to escalate the situation "I think the police will step up their game in the search for her because she might have some info about Jake's attacker."

He leaned over to reach the ashtray and put out the stub of his cigarette; without looking me in the eyes, he said, "I hope you're not hinting that Donna is a suspect."

I felt so awkward. "No, I'm just hoping she might have some info that would lead to the killer."

When he looked up, he gave me an icy look. It almost felt like I was talking to someone else.

By the end of the conversation, I could tell he was very annoyed with my questions and comments and couldn't wait to get me out of his house.

As I walked back to my parents' house, I thought, What did Brett mean when he said it was "dangerous" if Donna didn't take her meds? Could she have been the one who hurt Jake and then fled the scene? Is that why she was making it a point of not being in touch with her father?

I couldn't help but feel sympathy for Brett, no matter how unfriendly he was during our encounter. But Donna seems like an ungrateful brat! She sucked the life out of her poor father. I was hoping that things weren't going to get even more complicated.

After my short visit to Brett, I called Glenn Weaver, the lead officer on the case. He knew my dad back in high school, so they have this shared history and have been friends since I was a kid. But Glenn was never a regular guest at our house. They had their own guy thing, watching games at pubs or hanging out at Glenn's since he's a bachelor. I remember my dad inviting him a couple of times over during the holidays, but he had always skipped those invitations; eventually, my dad stopped. They were friends in high school in California, and many years later, they ended up in the same suburban community.

After I explained what I'd seen on Jake's phone and what Brett had told me a few minutes earlier, he took some time to respond. I guessed he was taking notes.

"Do you know anything about her disappearance?"

"We're talking to the people in the area, and a few of Jake's classmates mentioned a girlfriend, Emily, I believe. But nobody mentioned anything about Donna Howe. I will look into this," Glenn said.

"I think you should investigate her involvement in my brother's death," I said.

"Emily?"

"No, Donna," I said. "Could she have been the one who hurt my brother? Did she try to kill him and escape?"

"Let's not get ahead of ourselves. You said that Donna has a history of mental illness. As I said, I will look into this, but I need you to steer clear of any involvement in the detective work, Caleb. This is our job. And you've done the right thing by coming to me with this info." He paused and said, "We're gonna need to confiscate Jake's phone and laptop."

"Of course. I'm gonna let Dad know," I said.

Since LIV won't hand the material over to us, I've been trying to make sense of possible triggers that can prompt the Phantom stories to appear. I tried to guess Jake's answers to the questionnaire for the Epilogue subscription. I learned that a hashtag with 5k posts or more qualifies as one type of these triggers (there are like twenty of these conditions that define a trigger for this purpose). So, I asked everyone I know—family, friends, and friends of friends—to post something with the hashtag #thedean. We held a few press conferences, we spoke to the media, I was even interviewed by the TMD.

I need answers, because I can't make sense of what is happening.

#4 When Did it All Begin?

My addiction story started at an early age. It began as early as the day I was born.

The waves that carried me through that awful journey crashed hard on me, and I was left alone in a massive ocean to fight for my life, trying to sneak in short breaths between the constant attacks.

The very first time I dipped my toes into that wild ocean, I was only fifteen.

It's overwhelming the way addiction takes over everything. It all seemed like fun and games until my life got complicated.

I didn't think I needed help. I was a kid, putting mine and others' money toward my amusement, so what? After all, I was entitled to some fun, right? I thought of it as a rebellious act against this unfair world as I had to struggle early in life with family drama.

The lying was continuous and went on for a very long time. I took money from my father. I took money from friends and then lost them forever because I avoided paying them back. They chased after their money for a while. Some of them gave up. Others decided to ignore it because they felt bad for my sick mother (a lie I usually told to get out of situations like these), or because they wanted to help, or because they were afraid of me. I had transformed into the "bad kid" whose influence was avoided by any means. I remember thinking, When did this happen?

My father tried to make me feel guilty for lying to him, but that didn't work. You'll see why. I have so much to tell you about my father. I vaguely remember myself as a child; I loved being around him. Bedtime stories were always a highlight for me. We had all these books for every day of the year. He did all the voices and was an excellent storyteller.

If you're that good at telling stories, you're also probably a good liar.

He made me believe he was a good person, a loyal husband, and a caring father. The irrational side of my personality started to take over every time I felt so gullible with every disappointment. Eventually, I became what I am today. An outcast. A social creep. An addict.

Here is an important piece of information, though. One thing you must know about addicts is that they always justify their actions.

No matter how outrageous that can be.

Caleb Bodkin

Sep 25

I'm at the café just a few blocks away from our office building. The café is abuzz with chatter as people catch up on the latest office gossip or discussing their weekend plans. I'm halfway through my salad when I get a call from Dad during lunch break. When I see his name flashing on my phone screen, I leave my salad and walk away from the table for some privacy.

"Excuse me, I gotta take this," I say to Tobey and Ananth.

"They've got some info on the missing Howe girl," Dad says.

"What happened?"

"According to Brett and previous police reports, this is not the first time she's run away," Dad says.

"Do they think she has anything to do with Jake's death?" As I ask my question, I glance at the table where I was sitting. Tobey's eyes follow me as if he's checking to see that everything is all right. I nod to avoid any questions afterward. I haven't told Tobey much about the case, and he's been respectful enough not to pry with too many questions. I did tell him, though, who the mysterious D.D. is. I have grown close with Tobey, who joined as a financial analyst upon graduating from the University of Washington. He's shown genuine sympathy toward my loss rather than curiosity.

"He was kinda hostile toward Glenn and told him to stop dragging Donna's name into Jake's messy situation." Dad's disdain is evident in the way he says, "messy situation."

"Something is not right with that girl. I think we're onto something solid here," he continues. "She was last seen on July 11, two days before Jake's death. You know that Jake was expecting Donna to come over an hour before he died." Dad's voice breaks. Hearing my dad sobbing, I get emotional and blink tears away to avoid public humiliation.

"You saw the messages when that video was posted, and you were the one who told the police about Donna's possible involvement ... I know she's involved. I'm just waiting for the solid evidence and for the police to find her."

"So, is she officially a suspect?" I ask.

"Damn right she is! I'm going to kill that psycho bitch!" Dad yells.

I try to be the voice of reason by asking logical questions but inside I feel just as angry "But how did she do it? The autopsy results said that Jake had nothing in his system; how could she attack him? I remember her being tiny, short, and skinny; how could she hurt Jake so badly without him defending himself?" I'm talking more to myself than to my dad. I notice a lone businessman who sits quietly at a small table in the corner, typing away on his laptop while sipping a cup of coffee, looking at me; he takes a little longer than he should, staring at my face. So I lower my voice.

"The police said that Jake's attacker tried to kill him and fled through the window. But since the garage door was open too, this can only mean that Jake must have let them in himself."

"So it is fucking Donna!" My voice becomes louder involuntarily, and I'm thankful for the loud milk frother and the conversations overlapping around me. I'm disturbed and ... hurt. Hurt because she had fooled my little brother, and I wasn't there to stop her.

My dad tells me that since my last conversation with Glenn, the police confiscated Jake's phone as evidence. However, I can still access his data from my MacBook since I transferred everything to my laptop to make sure that I have a backup.

I go back to the table without my appetite. The guys are getting ready to leave as the lunch rush begins to wind down, and people start to filter out one by one.

"Is everything okay?" Tobey asks.

"Yeah, I just need to make one more phone call. You guys can go ahead. I'll follow in a few," I say.

I don't really need to call anyone. I just see two notifications on my home screen, which makes me stop in my tracks.

"Full_Metal_Jake has a new story."

"Today is Eveline Murphy's Birthday"

Jake's Phantom shared a memory of us with Eveline. That night we were at Suquamish Clearwater Casino Resort. We went there for a family vacation with my parents, Aunt Carla, Uncle James, Eveline, and her boyfriend. I was nineteen, so I wasn't old enough for a bar then, but old enough to gamble. I tried it, made seventy dollars, and figured I'd treat Eve and her boyfriend to a joint. I'd been there before, so I knew where to look for it.

I vividly remember that night; it was my last day of spring break before I had to head back to Berkeley, where I was still doing my undergrad. It was around two a.m., and we were high and couldn't stop laughing over something silly, which I don't even remember, but I do remember trying to order coffee to sober up and couldn't even get the words out. It was hilarious. The video shows us laughing and ends with Eveline's boyfriend, I think his name was Nate, shaking his head disapprovingly at Jake and saying, "why are you still up?"

The trigger for that video must have been Eveline's birthday. Jake tagged along; of course I wouldn't let him smoke, so he filmed the whole thing, but we were all too high to notice. For a while Jake used the video as blackmail material every time we had a fight; and it worked, until one day I walked in on him trying to touch one of my dad's old "precious" guitars, and so we were even.

I go to my camera roll and scroll back to that night. I see a series of Jake's stupid selfies, making silly faces, instead of taking our group pictures for Eve's birthday when we asked him to. The 'Live' photo feature awakens a lot of forgotten details about Jake. The subtle movements as I swipe between the pictures bring him to life, and I notice a teardrop on my phone screen. I try to go to the bathroom for some privacy as a wave of sadness overwhelms me, but there is a long line waiting, instead I wear my shades and walk around the building for a few minutes to calm myself down. I call Eveline to wish her a happy birthday. She starts crying when she hears my voice.

"So what happened with LIV, anyway?" she asks, once she'd calmed down a bit.

"Nothing. Basically, they get to keep Jake's content, and we have to wait for it just like everybody else," I say. "We're suing LIV, but things take much longer than they should. Glenn told my dad that once they receive the medical report from the exhumation autopsy proving that Jake had been attacked before the stack fell on his head, things will move quickly. We may even drop the case against LIV because it's gonna turn into a murder investigation."

She pauses for a few seconds.

"Wow…Who reported his death anyway?" she finally asks.

"It was Andrew. He told me that when he announced Jake's death on the band's page, he received a follow-up message from LIV. The message was to confirm that Jake, the owner of one of the accounts mentioned in the bio for the band's page, had passed away. And since it has the verified badge, Jake's death was confirmed."

"We have to try harder," she says. "What if the autopsy results aren't in our favor? What if they are inconclusive? We should put pressure on LIV to hand in the evidence."

"You're right," I tell Eve.

Of course, I don't mention any of what my dad had told me just minutes ago to Eveline. But that phone call does help to ease my stress. I throw the rest of my salad away and return to my desk.

Brett Howe

Sep 30

www.strengthcircle.com

Online Support Group: Parents of Troubled Teens/Addiction & Recovery

> *If you or someone you care about is dealing with prescription drug abuse, this community is here for you. Share your experiences, find support, and connect with others who are facing similar challenges. You don't have to face addiction alone. Ask questions, offer advice, tell your story, and find hope for recovery right here.*

775 Members   **2,211 Posts**   **6 Online**

I've been living in Red Hills for the past three years. I know I have my flaws, and I know that I may seem unapproachable or unfriendly at times because I mostly keep to myself. It may not be so obvious, but I am thankful to be part of a good community here. Despite Donna's painful experience at the local high school, I remain a good member of the community and avoid trouble at every chance.

I guess what I am trying to say here is that I need my space now as I deal with the disappearance of my daughter. I can't find the words to describe how I feel as I get up every morning and try to work away my worry and fear. I am trying to keep myself distracted because otherwise, I am going to go crazy! I don't know what to do with myself when I come home to an empty house in the evening. It is not the loneliness; it is the struggle with the uncertainty of the whole situation!

So please, I don't wanna seem rude when I say this, but unless you know where Donna is or can contribute to the search for her, please don't barge into my life asking unnecessary questions that will do no good to anyone.

I say this because the investigation team in Jake Bodkin's case came looking for Donna. They came looking for my daughter "to ask her about her involvement in Jake Bodkin's death," as the obnoxious detective put it.

"I should ask you where my daughter is since I reported her missing two months ago!" I basically yelled at the guy; his name is Glenn Weaver, he's the new detective on the Bodkin case.

I warned the detective that if my sick daughter harms herself because of their reckless actions, there's gonna be hell to pay! I mean, isn't it obvious that the Bodkins' kid was going through serious issues?

Because my daughter has been a victim of bullying, be it online or in person, I choose not to believe everything I read about their son because I know that most of the stuff you find online is nothing but meaningless junk, written on a whim by someone who has nothing better to do. There are rumors that he was involved in cult rituals related to the crazy music scene he was a part of. There is also the widely popular theory that he killed himself. Some people are saying that the whole thing was related to drugs. I understand that these speculations are offensive to his family, especially if they've been lucky enough not to have dealt with bullies up to this point.

That's precisely why I don't bother anyone!

Jake asked for this much attention in life and death, so they should deal with the consequences on their own.

"Our investigation is still ongoing; I am trying to get to the facts in time to do some damage control since the discovery of this evidence emerged a bit too late. If this were my crime scene since day one, none of this would have happened," the detective bragged.

He then looked me in the eye and said, "Mr. Howe, it's best for you and your daughter to be cooperative and speak up sooner rather than later. I advise you to tell us if you have any clue where Donna is."

The guy was obnoxious and arrogant. The way he spoke to me was so inconsiderate and condescending.

I want to ask everyone to keep my daughter out of any unnecessary mess.

My Donna is suicidal and is on heavy medication. She tried to end her life before. So please don't make it any more difficult for my girl.

I think we all should start to face the situation for what it is instead of living in denial.

@couchpotato thanks for your messages. Unfortunately, Donna does not use social media. Her therapist told me it is due to a lack of self-esteem, especially after all the bullying she endured in high school. Honestly, though, I think she doesn't want me to be able to reach out to her whenever I want or to have that comforting feeling of knowing where she is or what she is up to.

Thanks for all the suggestions and constant support.

Caleb Bodkin

Oct 1

My mom tells me to read what Brett wrote about "keeping his precious daughter out of any unnecessary mess." One of Jessica Bartlett's book club members is also a member of the "parents of troubled teens" forum, and she told Jessica about Brett's angry posts. Mom says that Jessica has been a great help in the days since Jake's death.

I know that part of Jessica's generous act of compassion is an attempt to avoid her cheating husband. She always tries to busy herself with anything but her own business. I guess it is too painful to face her reality. But, of course, I didn't bring this up to my mom because I am thankful for whatever and whoever it is that helps her. Like anything new, some people are against this feature, including my dad and me, thinking it is useless and morbid. While others, like Mom, are in favor of anything that might offer them comfort and consolation, no matter how fake it might be—at least in my opinion. Especially people like my mother who are not active on any social media platform. She's one of those people with an old Facebook account, which she never checks or uses, with two old photos in her profile picture album.

"Well, I'd like to tell him it is a bit too late for that! considering how fucked up his daughter is, being an addict and a suicidal maniac!" I tell Mom.

"Glenn said it is only a matter of time before we get the data from LIV. Once the investigation into Jake's case is ruled as a murder investigation, the company will have to hand in the data." She pauses.

"What's wrong?"

"If the exhumation autopsy results do not conclude that Jake was attacked, there won't be a murder investigation, and LIV can keep the data without question," she says.

"I know, that's fucked up! I can't help but think that the killer could be in one of those videos! What did the lawyer say?" I ask.

"Hawkins said that it is not an easy task to get these files. The privacy policies of these social media platforms include many terms and conditions that protect the company more than the user, and most of us check that box without even glancing at the terms. I'm sure that the LIV people are enjoying the attention also. Anyways, are you coming tonight?"

"Yes, I plan to be there around seven. What time is Hawkins coming?"

"Eight thirty, don't be late."

The drive from Seattle to Red Hills takes forever with the rush hour traffic on I-90. However, as I pass through Mercer Island, the traffic starts to ease up. As I continue eastward on I-90, I pass by scenic vistas of Lake Washington and the surrounding mountains. The sky has started to take on a pink and orange hue as the sun begins to set, casting a warm glow over the landscape.

As I approach the Red Hills area, a misty rain begins to drizzle down. I start to see the foliage along the side of the road changing color from green to orange, red, and gold. The air gets cooler and crisper as I move closer to the mountains.

When I reach our quiet residential area nestled amongst the trees, a feeling of sadness washes over me. I used to love coming home on the weekends. I'd just relax with my family and see some friends from high school. But recently, the sight of the familiar streets lined with quaint shops, cafés, and restaurants, all illuminated by warm, golden light, and the houses decorated with pumpkins and wreaths, has been nauseating.

As I step out of the car, the first thing I notice is the silence that hangs heavily in the air. Our cul-de-sac is empty, and the only sound I can hear is the rustling of leaves as they swirl in the gentle breeze.

Approaching our house, I see one light on in the living room and another in the kitchen. I fumble with my keys and open the door, stepping into a warm, dark foyer. The silence is deafening. The sadness and emptiness of the house seems to intensify, and I feel like the walls are closing in on me. I take a deep breath, trying to calm my racing thoughts, and resolve to focus on the questions I had prepared for the lawyer. Dad is in the living room, typing on his laptop. Mom is nowhere to be found.

"Where's mom?" I ask.

"She's at the Bartletts', as usual." He raises his eyebrows as if to say, Where else could she be?

As I settle on the couch, I can't shake the feeling that the house is too big and empty without Jake.

"Where's Fen?"

"With her."

I can't hide my disappointment. My dad shrugs and takes a call. I make herbal tea while waiting for Hawkins. It's almost eight p.m. A few minutes pass, and then I hear the front door unlock. The rain has picked up in the last thirty minutes or so, and my mom's hair clings to her face in wet strands, droplets of water dripping from the end of her nose, and her shoes squelching on the hardwood floor. Her eyes scan the dimly lit living room as Dad and I sit in silence, each of us lost in his own thoughts. When she sees me sitting on the couch, sipping my tea, her face involuntarily lights up.

"You're here? How was traffic?" she asks, attempting a bright tone.

"As bad as always," I say. The dim light in the room darkens the shadows under her hanging eyelids. Dehydration and lack of sleep have drawn deeper wrinkles around her eyes and lips. Where did the vibrant, resilient woman I've known all my life go? I look away to avoid revealing these thoughts.

She makes her way to the bathroom to dry herself. Fenrir shakes off the rain from his fur and pads into the living room. His tail wags excitedly as he sees me. I pat the cushion next to me, and he jumps up onto the couch, snuggling close to me as I rub him dry with a towel.

At eight fifty, the doorbell rings.

After Hawkins apologizes for the delay, he proceeds to business right away. He explains the plan in case the exhumation autopsy results don't work out.

"As Jake's family, you get to inherit the money his accounts generate after gaining a huge following. According to the terms and conditions, Jake allowed LIV to use his account for advertising, which means you are entitled to the proceeds as per the percentage in the contract. The amount could be significant," Hawkins says.

"Please. Let's not discuss this. I want to know more about the steps we need to take to get a hold of Jake's Phantom videos," Mom says.

"Right, I understand. However, the videos we're after are good enough for the exhumation autopsy but not enough for a murder investigation." He pauses to turn off an alarm on his Apple Watch. "If, for whatever reason, the exhumation report does not indicate that Jake was attacked and that his wounds which we see in the video from his

Epilogue post were self-inflicted, then the content he previously agreed to record and publish will become irrelevant." He drops his gaze for a second. "Maybe it would be wise then to drop the case and accept the money from Jake's account. Because Mrs. Bodkin, this will be a long, expensive, losing battle for you."

"My son was attacked! Have you seen the video?" Dad says.

"Nothing proves that someone did that to him. There were no witnesses, there was no weapon recovered from the scene, and there was no proper investigation conducted on the spot because everyone thought it was an accident. LIV's legal team could argue that the wound was the result of a failed suicide attempt and therefore Jake's Epilogue content is irrelevant."

We all sit in silence for a minute, trying to process what Hawkins just told us. Frustration and anxiety start to build within me. What if the exhumation report concludes no one harmed Jake? We'd be left with no choice but to move on, knowing that crucial evidence might still be stored on some Cloud server. I picture LIV going out of business years from now, their data acquired by another company. What if that new entity combs through the Cloud and uncovers a direct lead to the killer? Jake's case could end up being one of those that are solved years later—or, even worse, become a cold case forever.

"We all know how critical this evidence might be in this case, but we still have no power to force LIV to do anything about it; we do not even have a subpoena. To get such a document, we need to prove that Jake was, in fact, attacked," Hawkins says, interrupting my thoughts. "The police and prosecutors know it. They routinely use private social media content at trial."

He goes on about some law from the eighties regulating the internet; how defense teams generally cannot get their hands on such evidence because of that law.

"The primary goal of the Stored Communications Act was to prevent government and hackers from accessing this info. But they didn't think outside of the box. Nobody thought some third parties might need the information for legitimate reasons. The law still stands today because there were concerns about the Fourth Amendment. Law enforcements are expected to take particular measures, such as obtaining a court order, before making companies share users' nonpublic content."

"But the content could be helpful in several ways. There could be something there that would lead to possible suspects in this case. Why are they doing this? What good could it be for them? He's only one guy!" I exclaim.

"LIV refuses to disclose the content, referring to the Stored Communications Act. They want to reemphasize to the public that their data is safe and sound. They want to show that they acted responsibly in refusing to disclose people's private content," Hawkins says. "The laws regulating the internet are outdated."

"So what are they saying here? We have to sit and wait helplessly while evidence of Jake's murder is sitting somewhere in their clouds until god knows when it appears! Waiting for chance, hoping for good luck?!" Dad says.

The sound of raindrops tapping against the window provide a steady background noise to the heated conversation taking place.

Hawkins continues, "Take it easy, Mr. Bodkin. The good news is that the case will most likely turn into a murder investigation soon, which will involve the police retrieving this information without major obstacles. But for the individuals trying to access social media evidence, privacy protections prevail. So, Jake's right to privacy prevails." He stops to let us process what he's saying. "They argued that the family can access content through other routes, for example, by instigating triggers for content by the dead. I know it's ridiculous, but in the meantime, I suggest we play by their rules."

"We should try, but we don't know what we will get, and it is not easy to predict," I say. "I've been trying to deal with my grief more productively by prompting messages from Jake. Anything that can lead to his killer. I even asked his Phans for help."

Hawkins shares more general details about the dates and upcoming procedures for the weeks ahead, advising us to be prepared to provide additional information to the authorities if needed, and then he leaves.

"How did such an idea appeal to Jake?" Mom asks.

"Something is off. He didn't mention it to anyone. But apparently, he took it seriously enough to record all these videos. And he actually paid almost one hundred dollars for it! I tried to sign up because I wanted to know more about how it works. I was hoping I'd find a way to get the data faster. Basically, they ask about the important dates in your life, interests, social circle, highlights, regrets, beautiful memories, apologies, thank yous, and any deathbed confessions. It was all very personal. It took me a long time to finish the entire questionnaire. I stopped right before they asked for the payment."

The following day, my parents and I ask everyone we know to spread the word and use a set of hashtags on their LIV accounts, family, friends, and friends of friends. We use the band's official page. I even respond to web detectives obsessing over Jake's case, such as Trish_ona_mish. We might know more if we get people to discuss that specific topic and trigger Phantom Jake to post stories.

It works. After a few days, we start seeing more activity.

A part of me is worried that something else will resurface ... something a lot more sinister and upsetting.

There is no question that Jake's death was not an accident. We know he was attacked. We're only waiting for the results of the official forensic analysis to convert it into fact rather than opinion.

Unfortunately, there are a lot of things that were overlooked during the first investigation by the police. And now that I look back, things did seem out of place, but we were all under the impression that this was an unfortunate accident. For example, some blood at the crime scene might have belonged to the killer. When the death is no longer considered accidental, the blood that stained several places within the garage doesn't make sense.

But there is no way for the police to find out because Jessica called my mom when she found him. My mom was there before the police as she was walking Fenrir only a few blocks away, and she and Jessica tried to remove the broken equipment on top of Jake. They thought that he was still alive and that there was some hope of saving his life. But after seeing the footage of zombie Jake, it made more sense that the blood was on the guitar, the seat where Jake usually recorded his YouTube videos, and all over his path from that spot to where he ended up dead.

I'm so angry at myself for stalling to come home after I got the offer. Had I been home, I could have helped stop the attack. I am so angry that I've been fooled like that.

I'm angry at my parents for not following procedures upon discovering his body.

I'm angry at the police for not doing their job while under the assumption that he died in an accident. Everyone just assumed that he died because he was a foolish teenager pulling a Jackass move.

I mean, think of all the lost evidence!

Brett Howe
Oct 10

www.strengthcircle.com

Online Support Group: Parents of Troubled Teens/Addiction & Recovery

> *If you or someone you care about is dealing with prescription drug abuse, this community is here for you. Share your experiences, find support, and connect with others who are facing similar challenges. You don't have to face addiction alone. Ask questions, offer advice, tell your story, and find hope for recovery right here.*

782 Members   **2,235 Posts**   **10 Online**

Until the tragedy of Anastasia's death turned our lives upside down, we had a very normal life. You didn't have to know either of them to have your heart broken at Anastasia's funeral. Donna locked herself up for two weeks in her room. She wouldn't eat properly, speak, or go to school for a whole year. She had to be homeschooled for a while.

"Create a new chapter with her. She doesn't feel like there is a connection between you and her, and she misses her mother dearly. A move will develop this connection and a foundation for the attachment between you and her, which you desperately need. She has to depend on you in this new environment, and this is a golden opportunity for you to shine as a parent and show her the love and support she yearns for; you can be for her what her mother had once been," her previous psychologist, Dr. Zheng suggested, after we had exhausted every trick in the book.

We moved from Tampa to Seattle once I found a job, which was almost six years after Anastasia died. Since then, our lives have not been the same. Donna became hostile toward me. I wanted to get away from every memory of her mother, which surrounded her daily routine. I thought a fresh new start in a new place, new town, new home, with new friends could do the trick. Or at least give me the boost I was looking for.

It's been three years since we moved to this town. Donna hates me more than ever. She hates this town and everyone in it. She told me more than once. And you know what? I am starting to see her point. People in this town have nothing better to do but discuss my daughter's private life.

Don't get me wrong, I do sympathize with the Bodkins, and I pray for their peace of mind and the ability to move on and cherish their son's memory. But I would like to draw the line at causing any harm to my own family.

What the hell is wrong with people? My daughter is missing! Is this how they treat a missing teenager's case? The police continue to fuck up consistently! First, they fucked up Jake's case, and now my daughter could be in danger while they sit and watch people bully her online!

While I am grateful for the continuous support that many online community members offer me during this hard time, I am appalled at the scumbags who have nothing better to do than troll others online. My daughter was bullied out of high school and was tormented by social pressures imposed by unrealistic standards set by this generation of fake culture.

I will NOT let this continue.

One more thing, I hope to god Jake did not hurt my daughter before killing himself!

There I said it!

My daughter is under attack. They are saying the nastiest things about her, making assumptions that are too hurtful to read, and distracting the authorities from finding her. I am not going to stand by and hope for the best. I will continue to organize search parties, hire PIs, go to the end of the world to find her! She is my one and only!

This is a message to everyone: if you have nothing useful to say, then just back off!

#5 Who's the Real Psycho Here?

Being an only child is not a good thing if your parents think of you as a sponge for their energy, especially when that energy is negative most of the time.

Over the years, while living with the two most selfish people on this planet, I was given a different treatment depending on the situation and the issues they had been facing at the time.

When I was seven, I won first place in my art class. Our teacher gave three gifts to the three kids with the best Mother's Day card. Mine was the best; I'll never forget the tenderness I felt beaming from my mother. On that day, I felt like the golden child.

Fast forward five years, I grew into a troublesome teenager, and thus, they treated me as an obstacle. So I was the reason for everything that went wrong with their lives. When you feel responsible for your own decisions and that you need to stand up for yourself and justify your actions, that means your childhood days are over. My parents started fighting like crazy. Now that I think of it, the timeline is all a haze. Maybe the fights have always been part of their relationship, but I was too young to tell or remember. My mother blamed me for it. Classic scapegoat child story. She would talk about me to her friends, neighbors, and even acquaintances as if I were the enemy. She made me sound like the evil child plotting to ruin her life.

With my father being absent for most of the day, I remember feeling more like a partner than a child when I was only ten. Our relationship was unhealthy, to say the least. She depended on me emotionally and expected me to sit there and take whatever she threw at me. She would sit and discuss her adult problems, loneliness, financial troubles, and insecurities with me. I didn't even understand what she was talking about half the time. Still, I had to sit there and listen, and if I didn't show her any sympathy, she'd flip and lock me in my room for hours to "think about my ungrateful behavior."

By age twelve, I had become invisible to everyone around me. I couldn't tell if I was a good or a bad kid, in all honesty. I often wondered if I'd had any siblings, would she still treat me so badly? As if I am this terrible, disrespectful, heartless child? I realize now that my mother most likely suffered from bipolar disorder. I am not a psychologist, but she exhibited some classic signs or at least the symptoms we learn about through mass media. Regardless of the accurate diagnosis, I am sure she was not right in the head. One day, she would take me to the park or the beach or watch a movie and buy me ice cream. The next, she wouldn't speak to me and call me the worst of names. The fluctuation between the two characters was so confusing when I was younger I couldn't understand. She blamed me for everything that didn't go her way. She'd say things like I'm disrespectful, a terrible child, I don't love her, etc. Of course, I was in the wrong, no matter what.

She was not cut to be a mother. I know this sounds cruel but losing her at an early age was almost a relief because being a single parent (although my parents never officially divorced) for an only child was the worst possible combination for my mother's mental instability.

So yes, I blame my father for what I went through during my childhood and teenage years.

They both saw it coming ... they both deserved what was in store for them.

PART THREE

Trish_ona_mish
Oct 31

Log from www.crimebc.com/idiedazombie
HAPPY HALLOWEEN MY MISHIONARIES!!
I KNOW! I've been bad ... It's been a WHOLE FREAKIN WEEK OF SOCAL, VEGAS, since I last posted here! BUUUUT I HAVE NEEWWWWSSS!!!
I KNOW WHO DD IS!
It is none other than Jake's neighbor, Donna Howe!!
WAIT ... you all know that by now, sorryyyy haha!
Seriously though, THE BIG news I've just found out (& confirmed, here's the link) is that the results of Jake's autopsy are finally out! Here are the deets:
JAKE WAS REALLY ATTACKED BEFORE HE PERFORMED THE FINAL STUNT!!!!
The news article here explains how the police arrived at that conclusion:
"The loss of soft tissues and bone fragility were major obstacles in this analysis. However, the dry bone study showed defects in the skull, suggesting injuries by a weapon. Post-mortem CT with three-dimensional (3-D) reconstruction provided more details about the characteristics of the murder weapon and allowed us to speculate about the number and

the traces of potential blows. However, the vitality of these injuries, the final, fatal blow, and the distance could not be determined. Likewise, the type of the weapon could not be clarified. It is suspected, though, that it was an axe or a hammer. Despite all doubts, the forensic explorations have allowed to deny the proposed cause of death after more than three months of burial." Source: NBCNEWS.

Here are more details from other sources:

- According to forensic medical experts, Jake's odd behavior in the video was due to the severe damage the outer layer of his brain had sustained. This part of the brain is responsible for complex thought and reasoning. It makes up about 75% of the volume of the human brain. It was almost completely damaged.

- As a result, the part of the brain responsible for instincts and routine habits took over completely. This meant that he was completely unaware of what happened to him.

- Once his theme song came on, he followed his usual steps when recording an episode for his channel. He switched on his phone, grabbed his guitar, and started playing. Then he jumped on the wall for the show's closing stunt. The trigger song was in the queue or Jake's favorites playlist.

- Since Jake was not physically capable of performing his usual routine due to a prior attack on his head, he slipped while jumping on the wall of stacks, causing the heavy equipment to fall on his upper body, killing him.

It was probably a coincidence that this recording went to the Epilogue content. Jake was maybe in the middle of a recording session when he was attacked. Someone attacked him, left hurriedly, and the music kept going. Once "Domination" came on, Jake's senses were awoken in a familiar environment, thus carrying Jake through his usual routine when recording his episode. But he couldn't understand that he was in danger, bleeding, performing a dangerous stunt while unwell. He didn't register that he needed help. He was a zombie for the last minutes of his life (hence the name of this forum).

The obvious question here is, who did that to him in the first place?

Whoever did that had intended to kill Jake for sure. The good news is that now the police can get the data from LIV with a court order because this report proves that Jake was attacked and that content is evidence.

On another note, I've done some digging on Donna Howe and found info floating on the internet about her, although it was not easy since the weirdo has no online presence. No Insta, no LIV, Facebook, Snap, Twitter, TikTok ... nothing. Fuck me, isn't she like nineteen?

So weird! (Mishionaries, this is your homework: find DD's digital footprint.)

AAANYWAYZZ let's zoom in on this mysterious DD who stole the heart of our favorite metalhead ... (disclaimer: all the info about Donna I've managed to find are from unofficial comments and accounts by locals from her area)

Donna and her father, Brett, moved to Red Hills three years ago. She is almost a year older than Jake. She went to Red Hills High for a while and then was homeschooled.

She's a druggie, psycho, suicidal, the whole package! Jake sure knew how to pick 'em!

Wait, I'm not done! Here's the plot twist: she is MISSING!!! I MEAN! WHAAAAT!! Since when, you ask??? Since Jake's been dead!! Yeah ... it doesn't get more obvious than that...

THE SOUND OF TUNING OUT

Jake and Donna were in love (or so he thought, poor thing), and apparently, the relationship was under the radar. No one knew the two were dating (WTF?), including their families and friends.

Her dad reported her missing on July 12, a day before Jake's "accident." But because it isn't Donna's first time going AWOL ,the police didn't think much of it.

The note: She left a note in her bedroom before disappearing. The message was an excerpt from William Wordsworth's poem "Ode." To me, it sounds like a goodbye (suicide?); she does have a history of self-harm.

Three days ago, I asked my Mishionaries to give their votes on the most likely theory, and the results are (drum roll):

Theories:

1. She killed/tried to kill Jake and is hiding somewhere: **47%**

2. She killed/tried to kill Jake and killed herself somewhere: **31%**

3. She had nothing to do with Jake's death (either he killed himself or someone else attacked him), she is fine, and had just run away somewhere: **14%**

4. She had nothing to do with Jake's death and is in danger ... somewhere! **8%**

Wow! Our minds are synchronized! I am so proud of you!

All the evidence so far points toward Donna being as Darko as her bullies once claimed her to be!

The one thing making me disregard the last two scenarios is that, according to her dad, she has never been away from home that long. EVER!

It makes sense that she went away for good this time because she knew that there was no coming back from what she'd done. JMO

Below are the links to the latest news coverage/the sources for the above info.

Also, I'm starting a YouTube channel dedicated to Jake's Phantom stories for further analysis and contribution by my fellow web sleuths.

#catchDonna #whereisDonna #mysteriosd #mydd #Donnadarko

SEE YAS LATER!

Caleb Bodkin
Nov 1

I have always been defined by my condition. While Jake had rightfully claimed "the cool kid" title in the family (that statement still applies even when all cousins from both sides are included), I was the "miracle."

During my high school years, I had a good group of friends, a cute girlfriend, got good grades, went to a good business school afterward, and now here I am, starting my career at a Fortune 500 company in Seattle! So I'm better off than most of my classmates.

While I believe I did well, my performance in the past twenty-four years has been nothing extraordinary. After all, I'm just an average guy doing average things, just like most of the population. But I guess my HPP diagnosis has upgraded me from being just another guy to a "source of inspiration."

In all honesty, I don't feel special but rather privileged because I live in a place where everyone understands my condition and does their best to help out. Growing up as an Average Joe, I never thought that any death in this family was going to be investigated. The most likely reasons that could cause a guy like Jake or me to die were cancer, a heart attack, a stroke, or maybe a car accident. This conclusion lived in my subconscious, derived from my predictable circumstances. That's why Jake's accident was a shock. But still, nobody suspected foul play because, again, we are normal people, leading normal lives, who get excited when their son/brother/cousin knows how to play the guitar and performs for strangers.

I also imagined that we would have more time together. Much more time...

When Jake's autopsy results came out, the outcome was tough to digest. First, they x-rayed his skull to check for consistency in his injuries with the presumed accidental cause of death. The analysis revealed that he had been hit on the head before the amp stack fell on him. The report said something like an axe or a hammer.

"Is there any tool like that missing from your garage?" Glenn asks Dad as we all sit around the dinner table to hear the investigation updates following the autopsy. Although the results came out on a Tuesday, I still drove to my parents' house after I was done with work because Glenn wanted to speak to all of us about what this new information meant for both cases: Jake's murder investigation and data acquisition from LIV Inc. These developments are mainly based on the autopsy results.

"No, but I can look again. We don't own an axe, and I used the hammer just yesterday to pull a nail from the wall," Dad says.

"So the reconstruction of the skull revealed that the perpetrator hit Jake on the head, with an axe, most likely, more than once, and assumed that Jake had died." He pauses to sip his coffee.

"Except that Jake was not dead. The blows to his head had caused enough damage to his brain to make him incapable of understanding what was happening to him, but he could still move. You saw the report, right? Did you understand it? The part where they explain the human brain and how one side was intact, and the other was damaged after the attack?"

My mom starts crying. Dad nods, tears filling his eyes and escaping through the corners. I get up to bring the tissue box from the other room and to give myself a few seconds to compose. Glenn then continues explaining.

"I'm sorry this is hard for everybody, but I have to explain it." I nod for him to continue.

"I understand that Jake had a specific theme song for his show, right?"

"Yes, that song by Pantera," I say.

"Exactly. When the song came on, he woke up bleeding and followed in his usual footsteps. He acted like a shadow ... and that stunt he did to end the show ... He did it clumsily, and you saw what happened next."

Fenrir comes into the room and puts his paws on Glenn's thighs for attention, causing him to nudge the coffee cup and spill a few drops on the table. Glenn pauses to wipe the drops from the table surface with a tissue. "Sorry about that."

"So we suspect that Jake was recording a video to be added to his Epilogue space right before the attack. That's why the video he recorded next went directly to Epilogue."

"Makes sense," Dad says after he calms down.

"They must have come in through the door, which makes Donna Howe our number one suspect since Jake was expecting her, according to their message exchange. Her disappearance is treated more like a 'criminal on the run' under these new developments. Of course, this is not official or public ... yet, but from the looks of it, she seems like the most likely suspect here."

"I can't believe it," I say.

"It's hard to believe. A very rare outcome, but it happened a few times before. There was a guy in upstate New York who woke up after an axe attack on his head. The guy woke up to the alarm clock, got up, got ready for work, and died a half hour later at the bottom of the stairs leading up to his front door."

"That is bizarre," Dad says.

"So what's next? How are we going to catch her?" Mom asks in between sniffs, fighting the urge to cry some more.

"As I said, we will intensify our efforts to find her. Even if she wasn't the attacker, maybe she can lead us to them," Glenn says.

"What about the Epilogue content?" Dad asks.

"Yes, we are getting a court order in a couple of days once we complete the procedures, and that should force LIV to hand over the info at once," Glenn says. "We can see if there is any evidence in the content hidden there. My tech expert also told me that this will allow us to figure out the exact time of the recording and maybe the trigger that Jake set for this video, which may give us some clues as to what he and Donna may have been up to or mixed in."

After Glenn leaves, I take Fenrir out for a walk. The house is very depressing, so I need fresh air. It was around nine thirty p.m. ... The neighborhood is so quiet, I can hear my own footsteps echoing in the cold night. It's freezing, even for Red Hills, which is generally chilly and wet. I zip up my windbreaker and decide to walk back and have a cup of warm tea on the porch.

I make myself a cup of ginger lemon tea and sit in the wooden rocking chair with Fenrir by my side. I allow myself to drift for a while on a wave of memory. Jake and I were sitting on this very porch, catching up; I was telling him about my new internship, which was scheduled to start after Christmas break. I was due to complete my MBA program last April, and based on my performance, my bosses would decide whether to hire me as a full-time employee. I got the offer by the end of my three-month internship. I didn't tell anyone. I was saving this surprise for later in the summer after I finished all my arrangements to move from Berkeley to Seattle. This summer was all about good news and reuniting as a happy family. I never got to share the good news with Jake about my new job in Seattle, that I'd be moving there in September as we'd talked about.

THE SOUND OF TUNING OUT

Jake was telling me about his newfound interest in sound equipment. He wanted to pursue a career in sound engineering.

"I don't know if I'm comfortable in the spotlight. I prefer to enjoy the perks without the attention," I remember him saying.

Also, what happened to one of his classmates, Hunter Jenkins, scarred Jake for life. Hunter was only fifteen years old when he killed himself. Although Jake wasn't that close with him, the story of Hunter's suicide shook up the whole community. What they did to him was cruel, and what made matters worse was that the kids who bullied him were never properly punished. The community never healed because everyone felt like the bad guys could get away with anything, no matter how drastic the results may be. The things they posted about Hunter, while he was alive, were disturbing, to say the least. No one wanted to discuss it, but everyone dealt with it differently. Everyone was suffering on their own. Jake pulled the brakes on his online activity afterward; he kept his YouTube channel, LIV, and Instagram accounts active because of his band, but he used social media strictly for his music. Nothing about his personal life. Nothing about who he really was.

So why did Jake subscribe to Epilogue? And why the secrecy?

Brett Howe

Nov 4

www.strengthcircle.com

Online Support Group: Parents of Troubled Teens/Addiction & Recovery

> *If you or someone you care about is dealing with prescription drug abuse, this community is here for you. Share your experiences, find support, and connect with others who are facing similar challenges. You don't have to face addiction alone. Ask questions, offer advice, tell your story, and find hope for recovery right here.*

803 Members **2,305 Posts** **15 Online**

@Lisasmom Thank you for your kind words. You're right. It may have been a good idea, but not right now. I'm not sure that giving her space is the right approach under the current circumstances. I am terrified for her safety. I am heartbroken that my daughter said she didn't want any contact with me, and yes, she is an adult, so I guess I can't do much but give her time and space. I'll try to show her that I respect her decision regardless of the pain. But not now.

My main concern right now is to make sure that she is safe and healthy.

THE SOUND OF TUNING OUT

While everyone is too busy looking for someone to blame for Jake Bodkin's death, I am sick to my stomach with fear that whoever tried to kill Jake is now after Donna, and that's why she may have decided to go under the radar.

@Steph1965 That's the only reason I think the two cases (Jake's death and Donna's disappearance) could be linked. My Donna wouldn't hurt a fly; she is a very tender soul. Also, she is a petite girl, and her body is weak mainly because of her unhealthy diet and heavy medication. She couldn't have been the one that attacked Jake!

#6 What Was That Vision I Saw?

I miss Granny so much. I guess I'm most excited to see her at the end of this journey...

Talking to Granny was like stepping into a different dimension. She came from a different time and never really kept up with the rest of the world. She barely spoke English, and I could communicate with her using only a few Russian words.

I couldn't even blame her for leaving me when I was only twelve. She died at the age of ninety-two. Unlike my mother, she put up a good fight against time and her shitty living situation; with her tiny, frail body, she didn't stand a chance. She was the strongest person I knew, and I loved her so much. When she died, I left home for days. I would only show up around dinnertime and go straight to my room. I wanted to stay away from my parents. I wanted to stay away from everyone. I even contemplated suicide because I wanted to be with her forever.

One night, she came to visit me in my dream. I was on a swing under a tree on a farm. The sky was dark, and there was no one around. Suddenly, someone pushed me, making me go high up. I giggled because I was enjoying the thrill. I turned my head to see who was pushing me and saw Granny. She looked angry, had bloodshot eyes and disheveled hair, and wore a dark red dress. When the swing moved closer to her, she grabbed both sides of the rope and brought the swing to a complete stop. She held my head and whispered, "Ona smeyetsya," which means "someone's laughing."

And then I heard a low, guttural chuckle that became more intense by the second until it became a high-pitched cackle. It sounded distorted and echoey, as if coming from a far-off place or a place that no longer existed. My grandma was no longer there, and I started to hear other eerie sounds, like whispers or moans. When I woke up, the room was pitch black, and I was shivering from cold and fright. Also, I had wet the bed.

The next morning, I burnt the mattress to save myself the embarrassment.

I silently thanked Babushka for chasing these nasty thoughts out of my head.

Of course, my subconscious then chose a word I understood in Russian. It didn't make any sense and didn't signify anything. But somehow, I never got over that disturbing sound.

Maybe, because it had reminded me of one of the most terrifying Russian folktales, the Rusalka.

Trish_ona_mish

Nov 6

WE ARE ALL "ON A MISH" NOW!! The hunt for Donna Howe began the minute the autopsy results were made public. Her pictures are all over the news. Anyone with info about Donna CALL THE HOTLINE NOW!! Donna's involvement in Jake's murder has not been confirmed with any physical evidence YET, but guess what? WE CAN CHANGE THAT!

The major development here is "The court granted permission for additional DNA testing on items from the crime scene. The court also ordered all content from Bodkin's Phantom account to be handed to the police as evidence." Source: USA TODAY

OMG!!! THE MOMENT IS NEARLY HERE!!! We will finally know who (or what *wink wink* – shoutout to the paranormal investigators of the internet haha!) killed Jake!

I would like to thank the user Woodsy09, who used digital software to recreate the Bodkins' garage according to info scattered all over the internet. You can view the 3D model here. It includes details like the dimensions, the entry points, and possible sighting points by neighbors and witnesses. Because of the position of the garage, the extra work done to muffle the noise from Jake's musical instruments, and the surrounding greenery, eyewitnesses are not a huge possibility here; also, no one has come forward so far. It also shows that the backyard of the Bodkins' home extends into the woods.

The family dog was out for a walk with the mother. Both parents have alibis that were confirmed by the police. Jake's brother (Caleb) was in Seattle, also confirmed by the police (phew!). Meanwhile, we still don't know where Donna is. (Seriously! Find her on the internet! She must be here somewhere!!)

ANNOUNCEMENT: Whoever finds Donna online gets a FREE Tee from my Merch on CrimeBC's store!

Caleb Bodkin

Nov 6

I have been trying to figure out some mysteries on my own. Not the obvious ones, like who killed Jake, but things that relate to Jake's behavior in the weeks leading up to his death. For instance, why did Jake sign up for Epilogue? Was it Donna's influence? And second, how did Donna and Jake end up together?

Unfortunately, this means I have to talk to Emily.

"I need to talk to you about Jake. Can I stop by?" I text her.

Almost five minutes later, she responds, "Sure! When and where?"

"I'll come over in about twenty. Does that work?"

"okkk xxx!!" she answers.

The enthusiasm is mainly for the possibility of new content for her stories. It has nothing to do with Jake or me. But I don't care as long as it gets me going in the right direction. I understand that teenage couples don't need to make sense, and I know how teen boys can be mesmerized by Emily's looks and style, which leaves little to the imagination. But Jake was way too cool for her in my opinion.

It's too cold and rainy, so I drive to the Illingworth house. It's a short, ten-minute drive. When I make it, her mother greets me and leads me to their living room, where I wait nearly ten minutes for Emily to show up.

The interior is warm and cozy, complete with a fireplace and the sweet and spicy scent of a pumpkin-cinnamon candle. The Illingworths live in a classy brick home. I've always loved the corner lot perched above surrounding homes, which gives privacy and fantastic views. The house is pretty cool, with a lovely pool in the backyard. Jake told me once that when her parents were away, they would drink on the deck, watching the sunset. I look at the pool. It's a bleak and depressing sight, covered with leaves and insects since the water was frigid, making the pool useless for the time being. The cold wind blowing and the rain falling makes the atmosphere harsh and unnerving. The outside doesn't look like a place to relax and have fun.

Although Jake and Emily had little in common, they both had an artistic side. Jake had his music, and Emily has her photography. I look around the living room and see beautiful photographs decorating the walls, the mantelpiece, and the shelves. They're mostly close-ups of random objects, like tapestry, tiles, or exotic-looking embroidery. They look like they belong in a modern art studio. It's obvious that her parents are proud of her talent but aren't encouraging her enough to pursue it. She does have a good eye for it. The lighting, editing, and even the angles she chose makes the most mundane things around us seem like an incredible piece of art. I've always wondered why she couldn't focus on this gift for her blogs and decided to go for the generic, meaningless junk. Instead, she's opted for having an account called "Aesthetic Doll," which mostly contains photos of make-up products, slutty outfits, and pancakes. In her pursuit of fame, attention, and quick fortune, she acts like an idiot on social media. What a waste!

I've always believed she faked her interest in Jake's world to be closer to him. She was trying to appeal to the same crowd he did to increase the number of her followers. Jake also didn't fit in her inner circle, made up of wannabe TikTokers and boys who like to do these weird challenges on social media with their girlfriends. After Jake's band made a big breakthrough locally when it was in the lineup for Rockverse Music Fest last year, there were some talks with producers about a record deal for the group. So, knowing Emily, that was probably her favorite thing about Jake.

I hear Emily approaching and talking to someone. I keep my head down and ignore what she's saying to avoid prying on her conversation.

"Hey Caleb!" She hugs me in a lousy attempt at showing sympathy. "How are you holding up?"

"Trying to be okay, I guess."

"We all have our ways to cope with this tragedy, and you know what I'm like. I'm outspoken and like to communicate my feelings during these hard times. It's healthy. Maybe you should try it out." She cocks her head to the side in an attempt to look innocent and cute.

"I wanted to ask you about your relationship with Jake; when did you two break up?"

"We never really broke up." She tries to hide her shock but fails.

"At this point, everyone knows you broke up a while before he died," I say. I admit that I'm enjoying the look of hurt on her face a little too much.

Her expression changes into something more genuine, with a look in her eyes that challenges me to continue with these implicit insults.

"Well, it helps to share my thoughts with other girls who grieve their cheating boyfriends and try to take care of my mental health."

"Excuse me?" I interrupt her.

"It is what it is … Your brother didn't break up with me, officially. I thought he was playing hard to get after we fought over something stupid, that's all!"

"If you really care about Jake, Em, you'll help me out because I am sure as hell Jake's death wasn't an accident. It wasn't a suicide. Someone hurt Jake but didn't get to finish the job."

She pauses. She pours herself a glass of lemon water and chugs it. She doesn't even think to offer any to me.

"Honestly, he hadn't spoken to me for weeks before he died. He was being a jerk for a while, completely ghosting me. I knew there was someone else."

I don't say anything.

"Do you think she killed him?" Emily asks.

I stay silent, but of course, the answer is yes. Honestly, there is no other person of interest I can think of. And after seeing Jake's face before he died, it makes more sense that someone with mental issues had done that to him.

"Who do you mean?" I ask Emily.

"You know … Donna Darko?" she continues. "I mean, if you ask my opinion, a junkie like Donna wouldn't be able to finish the job. She was probably too high to even realize he wasn't dead when she left him."

On my way home, I think about Emily's unpleasant take on things. It makes sense that it has to be someone not strong enough to finish the job. Also, he must not have expected it; otherwise, he would have defended himself. As much as I'd hate to agree with Emily, what she said echoes my thoughts for the past few weeks, ever since I saw Jake's death video.

I check Emily's TikTok account. In her latest posts, she's been playing the victim and trying to get sympathy points. And, of course, some of her stupid followers are giving her what she's fishing for. She even cried in one of her videos while talking about the moment of truth when she found out that Jake was "cheating" on her. I cringe so hard that it feels exhausting just watching these videos. I close the app, feeling more irritated than ever.

The fact remains that Donna is still missing. It's been three months since anyone had seen or heard from her. Did she do something unforgivable this time that she had to hide indefinitely?

Is Brett hiding her somewhere?

I know I would do anything to protect Jake.

Brett Howe
Nov 9

www.strengthcircle.com
Online Support Group: Parents of Troubled Teens/Addiction & Recovery

> *If you or someone you care about is dealing with prescription drug abuse, this community is here for you. Share your experiences, find support, and connect with others who are facing similar challenges. You don't have to face addiction alone. Ask questions, offer advice, tell your story, and find hope for recovery right here.*

950 Members **2,465 Posts** **26 Online**

This is a very hard time for me. The idea that my little girl is out there without her medications, possessed by dangerous thoughts while getting bullied nationwide, scares me to death. Donna has been bullied all her life by losers who have nothing better to do than get into my family's affairs and damage innocent people's lives and reputations.

Thank God Donna isn't into social media; otherwise, the stuff people have been writing about her online might tip her over the edge. I'm trying to make people understand that attacking a helpless, sick girl will not bring Jake back and will not give them any answers.

My girl needs help.

She is the one person that makes me cling to this miserable life I have. My daughter is the gravity that keeps any traces of happiness from slipping away. I feel like I'm floating in a black hole. Nothing is familiar, and nothing is giving me a reason to stay. I feel like letting go and swimming into nothingness. Maybe the darkness is misunderstood. Perhaps it offers comfort beyond our comprehension, beyond our limited existence, and that's why we're afraid of the dark. Until Donna shines the light at the end of this very long and dark tunnel, what's the point?

I am not discussing the case with anyone.

I am not even talking to the neighbors.

Once my Donna comes home safe, I am leaving this damn town forever!

Text Exchange Between Jake and Donna

Apr 5

JB: Do you know what happened to Jonah and Tyler after they got expelled?

DH: No ... not even curious tbh

JB: I guess there's no use in knowing...

DH: Hey, did you know that Donnie is Jake Gyllenhaal's character, and the guy in the rabbit costume with the fed up eye is called Frank! What a bunch of idiots!

JB: They didn't even get their insults right!

DH: Haha I know! I actually like Jake Gyllenhaal. I don't mind being Donna Darko

JB: Deal! From now on, I'm gonna call you DD!

DH: jerk...haha

Trish_ona_mish

Nov 10

Fam! NOT COOL what's happening here and all over the internet! We still dunno what the deal is! We can't go canceling people without solid proof! This is bullying!

I am asking my Mishionaries to stop judging people without enough info! Please, the last thing I wanna do is to start losing members of this lovely community

I had to block some toxic people on here, and it was just not pleasant!

The Tea: Donna's father (Brett Howe) has organized search parties. I have decided to join the search party during Christmas break unless she comes home or the police find her by then.

One witness came forward with a tip on Donna's whereabouts … that's what I read on one of the local news websites (click here to see the story). I dunno how reliable that source is, but we can consider it as rumors for the time being.

I thought it was worth mentioning.

Again, remember, we are not bullies!

Bye now!

Caleb Bodkin

Nov 28

This isn't really a typical Thanksgiving dinner. My parents don't want any visitors, so no family are coming over. My parents refuse to cook, watch football, or engage in any typical festivity. I agree with them, because we are not ready for the holiday season. We do not want to move on.

We sit at the dinner table, each trying to be present for the others, but unable to stay in the moment. The uncomfortable silence hangs in the air, broken only by the occasional sound of utensils clinking against plates. Every word sounds like a forced attempt at an unnecessary conversation.

"Glenn was telling me today about the whole case against LIV," Dad says. "In most cases, the police send the platform a search warrant or a subpoena for data acquisition. However, he said that they have 'emergency requests,' where they will hand over data outside of the legal process when police claim a case involves death or national security matters. Apparently, the police have been relying on these companies much more in recent years."

Dad knows that we are not particularly interested in the process, but we have nothing else to say to each other. Mom is silent. She barely touches her coconut vegetable curry, which I cooked. I did the cooking this year because, as I said, we are avoiding any previous traditions. She's just drinking her wine and staring into the glass doors that lead into the pitch-black wilderness.

I try to make eye contact with her, but she doesn't look my way. "Yeah, I spoke to him just two days ago. He said that there's a unit which includes some former police officers, retired secret service agents, and cybercrime investigators, which handles law enforcement requests through an online portal." I sip my drink.

Nobody speaks, so I continue.

"Glenn said they can essentially ask for every piece of detail, photos, IP address, location, posts, even deleted material. This is lucky in our case, but I must admit, I feel uncomfortable sharing too much online, knowing that someone can access it if they want to."

My dad nods and eats a piece of broccoli.

I am a pretty good cook. My condition has compelled me to be very careful with my diet, hence my interest in cooking healthy food. I scan the speed at which my parents consume their dinner and try to gauge their reaction.

I know that the quality of their dinner is beside the point. But it is too much to focus on the pain 24/7. So I shut up and eat.

"This is good, thanks, son," Dad says.

I smile and nod.

"I mean, it beats that awful lentil salad I tried to make a couple of years ago," he says.

"I don't know if you're trying to insult my cooking or compliment it, Dad." We both laugh. "You know Jake and I tried to feed it to Fen afterwards, and he gagged?"

"You know you and your brother can be assholes sometimes," Dad says, the smile quickly fading as he realizes that he's just spoken about

Jake in the present tense, and just like that, the mood suddenly returns to its earlier darkness. I see the tears on Mom's cheeks.

"Anyway, this tastes good. Thanks son," Dad says looking down at his plate to avoid any more conversation.

"I'm joining the search party for Donna." Mom's voice cuts through my thoughts and brings me back to that unpleasant moment. She is not making eye contact with either one of us.

"Are you sure this is a good idea?" Dad asks.

She sniffs and wipes her tears. "I don't see why not," she says, raising her eyebrows, and for the first time this evening, she makes eye contact with my dad, with a defiant look on her face. Has she made it from denial to the next stage of grief? Is she angry now? Is that good?

I know there's no chance to have any normal conversation tonight, so I decide to finish my food, clean up, and head out somewhere. I have no particular place in mind but I can't stay in the house any longer.

"Hey man, what are you up to?" I text Matt, one of my best friends from high school.

"Hey, not much, just chilling with Ian at Dad's place in Red Hills, are you in town?" Matt types back.

"Yep, unfortunately. Parents are being a real pain."

"Ugh, I feel you, wanna stop by?" Matt asks.

"Cool! I'll be right over, want me to bring anything?"

"Just yourself," Matt replies.

As I text him back, I allow myself to enjoy a brief moment of excitement and nostalgia. It is natural to be happy to see old friends, but I can feel guilt lurking in the shadows, as prospects of having anything normal start to materialize.

Matt, Ian, and I used to be so close in high school and stayed in touch over the years through social media. Matt lives and works in Redmond, and Ian is in Tacoma. Both Matt and Ian are home for the holidays.

Though I know where they live, what they do for a living, and even what their girlfriends' costumes were this Halloween, I hadn't spoken to them since last Thanksgiving.

I walk with Fen to Matt's place; it's a short, ten-minute walk, but the freezing temperatures make it seem longer. When I arrive at Matt's place, I find that Ian is still there.

The three of us huddle in a circle around the fire pit in Matt's backyard exchanging rants about our miserable situations. I'm definitely ahead in that race, but still, misery loves company, no matter how inferior. There is no real drama going on in Ian's life; he's just craving some old company.

"I felt bad for Donna Darko when I heard the story of the bullies who sprayed her face. But I'm losing all sympathy for her the more I know about her." Ian says; he's been following the case closely.

"I don't know what the heck Jake saw in her," I say.

Matt shakes his head and says "I don't understand her crazy tendencies. The part where she gave up on life and everything and went on to become a weirdo. I understand it's hard to lose your mom so early, but she still has her father, who seems like a decent guy."

We sit in silence for a couple of minutes, Ian is checking a notification on his phone, Matt is sipping his drink, and I listen for a moment to the soothing sound of the crackling fire, the soft rustle of leaves and chirping of crickets. I pick up a stick and move the burning wood inside the pit, embers spark and glow brighter and small pieces of ash rise into the air. I watch as one delicate flake lands gently on the concrete blocks that encircle the pit.

"Have you guys checked the Epilogue thing on LIV?" Matt asks disrupting the calm of the moment.

"Not really. But my girlfriend told me that she's signed up and is uploading a lot of content. I told her to keep me out of it. This is not just a normal post," Ian says.

"I tried to subscribe. Went through the whole registration process and believe me they ask a lot of questions. I'm just trying to understand why Jake was interested in subscribing," I say.

"Maybe it was Darko's influence?" Ian says as he slips his phone back into his pocket.

"That's what I think. I mean, Donna is weird and depressed, and her reputation as mentally unstable has always surpassed her, so I can understand it if she was into this kinda stuff, but the weird thing is, she doesn't have any social media accounts," I say.

"That's odd; how old is she again?" Matt squints as he looks in my direction, confused.

"Nineteen," I say as I draw my chair closer to the fire and extend my hands for extra warmth.

The way Ian keeps referring to Donna as Donna Darko pulls us into reminiscing about high school days, the stupid things we used to do and the things we didn't but should have done ... we end up stalking some of our old classmates on Instagram and LinkedIn to see what they're up to and how successful they are. Their posts showcase promotions, marriages, and travel adventures, sparking a mix of nostalgia and envy that draws us deeper into our own stories.

Matt drops Fen and me home afterwards, as the rain starts to pour, and the ten-minute walk becomes out of the question. Somehow, our conversations leave me uplifted and it is a welcome change from the disappointing start to the evening. When I get home, both of my parents are in bed. The whole house is dark and very quiet. I am back in the depression zone.

Jake and I were lucky to have grown up in a close-knit family. Indeed, we had the usual bickering and casual arguments that sometimes escalated to fights, but we were all happy with where we were in life and satisfied with who we were. Holidays were packed with precious family memories, and although the connection between all the cousins may have faded in some instances, it still felt natural once we all met up.

It's hard to be in our house without Jake. The silence is deafening. I hear my mom's sobs through the bathroom door.

I go to bed, relieved that one of the worst days of my life is finally over.

Brett Howe
Nov 30

www.strengthcircle.com

Online Support Group: Parents of Troubled Teens/Addiction & Recovery

> *If you or someone you care about is dealing with prescription drug abuse, this community is here for you. Share your experiences, find support, and connect with others who are facing similar challenges. You don't have to face addiction alone. Ask questions, offer advice, tell your story, and find hope for recovery right here.*

1,011 Members   **2,520 Posts**   **22 Online**

@Teenwhisperer Thank you for your support. I am cooperating with the authorities in every possible way, because I know that the sooner the truth comes out, the more likely Donna will come home to me. I was thinking about what you said regarding setting boundaries and trying more forceful methods to raise my daughter. Frankly, I've never tried to discipline my daughter by setting limits or consequences for her actions. I always felt sorry for her because she grew up without her mother. I needed to compensate for the loss she had to suffer so early in her life. The trauma of losing her mother was compounded because she was at the scene. I couldn't be firm with her after such a harrowing experience. It was too much for a grown man like me to take, let alone a delicate soul like Donna.

Donna and her mother were very close. Because of my long working hours, they only had each other. So, while I agree that discipline can help teenagers understand what is expected of them and what the consequences will be if they do not follow the rules, I do not think this approach applies in Donna's case.

The police are finally doing their job; they are following every possible lead, eliminating all possibilities that do not add up. I am certain that Donna's name will be cleared in a matter of weeks because we had nothing to do with Jake's death.

It is normal for two teenagers to fall for each other. They were neighbors with a lot of time on their hands. It was their summer vacation. So what if they went hiking a few times? And while you're all analyzing and playing detective, here's a thought: maybe Jake hurt Donna one way or another, and that's why she ran away. So let's keep an open mind and consider that Jake may have been the villain here.

#7 What Happened That Summer?

Summer has always been the toughest season for me to fight the urge. Time moves slowly during summer, especially in the suburbs, and boredom is a strong instigator. Every night, I'd lie in bed playing different scenes of my life in my head and realizing that I was going nowhere in life.

One summer, I met someone. I can still hear that song sometimes. It was, although dark, the soundtrack of our relationship...I would have led a very different life if not for that relationship. It showed me a new world which I never knew existed. It changed my life. Made me quit for a while, made me a better person, and brought out the good in me.

Temporarily...

But that same summer, I did something unforgivable.

I'll never forget the sound. A crack. I saw blood; his eyes rolled back and finally closed. He was still.

And I ran.

I was so scared over the next few days. I hid in my room and didn't leave the house.

I've come a long way since that day.

Like anything else, killing is only hard the first time.

Trish_ona_mish

Dec 17

T-minus four days until my trip to Red Hills Ridge!

I will make the three-hour drive from Portland to Red Hills Ridge in two hours and thirty minutes, planning to break my record.

Buckle up! Time for a road trip!

Lots of you have been asking me about my prep for this journey. Well, I have packed a few comfy and warm items. Following the heavy rain that continued throughout November this year and the power outages, and considering how cold this December turned out to be (even for that area), I'm not taking any chances.

I've packed my flashlight, batteries, thermals, favorite snow boots, and sunscreen (actually, I packed my whole skincare kit because we are not savages here!).

Vibe check: Please share your road trip playlists!

I just hope I'll be able to get a minute with Donna and get a statement/video before the police show up.

This case is so sus!

Text Exchange Between Jake and Donna

June 6

JB: Thinkin' about you. You seemed out of it yesterday
DH: The meds. They do that sometimes
JB: I still think you should go easy on the meds
DH: I have...But OK doc
JB: (middle finger emoji)
DH: TBH...You're the reason I'm still in this town
JB: I can't wait to go to college with you
DH: Me too
JB: Have you listened to that song I told you about?

PART FOUR

KING 5: CRIME

<u>K5: Body Identified as Missing Woman</u>
The body of a Red Hills woman reported missing since July was found yesterday
Author: KING 5 News (KING)
Published: 12/23/2024 5:52:09 A.M.

Remains found by authorities searching for Donna Howe, Jake Bodkin's girlfriend, were confirmed to be hers. She was identified through dental records.

The result was reported by the King County Medical Examiner's Office. The remains were found after a private search and rescue group had found an item belonging to Donna on the Douglas Fir Creek Trail Wednesday after more than five months of searching for Howe. Earlier this fall, Donna was declared a person of interest in the Jake Bodkin murder.

Donna Howe was last seen outside a supermarket close to the beginning of the hiking trail on July 11. Her father, Brett Howe, had officially reported her missing on July 12. She was 19 years old at the time of her death. Her father saw her on the morning she went missing. She said she was going for a walk. Mr. Howe left around 7:30 a.m. to attend a business conference in Seattle. He had not saw her since.

A spokesperson for the police told K5 News earlier Thursday that the remains were "skeletal."

"The Red Hills Police Department would like to thank the media and everyone who helped with the search over the last six months," said King County Sheriff James Martin "We extend our deepest condolences to the family and friends of Ms. Howe, who was in the prime of her life," he continued.

After she was found, a recovery mission was launched for Donna, and authorities requested that people remain out of the area until their mission was completed.

Brett Howe commented, "Sometimes there are just no words for a broken heart."

Text Exchange Between Jake and Donna

July 12, 10:03 a.m.

JB: Where are you? I'm worried about you.
    DH: Sorry, this new medication is making me drowsy all the time. What's up?
    JB: What new med? I thought you stopped it all
    JB: Is your dad home?
    DH: Yeah it's Saturday
    JB: Are you home?
    DH: Why?
    JB: So your dad put up a post saying you're missing. Where you at?
    DH: Where did you see it?
    JB: On the support group.
    DH: Oh…right, I need to see you.

Caleb Bodkin
Dec 22

This is not a coincidence. No fucking way!

The majority of the people around me and on the internet think she killed Jake and then killed herself because she was a lunatic. Maybe, but I was way more suspicious of her before she was found dead.

The police are looking into anything that would verify the exact time of her death. But, of course, there is no way to know that after almost six months. So they are on the lookout for any evidence that she was, in fact, alive on July 13, when Jake died. They are looking at the CCTV cameras in the area, her phone records, any witnesses, her online activity, etc.

I'm trying to go over this in my head. Donna was planning for her future with Jake. She was all flirty with Jake the night before she went missing; she went to bed and woke up the following day determined to kill Jake; then she finished herself off in the woods? That doesn't make any sense.

This could mean that a new mysterious person must have killed them both. I am beyond frustrated; we are officially back to square one.

Who would want to kill Jake? And kill Donna? And why? There would have been a trail somewhere leading to the killer. Jake didn't have secrets aside from Donna. I looked at all his messages and emails, nothing.

No one had a clue where Donna could be. The only reason that narrowed down the search area was the message she sent to Jake on July 11.

"Meet me in 30, our spot."

The police approached his friends to see if they knew what Donna meant by that. Andrew didn't know about that specific location; however, he could point the police in the general direction. Andrew was the only one who knew about Jake's relationship with Donna. He told the police that Donna and Jake usually met near one of the hiking trails beside a creek, which limited their search to three trails. He said the three of them had gone on a hike once to a place that Donna described as "tranquil." However, the trail is often marked by only a barely visible path that has been packed down by hikers, making it easy to miss. It took the police and the volunteer search parties a while to find her body.

Once the search party found Donna's bracelet along one of these trails, the police returned to the spot with cadaver dogs and intensified their search. An hour later, they found her body partially covered with leaves as they went into a hidden trail that led to a tiny opening under the trees. Surprisingly, not even wild animals had found her.

The cause and manner of death are pending toxicology results. Unfortunately, the remains were badly decomposed, and despite the efforts, it might not be possible to determine the exact cause of death. A possible cause of death is a lethal overdose, considering her addiction problem. But there was no physical evidence around her body (such as needles or substances) to indicate that, and no weapons were found either.

The medical examiner said the circumstances in which the body was found were suspicious. It's unclear whether the coverage of her body with branches and bushes was done by someone else to conceal it, whether natural conditions had led to the movement randomly, or whether she had done it herself. Investigators noted that evidence of some types of traumas, like asphyxiation, could have been destroyed by the passage of time.

The police are looking into the messages between Jake and Donna, new and old.

They couldn't find Donna's phone anywhere, which is another suspicious fact in this case. I mean, even if she killed herself, why hide her phone? Why get rid of it? She might have done that as a bluff if she were found alive. But she is dead! So why try to cover her tracks?!

And now everyone is talking about her last poem, which she left in her room the day she disappeared.

Some think the two deaths weren't linked. I can't accept that, though.

My life is on hold for now. I can't think of anything, and I can't do anything but go over the evidence in Jake's material.

The police have gained access to the content from LIV for Jake's Epilogue account. They are studying every entry, according to Glenn.

We're still trying to figure out the meaning behind that message she sent to Jake on July 11.

"It fell off."

Brett Howe

Dec 29

www.strengthcircle.com

Online Support Group: Parents of Troubled Teens/Addiction & Recovery

> *If you or someone you care about is dealing with prescription drug abuse, this community is here for you. Share your experiences, find support, and connect with others who are facing similar challenges. You don't have to face addiction alone. Ask questions, offer advice, tell your story, and find hope for recovery right here.*

1,452 Members **2,860 Posts** **45 Online**

When Donna was thirteen, I sent her to a therapeutic wilderness program for ninety days. And when she was sixteen, I sent her to a residential treatment program for sixty days. At the time, I thought I was doing the right thing for my daughter. But, by then, she had already been using drugs, and I worried that she would end up in jail or dead. I don't think these programs were helpful, in Donna's case, at least. Not sure what would have happened had I not sent her to these programs, but I saw no improvement after she completed the period.

Now, after all these years, I see that they left her disturbed, lost, and feeling detached from the world. They have turned her into an outcast. An easy target for bullies. Eventually, she had to be homeschooled.

I have a reason for sharing this. I want to warn parents who think these programs will help. They won't. On the contrary, they did considerable damage and left my daughter traumatized.

I feel like I'm on autopilot. I'd reached out on here before and tried to take everyone's advice. I got my daughter into therapy, tried to listen more, and tried to do what she wanted. I thought I was seeing some progress this summer. She seemed calmer and even nicer to me, which had never happened before.

I thought she was okay.

She's gone. She was the one reason I woke up in the morning. The one bright color I could still see in my colorless world. Her problems gave me a purpose to live for; they lit a flame of hope that kept me warm on the inside. That hope distracted me from my own depression. I didn't even get to tell her everything I should've. We didn't do everything we were supposed to do. I was going to take her to Europe this Christmas. We talked about going to the Strasbourg Christmas market. I was going to enroll her in college.

Neither of us is ever going to get that. And it's my fault. I did this. I should've been better; I should've listened more.

I am going to stop my online activity. I am seeing very negative things being circulated about my daughter and me. Nasty things are being said by people I've never met and never will. People who know nothing about us feel entitled to pass harsh, incriminating judgments blindly. She meant everything to me, yet some random loser in the middle of nowhere thinks he had me and my daughter all figured out, disregarding her precious life and calling her all sorts of awful things.

This is not the place for me or any parent mourning the loss of their child. This virtual world is a dangerous idea…it is poison.

This is my last post here.

This is my last post anywhere.

My life stops today…

I continue to breathe, but I am dead.

#8 What Did He Do?

At thirteen, you start seeing your parents as real people, two individuals with problems that they have never shared with you before. You begin to peel the layers and reveal the truth about their flaws, which is almost like a revelation.

The closer you get to the line of adulthood, the fainter their sound becomes until it dissolves into background noise that you try to block constantly. Eventually, that noise blends into the fabric of your world, and you can't hear it anymore. I keep wondering, did I stop hearing it because it faded and became irrelevant, or because it came to be a part of who I am?

The older I grew, the stranger my family dynamic seemed.

One night when I was only eight, I remember it was a very cold night. I was home alone.

"I'll be back in twenty minutes. Behave yourself. I am just going to grab the refill for my prescription," my mother said, before locking me in our two-bedroom house.

Two hours later, she came home crying so hard her whole body shook. I had slept on the couch while watching TV. The slam of the front door woke me up.

My mother sat down on the chair in the kitchen, crying and crying.

"Mommy, are you okay?" I asked her.

"Go to sleep. I am busy," she said, not even glancing at me. She smelled of cigarettes and rain. I did as I'd been told and went to my bedroom.

Around midnight, I woke again to a loud banging noise that I had initially mistaken for thunder. It took me a minute to realize that someone was banging on the front door. I slowly opened the door to my bedroom and walked to a spot where I could see the front door from the first-floor landing.

"Go away! I never want to see you again!" she told my father, who sounded angry and drunk.

I was shocked because I thought we had led a seemingly normal family life up until that point.

I later found out that my father had cheated on her with some woman who worked at the local bar just a few blocks from where we lived. From that moment on, they began to fight constantly. And with that, I was introduced to the worst versions of both.

After a while, they started dragging me into their fights. Bad grades followed, and rebellious behavior at school, fights with other kids, anything that would tell my parents to stop being so selfish and to pay some attention to me. Eventually, when I gave up on having a caring mother or a considerate father, I grew silent and distant and mostly kept to myself.

One month later, I came back from school and was greeted at the door by my father.

"Daddy is home," he said. I was so happy that day because I thought that maybe we had all learned our lesson and could move on and be happy. In reality, though, this was the introduction to a cycle of events that would define my childhood and teen years. I felt sick every time a new version of the same act happened.

That part of my life taught me that half of the emotional pain when you go through a traumatic experience lies in expecting it. It was cruel. The other half is watching the events unfold exactly the way you'd expected them, which made me lose respect for my mother and myself. She took the bait every time. Although I was very young back then, I was still smarter than my mother. I don't know if smarter is the right word here, maybe I saw things for what they really were. I also learned during that phase that grown-ups tend to add layers and layers of sugar to reality until it fucks up with their taste buds. It turned out that what had happened that night was the beginning of a pattern rather than a one-off.

Toward the end of the school year, I believe it was May, I was getting ready for bed, my mother was out, and my father was downstairs watching a game. There was ice cream in the freezer, and I went downstairs to see if I could sneak some in before bedtime. My father never really paid attention if there was a game on. When I descended the last few steps, I saw the living room was empty. I snuck into the kitchen and ate quick mouthfuls of the chocolate peanut butter swirl from the Ben and Jerry's container. I suddenly dropped the spoon when I heard the front door open. I thought it was my mother, which meant I would be in trouble. Quickly, I rinsed, put the spoon away, and ran to the stairs. I stopped when I caught sight of my father opening the front door with a small suitcase in his hand.

"Where are you going, Daddy?" I asked

"I'm sorry. Daddy has work to do. Go to bed, and don't do anything you're not supposed to," he said, locking me in the house.

Even to my nine-year-old self, he sounded shady and irresponsible.

The next morning, my mother's eyes were red and puffy. She didn't speak to me or even prepare my breakfast.

At first, I blamed myself because I thought I might have disappointed him. But now I don't think like that anymore. Somewhere down the line, my hate toward him vanished with nothing else to replace it. So that part of me became empty, which, in my opinion, and based on my experience, is way more serious. I grew into a callous, selfish, uncaring teenager.

I started to analyze the facts about these two individuals who happened to be around as nature took its course, and I became an adult. My mother had no self-esteem, being from a foreign country, not having relatives or real friends where we lived, and having no source of income to support herself were all reasons for her struggles with herself. She was completely dependent on my father. My mother was basically his cook and maid, and he slept with another woman behind her back. Seriously, I am disgusted with myself when I think about the household where I grew up. That was the time I discovered how messed up our family really was.

A couple of weeks after that, she seemed to be better. She wasn't crying anymore, nor did she fight with me over every little thing. That looked like she made progress, right?

The truth is, it's hard for a kid to make a distinction between stability and numbness. Like me, my mother was not okay. She hadn't moved on…her depression had evolved to the next stage of complete nothingness. She stopped being angry at my father; she stopped taking it out on me…she stopped being anything at once.

While my father was too busy chasing one woman after the other, my mother was dwelling on the fact that she had no life. I was left to fend for myself. I needed to exist in the midst of living in the delusion of a family.

And that is how I started a journey of real struggles.

No matter where my life had taken me, and no matter what you might say, I am the real victim here! My parents chose to sacrifice my youth for the sake of their selfishness! I was still a fucking teenager! I had to learn by myself how to live with a miserable woman who abused me and shared dark thoughts with me…

Trish_ona_mish

Jan 4

It's been three weeks since my last post. My Mishionaries know this is the longest I've gone without posting any update. Ngl, I just wasn't ready to spill the tea ...

Also, a lot of you know what I am about to say here, but here's the whole rundown of what went down on December 21.

Last month, I went to Red Hills Ridge to help with the volunteer search for Donna Howe. I booked a room for two nights at the Mountain View Motel but ended up staying for only one. I'll get to that...I was planning to do some investigation on my own once I was there.

After checking into the motel, I spent the first day cruising around the area and snapping pics of the key spots that keep popping up in this case. First stop was their high school, but obvi, it was closed. Next, I tried to chat with Brett Howe and the Bodkins, but they were a total no-go. After that, I went to the grocery store where Donna was last spotted. Found this lady in her fifties running the joint. She wasn't the one who saw Donna right before she went into the woods. "Sarah, my daughter, she was the one who saw Donna Howe. They were friends at some point," she said.

"May I speak with Sarah, please?" I asked.

"You look too young to be a reporter. Why are you exactly here?"

"I'm not a reporter. I have a true crime blog and podcast; I'm here to cover Donna and Jake's case. This is for my thread on CrimeBC."

She looked like she didn't know what I was talking about. I knew I was going nowhere with this, so I decided to dip and grab some grub and caffeine. The front desk lady at the motel suggested this dope spot called Roasted, so I headed there.

I don't know whether this is normal in Red Hills Ridge or it was mainly because of the gloomy winter weather, but I literally felt like I was walking through a ghost town. Super depressing vibes everywhere I went. There were barely any Christmas decorations in the houses near the Bodkins' and Howes' residences. The whole block looked barren of any seasonal celebrations.

Understandable but unnerving.

Jake's brother gave me a short interview while waiting for his coffee. Yes! I ran into Caleb Bodkin at Roasted (delicious coffee, by the way, and super friendly staff!). I don't know Caleb from anywhere apart from news reports and shared memories by Jake's Phantom account on Insta, but it felt like I was talking to a shadow of someone's existence.

On another note, he's taller than I thought.

I introduced myself; he recognized me. I wasn't sure whether that was a good thing. I was worried that he might think of me as an intruder. So it was a relief when he said that he follows my blog and isn't bothered by my coverage of the case (phew!). I DID want to help with the search, but I also wanted to get more perspective on the lives of the residents, including Jake and Donna and their social circle. According to Caleb, there was no common denominator at all except for the geographic location. The two lived in parallel worlds, although they were neighbors. Up to six months before Jake's death, he had never spoken to her in his life. Not even at Red Hills High, where they both went (briefly in D's case).

THE SOUND OF TUNING OUT

He even gave me a quote to include here!

"Mourning my brother under the public's eye is not easy, and finding out that we all messed up at the beginning is very disappointing, but I'm thankful because if it weren't for that Phantom story, Jake's killer could have gotten away with murder. But we can't move on without finding out the truth."

About Donna, he said, "I don't know her, and I hope she had nothing to do with Jake's death because he loved her. I also hope she comes home safe."

Our convo lasted about five minutes. He got his coffee and left.

There wasn't much to do in the area. I returned to the motel to work on other projects and take a break from the harsh cold outside. The temperature hovered around freezing, with light misty rain falling intermittently. The trees were bare, their branches stretching out toward the gray sky, and the streets were quiet and empty. I bundled up in a warm coat, scarf, and gloves. When I stepped out, my breath came out in visible puffs as I exhaled. I had to walk carefully to avoid slipping on the wet pavement. The rain was turning into sleet, making my short walk even more treacherous. I went to an Italian place called Nonna's Cucina. It is a cozy, family-friendly spot, the perfect escape from the freezing December night outside. As soon as I stepped in, I was hit with the warm aroma of garlic, tomato sauce, and freshly baked bread. The interior was dimly lit, with soft lighting that cast a warm and inviting glow over the space. The walls were decorated with photos of Italy, and the sounds of Italian music played softly in the background—the typical American idea of the Italian experience.

As I waited for my food, I could hear families chatting and laughing around me. Children giggled and played games at the table next to me, while their parents sipped on glasses of red wine and enjoyed a peaceful evening out.

I was hoping to meet some of the locals. While there, I introduced myself to a group of teens who were two years older than Jake and didn't really know him.

The night was a total snooze-fest, and to top it off, the food was just meh. I was totally bummed out and went to bed feeling super disappointed on multiple levels.

The next morning, I went to the meeting point of the search party to start my mission for the day. I wasn't hoping to accomplish much, as I was almost sure that Donna was hiding far away.

I saw a helpless, grief-stricken father when I met Brett Howe. The image of him standing at the beginning of the hiking trail, looking defeated, exhausted, and definitely older than fifty, is going to stay burnt into my brain forever. He started his speech by thanking those of us who had gathered to help search for his missing daughter.

The turnout was not great. Given the bad reputation that Donna had sustained as a troubled teenager with drug abuse and possible involvement in the death of a very popular kid, you could guess that she was not everyone's favorite. Also, judging from the online community's reaction to the latest news about Donna's relationship with Jake and considering her battles with mental illness, people were not expecting to find her. Everyone thought that she was long gone, and while people sympathized with her father's desperate (and persistent) attempts to find her, very few people were ready to sacrifice their holidays for this purpose.

The temperature continued to drop the night before, and the rain slowly turned into snow…It had snowed early this year; usually, December is a rainy month. The town legit looked like something out of a fairy tale or a winter wonderland! It was so magical. But the somber vibes overshadowed any natural beauty the place offered.

In total, we were nine. It had the sad feeling of going to someone's funeral and the turnout being so little that you'd feel embarrassed for the

THE SOUND OF TUNING OUT

family, and you'd be a little happy that the person of interest is dead, so they won't see how little influence they had left on the people around them.

Here is the list of the members of this search party:

- Brett Howe

- Sarah. (She worked with Donna at the grocery store at some point, and the two were friendly- the girl I spoke about above); she was the last person to see Donna.

- Two guys from Brett's work (Aaron and John)

- Two members from church (Linda and Greg)

- A neighbor – I think her name was Jessica or Jessy

- Yours truly

- And... Are you ready for this? Diane Bodkin! Jake's mother!

It seemed like nobody, Brett included, recognized me, and for that, I was thankful. I think he remembered me from the day before when I tried to interview him because he hesitated as he gave me the Google Maps printouts. At some point, it looked like he was gonna say something to me, but I pretended to be on my phone to avoid the awkward conversation.

The Google Maps printouts had sections gridded with a marker to signify the zones we were supposed to cover. So I took my printout and went to my assigned zone in the southern part of the area. We went in teams of two. My partner was Sarah. I was so happy that I was gonna get a chance to ask her all my questions. I think she was around my age, early twenties. I assumed she must have been a close friend because she looked so sad, cheeks flushed and head bowed. I felt terrible for her. It was a shame to experience loss so early in life.

The town is small, with a population of only seven thousand people, but the surrounding woods are massive. So it took us a while to get to the starting point. Around twenty minutes, to be exact. During that time, I tried to break the ice with Sarah. I introduced myself; she said she knew who I was and occasionally watched my videos and read my posts. At first, she was pretty quiet and not really feeling like chatting it up with me. I was starting to doubt my entire decision to make a fool of myself by imposing onto these people's lives. I haven't felt this out of place since I walked into Saks Fifth Avenue with my BFF a few years ago during NYFW (which, btw, is so not my scene, but that's a whole other story!).

The printouts we had with us had pictures of the clothing Donna was last seen wearing: a plain gray T-shirt (with lime green Under Armour logo), black yoga pants, white Nike sneakers, and a yellowish orange and blue friendship bracelet.

"She always had that thing on…I have never seen her without it," Sarah told me when she noticed that I was checking the items on the paper.

"What?" I asked.

"That bracelet; she told me that her mom gave it to her years ago," Sarah said.

Two more cars had parked. Four or five more men exited and started walking toward the woods. They were not part of the search group. But seeing them with their backpacks and hiking gear reminded me of the time I went with my brother and a couple of friends to the Franklin Falls trail two years ago. It was right after Christmas, so the falls looked like something from a fantasy movie in the winter when they were completely frozen.

Despite the depressing vibe, I gotta say, the scenery from the mountains by Red Hills Trail was straight-up breathtaking. I mean, the landscapes around us were just like, whoa. The mountains are dusted with snow, pretty streams, and greenery blanketed with the beautiful white coat, the outline of mountain tops, and the trees in the background. Somewhere among these snow-covered summits, skiers were enjoying the season and were cozying up next to a fire in these lodges, enjoying hot cocoa and creating beautiful memories. The cheerfulness of the season, coupled with the beauty of the scenery, somehow further dampened my mood.

If you Google this trail, you'll probs see that it's like around two miles in total. However, the forest road closes during the winter, and you have to hike around five miles. This meant Sarah and I had to travel deeper into the woods.

It was getting colder by the minute. The clouds covered the sky, and it was definitely going to rain soon. Although it was only ten a.m., the dark skies above us made it feel like it was much later in the day. I also realized we were doing this search on the shortest day of the year. We had only six hours until sunset. Also, the wind was hella strong, making us freeze our butts off even more. I totally get why some peeps would rather Netflix and chill than go on hike in this mess.

The ground was muddy; I was glad I had my good hiking shoes on. Around me, each member chatted with their partner as they walked toward the gloomy scene of leafless limbs.

We continued toward the trail. I had downloaded the map on my phone but kept the printout for extra safety measures. My leggings were already moist, and my legs began to hurt from my high pace. On the edge of the wood line were thick bushes. I strolled along the first row of pines. I was looking at the ground most of the time, searching for an anomaly poking through the white. Finally, I saw the trail that led into the mouth of the pinewoods.

"Why are you, like, actually doing this? It's kinda hard to believe that you didn't even know Donna, but you're still driving all this way just to find her. I mean, let's be real, you're not some kind of angel or anything, we both know that," Sarah said.

"You're right. I am a criminology major because I love finding out the truth. This is a passion of mine, and I do this to satisfy this passion, but I also am a good person who wants to use this passion in helping others."

"You're also a Gen Z hungry-for-attention influencer," she said before walking ahead of me; I guess that was her way of ending the convo.

"I'm not an influencer. Not everyone on social media is an influencer, actually," I said as I quickened my step to keep up with her pace. My agitation was evident in my tone. I hate it when people call me an "influencer"! I am not looking to influence anybody!

She stopped to face me. "Was it you who showed up at the store yesterday?"

"Yes."

"Whatever. Just know that real people are involved in this." She paused. I thought that was the end of it. "And if we actually find something here, don't go sharing it on any platform. That could totally screw up the investigation. Let the police handle it, not you."

With that, she started toward the trail. I followed.

"So, were you two close?" I asked after five minutes of walking down the trail in awkward silence.

"Not really. Donna isn't close with anyone." She paused for a while. I thought she wasn't going to speak again. Then she half-turned her face toward me.

"We used to work together and live in the same town. And you know what? Despite all the crap people say about Donna, she's not, like, some weirdo or evil or anything. She's actually a sweet girl who keeps to herself 'cause she's been bullied her whole damn life."

Silence again.

I listened to the sound of our shoes crushing dried leaves and twigs as we walked toward the marked spot on the printouts—an occasional splash when Sarah accidentally hit a puddle followed by a muttered curse.

"I feel bad for her. I feel like maybe she is hiding somewhere, not sure what to do, probably thinks she's going to jail," I said to Sarah after a while.

"Yeah, I feel bad for her in general," she said.

One thing I love about hiking in the winter is the complete silence and isolation. No bugs, no bears, everyone abandons the woods, and they are left for me to enjoy. Finding the right trail on this route was a bit trickier, so I was thankful for bringing a map and knowing how to use it to find where we were and needed to go. We started down Creek Road, paralleling I-90. We passed under I-90. I paused and looked behind us at the gorgeous view underneath the overpass.

We went gently downhill on the closed Creek Road for about a mile, going through the forest with views of mountains here and there. The hiking trail curves through a vast wooded area, starting as a faded groove in the underbrush that can easily blend into the surrounding landscape, surrounded by towering evergreens whose branches sag under the weight of frost. The ground is uneven, with roots and rocks jutting out, making the trail appear more like a random collection of forest debris than a designated path. Finally, we reached a large hairpin curve with a big view of the valley. Somehow, we lost the trail and kept walking for a while before we realized, and decided to return to the curve.

It started to rain, and it had gotten significantly colder as we'd already walked through the last hour of daylight. That little unintended detour delayed our arrival. By the time we arrived at the meeting point again, there was nobody. Frustrated, wet, and cold, we both decided to part ways.

I headed to grab a sandwich at a place called Submerge. The smell of bread and the warmth of the heating system hugged every piece of me, and it just hit me how hungry and, tired and cold I was. I was about to order when I saw Aaron from the search party earlier; he was waiting in line, too. I nodded, placed my order, and waited in the pick-up area; he stood next to me.

"Hey, how did it go?" I asked him.

He looked so grim suddenly.

"It's crazy; I just finished at the station. The police are going to the site soon," Aaron said.

"I'm sorry, what?" I said, looking clueless.

"Oh." It hit him that I had no idea what he was talking about. He looked around before telling me, "We found Donna's bracelet in the woods. Things don't look good."

"What!"

"Where were you?" he asked.

"We lost our way, and by the time we made it to the meeting point, it was pouring, and no one was there. So we were like, okay, guess nothing went down." I held my tongue from saying nobody even cared about us being MIA!

"Poor Brett, he's distraught. I didn't want to leave him at the station all by himself, but I had to make it in time back in Seattle. I haven't done my holiday shopping yet," he said.

Everyone knows I'm a spiritual girl (you've seen my crystal collection! #crystaltok). At the time, I didn't know that she was dead yet, but I had a bad feeling about what I had just heard. I longed for my favorite amethyst crystal; it is essential for my emotional stability.

THE SOUND OF TUNING OUT

By the time I finished my meal, the rain had slowed down, and I decided to drive back to Portland. I was too freaked out and too upset. The whole drive back, I kept looking behind me. I felt like Donna was going to pop out of the woods somewhere, all bloodied and blue ... Every scenario from every horror movie I've seen was jumping at me and attacking my thoughts.

Almost three hours later, I was back in my studio apartment, checking my phone every second for news updates about Donna.

The following day, at seven a.m., I woke up to the news. The police found Donna's body about a mile from where they found her bracelet. It was hidden underneath dead branches. The entry to the spot where they recovered her body wasn't accessible due to a huge broken tree. Maybe that's why she loved that secluded spot.

My mind had not yet registered what my eyes saw for the first few seconds. My brain cells did not make the connection; I almost passed the news article notification on my home screen without thinking. And then the sudden realization and the fear I felt afterward. I was crying, and I was cold. Very cold. And it had nothing to do with the weather. Being a criminology major and an amateur detective, I've been reading about crimes and criminals, disappearances, murders, etc. But the real encounter of a possible homicide is nothing like reading about it from the comfort of your home. I felt so exposed and so vulnerable. Like I mistakenly walked into a trap.

The police could not determine the cause of death due to exposure to natural elements and the passage of time.

The discovery of Donna's body only added more questions than resolved any mysteries.

Donna was texting Jake AFTER the day she went missing.

Her last text to Jake was on July 13 (link to the source below – not verified yet)

One hour later, Jake was dead.

Did she kill him and run away to hide in their favorite spot?

When did she exactly die?

How?

Why?

The most disturbing thing is that these details are almost impossible to find out after six months.

Thanks for hanging out with me today, squad. I needed the company.

See you in the next one!

Caleb Bodkin
Jan 26

I walk down the streets of the Central Business District, longing for the warmth of the spot where I meet Tobey every morning to pick up our coffees before we head to the office. It is freezing. I think it was around thirty-five degrees this morning. The sky above is overcast, with clouds stretching across the horizon. Smears of blue hint at possible moments of clarity later today. The inviting aroma of freshly brewed coffee as I occasionally pass by different coffee shops is a pleasant distraction from the grim morning air and the depressing thoughts in my head.

When I finally make it to the café, I can barely open the door as the line of people waiting to be served pack the small space. I squeeze behind the last person in the line and wait. Tobey, who had been vaping outside, joins me as he sees me coming in. The line moves quickly, and before I can enjoy the warmth of the indoors, we are out on the street again, walking toward the office. He is careful not to bring up the case unless I do.

"They caught Donna on a surveillance camera on July 11. She was walking into a small grocery store at the edge of the woods before entering the area leading to the hiking trail," I say as we exit the café and walk toward the office building.

"You mean where the police eventually found her body months later," Tobey says.

"Yes. The video shows her walking in, and then almost ten minutes later, walking out, texting … she was texting Jake, I know from the time of the text." We pause at the light, as we wait, I continue "She bought Reese's Cups. I know that everyone loves peanut butter, but I can't help but think that she bought Reese's Cups for Jake. It was his favorite snack. That, and the fact that she was texting him to come and see her," the light goes green, and we continue our walk.

"But she had her phone on her, so where is it now?" he asks as we step off the curb.

"We don't know. I don't know where that leaves us. The log from Jake's phone showed that Donna was the last person to see him. I'm afraid we reached a dead-end with the investigation," I say as we go through the revolving doors at the entrance of the office building.

"This killer chose their lucky day to commit a murder," Tobey says.

"If she were really the killer, I don't know how lucky she was since she ended up dead," I say. "If she had anything to do with my brother's death, the blame falls on Brett! He should have had her admitted or locked up somewhere, because she was clearly a danger to society and herself!" we swipe our ID badges and head to the elevators.

"In all honesty, the girl in Jake's stories and camera roll did not look like a murderer. It could have been someone else, someone they were both tangled up with, like a drug dealer or an addict. One of Donna's acquaintances," he says as we wait. The elevators are usually packed and slow.

"Why would they kill Jake?" I ask.

"All I'm saying is that what they found is not enough to conclude that Donna had anything to do with it. We can't even know she was at your parents' house. Maybe she flaked and went to the woods to kill herself. There's no trace of Donna anywhere near the crime scene."

THE SOUND OF TUNING OUT

The elevator dings and we step into it with at least six others. I stare into the metal doors in silence.

"Why would she toss or hide her phone if she were to kill herself?" I say as we make it to our cubicles.

"I agree, it doesn't make sense, but she was a druggie. They are not the most rational people," he continues as he unpacks his laptop bag. "Did she look like she was on something? Was she nervous? In a hurry?"

"I don't know. I didn't see the footage. Glenn told me about it. It will eventually find its way to the internet."

"I'm sure."

#9 What Did She Do?

We think of our own death as a mysterious event in the far future. Time and place unknown. Circumstances unknown. Reasons unknown.

Not me, though. I died a while ago. I no longer exist in this world. I was a ghost before I even knew it.

Once you finish reading these messages, you'll arrive at the same conclusion I had at the time, that she was right. I won't spoil the ending for you. This is more like a teaser. Now, let's get back to the point where we stopped.

One beautiful spring day, I got home from school starving. The house was very quiet when I walked in. I called out to my mother. No answer... it's nothing new, I thought.

The nagging feeling of having money in my pocket and wanting to indulge my weakness made me resolve to have a quick lunch of a Snickers bar and a soda can before I headed out again to my usual spot.

Six hours later, I came home, exhausted, famished, angry, and out of thirty dollars ... I wanted to pick a fight with anyone, to take out my frustration and anger on someone. So I walked into our house. All the lights were out. No one was home clearly.

I ate a bowl of cereal and went to bed, still starved and angry.

The next day, I came from school to an empty house again ... no sign of my mother. She usually drank alone in her room, so it was not unusual for me to easily avoid her for a few days even though we lived in the same house. But this time, it felt different.

Usually, I would see a sign that someone had been there other than me, a half-eaten bag of chips in the living room, the TV still on because she had forgotten to turn it off, the water running in the kitchen for the same reason.

Not this time, though. I could feel the air so still, undisturbed, just as I left it that morning.

I went upstairs to her room.

At first, I didn't see her lying so still on the bed under the covers. She had lost a lot of weight, and she was a short, petite woman to begin with. She was sleeping on her side, facing the window that looked out to the street.

"Mom, are you okay?"

No answer.

I walked over to turn off the lamp on her bedside table. I saw an envelope with two papers inside. One had my father's name on the back of it. I didn't cry. Instead, I reached out to my mother's wallet and looked for money. She had close to fifteen dollars on her. I took them and called 911.

The letters at the scene confirmed the suicide. I kept the one with my name on it, never telling a soul about it, and gave my father his.

My father was telling people, including me, that my mother passed in her sleep, a heart attack due to her anxiety and depression medication. He wouldn't talk to me about any of the details of her death. It did not feel like he was protecting me from the painful truth. It felt like he was treating me like an outsider, but I was used to that anyways.

Two weeks after the wake, my father's mistress moved in.

PART FIVE

Trish_ona_mish

Excerpt from the transcript of episode 506 – published on Feb 20

Hello and welcome everyone! I have a few updates on some of the major cases that I've been following for the past I dunno months now! We're gonna discuss some new and existing material from the Jake and Donna case, Kim Bennett's case, and the disappearance of Kate Chen.

Let's begin with the tea on Donna Howe. Donna and her dad were not on good terms. It's all over the media! People are speculating that Brett was abusive toward her in every way possible—sexually, physically, and emotionally. But honestly, when I met him during the search, he didn't seem like the abusive type to me. What do you guys think? Let me know in the comments! Although, really, what can you tell from meeting a guy once?? Hahaha Not much! Believe me! I KNOW! At 23 and after a series of failed relationships and dates through Tinder!

The police confirmed Brett's alibi. He was attending a conference in Seattle the last day Donna was spotted. Her last appearance was on a CCTV recording at around 8:57 a.m. on July 11. I saw here, on Reddit and Quora, that some of my fellow web detectives are trying to investigate Brett even further.

Let's freeze the screen and zoom in on Brett Howe:

THE SOUND OF TUNING OUT

Facts: He is 49 or 50 years old, has no former criminal history, no history of mental illness, and works as a Director of Finance at a boutique firm in Seattle. His wife died in 2015. So I heard from some peeps in the Red Hills community (they wanna stay low-key, though) that he never got hitched again and wasn't really into any serious relationships. #singlelife #noregrets

Online footprint: His online presence is very limited (duh, he is 50!); he's on Facebook (again, DUH, HE IS FREAKIN' 50) and LIV (recently created). Both accounts are private, but someone on his friend list (we don't know who) has shared the complete contents of his accounts for some old hard cash. Like seriously, they shared EVERYTHING—pics, posts, updates, deets, and even his personal email! Ugh, not cool at all. He is also a member of an online group for parents with troubled children. I've been reading his posts on the support group. His concern, sadness, and grief seem genuine to me.

Questions: Why would he kill his daughter? AND Why go after Jake?

Possible scenarios: (once you vote, please answer relevant questions in the comments section)

- He's had enough! He couldn't deal with her anymore. (But what about Jake? How does he fit in all of this mess? He has no reason to go after some guy she's been seeing for a couple of months.)

- Donna and Jake attacked or threatened him; maybe they went after his money or something. (impulse/self-defense)

- Donna and Jake uncovered something, and Brett wanted to keep it hidden. (Like what?)

JMO he doesn't fit the profile of a killer. Also, what does Donna's message to Jake mean? What "fell off"?

Of course, these texts were also leaked by someone in the community, probably from the police. I am so intrigued every time a piece of info is out in the open, but I also don't want someone's hunger for fame and fortune to put this case at risk.

Now, moving on to discuss Kim Bennett's statements in her legal battle against her parents...

Caleb Bodkin
Feb 21

It's Friday, thank God. It's been a very long, exhausting week, and I'm looking forward to relaxing and unwinding. I step into the foyer to the awkward silence between my mom and dad. My parents have been acting like two teens bickering and fighting all the time; it's emotionally draining. I don't even bother asking what's happening. It's obvious that they are in the middle of a nasty argument. I don't feel like being trapped in this anxiety-provoking environment, waiting around for the next argument to erupt so I can make them feel better about themselves and their lives. So, I call Matt, he's visiting this weekend for his dad's birthday, and we agree to meet at Wicked Joe's, one of Red Hills' favorite hangout spots.

    I push the door to the bar, to the sound of a live band. I make my way between couples swaying together on the dance floor, friends around high-top tables and groups of familiar faces. I recognize the band playing as Unreleased. My stomach tightens, a cold, sinking feeling, and my mind races back to when Jake stood in that exact spot, guitar in hand, alive with energy. I swallow against the ache and I wave at Andrew and the guys and step outside to find Matt sitting, head down, staring at his phone screen, wrapped in a blanket, with a vape in his other hand.

The patio is lit by string lights, casting a warm glow on the small gathering of patrons, the steam rising from the mugs of hot cider and cocoa as people sip their drinks and chat. The chilly evening air is offset by heaters and the warmth of the crowd, creating a cozy and intimate atmosphere. It is lovely.

"Hey, do you mind if we sit inside? You know how the cold makes my muscles weak," I say.

"I'm so sorry, man, I totally forgot; let's go. I just wasn't sure you wanted to be around Jake's old band; I had no idea they were playing here tonight," Matt says, looking extremely embarrassed.

"It's fine. Let's go inside, I'm starving," I say.

We go in, find a table, and catch up on work and the drama in our lives. It's time for the band's break. The sound of lively chatter and laughter fills the air. Andrew comes over.

"So Maddy is the guitarist now?" I ask, referring to Madeline Davis, the band's drummer.

"Yeah, you know, it was Jake's idea. He was always teasing Maddy that she's the second-best guitarist in the world. After him, of course." Andrew puts his hands in his pockets and looks down, embarrassed. "This is our new gig; they have us playing every Friday."

"Nice. I've always liked Maddy. She seems cool," I say with a smile.

"Yeah, I'll come to see you after the show if you're still here," Andrew says, before joining the rest of the band on the stage at the back of the bar.

We get our drinks and burgers. The place is busy, but the general vibe is laid back. After the band is done with their show, Andrew joins us. He waits until Matt has to use the bathroom before talking.

"The police came asking a lot of questions about Donna and Jake's relationship."

"When?" I can't hide the surprise in my tone.

"This morning," he continues, "I told them everything I know. You know, they asked me not to say anything to anyone about the investigation because it will help them rule out who knows what when some details are kept from the public. But I'm sharing everything I know with you because it's different."

"Can I drop you off after? Maybe we can talk then?" I ask.

"Sure, but I can't stay too late."

"I know, I'm beat too."

After an hour or so, we head home. When we get into the car, I turn the heat on full blast. We drive around for a bit before dropping him off so we can catch up on the investigation news.

"Okay, so this guy Glenn Weaver showed up at our house earlier today and asked me a bunch of questions about Donna and Jake, when they met, where they went, what we did when we hung out, what drugs we used … my mom was so furious with him, but I told her it's all good."

"What else did Glenn say?"

"He asked if Jake had an Apple Watch."

"That's weird. Where is he going with this?"

"I know, right? I told him he didn't," Andrew says.

I make a note to myself to ask my dad about this. Maybe Glenn told him what he was after.

"I don't really think Donna did it, but there's definitely some kind of connection between her and this whole thing," Andrew continues.

I stay silent for a while. I don't wanna argue with Andrew, but all I can think is, Who else could it be?

"Donna cared for Jake. I don't know if she really loved him. We hung out a few times, not enough for me to judge. But she shared a lot with Jake and complained about her father. That much, he told me." A look of sadness crosses his face. "Jake really loved her, but I doubt it was mutual. She seemed too distracted."

"Maybe you can help me understand this better. But how did he fall so hard for Donna so fast?" I ask.

"I dunno. I've never seen Jake talk about a girl the way he did about Donna. I remember giving him a hard time about it the first time he told me he was seeing her. He didn't take it well, and I never really joked about their relationship after that," Andrew says.

We paused for a while, looking at the passing scenery and the serenity of the night, so tranquil.

"And why the secrecy?" I ask Andrew.

"She didn't want her father to find out. I don't know exactly why. Also, Jake didn't want to hurt Maddy's feelings; we all know she has a thing for Jake, like a crush or maybe real feelings." He pauses. "I mean, Jake and Em were a thing, but he didn't really care for her, and she had other plans. By the way, have you seen her latest posts about Jake? She's playing the victim now."

"I never really understood why Jake would date a girl like her. Anyways, she has nothing important to say," I tell Andrew.

"She's all 'Oh, my bf cheated on me with this dark weirdo, I forgive them, I am the bigger person here...' All that bullshit. It's nauseating," Andrew says, in a tone mimicking Emily. It is a lousy but kinda funny impression.

A laugh escapes my mouth involuntarily.

We are silent for a little while. The soft glow of the dashboard illuminates our faces, and the gentle hum of the car's engine provides a comforting background noise to our conversation. The contrast between the frigid temperatures outside and the warmth from the car's heating system is relaxing. "I thought Maddy had gotten over her crush on him," I say.

"Not really. She doesn't talk about it, but I know her well. Jake cared about Maddy and didn't want to hurt her feelings. He thought that we were gonna part ways after we graduated high school, and things would be resolved on their own," Andrew says.

The idea of Jake graduating high school and starting a life elsewhere downs my mood and makes my throat tight.

"Did he tell you about his plans after graduating high school?" Andrew asks.

"Yeah ... that was the last time we had a serious convo ... I was packing my stuff after spending the Fourth of July weekend here. He came into my room and had this intense look on his face. I'm sure it's nothing, I told myself." I pause and focus on holding back my tears. After a few seconds, I continue, "He talked about ditching the whole idea of being in a band and just going to college to become a sound engineer. I asked him if he had told you and the guys. Now that I remember, he said, 'Yes, I told Andy and some friends,' and I remember thinking, Who else other than the band? It didn't seem important at the time to ask about who knows what."

Tears start to rush down Andrew's cheeks. "I was a little angry at him at first," he says. "I wish I'd reacted better. My parents are making me go to college anyway. He didn't get to tell the rest of the guys. He only told me."

"Never in a million years could I have guessed that the other person he told was Donna Howe," I say. "I remember telling him, 'You're gonna shatter Dad's dreams of touring with the Foo Fighters one day.'" We both laugh with tears in our eyes.

The memory lingers, and I start recalling more details from that conversation. I sensed that something was off, like he had more to say but didn't. I almost teased him about it but decided against it.

"A day before Jake died, he came to see me and was very upset," Andrew says, breaking my train of thought.

"What for?"

"He said that Donna was acting weird, like she was dodging his calls and texts. At first, I didn't think much of it, back when we thought that it was just an accident, but after they found her body, I thought that maybe there's more to it,"

"What do you mean? I read the texts between Jake and Donna; she said something about taking a new type of medication that kept her drowsy. Maybe that's why?" I say.

"Now I'm thinking, what if she was dead?" Andrew says.

"But she texted him after her dad says she disappeared."

"Maybe it wasn't her using her phone."

"Did you tell the police about this? The last time Jake talked to you about Donna being a little off?" I ask him.

"Of course, and they asked me in much more detail about this last convo this morning. Anyway"—he shakes his head as if to rid of an unpleasant thought—"I found it weird because she told him that she had been going easy on the meds since meeting him. A week or two before he died, they went on a date in Seattle; it was their first official date, dinner, and a movie. I remember he was very excited. He told me afterwards that she had been sober for almost three months and was off her meds for two months, if I remember correctly." He pauses to unbuckle his seatbelt. "So, what she wrote to him in that text doesn't make sense."

Trish_ona_mish
Mar 8

OMG, guys! Did you hear? Brett totally deleted or deactivated his Facebook account! I mean, why would he do that? Is he hiding something juicy from us? Let me know your thoughts in the comments below!????!! Okay, I'm seeing some of you in the comments saying stuff like, "Omg, this is such a violation of his privacy." And, like, yeah, maybe you have a point there. I was scrolling through the comments, and some people were being so harsh on this grieving dad. Like, seriously? Can we give him a break? He's already dealing with so much and doesn't need the added stress of everyone judging him. Let's spread some love and positivity instead of hate, you know?!!

I reached out to my special tech-savvy forces (the Watsons of you who have IT expertise). I was told that if a police authority has a case where they need access to a "deleted" Facebook account, they will get a judge to sign a warrant and present that to Facebook. Facebook will then search their servers and provide the messages.

Listen up, fam! Here's the deal: when you post something online, you gotta assume that it's out there for good. Even if you delete it or your whole account, it could still be available to law enforcement. So be careful with what you put out there, and always think twice before hitting that "post" button! Like the case with Jake's Phantom account on Epilogue, the police can access all the entries. They are using the content in their investigation. (We still don't know what came of that.) It is true, though, that Brett, like his daughter, was cyber bullied a lot.

Calling all fellow amateur detectives here! Please share your thoughts and findings. Our file here is huge, and mayyyybeee it can actually help the police to catch the killer!

View 9820 comments

TheWiz654 (admin)

Any time a group of people gets together, there are bound to be disagreements. This forum is no exception. We are in no position to tell you what to think of ideas you see expressed here, but in our Terms of Service, we do lay out the rules about how you can post here. If you find that there is a fellow user whose thoughts you find offensive, you should add them to your Ignore List. When you put a member on this list, you will not see their posts, and they will not be able to send you private messages. By all means, if someone violates the Terms of Service, use the Report link (at the bottom of a post) to let us know.

LuvmyPug

Thanks for bringing this back up.

Mr. Snowball

The father sounds sketchy to me...

Mary Smith

Go find a job! Let the real police handle this case. Leave the poor man alone!

Mr. Snowball

Please block this nasty bully. We don't need her negative energy. This is a space for free speech.

Mary Smith

THE SOUND OF TUNING OUT

You are the true bullies barging into someone's life like that, analyzing his every move trying to create the boogeyman when there is none! The girl was crazy!

Hart856

Mary Smith??? Really? Can this account be more fake?

Cancan_lx

Dude, they always go for the most generic names! LMAO

Caleb Bodkin

Mar 10

The results from the toxicology report of Donna's body came out yesterday. There were no traces of drugs found in her system. This confirmed what Andrew told me about Donna laying off the meds for a while, as she had told Jake. They found no evidence that she had been stabbed, shot, or sexually assaulted. However, the state of her body made it even harder to determine anything.

There's some evidence to suggest that she had suffered compression of the neck. This means strangulation is a possibility here but not a definite one. It was hard to conclude whether she had suffered any head injury; however, that doesn't mean she wasn't physically attacked. Maybe they hit her on the head and then killed her while she was unconscious. I hate to think of what else they could have done to her while she was out. So, officially, the cause on Donna's death certificate is undetermined.

Glenn told my father that Brett is a suspect, not because there's any evidence against him but because, typically, in these cases, the investigation starts with those closest to the victim.

I personally don't like the guy. I mean, he said a few nasty things about us online and is acting all hostile toward us, like Jake was the reason his daughter died when, in reality, it is the other way around! But still, he is a dedicated father who never remarried or even had a girlfriend. As far as we can tell, he moved cities, changed jobs, and paid a lot of money to fix his daughter's mental and emotional issues. He's cooperating with the police as far as we know and providing every piece of evidence they asked for, including searching his house and car.

Just before New Year's, I was at Donna's funeral. It was packed because of all the media attention on the case, the connection created through Jake's Phantom stories, and the picture the media painted of a doomed love story between two teenagers from the Seattle area. Some online forums went as far as calling them the new Kurt and Courtney. Brett was hysterical that day. But amid all the drama, I saw Emily filming at some point. I hate what my generation has become. Narcissistic, judgmental, prying, and insecure. These are the main things that feed the social media frenzy. It is anything but social. Just incredibly selfish and self-absorbed.

Andrew was there too. Once my dad saw him, he wouldn't let him go without having dinner with us, which turned out to be a good idea. With the constant fighting between my parents lately, we've rarely been sitting at one table as a family. They both behaved in the presence of a guest.

When Andrew was sitting there, it felt like one of the old times when we would sit with Andrew while Jake was upstairs, getting ready to leave with him. Andrew would sit with us at the table for five or ten minutes, finishing Jake's plate. We would talk about school, the band, and the Seahawks.

When he left, I went into my room and cried until I heard someone whispering in my ears. I couldn't turn my neck or look around. I could only look ahead into a blurry frame that showed my bedroom window, with the faint streetlight shining through just enough to create a silhouette of my desk and chair.

It was very dark, which intensified these whispers.

I didn't know what was being said.

I started wiggling my toe. I tried to keep that momentum going until I fully woke. It took extreme effort, and if I didn't keep the effort constant, I had to start all over again. It was like being buried alive, screaming for help but getting nothing but silence.

I couldn't do it, and I couldn't move my toe, I couldn't scream, and even breathing felt like an added effort. All the while ... I was thinking to myself, if I managed to wake up from this nightmare, there was no way I was going back to sleep!

This time, the episode lasted longer than usual. The whispering wasn't making it easier because I couldn't focus my energy on waking up. I was too freaked out to focus. And then the whispering stopped, and I saw an outline behind the windowpane. A dark shadow of a face, but I couldn't see its features. Then, a hand crept up along the edge of the window frame; their fingers started to fold around the rim, attempting to climb into the room. I tried to scream; I thought I was making a noise because I could hear myself screaming. I didn't sound like myself, though. I sounded like an animal, suffering, screeching. It was getting harder to breathe. The noise was getting louder, and the shadowy figure had crept through the window and was now crawling on the bedroom floor. It reached the foot of my bed, then stood up, and I suddenly realized they were much taller than I had imagined, with long, disheveled hair.

It came closer, standing right next to my head. Fear wrapped its claws around my heart, and I felt like it was going to give in and stop at any moment. My muscles refused to acknowledge this fear, and I couldn't even turn my head to see what or who was standing right there.

And then, for a second, I could hear it clearly saying, "Watch."

The raspy screams continued as I fought for each and every breath. Something was closing in on my neck, suffocating me, stopping the air from flowing into my lungs.

THE SOUND OF TUNING OUT

With a sudden jolt, I woke up, like I was jumping from underneath the water's surface after being trapped for a long time, struggling to stay alive.

In reality, though, I only opened my eyes, barely moving any muscle. I knew that because Fenrir didn't even flinch. He was sleeping on the floor next to my bed.

When I woke up, I scanned the room quickly, not expecting to find anything but more of an instinctive move. My eyes rested on the picture of Jake and me in the Grand Canyon.

Then I remembered when I was on vacation with my family, and My parents had booked a separate room for Jake and me. It was tiny, and our beds were very close to each other. When I woke up from my sleep paralysis episode, Jake was still awake, and I was mad at him for not waking me up when he saw me struggling in my sleep.

"You weren't moving or making any noise," he said. "You were just asleep."

I was too terrified to go back to sleep.

My sleep paralysis has never been a serious condition, but it is disconcerting. It is common knowledge that when you suffer one of these episodes, you encounter a creepy fragment of your imagination, which can be a dark shadowy figure. It's constantly been changing and never maintained the same form because it is not someone or something; it's only your mind playing tricks on you. Lately, though, the figure has more of a consistent look. It freaks me out every time I see it.

My sleep is not the only thing that's been fucked up since Jake's death. My PP attacks occur more frequently, lasting for a few hours or sometimes days. During these attacks, my reflexes are entirely gone. And I surrender to sleep, and the cycle continues … the fog thickens. Talking about them helps me to keep track of what is real and what happens only in my mind. So, I've started logging my dreams, my brain fog episodes, my emotional state, and what actually happens in my life, my job, my family, and the investigation into Jake's and Donna's cases.

#10 What Did I Do?

Looking back on the days that followed my mother's demise, I realize I was still a naive child, no matter how malevolent I thought I was. Surely, a woman with any functioning brain cells would not last with a cheating drunk, no matter how desperate she was. Men like my father are self-destructive; I shouldn't have bothered with him at all.

I tried to drive my father's girlfriend away by making her life miserable. I was very rude to both of them, made a mess in every way I could, and made a habit of stealing her stuff. But, of course, I didn't do those things because I wanted revenge for my beloved late mother. Not really. I did that because I hated my father and wanted him to suffer.

Eventually, she left. He was cheating on her; she found out and left him.

One day, I decided that a trip to go out and let loose wouldn't hurt. I went to my usual spot, a bar off the beaten path. The whole setting of that place calmed me down. From the music to the smell of cigarettes and the ambiance in general, I could feel the tension easing. I started going there whenever I could. It felt like a small hidden haven where I could blow off some steam and enjoy my favorite "hobby," as I used to tell myself. It was a bad night because I had lost almost one hundred and fifty bucks, so I stepped outside for a cigarette and an older guy, I think he was in his fifties, followed me. His name wasn't really Mr. Smith; I didn't know what his real name was; this is just a name I've given him for the purpose of writing this.

"Bad night, huh?" he asked.

"Yeah," I said, looking out onto the lights beyond the parking spot of this ghetto joint two blocks off the highway. It was very quiet; you'd feel like this was a dimension that sucked you into this dark place. Only the lost souls and those with no place to go or anything to lose came here.

"How old are you?"

"Twenty-one," I lied.

"Of course, you are..."

I gave him a side look like I was ready for trouble. "I just left my asshole dad at home. I'm not looking for another asshole out here."

"Relax, I'm not gonna tattle..." He put his finger on his mouth as if to hush a little kid. "Addicts of all sizes and ages are welcome here." He let out a loud laugh, which morphed into a disgusting cough.

"I'm not an addict. I know what I'm doing," I said.

When he regained his composure, he sounded different; his voice was deep, and his tone was serious. He dragged his body toward mine and got too close, invading my personal space. "Please ... being young doesn't necessarily mean that you're stupid." His stale breath of alcohol and cigarettes filled my lungs as I was not ready for this close encounter. My instant impulse was to push him as hard as I could. But was it all because of the sudden rush of bad breath, or was I taking my anger out on this miserable jerk?

"What the fuck is your problem!?" I pushed the guy so hard, he fell to the ground, hitting his head.

I know our memories of sounds are not as vivid as the visuals, but that sound still rattles my brain every time I recall it. I ran to my car and hid in my room for the next two weeks while keeping a close watch on the

THE SOUND OF TUNING OUT

news and obituaries. I saw nothing, so I chose to believe that Mr. Smith was probably okay.

Trish_ona_mish
Mar 16

Hey guys, I've been getting some messages from my Mishionaries about some negativity in the comments section. Apparently, there's this one user who's been plain offensive. Not cool! We gotta keep it civil and show each other some respect. Remember, there are families out there who have lost loved ones, so let's be considerate and try to vibe with each other.

Look, I get it. It's okay to doubt the persons of interest in this case or any other ongoing investigation. But, at the end of the day, we are coming from a good place, trying to help out and bring justice to Jake and Donna. Let's not forget why we started this whole chain in the first place—their killer is still out there, and we need to stay focused on finding them.

Many of you are analyzing the details of every picture and entry by Brett Howe. As a guy in his fifties, he's not very active on social media, which makes sense, but we do see random posts; some political, other religious, and business news articlllllllllllllllllll... (sorry fell asleep on my keyboard from boredom, haha).

Hey, shoutout to my squad of Mishionaries! I gotta give you some major props for all the intel you've been sending my way. I did some digging of my own using publicly available sources like news reports and university records, and I was able to confirm a lot of what you sent me. So without further ado, here's the down and dirty on what I found:

Brett graduated with a business administration degree in 1998. He met his wife, Anastasia Howe (maiden name unknown), in college and married in 2002. Sometime in the early 00s, they moved to Tampa, where they had Donna. She was born in 2005.

Brett has a LinkedIn profile (still active btw). He's been working as a Finance Director in Seattle since October 2020 and has been working in Finance for more than 25 years now.

Brett's Alibi: People mostly focus on his entry from July 11, the day Donna disappeared.

Yesterday, I had to meet my friend in Seattle, and I went to the said conference room that shows in the background in Brett's selfie from the conference on July 11.

Click here to view the pictures for your reference; it looks like Brett was at the Alaska Club Ballroom at Courtyard Seattle Downtown where the conference took place. I've compared the items in the background in his pictures, such as the carpet, tables, walls, and windows. Also, I checked the history of events held at that specific hall; there was an event held that day under the title "Innovation in Finance" (YAWN YAWN AND YAWN). I've also found a lot of other finance professionals who checked in the same conference room that day as well.

It's safe to say that Brett had a solid alibi.

Donna's Text: The secret message between those two lovebirds has been finally decoded! And let me tell you, I was legit bawling my eyes out when I read the backstory. Sometimes, I feel like Donna was misunderstood all of her life. She was a lost girl who didn't know how to cope with the massive loss she went through. (I know I sound like an echo of Jake's first Phantom story here, posted on 7/16.)

"It fell off."

She was talking about the bracelet the search party found before finding her body in the woods later that day. Remember what Sarah Blackwell said to me that day? She said Donna loved the bracelet and wouldn't go anywhere without it. This is a friendship bracelet. So you tie the bracelet onto your friend's wrist as a symbol of friendship and make a wish for something at that moment. The moment at which the bracelet falls off on its own, the wish will come true. So Donna was referring to the bracelet, which must have fallen off before she was attacked/killed herself. The bracelet was given to her by her mother, according to Sarah.

She had made a wish with her mother the day she bought that bracelet.

How do I know all of this? Well, someone leaked this info from the police investigation.

How did the police figure this out? A hidden diary? Jake's phone? Or perhaps the Epilogue content? I have no clue.

Now the police have access to all the material from Brett's deleted Facebook account and the content from Jake's Epilogue, so maybe there was something in there that told them all the deets about this super sad backstory. Although we have no source to confirm this info, it makes a lot of sense, so I'm betting my favorite pajama pants that this analysis is accurate.

Keep at it! #JakeandDonna #idiedazombie

view 4380 comments

SleuthySill

Someone is hot for that perve! haha

Mary Smith

It is perfectly normal to post about your workday. So what is the big deal? Get a life! Stop attacking Brett!!

SleuthySill

Idk. That post looks out of place. I mean, the guy never posts any pictures of himself and never shows any social interest, and yet he goes to this boring conf for work and feels the need to show where he is and what he is up to!

Sgr120

Is it just me, or is Glenn Weaver hot?

Tania43

Yessss!!

Caleb Bodkin
Mar 18

"He knows something," Mom says. I'm in my kitchen talking to my mom while preparing my dinner.

"Knows something like what?"

"I don't know…" she says with hesitation.

"Look, Mom, this doesn't sound very logical to me. People are harassing him left and right," I say as I fix my Airpods.

"Now that I think about it, it doesn't make any sense that he would break down and cry the way he did at Jake's funeral for no reason! At first, I thought he was hiding her somewhere because I was certain she was the one who had killed Jake. But now…" She trails off the way she always does when she's unsure whether to tell me what's on her mind.

"Just say what you wanna say, Mom, please. It's been a long day."

She lowers her voice, using her very serious tone. "We don't know what he's been doing to his daughter. Nobody ever listened to her. The only one who did was her therapist in Florida, and she had nothing against her."

"So what are you suggesting? He killed his own daughter? And why would he go after Jake too?" The thought is too distracting. I put down the knife and look out the window. The view isn't great, mostly of the backside of the buildings crammed in front of my apartment building,

THE SOUND OF TUNING OUT

framed with the black aluminum border of my window. I gaze past a sliver of an open space, giving a glimpse of the main street from my vantage point. I look for any sign of other people, the bustling city life, to distract me from that suffocating thought. The thought of Brett killing his own daughter. It seems to dim my tiny studio apartment even more, and I hope to escape the darkness. The sight of people walking, and car headlights was a reminder of the life that happened beyond this dark storm I am caught in.

"I'm just saying that I don't know what happened, and I don't trust the guy," she says.

"Did Dad talk about the possibility of Brett's involvement in the murder with Glenn?"

"I don't know, probably." She pauses for a long time. I'm distracted by the pain in my eyes from chopping onions. She finally speaks, "We barely see each other anymore. But the last time we spoke about the case, which was this Saturday, right after you left, he said that I'm looking for someone to blame."

I know this. Dad told me the same thing just yesterday. Of course, I don't tell her.

It's sad to watch them at each other's throats like that. When will this phase end and what good may come from it? I keep hoping this will prove to be another case of the "what kills you makes you stronger" type of thing. Maybe in a couple of months, the police will solve the case, and my parents can move on and realize they need one another more than they know. My parents love each other. They absolutely do. Always have. My dad once told me that he fell in love with my mom because she is everything he isn't.

My dad is indeed smart and hard-working, but when it comes to physical activities, he is lazy and doesn't care much about his figure. He is passionate about music and adventure, which entails traveling on wheels.

Oh, and he is definitely into wheels. And since my mom is an environmental engineer (and kind of a hippie), she isn't into anything that could jeopardize the sustainability of this planet, like, say, cars. My mom is very successful. She chose this career path because she loves nature. She's the outdoorsy type who signs up for hiking trips and marathons just for fun and barely has time left for online activity. She thinks of the whole cyber world as a minefield for porn, scams, and fake news. She grew up with two like-minded siblings who continued to explore the landscapes on foot, hiking, white water rafting, biking, etc. Every year, my mom, her two sisters, and Fenrir go on a wilderness adventure for a week or two. They disconnect entirely from their lives and enjoy nature and their favorite sports activities. Last year, they biked to LA in three weeks. Her sisters have social media accounts, but my mother was never into the self-absorbed act of posting every little or big milestone. She still prefers the old-school camera to her iPhone when she travels.

My parents have the perfect combination for a relationship where the interests match while the personality traits are the opposite. If you're lazy, you need an active partner to keep you motivated because when someone is good at something, they make it look easy enough. If you have a bad temper, you need someone who can absorb that temper and show you how messed up your reaction was in handling the situation. If you're impatient, you need a tolerant partner to even out the equation and restore balance in the environment where your kids are brought up.

Neither Jake nor I are as physically capable as our mother. The one healthy kid inherited my father's musical interests and talents, while the other kid has a chronic condition that qualifies as a disability. So my mother couldn't share her passion with either of us, hence the strong bond with Eveline. But my disability forces me to eat healthy and keep a close watch on my vitals, so there's a window for my mom and me to have discussions about healthy smoothie recipes, the latest trends in the food industry, and ideas to keep my potassium levels as acceptable as can be.

When I look at my parents right now, I have the urge to block them both out of my life. They can't handle the loss like grown-ups are expected to. I've always asked for their advice to know what I'm "supposed to do," but not lately. They're like a deformed version of a once-beautiful face. Unpleasant, borderline scary. I'm scared of being with someone and then hating them the way Mom and Dad hate each other right now. I feel like a child when I'm with them. I try to avoid any topic that might start an argument between them. These days, Brett is the hottest topic of disagreement. Whenever Glenn comes over with any news, Brett trends again as the topic of discussion in my parent's living room.

"I expect the police to be looking into Brett's possible involvement. Glenn said they had been questioning him, searching his house and car, a while ago," I say. "What matters to me, Mom, is why the police would waste resources and time on someone when he has an alibi on both days when Donna and Jake died. Seriously!" It's my turn to sound angry and frustrated because the police insisted on fucking up the investigation.

"I disagree. I think they're not looking hard enough," she says.

I'm too hungry to wait, so once I finish preparing my dinner, I end the call and have my stir fry in silence. I don't even turn the TV on, too much on my mind.

After washing the dishes, I'm getting ready to hop online to play a quick game to keep my mind off things when Glenn calls.

"Did Jake ever mention that his phone had been stolen?"

"Not that I know of. Try asking my parents, though. Why?"

"Just something that we are looking into right now," Glenn says.

"I hope you're getting somewhere with those random questions."

"What does that mean?" he asks with a hint of annoyance in his tone that he tries and fails to mask.

"Just letting you know that Mom will not tolerate any more mistakes."

"Listen, we're doing the best we can." He pauses briefly to calm himself, then continues, "Things are moving. Just have some patience."

"Dad told me that Donna's former psychologist is flying in from Florida next week."

"Yeah, we're hoping Donna shared some info with her before she died. Any new acquaintance, threats, dark thoughts…" Glenn says. "She was emotional when I spoke to her. She said her relationship with Donna went beyond the typical patient/doctor relationship. Donna had stayed in touch with Dr. Angela even after moving to Washington, so she must be the best judge of Donna's character."

I've been thinking about meeting her ever since my dad told me that she was coming. Glenn told me where she is staying, some boutique hotel in Seattle. I am going to try to talk to her.

I wonder if Donna mentioned Jake to her at all.

Text Exchange Between Jake and Donna

Jul 11

DH: Meet me in 30. Our spot.
DH: It fell off!
JB: Sorry just woke up
JB: Where are you?
JB: U ok?
DH: Yeah I'm OK. I'll text u later
JB: Wanna meet up?
DH: Maybe later, I'm exhausted.
JB: What happened?

Trish_ona_mish
Mar 18

HAPPY ST. PATTY'S DAY!
Thank you all for your kind and encouraging words! Without the dose of reassurance that I get from my Mishionaries, I wouldn't have been able to do this!! This is not just me! It's the endless dedication and priceless efforts by all of you in this community of web sleuths! Your commitment to the pursuit of truth and justice is truly inspiring, and I feel so lucky to be a part of such an incredible group of people.

I knew it! There was no way in hell that a nineteen-year-old did not have any social media presence at all! No freakin' way! No matter how complicated her life might have been. Like, even if she's not active all the time, there's gotta be some sort of online footprint. This whole situation is just WILD!

I admit it took me a very long time and excessive dedication to find out that Donna was the owner of the LIV account "Sullen_Girl05."

Jake followed 864 accounts on his Insta. I went through each and every one of them and traced it to a user. This account stood out as an outlier. Most pages or accounts he followed were owned by teens from his community or were related to the music industry—specifically the metal genre—sports, video games, typical boy stuff. This one had dark poems and pictures of waterfalls or natural bodies of water. The profile picture shows blue eyes; they look like Donna's.

The bio had one sentence.

"It's calm under the waves ... in the blue of my oblivion."

This is a quote from a song called "Sullen Girl" by Fiona Apple. We know that Donna loved the artist because of that Phantom story where Jake did a metal cover of one of Fiona's songs. I heard she loved her because Fiona Apple was her mother's favorite singer (aww). I started listening to her stuff lately; I can see why Donna would be into her music regardless of her mother's taste.

I emailed Caleb Bodkin and tried to explain my findings to him. I didn't expect him to answer me, at least not immediately, so I called the police tip line and gave them the info.

One day later, BOOM! Caleb emailed me back, saying he saw my message and had already spoken to Glenn Weaver about it. They're on it, people! He even thanked my followers and me for our consistent efforts. How cool is that?!

I am so happy to be of any help, and I will continue to work so hard on this case and others and help the families and the authorities get the justice we all pray for.

This account does show a stable, talented, and soft side, not what the media had painted about Donna.

But most importantly, the police announced (or Glenn Freakin' Weaver) that this lead has shed light on some new material that could lead to new evidence in the case!

So thank you, thank you, THANK YOU for all your support! Let's keep this momentum going and continue to make a difference in the world. You guys rock!

I'm too excited to type anymore!

P.S.: Here is a picture of the new Williams Family member. A couple of weeks ago, I met this cute ball of fluff in an alleyway behind a deli near my apartment building. I started feeding her every morning and evening. Today, I decided to take her home, and I named her Donna because of her striking blue eyes ... she gets along just fine with my beautiful LovePug! Isn't she lovely!

Caleb Bodkin
Mar 19

I go to the Azure Haven Hotel, where Dr. Zheng is staying, and ask the receptionist to call her. At first, she asks to speak to me on the phone to confirm that I'm not some nosy reporter. Then, when she confirms my identity, she's reluctant to talk to me because she's not meant to discuss the case with anyone but the police.

"I'm curious to learn more about your brother, though," she says. "Let's make it quick. I'll be in the lobby in five."

I sit on the couch in the lobby and order myself a drink. It was seven forty-five p.m. The guests are coming in and out. I can tell by how they dress and the few conversations I overhear that most guests are in town for business. No families for sure, only professionals as far as I can see. Also, this isn't not the season for tourists. The black leather couches are deep and uncomfortable. It's a modern, cheaply done setting but good enough for a quick trip. I keep an eye on the elevator. I looked up her profile on LinkedIn to know what she looks like. Finally, after ten minutes or so, she comes walking toward me with a tiny cat in her hand.

"Caleb?" she said.

Her profile picture does not do her justice, as Dr. Zheng is very attractive indeed. She must be in her mid to late forties; I made that educated guess because I saw on her LinkedIn profile that she has over twenty years of experience in the field. Had I not known that piece of info, I would have been easily fooled into thinking she was thirty-five or even younger! She is slim and elegant, with straight black hair and sharp features. It is easy to guess that she is well off and in control, even if you know nothing about her. She has a strong presence. But when she speaks, she is very soft-spoken, which makes her even more attractive, if that's even possible.

Her cat is in her lap; she's stroking her and massaging her head between her ears.

"This is Bianca. I don't go anywhere without her. This is why I chose this four-star hotel. I always look for pet-friendly places."

"Thanks for meeting with me."

"I'm following the case and the news closely because I'd been worried about Donna." She drops her gaze for a second, a flicker of helplessness breaking through her composed exterior.

"I need to make this short," she continues, her expression serious, "and I can't share any private information about Donna or any of the info from my interview with the police. But I agreed to see you because I have questions of my own as well."

"I can't share a lot of info, but I guess we're here for the same reason," I say.

"Which is?" She narrows her eyes and lowers her voice. It's intimidating because, knowing what she does for a living, every question feels like it has an underlying message.

"Hearing the other side of the story?" I manage.

She flashes a gorgeous smile and says, "Donna is not the other side." She shifts in her seat and fixes the cushions behind her in an attempt to get more comfortable. "Jake talked about you to Donna all the time. It even made Donna want to have a sibling just so she could have what you guys had." She pauses. "Donna wanted to meet you."

THE SOUND OF TUNING OUT

My eyes start to sting. I panic as I realize the familiar feeling of tears rushing into my eyes.

"I'm sorry. I didn't mean to upset you," she says, her voice softening.

I shake my head as if to rid my face of all the sadness and weakness. "No, it's okay. I'm still dealing with it."

"I know. Me too." She continues. "Had you met her?" her voice barely above a whisper.

"No."

"Did Jake talk to you about Donna?" she asks, leaning in slightly, her tone probing but not unkind.

I shake my head, looking down with my lips pressed into a thin line. Disappointment and regret well up inside me, and I choose to let my silence speak for me instead of words.

She looks at me with a mixture of empathy and curiosity "Do you feel betrayed in a way? Like you believed your relationship with your brother was one thing, but it turned out to be something entirely different?"

The question strikes a chord deep within me, and before I know it, the words spill out. "I'm too scared to go down that road because I don't want to know that I did something that made him think he couldn't trust me." I pause, surprised at how much I've revealed.

We don't say anything for a while.

"Do you want a drink?" I ask.

She gives me a sad hint of a smile as her features speak of all the compassion and gratitude before her lips do.

"No, thanks."

Her confidence and facial expressions make me feel like a kid playing an adult. I don't know what about her makes me so vulnerable.

"I'm curious whether you have any theories on who killed Jake," I say.

"I don't know..." She pauses for a second. "She didn't kill him. I know that for sure."

Does she really? How can she know whether her crazy teen patient killed her boyfriend? I know the police said she was possibly killed, but I fail to see any other connection between the two deaths.

"You were close with Donna? Other than being her therapist?"

"Psychologist. And yes. She was like the daughter I never had," she says. "Honestly, when they found Donna's body, I was shocked. I thought that she was on her way to me. She always spoke of coming back to live in Florida." It's her turn to look emotional.

"What was she like? What were her interests?"

She looks down at her cat ... Like she's having a silent conversation with her. Then she puts her on the couch next to her, crosses her legs, and continues.

"Donna spoke about Jake a lot. He had a positive influence on her life. She was thinking about going back to college with him next year. They both wanted to move to Florida."

"Why Florida? Jake has never been."

"They talked about Full Sail University. Jake was interested in a program there. Donna was gonna study creative writing. And Jake was into sound engineering/audio production." She pauses to check the screen of her phone. I don't know whether she's checking the time or a notification. "She was a shy girl, isolating herself from the world; she was terrified of people. She loved poetry, literature, and water sports. She used to tell me how much the sight of water relaxed her and how much she longed for Florida for that same reason." She pauses again to calm herself, as she's getting visibly upset and emotional.

"Were they in love?" I ask her. I start rubbing my temples as a headache kicks in, and I feel tired and numb. I recognize the signs of a PP attack and choose to ignore them.

"She loved Jake but not the same way. I think he was to her everything she never had: the best friend, the brother, the boyfriend, the neighbor, the classmate, all the typical social titles in a teenager's circle bundled up in your brother. Donna was deprived of all the basic social interactions we take for granted."

"If she were such a big deal to him, why not tell me?"

"I think he was protecting Donna. She was a very private girl. She didn't want him to publicize their relationship," she says.

"You know why?" I ask.

"I can't share that info with you, Caleb. But I can assure you, it had nothing to do with Jake. She had her reasons."

"You mean her dad?" I remember my conversation with Andrew the other day.

"It's hard to keep a secret these days," she says with a faint smile that confirmed my suspicion.

"What is Brett's deal? They lived next door, and we barely heard or saw them." I'm getting agitated. "I am so lost. I don't know what to think or what to say. Between Jake's videos on Epilogue and his relationship with Donna, I don't know what to expect anymore. I can't help but wonder why. I thought we shared everything." And I'm getting emotional, too.

"She told me that he loved her, and she believed him." She remains silent for a while. I'm unsure why and am about to excuse myself when she says, "I really wanted to meet your brother. From what Donna told me, he was a genuinely nice guy. Caring and observant. He paid attention to details and was very focused all the time. At least that's what she told me on many occasions. She was so fragile and suffered from severe depression. Her issues were very real and came from the detrimental experiences she had to go through as a child. The only person she had ever hurt was herself."

"You mean her mother's death?" I ask.

"Yes. That, and other things."

"Bullying?"

"Seems like you've done your homework," she says, with a smile and a tone that teachers often use when their students, surprisingly, get the right answer to a trick question.

"Do you think she killed herself?" I ask, and as expected, she seems uncomfortable.

"I can tell you this much. I wanted to meet your brother because I felt like she was moving forward for the first time in ten years. She had a plan that involved a future. A term she was not accepting since her mother had died."

I bow my head. I'm feeling weaker, and my toes are numb. I'm pretending to listen, but I can feel the tears running down my cheeks, and I'm not going to raise my head because I don't want her to see my face. It's so embarrassing.

I know this is absurd, but I think a tiny part of me is embarrassed to cry in front of a hot lady. I don't know. Something about her is intimidating and reassuring at the same time, the way any good-looking woman makes me feel. Is it her confidence? Her eloquent sentences and steady yet soft voice. She knows what she's saying and is not wasting a breath on useless conversation. I'm not used to that.

"Caleb, are you okay?"

"Yes, I'm fine," I say, cradling my head.

"I recommend you seek professional help. What you're going through is not the typical grieving process. You must focus on yourself, your well-being, and your mental health."

I look up with a resigned smile on my face. "You know, at puberty, I had excruciating muscle cramps. They were triggered by my bad diet and the cold weather in the suburbs of Seattle. My muscles would turn rock hard. It took a while for the doctors to figure out what exactly was wrong with me. They thought it was psychological at the beginning. I saw a therapist from when I was twelve until I was fifteen. A year later, they finally figured out what was wrong with me."

"What was that?" she asks.

"Hypokalemic Periodic Paralysis." My voice is shaky, and my eyes are teary, but I continue, "So, with all due respect, I don't think talking about it will solve the problem here. I just wanna know who killed Jake."

She picks up her cat and starts to stroke its back again with a concerned look on her face.

I fidget with the dead skin around my nails for a second, trying to hide the now streaming tears on my cheeks. Finally, I get up, thank her, and walk as fast as I can out of the hotel, onto the street, and toward the parking lot.

I feel so awkward.

Trish_ona_mish
Mar 21

MISHIENARIES!! I KNOW WHAT YOU'VE BEEN UP TO!!!
You've been stalking Donna Howe's account, haventcha?!
Last time I checked (about ten seconds ago) Sullen_Girl05 had close to 3,000 followers!!!
Let me be frank here, the account is pretty boring, especially if you're not into poetry. I personally DO NOT enjoy poetry, classic lit, or reading whatsoever! I prefer visuals. I wonder if Donna subscribed to Epilogue... But you know me. I don't spend much time fantasizing and planning. I'd rather just do it! So I reported Donna as dead on LIV. Now we have to wait and see if they will accept my request to Phantomize her account (I sent links of her obituary and other news articles to confirm her death since I can't get my hands on other documents they typically ask for). Idk if this will be enough because in order to switch the account from the regular to the Phantom status, you need to provide docs like a birth certificate, death certificate, and relation to the dead person. But I'm hoping it will be different with Donna since she's famous now. I also called the tip line and suggested that the police ask LIV for Donna's Epilogue content (if it exists).
So, basically, we're stuck waiting for months until the authorities give the go-ahead to seize LIV's content. It's ridiculous, considering they

THE SOUND OF TUNING OUT

took forever to get Jake's content, even though it was obvious he was murdered. In Donna's case, it is going to be even more difficult because her death is not a homicide yet. Thoughts?

Dan-90K

what if we try to use hashtags like Jake's brother did?

Joshua_cl

how? We don't know anything about her

Prad_09nm

agreed

King_Pong12

Fiona Apple stuff?

Charlotte.dmond

the dad should report her as dead. He must want answers unless he doesn't want others to find out more

Patel_G

it won't work unless LIV switches her account

Breakmysoul_5201

but what if Donna is a suspect in Jake's case? Can't they get the data on that basis?

#11 Has it Always Been This Dark?

You know that saying, "It is darkest before the dawn"? Well, that summer was one of the darkest times in my life. It had become impossible for me to live with my father. We fought every day.

But I did see the light at the end of a very long, dark summer. I saw the dawn slowly crawling in the background, illuminating the path and leading me to my victim.

Innocent, oblivious, like a sitting duck, waiting for me to launch my attack.

Do you know how they tell you to break down a massive project into smaller chunks that are easier to digest? They say it will help simplify a big plan and make it more achievable. Then, before you know it, you're done with the big assignment.

My big project was to be a good person. My first small task was to go on a date.

Luckily, my date's goals overlapped with mine. That helped me overcome my sickness and get over the dire situation at home. I was drawn to the determination and understanding I found in myself once I was in that relationship. The support I found was a shining torch of hope. I started to look for the solution rather than the cause of the problem, which was more manageable and productive.

THE SOUND OF TUNING OUT

After finishing high school, I took a year off to stay home, prepare for my tests, and apply to colleges. The series of successful dates, good scores on my exams, and staying clear of bad habits day by day created a chain reaction that paved a path ahead. I imagined myself walking along this route studded with milestones of triumphs like a college degree, a good job, a family of my own, you know, the standard ingredients for human satisfaction.

It was hard to admit that I was sick and seek treatment. The more I stayed at home, the stronger self-pity I felt for myself. It took me a while to recognize that what I had was considered an addiction, not just meaningless fun.

Text Exchange Between Jake and Donna

Jul 12, 12:53 a.m.

JB: I need to see you, I can't stop thinkin' about what you said to me. About your mom, this is huge!

JB: Did you make that post?

JB: Maybe you can head off before me, start a bit earlier?

JB: Hello! Please answer, I'm so worried. Just saw your dad's post on the forum. CALL ME!!

Jul 13 11:05 a.m.

DH: Where are you? We need to talk.

JB: Garage, recording, wanna come over? No one is home. We have about an hour or two.

Caleb Bodkin
Mar 22

Feeling weak, I walk out of the hotel lobby and onto the street. I felt the tingling in my legs while sitting with Dr. Angela. This initial warning sign usually indicates that a full-blown paralysis episode is about to occur. It's my fault. I ignored all the subtle warnings my body had given me. Thinking about Jake and trying to understand what was going through his mind, I was so mad that I never got to ask him about so many things before he was killed.

My body feels like it was too heavy for my legs to carry. I'm sweating on this cold night. I can't move my legs; the next thing I know, I'm on the ground. On the street, crying and asking for help.

I lay there on the dirty ground all by myself. It's eerily quiet in that alleyway, although it makes sense because unless you are parked in the building at the end of it, you never have to walk in it. I wait for someone to help. A homeless guy approaches me. He doesn't say anything, just takes my wallet and takes off. I try to move, I yell for help.

I wait on the street for nearly ten minutes before a lady comes and calls 911 for help.

I was in bed for the next two days. Couldn't move, the potassium IV attached to my arm, I felt helpless and worthless. Just lying there in the same bed I had when I was a high school kid. In and out of sleep paralysis episodes. Barely able to eat, barely able to use the bathroom. Listening to my parents fight day and night and then dealing with the awkward encounter when either one walked into my room to check in on me.

Four days after I had the PP attack in the street, I can move, and I'm feeling better, but my boss thought it best to work remotely until the following week. He's paranoid that someone will think him unfair or intolerant of my disability. So I spend my solitary confinement at my childhood home, remembering Jake. Not just having flashes of memories but concentrating hard enough to get the little things that we never think about but actually make the person so real in our heads. Like the face he made every time we disagreed on something, the way he cleared his throat before he started to play the guitar even though he didn't really sing, the way he constantly fixed his hat, or the sound of his laughter.

I think the last time I saw him. It was early morning, three weeks before he died. He was going for an early morning hike with Emily. "I didn't peg Emily for an early hike kinda person," I commented. It makes sense now because that was probably a lie. He rolled his eyes and asked something about my flight back and left. I couldn't remember the exact last word he said to me.

I remember looking at him that day and thinking how much he'd grown in the past year. He was wearing his signature Seahawks hat turned to the back. And then it occurs to me that I've looked for this hat everywhere but can't find it. I want it as a keepsake, a memory of my favorite person in the world.

When I wake up on Monday, my parents have already left for work. So I make myself breakfast, fire up my laptop, and work on a weekly report that's due later that afternoon. I work for about three hours before stopping for a short break. Then, I make myself a banana, avocado, and honey smoothie. There's no new story by Jake, but my finger taps on his profile, and I find myself stalking his older posts. One photo after the other.

I catch myself smiling at one particular photo of Jake and me from last year. Jake's band got to perform in the Rockverse Music Festival, an annual three-day music and art festival with several bars, restaurants, and retail shops alongside bands. You can only imagine how proud we were of this musical genius among the herd of average individuals who make up the Bodkins and the Bowmans.

We always joked about Jake being "the chosen one" as he broke the average Joe streak in the offspring. He was the youngest and most artistic, or rather the only one with a creative side. Jake was clearly an intelligent child, but his grades were not indicative of that because his true passion was in the world of music. His teachers loved him, though, because he was a very well-behaved, talented, and charming kid. The whole town was rooting for him. My dad was so proud of his prodigy son and had hopes for him to become a real rock star someday. The whole town believed that Unreleased was going to make it and be the pride and joy of this hidden suburban community known only for its proximity to Seattle.

I took a day off and attending the full three-day festival with my brother, his friends, cousin Pat and his wife, my parents, and cousin Eveline. It's one of my favorite memories. Not because he got to perform in front of thousands and not because of the mayhem, fun, music, drinking, and crazy fun stories, but because it was just so random and unexpected. Everyone who made it wasn't planning on doing so; it kind of fell into place last minute, and we were so psyched for this unplanned reunion. In the pictures, Jake was wearing his favorite Seahawks hat. I'm determined to find it, so I go to Jake's room to look for it, and then I look in the basement with no luck.

Frustrated and exhausted from moving and shifting the heavy boxes in our messy garage, I sit on an old couch to rest for a while. My gaze is fixated on a stupid keychain of a cartoon ghost, probably a dumb gift from one of Jake's classmates...

And then everything becomes a blur.

I can hear noises, like scraping, followed by metal being dragged on the floor. I see a blurry image of a figure in my room who looks like a tall guy with short hair, not the usual. He's moving around the room in a natural manner. I'm trying to get up, but I can't. Although right then and there, I know this was another sleep paralysis episode, I'm still nervous and scared. I try to wiggle my toes, move my head, or make any sound, but I fail. For a few seconds, I decide to give up and wait for my mind to go wild with the tricks it's playing on me. I'm just sick and tired of everything. It's been happening way more frequently lately, and I'm utterly defeated.

A few seconds or minutes pass, not really sure, which feels like an hour, and I start to think, What a lame ghost. My subconscious has grown so predictable and uninspiring. The mysterious figure, or sleep paralysis demon, does nothing but shift around the room, moving things.

I fall back asleep. I don't know for how long, a minute? Thirty? Or was it just a few seconds? But the next time I wake up, I hear a ringtone. Then I realize I must have left my phone on the cabinet next to the door when I entered the garage.

I decide to gather whatever strength I have to get to my phone and check who's calling. It could be work; maybe it's my boss asking about the weekly report!

THE SOUND OF TUNING OUT

As I open my eyes, I hear a whoosh and a thud. I stand up, rubbing my eyes, ignoring whatever fantasy noises my mind was creating, and I walk to the door where I thought I heard my phone ringing just a few seconds ago.

Nothing.

I try looking for my phone but can't find it. So I go to the landline and call myself. Then, I walk back to the garage to find that my phone had slipped behind the cushion on the couch where I had just been sleeping.

No missed calls or messages except for the one I had just dialed a moment ago. Weird...

Maybe not. I have a history of blurring reality with believable dreams right before waking up. So, I decide to make nothing of it.

But then, I look up and start my walk back to the kitchen, where I had left my laptop open. I stumble over something, almost falling over. It's an old tennis racket my father bought once and hadn't used for more than a month, tucked among the endless mess of historical personal failures that this family had known over the years. It fell out of a box marked "tennis gear," which also has a ukulele and some art supplies. This box should be marked, "It seemed like a good idea at the time." Geez.

The box is tipped over to one side. Beyond it, I notice the disruption of the forgotten clutter in our garage—overturned boxes and scattered tools. It suddenly hits me that the garage has been ransacked ... that I was not alone in the room this time ... and that Mr. Sandman was here for real.

#12 What Am I Supposed to Do?

I think I'm fucked...

I don't remember feeling anything like this in years...

I feel lost ... Clueless ... I don't know where to go from here...

Come to think of it, the last time I felt anything close to this was the day my mother died ... and I had to live with a pathological liar, a narcissistic asshole, a selfish prick.

It felt more like I was switching foster homes.

The saddest thought that crossed my mind today was that I have no use for money anymore but to satisfy these urges.

What's the fucking point, then? Why?

I've done this before, you know? I gave up on everything and everyone and lost every ounce of human decency in the process. What can I say? I needed the money. I thought maybe if I got away with it this time, I could start anew and be there for the one who mattered the most.

Here I am ... I've done it again.

I'm exhausted from thinking, trying, and fighting. I'm succumbing to my weakness. I'm gonna let my obsession take over my mind, body, and whatever is left of my soul. I'm gonna let the weight and shame of what I've done take me down with it, drag me to the bottom of this dark ocean until I die—drowning in my own misery, flooding dirty souls like mine out of this world.

THE SOUND OF TUNING OUT

I thought I was prepared to face every milestone along the way. Going down the same road again doesn't guarantee the same experience. I feel so numb. There is no coming back from it this time. I am waiting for this wave to wash me away.

PART SIX

KING5: CRIME

<u>Man Seen Entering Home of Murdered Teen Musician</u>
Seattle Police Seek Help Identifying Man Who Entered Home of Murdered Teen Musician
Author: KING 5 News (KING)
Published: 03/26/2025 8:23:09 A.M.

Police officers are looking for a man seen by eyewitnesses entering the house of the late teen blogger and guitarist Jacob Bodkin, the police department announced.

Officers received a call from Caleb Bodkin after he was awakened by the intruder around noon on Monday. When officers arrived, they searched the area but were unable to find the suspect.

"I got a call from my son around 12:20. He was very distraught," Frank Bodkin said.

No eyewitnesses saw the suspect, given that most residents were at work or school. The cul-de-sac where the Bodkins live was almost empty during the break-in.

"The door was locked," Caleb Bodkin said.

According to Caleb, when he woke up, "The guy was in the garage looking for something and moving around the room. He didn't see me asleep on an old sofa, hidden behind some boxes."

Caleb recounted, "As an HPP patient, I frequently have sleep paralysis episodes which sometimes feel so real." Hypokalemic Periodic Paralysis (HPP) is a muscle disease that is manifested by momentary episodes of paralysis, usually caused by low levels of potassium. Caleb continued, "When I woke up, I heard a ringtone and shuffling, but I thought I had a sleep paralysis episode. When I got up a few minutes later and saw the mess in the garage, I realized someone was in the room with me."

Brett Howe, the next-door neighbor and father of Donna Howe, whose body was discovered earlier this year in the woods surrounding the suburban community, gave a statement to the police as he saw an unfamiliar African American man in the area around the same time the Bodkins' break-in happened. No other leads have been found so far.

Frank Bodkin is warning others to be careful and asking for residents' help to identify the man who broke into his house.

"I hope someone recognizes him and gets him off the street," Frank said. "It could've been much, much worse."

Residents of the Red Hills Area said that despite extra patrols in the area from Seattle police, they still feel on edge.

Police said that they are doing everything they can to locate this individual quickly. The police are asking RH community to stay vigilant, keep doors and windows locked, and report any suspicious activity. Seattle Police Department is handling the investigation for this incident, and specific questions should be directed to that department.

Following the break-in, some residents believed the suspect to be involved in Jacob Bodkin's tragic death. While unconfirmed by the police, this new revelation has only heightened fears in the area.

"I try to stay alert all the time for any unusual sounds or movements in the surrounding area. I have also installed CCTV cams on both sides of the house, front and back," Jessica Bartlett, the next-door neighbor of the Bodkins said.

Residents say they hope for an arrest soon.

"I think everyone would sleep easier if he were caught," Brett Howe said.

Anyone with information that might lead to the identification of the intruder is asked to call the police tipline.

Caleb Bodkin
Mar 26

Why did he come back? This guy literally got away with murder; what was he doing back at the crime scene?!

There is no way this was a random break-in incident. He took nothing. From the looks of it, he was looking for something, specifically in the garage where Jake was attacked. So the only logical conclusion here is that he was looking for a missing piece of evidence.

The police agree with this.

It must have been his phone ringing! The screeching noises were probably him trying to move the freezer; it always makes that noise when we try to move it. He must have thought that no one was home. He'd been watching us.

When I realized that someone had been there for real this time, I left the garage, trying not to touch or move anything. I walked out of the house through the main door and circled the neighborhood a few times, the backyard, the front yard, and the wooded area behind our house. Then I went to check with Mrs. Bartlett; maybe she'd seen something.

"Oh my God, Caleb! What are you doing here!"

She sounded overly enthusiastic and loud. Maybe that was her idea of showing sympathy and support. It was weird.

"Have you seen anyone around here? Someone broke into our home!"

"What! Are you okay?!" she asked, terror and surprise both glowing in her eyes.

"I'm fine."

"Oh my gosh! Are you sure?"

I couldn't hide my impatience and exasperation at her persistence.

"The garage is a mess! I just missed them and was wondering if you've seen anyone around." Someone sneezed inside as I was talking. She suddenly looked even more nervous, stepped outside, and shut the door behind her.

"Have you called the police or your parents?" she asked.

"Not yet ... I tried to walk around to check for anything out of the ordinary."

"I'll keep an eye out for anything, and please call the police and your parents, or I'll call your parents!"

She was trying to get rid of me. Her body language suggested that. The way she softly led me toward the steps of her porch, folded her arms, and closed her robe tighter, all screamed, "Leave right now!"

Another noise came from inside the house. A sneeze and a cough this time, her eyes widened. She looked like she was ready to shove me and run into her house.

"I gotta go now. The electrician is fixing my fridge. I gotta see if he wants anything. Bye now, and stay safe."

Next, I went to see Brett Howe. I read some of his posts online, so I was reluctant to go given his hostility towards us, but I decided that it was worth it. Most likely, he would probably appreciate this piece of info more than anyone else.

As I made my walk back to the Howes' home, I called 911 and then my mom. I tried my dad too, but he didn't pick up, and then I remembered that he left this morning for a business trip. It didn't look like Brett was home, but trying didn't hurt.

THE SOUND OF TUNING OUT

I knocked on the door and rang the bell, but he didn't answer. As I waited, I saw his car parked in the driveway, and I remembered what my dad had said about Brett getting fired. He must be out in the neighborhood.

I went back home and waited for the police.

"Did the police come?" Mom called me again. "Maybe you should leave the house! What if he's the killer! I am on my way!"

I tried calming her down, told her I'd been around the block, and asked the neighbors. Whoever was there had already fled the scene and was on the run.

"Did you see what he was doing? Did you see his face? Can you identify him or describe him to the police?"

"I fell asleep on the old brown couch behind the boxes; I guess he never saw me and didn't think anyone was home. I must have made a noise, or maybe when his phone rang, he was nervous, but that's when he left. I checked the main garage door; it is locked, so he must have come in and left through the window," I explained to Mom.

My mom started crying. I was terrified, too. Fenrir sensed my fear and came to lick my fingers.

After almost ten minutes or maybe less, the police arrived. They took my statement. They went into the garage, took pictures, and looked around.

"We're going to talk to the neighbors and see if they saw or heard anything." the police officer told me.

I feel bad for Jessica Bartlett because everyone is going to find out that she's been cheating on her husband. What luck she has! She cheats, and the next-door neighbor's house is broken into. I guess, finally, she's paying back the favor to Mr. Bartlett.

I almost texted Jake, "Guess who's been a naughty girl?"

Trish_ona_mish

Excerpt from the transcript of episode 511 – published on Mar 24

What's up, squad! It's your girl, Trish, and I'm back with another lit episode of Trish_ona_mish. So, how's everyone doing today? I hope you're ready to dive into some juicy topics and have some real talk.

You all saw those crazy vids and pics of the cops swarming around the Bodkins' home, right?

I mean, it's a known fact that criminals often return to the scene of their crimes. Not your run-of-the-mill thief or robber, though. They usually dip out and stay low-key to avoid getting caught. But, like, if someone's motivated by revenge or something twisted, they might just risk it all to go back and relive their wicked actions.

It's messed up, but there are actually documented cases of these creeps going back to the scene of the crime. When it comes to some twisted individuals out there, it's not just enough for them to commit their crimes and get away with it. Oh no, they take it to the next level by trying to inject themselves into the police investigation. Yeah! You heard me right. Some of them are actually interested in police work, while others are just trying to see how close they are to getting caught. Then, you got these arrogant pricks who get a kick out of being right under the noses of the detectives working the case and not being found out. And get this: some of these sickos actually want to get caught! Yeah, their sense of inadequacy is so intense, they crave any form of attention or recognition, even if it means spending life behind bars or facing the death penalty. It's messed up, but unfortunately, it's a reality we need to be aware of.

Brett Howe, Donna's father and the next-door neighbor of the Bodkins' said that he saw an African American man roaming the forests behind the Bodkins' house the day their house was broken into. This will help us narrow down the list. Brett claims he doesn't remember much about the mystery man he saw. All he's saying is that the dude was tall and had some weight on him. That's it. Like, seriously, dude? That's all you got for us?

Following the same logic, the sicko might have been at Jake's funeral. That's why we're taking a closer look at Jake's funeral pictures/videos, which were leaked by fellow internet sleuths and some media sources. Let's try to identify any outliers in the service, and maybe we can pinpoint the killer.

Okay, peeps, listen up. If the police wanna get to the bottom of this, they need to start investigating all those cold-case murders in the area. I'm talking about a deep dive. They need to look for any patterns or connections in case there's a serial killer out there lurking in the shadows and getting away with it. We gotta do whatever we can to help the cops catch this monster before he strikes again.

#13 The Aftermath

A gambler never wins.

This is a fact that no one tells you.

I've had winning streaks a few times, but there is no sense in going on about the wins because I never get to keep any penny. It's silly to think I was ever "winning." I used to get so excited, but over time, that excitement grew into a dull feeling of numbness, it didn't matter that much.

I did quit for a while, almost a year. But I knew deep down that it was too late.

You never really get to keep anything because all winnings are short-term. Winning only extends the losing process for a gambling addict. When you place a bet, you've already lost. The outcome is beside the point.

Yep, gambling is never about money. It's an illusory high.

It was the behavior that made it gambling. My bank statement is the number one indicator of my problem. It consists of several fifty or one hundred dollar deposits over and over again. Does this sound like a sane move to you? When I looked at those statements, I saw that I clearly had a problem. It started as a coping mechanism with my exceptionally shitty home conditions before turning into a downward spiral. When the circumstances no longer applied to my living situation, the behavior resulting from those dark times stayed with me. Placing oversized bets without being able to stop, feeling a thrill when doing it, and chasing losses. My ability to make a decent amount of money and recover from gambling losses fast sort of enabled me to do it more.

I kept asking myself, When does the urge go away? I needed to regain some control over my life; I was not in control of myself when I gambled. I could see the irony in that, because my addiction to gambling sprung from my addiction to control and power. When I first started gambling, I was under the illusion that I had a real feeling of control. I was always "in the zone." I don't know how else to describe it.

Until one day, I realized it was controlling me instead.

I need to move on.

This doesn't feel like moving on, though. I am stuck in the same place. Always have been.

The weirdest thing happened to me yesterday. I got a call from an unknown number. The woman on the other end said her name was Larisa Pikul. She worked for a car insurance company and was calling about their latest promotions for car policies. She sounded so old, like my babushka; she even spoke broken English like her, much better than my grandma's, but still, the way she twisted the words and the sounds of letters was very familiar. I was hooked.

I surprised myself when I told her I'd pay her a visit this week to discuss her offers. I didn't pay attention to the address; I just popped the location on my maps app and followed the navigation instructions. After driving for some time, I realized I was near that awful place where I almost killed Mr. Smith. I freaked out, turned around, and went home. When I walked in, I locked the door behind me and noticed I was shaking.

I don't wanna go back to that place. So, I decided that I was going to ignore her calls.

But this morning, Larisa called again, and I answered. I don't know why. Am I that lonely? Desperate? Or is it nostalgia?

Maybe I can arrange to meet her somewhere else. Perhaps they have a different office in another location ... because there's no way I am going back to that place again.

My first impulse when I get marketing calls is instant hatred and irritation. But not with Larisa. I couldn't help but feel sympathy and understanding because she reminded me of my grandmother. She barely spoke English, but a mother's love knows no boundaries and cannot be held by a lack of oral communication. She would talk to me in Russian; all I could pick up from the sentence was my name. Whatever she lacked in words, she overcompensated for with kisses, hugs, and candy. I think my character would have been entirely different had I been brought up by my granny.

Meanwhile, Larisa scolded me over the phone and told me that she was extremely disappointed since I failed to show up for my appointment this week. I don't know whether it was her voice or accent that made me feel so guilty, but I wanted to make it up to Larisa.

I am going to try again.

I want to be a good person.

This newfound goal requires facing my fears and past and overcoming my weaknesses. Surely, these milestones shall not be mistaken for smaller tasks.

Running away from that small gambling joint where I almost became a murderer on the loose did not help anyone. I am not going to run anymore.

"I'm coming for sure this time," I told Larisa. I was determined to break down my huge goal into smaller, achievable tasks...

First step: Meet Larisa.

THE SOUND OF TUNING OUT

Transcript of an Interview with the Defendant on 6/30

Jul 12

DEFENDANT EXHIBIT A, PART I
Whereupon the following proceedings were had in the Seattle Police Department, Seattle, Washington, on June 30, 2025, and were transcribed from the video on July 12, 2025.
APPEARANCES:
Detective Micheal Smith (MS)
Detective Glenn Weaver (GW)
Sergeant Eric Barnes (EB)
Detective Alfred Gibbons (AG)
Detective Aiden Lee (AL)
Defendant (D)
Proceedings

GW: Do you want to sit in the blue chair? We'll just put a cuff on you.
EB: Are you right-handed or left-handed?
D: Right.
GW: Do you want coffee?
D: Yes.
GW: (inaudible) How do you take your coffee?
D: Black.

GW: All right, there's a video recorder up there, and that's for your and my protection. (clears throat) Before I start to talk to you, there are a couple of things that I want to make sure that you understand. You'll be treated with respect and dignity here because this is how we run things around here. Okay?

D: Yes, sir.

GW: Well, my name is Glenn. These are my colleagues Alfred, Michael, Aiden, and Eric. We are from the homicide unit; we have already advised you of your rights.

AL: It's really hot (inaudible). Be careful with that.

D: Okay, thanks.

GW: You were arrested yesterday for murder.

D: Yes

GW: You were put under arrest yesterday as you were driving on the highway.

D: Yes

GW: It looked like you were on your way to Canada. Is that correct?

D: I had some business to take care of there.

GW: What kinda business?

D: It's personal.

GW: How long were you planning on staying?

D: Not really sure.

GW: Because you packed quite a lot, I'd say most of what you have under your name; where exactly were you headed?

D: Saskatchewan.

GW: Wow! What for?

D: It's personal.

GW: And you were told that, you know, you're under arrest for two murders.

D: That's what they told me.

GW: Okay. So charges have already been laid, and we are doing a pretty thorough investigation. This means you have been formally charged with two murders. As you can imagine, the investigation is pretty significant; you know, you're more famous than A-list Hollywood celebrities, for Christ's sake (chuckles). Now, we have already advised you of your rights, is that correct?

D: Yes

GW: Do you want to talk to us then?

D: I want to help in any way.

MS: Okay, the police have gathered evidence and met with prosecutors, and based on the evidence as it stands now, they've decided that, yes, the evidence is significant enough to lay a charge. Do you understand that?

D: Yes

MS: What does that mean to you?

D: I don't know anything about those allegations. It could be a set-up. To me, they sound farfetched.

GW: We want to talk to you about a woman who made an allegation against you. I'm not saying the allegation is true, but she made an allegation, so we want to discuss that.

D: Who is this woman?

MS: Well, she made the allegation back in December, and the woman says you were with Donna Howe the day she died in the woods.

D: That's a lie. I know who said that.

MS: Do you know who I'm talking about?

D: Yes.

MS: How do you know her?

D: She is from the Red Hills Ridge area. She works at the grocery store.

GW: Why do you think she is making these claims against you?

D: I don't know.

GW: You don't know?

D: No.

GW: Do you own the vehicle with the license plate number BFL8400?

D: Yes

GW: Were you able to renew your car registration?

D: No.

GW: Why?

D: I had an unpaid toll penalty.

GW: Do you remember the date of the unpaid toll?

D: Not really. It was some time last year.

GW: Where were you headed that day?

D: I don't remember.

GW: Maybe if you tell us, we can try and confirm your whereabouts, and this will all blow over.

D: This is almost a year ago; I don't remember.

GW: That strikes me as odd because that day was not just any day. It was the day Donna went missing.

D: I would like to stop this interview and wait for my lawyer.

GW: Okay, absolutely.

Caleb Bodkin
Mar 30

The more I think about what happened the other day, the more I see it as a cleanup act, which means we must have missed something. It's driving me crazy thinking about the possibilities.

"Did the voice sound familiar?" Glenn asked, as he took my statement that day.

"No. All he said was, 'Hello,'" I said.

Or at least that's what I thought I heard. In all honesty, it was muffled. My memory is hazy. All I can say is that it was a guy. He didn't sound aggressive; his tone sounded casual. But, of course, I don't say that to Glenn because I don't wanna lose my credibility.

Luckily, Brett was walking around the area that day. He told the police that he saw a gray Toyota Sedan that he'd never seen before parked nearby. He also saw a guy in the woods around eight fifteen or eight twenty a.m. as he was out.

Yesterday, when I arrived home for the weekend, the air was charged with negativity as my parents were in the middle of a heated argument. Mom was reciting her rant about my dad acting irresponsibly all his life, up to the point when he rebuilt the garage and encouraged this dangerous behavior.

Dad yelled back an assortment of his favorite profanities and left; I was expected to deal with the aftermath of my mom crying and shutting herself in her room. They have been sleeping in separate rooms for weeks now. Things are getting worse day by day.

I wake up at five thirty this morning. I check in on Mom; she's sleeping.

Dad hasn't come home yet.

I decide to take Fenrir for a walk. However, the minute I step outside, I regret my decision. The freezing temperatures of an early March morning in Red Hills are way too much for me. So we go for a quick stroll instead.

At six fifteen, I'm in the kitchen making coffee. I try to focus my thoughts on something so dull to escape the events of last night, like watching the little drops of the rich dark brew fill up the pot, inhaling the caramelized nutty aroma of this fresh holiday blend filling the air, or choosing from the selection of mugs in the cabinet. I'm trying to block the negative thoughts surrounding every aspect of my life.

Fenrir is having his breakfast next to me on the kitchen floor. I pour the hot, steaming coffee into my mug, feeling the warmth radiate through my hands. I take a sip, savoring the rich, earthy flavor, and felt a sense of contentment and relaxation wash over me. I stand next to the window, looking outside onto the front yard, expecting nothing.

Halfway through my first cup of coffee, my dad arrives. As he parks his car, I see someone sitting in the passenger seat. When they get out, I realize that my dad's new drinking buddy is none other than Brett Howe. They talk for a minute as I stare at them in disbelief.

Brett catches my eye and waves at me, then heads to his house, and my dad comes in, bringing a wind of freezing air with him.

As he takes off his muddy shoes by the main door and hangs his coat and scarf, I stare at him open mouthed, hoping he'll tell me what he was up to with our next-door neighbor.

He manages a "Hey" before filling his cup with coffee and sitting across from me at the kitchen table.

"Is she up?" he asks.

"No. are you gonna tell me what is going on?" I ask him.

He simply shakes his head, and we drink our coffees in silence for a few minutes.

"I went for a drink," he says.

I stare at him expectantly, brows furrowed, lips pursed, I cant hide the shock and confusion and I don't try to.

"All right." He lets go of the coffee cup and leans back on his chair with his arms on either side as if giving up on being sneaky. "I ran into Brett there. At the tavern, I mean. He was drinking his sorrows away. We grabbed a beer or maybe five."

"O'Donnell's?" I try to soften my tone.

"The River Tavern, near that coffee place we went to that Christmas when we ran out of ground beans for the whole party." He takes a sip.

"Right. The coffee was delicious," I say, as my mind taking me back to that beautiful Christmas morning two years ago, one of the very few pleasant memories that do not include Jake.

"Meh … I dunno … I went there this morning. It's not as good as I remember it," Dad says.

"Maybe we liked it so much because it was the only place open on Christmas Day."

He gives me a side nod.

"Dad, I just don't understand. You ran into Brett and spent the entire night drinking and smoking? What on earth were you discussing—work and the weather??" I realize that I sound so frustrated and impatient.

He puts his index finger to his lips as if to shush me.

"Brett was telling me about the 'Organizational restructuring' at his previous company." He puts the last two words in air quotes and raises his eyebrows. "Which meant they had to let him go,"

"Wow."

"Yeah … You know? He seemed like a decent guy, very drunk but decent; the guy's been through a lot," he stares at me defiantly as he says this, "we of all people should understand, we share the same pain." He adds softening his tone "Anyway, I drove him back."

I don't say anything, not because I disagree but because I don't care about Brett and his feelings.

"He told me about the root cause of all his problems." He grimaces when he takes another sip.

"You don't like the coffee?" I ask him.

"Is it bad, or is it just me? I've never liked coffee after a night of drinking."

I clear my throat. "So what did he say the problem was?"

"He talked about how he lost his wife, Anastasia…"

"Oh…"

"Yeah. He said Donna blamed her mother at first. It seemed like she was angry with her. They had only one car between them; they couldn't afford another after his car had burnt in an accident a few years before. Every promotion had been put on hold for many reasons—mainly his poor communication skills as an introvert. The financial crisis played a major role in their economic setback as well. Anyway, he said their financial issues were a constant cause of problems between him and his wife, but it was nothing out of the ordinary."

"Uh-huh." I nod.

"Yeah, some people have it the hard way. Anyways, the worst part was that the day Anastasia died, she had come to pick him up from work with

Donna in the backseat. They were on the freeway, and they were arguing. He said the next thing he knew, he was at the hospital, wife dead, car completely lost, and daughter in a coma. Life was never the same after that."

"Oh my God!"

"You know what I think? I think it's not just mental or psychological, the thing that fucked her up after the accident." He put the mug on the table and got up. "I think when she was in the car that day, and she hit her head, her injuries did some damage, serious permanent damage, and they just never treated her."

"What are you saying?" I ask.

"I am saying that after the accident, her dad said she was in a coma for a week and had serious head injuries. Maybe that explains why she was crazy!" He starts to walk toward the guest room where he'd been sleeping lately. "I'm going to get some sleep. Don't tell your mom about all of this ... me going out with Brett and all. She hears his name, and something clicks. She goes wild."

He leaves me alone in the kitchen with my cold coffee and thoughts.

I can't believe it. I'm feeling bad for Donna. She had to witness her mother's death! At the age of what? Ten? Not only that, she suffered physically and mentally throughout her life because of one simple mistake by her mom, who was driving the car that day. She was lucky Brett made it out alive. Parents fight, not knowing the extent of the damage they could cause their own children. This sparks a terrifying thought: Is this what's happening to our family?

I decide that I have to talk to them. They've been going at each other for no reason, throwing hurtful accusations and making detrimental decisions at moments of weakness.

This can't happen to us.

I decide to learn more about Donna's history, so I look up the car accident that Brett was telling my dad about.

On September 15, 2015, Anastasia Howe was picking up her husband from work. Their GMC Envoy was traveling northbound on the road when it veered off to the right and left the road. The car rolled over until it stopped in the parking lot of a diner. Anastasia was dead at the scene. Brett was taken to the University Medical Center. His leg was broken and some ribs too. Donna suffered a head injury and was in critical condition. The news articles don't say much beyond that. It was even hard to find this much information. Besides an obituary and a few records from her university days, I can't find anything online about Anastasia.

Accidents happen to anyone. Brett wasn't even behind the wheel. Her mother was driving! How could Donna blame him? Dad said she did blame her mother in the early days after the accident. My thoughts and research were interrupted by my phone buzzing. It's Glenn.

"Still waiting for lab results."

"What did Jessica say?"

"About?" Glenn asks.

"About the incident. Who was with her that day? Did you check?"

"She didn't mention anything about someone being there with her."

I feel bad for snitching, but I can't risk it; what if this mysterious guy had something to do with it? What if Jessica was in on it? After all, she was the one who found Jake's body. I don't say this out loud to Glenn, but I press on the matter.

"I heard someone in there with her that day," I tell him instead.

"Did you recognize the voice?"

"No, he called out her name, and I heard a sneeze and a door shutting. She was also awkward, did not invite me in, and immediately closed the door behind her; we talked while standing on the porch, and she asked to be alone as she was busy. Oh, wait! I remember now, she said something about her electrician helping her with the fridge..."

"I'm gonna look into that," Glenn says. "Honestly, this is getting frustrating even for us, Caleb. This guy vanished without a trace. Like a ghost!"

And just like that, my mind recalls the last thing I saw before I drifted into sleep that day in my parent's garage, the stupid keychain in the shape of a ghost.

It's not there anymore

Trish_ona_mish
Apr 1

Quick update! My research turned up the following results:
Possible serial killers operating in the Northwest:
The Snohomish Killer, the Magnolia Park Killer, and the National Forest Ripper. I do think that the Magnolia Park Killer is an implausible candidate since they had only killed homeless guys and two sex workers. So our lovebirds don't fit the profile.
Other similar murders and attacks around Red Hills (I'm only including the killings with similar MO, trauma to the head or brutal attacks, stabbing, strangulation, excluding drug-related cases or shootings.)

- A 22-year-old male was found in a stolen car parked in the Lakewood neighborhood of South Seattle, MO: stabbing.

- A 911 caller reported discovering a white male deceased in an RV parked near South Forest Street and Occidental Avenue South. MO: trauma to the head

- A 20-something-year-old woman was found in Phinney Ridge earlier this month has been ruled a homicide. Police have identified the suspect as 41-year-old Curtis Wallace Jr. (5 feet 9 inches tall, African American, approximately 250 pounds). Detectives believe he may be living in Seattle or Portland, Oregon. (Strong contender)

- (Click here for the complete list of 12 cases)

For pictures from Jake and Donna's funerals, please click here.

Mishionaries!! We could be onto a major breakthrough here! This investigation could lead to more than just solving one murder or two! Seriously, you all rock! Your input is truly appreciated, and it's what makes our community so lit Keep doing your thing and making a difference. Let's keep slaying together!

#14 The Light

Last year, on Christmas Eve, I won nine hundred dollars, a nice chunk of cash. I headed to the mall on Boxing Day. I wanted to spend this money on random things, but I couldn't bring myself to do it. So I decided to spend all my cash satisfying this nasty urge.

Three months ago, I maxed out my card and even went into an unauthorized overdraft by several hundred bucks, which is not my first time.

I have sixty dollars to last me until the end of the month. The most dangerous thing is that I can increase my overdraft almost immediately, up to five thousand dollars. I have nothing left. Absolutely nothing. I mentally jot down a list of things under my name. A beat-up car, a drained bank account, random rags, and meaningless junk accumulated over the years—most of which carry painful memories that are better left alone.

The worst part of what I became is that I lost track of the money and the time I spent gambling.

Life had offered me things to hold on to and keep me away from this nasty habit, worthy causes to which I should have clung. They should have pulled me out of the mud.

But the more I found of these treasures, the deeper I sunk ... and the deeper I went in, the more helpless I felt. I guess I never really knew how to differentiate between means and goals. Because I've always thought of the goals in life as means to fulfill my addiction.

In a way, the reality of the financial losses I suffered over the years made me feel more like a human being who mattered. It's not the instant wins; it's also the losses and what's at stake the more dramatic my losses become. The losses made me feel like a real person.

My addiction was woven into every cell of my body. And before I knew it, I realized that I'd gambled away my happiness and lost everything. I was cheated out of my money and sense of reality.

But then I saw the light at the end of this tunnel. I recalled one tiny detail from the family's history. One forgotten property under my name in the middle of nowhere in Saskatchewan, Canada.

At that moment, I made up my mind to move there, farm the land, and live a peaceful life. It was a beautiful, quiet spot in one of the least populated areas in the country. My grandfather had that property, and we never made any use of it. It was also hard to sell.

So I think this is a sign. I plan to make the long drive to Forget, Saskatchewan, stopping along the route for gas and sleep only. It should take about five days.

One of the stops is going to be Larisa. With my upcoming move, I do not need to renew my car insurance policy. I plan to sell my car and buy a used truck, anyway. But I need to meet Larisa. I owe it to myself.

I've never been to that cabin. I'm sure it will need a lot of handy work before I can move in.

What the hell? I have nothing better to do. It's almost therapeutic to think about a secluded area with beautiful landscapes and my own space to fix my way—a paradise for rehabilitating ... even if I was never a fan of the wilderness.

All my life, I've been afraid of the woods. I've stayed in the cities and towns and avoided anything secluded. It is embarrassing, but it started with those creepy folktales that my grandma used to tell me. There was one particular scary tale about the Rusalka. It's a twisted take on The Little Mermaid where the nymph kills the men instead of the Disney version. What's the point of that story? Or what was the moral? I know that all those Disney movies came from creepy fairy tales, but even those had certain messages behind the protagonist's actions. This one has none! I hate it!

Almost all of these fairy tales involved the woods, a cabin, and a witch or some villain living in it. Over the years, I have grown to be that villain. And so that little shack in the woods seems to be a fitting destination. It's where I belong.

I understand the need for isolation because I can't face the reality of the situation by admitting to someone face-to-face that I am sick. I had done it once before, and it helped me for a while. I came clean and confounded in her. She came along as if to provide a living example of what I was dreaming about, and I jumped on the wagon and gave it my all. But the truth is that my problem is way deeper than this.

Caleb Bodkin
Apr 2

Serial killers? Really? I don't think so.

I mean, everyone is always complaining about the government and the tech giants watching our every move and knowing more about us than our own mothers, kinda like living in some Orwellian alternate reality. Meanwhile, Leatherface stands a chance to live in the shadows, roam the busy streets and neighborhoods of Seattle and kill people for fun under the radar?

Doesn't make sense. There's no place for serial killers in the digital age.

I know the internet wants a massive climax to this mystery/crime thriller, and they want some masked maniac to burst out of the shadows and start slashing around, but that is not happening.

This is not random. This is personal.

Tobey agreed with me. We talk about the investigation and the case every day over lunch. I try to keep it just between us. Also, I only mention public info or very minor details because I don't wanna risk the investigation in any way. I do trust Tobey, but one cannot be sure these days. I'm back in Seattle this week after taking almost one whole week of working remotely. Our company policy allows WFH for up to sixty hours per month. I've already used thirty-two this month because of what happened.

"And even if this is a serial killer, will they use the same profiling methods from thirty years ago? Even if they were to kill for fun and fame, they must be different now. They must attack soon or try to increase their status with social media," he says as he takes bites of his sandwich.

Tobey is a great guy, but man! Why does he have to talk between mouthfuls?

"Why would they stop at Jake?" he continues. I always struggle to listen and focus on keeping my gaze somewhere neutral, like my food or the people going in and out of the café, while he talks, because I want to avoid the repulsive sight.

Our discussion is interrupted when one of Tobey's colleagues comes to sit with us. I don't recall her name, and inconveniently, Tobey goes on without mentioning it. We have been introduced before. She obviously knows my name because I'm a celebrity here, but I'm too embarrassed that I've forgotten hers. So I decide to stay silent and pretended I have somewhere to go. She must think I'm a weirdo, but that's the least of my worries now.

I return to my desk, stare at the spreadsheet for fifteen minutes, thinking about the dream I had that morning.

I was sitting on the swing chair on my parents' porch and speaking to Jake. We both knew he was dead, but we were still talking as if death was just a trip to another continent. We were both smiling and for a second, I felt like I had time traveled.

"Do you know when I am going to die?" I asked Jake.

"What do you mean? You're already dead..." He didn't sound like himself.

Then, we both heard a sound, a rhythmic pounding on the floor. It came from inside the house and sounded like a stick hitting the tiles. I walked into the glass double door that leads to our family room where Fen usually hangs, but as I stepped inside, everything was wrong. I found myself standing before an endless bright hallway, without windows or doors. The rhythmic thudding I'd heard continued to echo through the floor, a persistent tapping that seemed to come from nowhere. The only thing visible was a single, distant door. Anticipation sent prickles racing down my spine.

A little girl walked in; she only looked about five years old and had piercing eyes and no mouth. She was using a cane as she walked toward me. I stared at her, dumbfounded, and as she approached me, I asked her name. She didn't answer, and I realized she had no ears. She continued to walk out of the house into the backyard, which was too dark now. Her eyes lingered a little too long on me, as if searching for something hidden within.

I looked for Jake. I walked to the end of the corridor while calling his name, and then I was in front of the door; it was locked. When I tried it again, I heard the sound of the cane again, except it was faster this time. I turned around and saw the same girl, but she looked a hundred years old, her face was all wrinkled, and her skin tone was gray. She lunged at me when the door opened. I went in and locked it behind me.

Donna was there. When she talked, she sounded like Jake.

"Watch out. He is awake!"

I asked her, "Who is awake?"

"He can hear you..."

She stared as if into me and finally said:

"I'm only here to watch."

Last night, Brett came over and stayed until midnight, talking and drinking with my dad. I felt a sting of pity for his endless losses. He was intrigued and asked so many questions about the incident … he sounded just as desperate as we are.

My mom calls me daily to complain about my dad, how he has changed, and that she needs to confront him about her recent doubts about their whole relationship. But most importantly, she cannot stand Brett.

"I tried very hard to raise you two to be responsible. You grew up in a healthy environment. But Jake was a baby, and she dragged him into the mud with her. So yes, I think she killed him in one way or another!" Mom says.

"He loved her, Mom. I think he truly did."

"Of course he did! Teen boys go with the flow and don't like someone or develop feelings gradually based on valid reasons. No, they just instantly fall in love. They're still developing physically and emotionally! Their emotions are NOT based on perspective and experience; they are just driven by instinct and self-exploration. Constantly on a quest to find the next adventure."

I don't know what to say to that. I know she's right to some extent, but she's getting agitated, and I have no energy for that, so I decide to change the subject.

"I keep forgetting to ask you about that promotion you were promised a couple of months ago, Whatever happened to that?"

"I've been thinking about my options lately," she says.

"What do you mean?"

"I was offered a position in San Francisco. It's a great jump in my career. I will be heading a team of engineers and technicians with a twenty percent increase in salary."

Great ... so, my parents are moving now? I transferred from CA to Seattle to be closer to them, and now they decide to move to CA!

Trish_ona_mish

Apr 5

The people have spoken! LIV changed Donna's account to the Phantom status!

You did it! We all did it! Thank you guyssssss

Well done!! Now that we succeeded with step #1 we should try and figure out the hashtags to use.

Let's play the guessing game!!

I have pinned a thread to the beginning of this page. I renamed it to "suggestion box." Feel free to add any # and REMEMBER: post the suggestions AND use them in LIV!

The police are still trying to figure out who the mysterious man is from the Bodkins' home invasion. No traces whatsoever. No fingerprints were found anywhere in the garage.

No one, besides Brett Howe, has seen the mysterious man. Or his car. According to an insider, the police are looking into the owners of similar vehicles; the number in the area is more than 3000, and it seems like it is leading nowhere. Guess we're lucky Brett was home that day!

This case has proven lucrative for many since the attention is worldwide now. A lot of people with insider info on the case are leaking the news for money and attention in some cases (i.e., Emily, who sold her pics and videos with Jake to local magazines—Not cool).

But that doesn't mean the tip didn't generate a list of suspects. For example, we heard that two African American men were thoroughly investigated by the police since their alibis were not accounted for the day Jake died, and I think they had attended the funeral.

We have to wait and see…

The public's attention to this case started to die down a bit since there was no real progress made in the investigation. And mainly because everyone is turning their heads toward the new stream of videos after the death of Big Ben (our favorite rapper in the last five years if not of all time!). Phans are drawn to the stories made by this young talent before he departed this world. Check out these cool remixes of his material released by his Phantom account. I was at a party two days ago, and they were playing his Phantom tracks on repeat (demos and side projects) more than the official tracks!

I mean, I was skeptical when I first heard of Epilogue, but now, I think I've switched teams. We can continue to live even after our bodies no longer function. After all, what are humans but a complex mix of reactions to the energies surrounding us, the tangible and intangible forces?

Since the dawn of time, we responded to the internal forces within our bodies and the external power imposed by our environments. We created solutions to the problems and became creative with these results. We formed strong relationships and identified love in the people around us, the land we live in, the pleasant weather, and the memories. We held on to this life, this comfort zone that we designed.

And like many other projects, innovation had started way before we even realized it. We started innovating before giving it a title. We created possibilities for growth that made us love this place even more, although it's not perfect, and it's full of misfortunes. We invested in medicine, transportation, and entertainment, making every possible effort to not only extend our temporary stay in this world but also make it as pleasant as possible.

Crowdsourcing has been part of human nature all these years; we've been doing it since the beginning of time. But we've been doing it across different time periods, logging events from the past and handing them over to the next generation to build on. We call this input "history," and we call the output "innovation." What reasons do historians have to keep those records other than laying the foundation for a better future?

And this bright future has always incorporated money and health. Because with these two, you can do whatever you want. We stay consistent with our targets to simplify the common goal, forgetting the details that change drastically over time.

We've only experienced life, and we simply don't know how to die. In the end, we are creating the afterlife, which we have always talked about, believed in, and even disagreed over.

I'm starting to see these Phantoms as an extension of the person's existence rather than a memory.

Ladies and gentlemen, this is an official announcement:

I have subscribed to the Phantom service!

I have signed up to live forever!

#15 The Grand Scheme

I started packing today. I took some clothes. No furniture, though. I also took some kitchen stuff like glasses, plates, and ashtrays. That particular ashtray was a souvenir from Russia. My grandma brought it as a gift to my dad when I was four or five.

Surprisingly, packing did not take that much time. Realizing how little I had left under my name after gambling snatched everything was depressing. This new isolation plan should help a lot with my financial difficulties. No rent to be paid, no loans to be repaid, just disappear and leave all my liabilities behind.

I am a coward. I know that damn well. I don't deserve this last ticket to paradise. But here it is for me to grab, and I will take it.

While packing, I stumbled upon an old fairy tale called Baba Yaga. And I started to read the story about the witch who lived in the cabin in the woods. She kidnapped a boy and locked him up in a cage. I knew it was stupid, but I could swear as I was reading it, I heard Nana's voice. It scared me, and I stopped. But I couldn't bring myself to throw it away, so I packed the book.

I felt much better after I was done. The sense of starting a new chapter certainly was refreshing. I sat on my couch, watching the game, knowing the White Sox were on the verge of something special—something no one had seen from them in a long time. Over the years, I mainly bet on sports and always enjoyed it. I'm not saying I am a good sports capper, but I remember making major hit streaks with big money at some point. I was pretty much unstoppable. When I got out of college, I graduated with a solid job and started making my own money. I could afford to gamble at that point because I had little to no responsibilities. I was single and only had my rent to pay. By that time, I had lost around 12-18k in my life. I lost paycheck after paycheck.

I now understand what made my mother kill herself... But even that, I am incapable of doing because I am a coward.

My phone rings.

"Are you coming or not this time?"

It's Larisa. The resemblance to my grandma's voice is uncanny.

"Yes, ma'am, I'll be there in three days." But, in all honesty, I don't know why I still deal with that company. They're so out of my way.

But I must meet Larisa. I have to say goodbye.

"Broken things can be fixed and healed. Nothing is too difficult or too dirty to clean," Larisa said.

I know I'd heard that line before. My grandma used to say it in Russian and I remember asking my mother what it meant. She translated it for me.

I try to ask Larisa where she had heard that, but she hung up. I start to doubt whether she had said it at all, or had I just imagined it?

It's all too bizarre.

THE SOUND OF TUNING OUT

Transcript of the Interview with Sarah Blackwell on 7/3

Aug 2

PROSECUTION EXHIBIT B, PART I
Whereupon the following proceedings were had in the Seattle Police Department, Seattle, Washington, on July 3, 2025, and were transcribed from the video on Aug 2, 2025.
APPEARANCES:
Detective Micheal Smith (MS)
Detective Glenn Weaver (GW)
Sergeant Eric Barnes (EB)
Detective Alfred Gibbons (AG)
Detective Aiden Lee (AL)
Sarah Balckwell (SB)
Proceedings

GW: You and Donna Howe were friends, right?
SB: Yes.
GW: When did you first meet?
SB: Spring of 2021. Donna worked at the grocery store where I had been working.
GW: How long did Donna work at the grocery store? What was it called again?
SB: The Hills Convenience Store. I'd say two months or so...

GW: And you've been working at the store since?

SB: Around five years now.

GW: How old are you?

SB: Twenty-two. My parents own the store; I'm just sticking around until I figure out what I wanna do.

GW: Okay. Can you tell us more about your friendship with Donna?

SB: At first, I thought Donna was a bitch. She had a very stern set of eyes, making her look like she was in a bad mood most of the time. Her reputation from her high school days didn't help either. I remember telling Mom once, "Goth Barbie is bad news." But then, one day, she overheard Mom going off on my little bro 'cause he was failing English, and Donna offered to help him out. After that, we got to know her a little better, and turns out homegirl was just hella shy.

GW: Did you hang out after working hours?

SB: Yes. Sometimes. She used to help my younger brother with his homework. He's three years younger than me, around her age.

GW: Was she friends with your brother? What's his name?

SB: Nate; no, not really; he didn't like people to know that we spoke to "Donna Darko."

GW: Why?

SB: Because people thought she was weird.

GW: And did you?

SB: No. I liked Donna. I thought she was smart and sweet. She only got hostile toward people who messed with her, like, duh!

GW: Did your friendship last after she quit her job at the store?

SB: No. She worked at the store for about two months and stopped coming.

GW: Do you know why?

SB: Damn, they said she relapsed or some shit. Next thing we know, she got sent to some rehab joint for a hot minute. We didn't talk after that 'til the day she went missing.

GW: Can you tell us what happened that day?

SB: She came in, grabbed a few things, and bounced.

GW: Did you speak?

SB: I asked her how she was doing, and she was all like, "Oh, I'm doing much better, thanks for asking!" And then we started talking 'bout meeting up and catching up sometime soon. She was looking so happy and like, super pumped! I've never seen Donna so hyped before.

GW: Earlier, you said something about people hurting Donna. When you two were somewhat close during her employment at the store, did she ever mention anything of that sort to you?

SB: Donna didn't say much 'bout her school probs. She said some dude named Jonah was making fun of her and stuff, and another jerk sprayed her in the eye with pepper spray one time. Like, what the heck?! That made her drop outta school and everything. Ugh, people can be so trashy sometimes.

(silence)

SB: But she was miserable at home, too.

GW: How so?

SB: Not gonna lie, she was working overtime and didn't even mind helping Nate with his damn homework, even though he acted like he was too good for her 'cause he didn't wanna be seen with a girl like her. But she didn't mind that, 'cause she wasn't tryna cross paths with her old man.

GW: Did she say why?

SB: Nope.

GW: Did she ever show any odd behavior?

SB: Once.

GW: Can you talk about it?

SB: On her last day at the store, Donna showed up late, looking like she just crawled outta bed and stumbled into the damn place. Her hair was a hot mess, and her T-shirt looked like it hadn't seen a washing machine in weeks. I had to help some customers with their crap, but when I came back, I saw Donna munching on some candy and sipping on juice like she owned the place without paying for it! And get this, and when customers tried talking to her, she just ignored 'em like they weren't even there. Then, half an hour later, I caught her snoring like a grizzly bear in the back. I tried waking her up, but she…

GW: What happened?

SB: She lunged at me! But I don't think she meant to attack me or nothing, 'cause she didn't seem like she was all there in the head.

GW: Did she physically harm you?

SB: She leaped forward and screamed, "Stay away!" She kept screaming, and we both stumbled over, and I ended up on my back with a few cereal boxes on top of me and some cans, which left some bruises on my shoulder and cheek. But I know Donna didn't mean to hurt me. It was an accident.

GW: What happened after that?

SB: After the incident, we sent her ass home, and the next day, her dad called, apologizing and saying that Donna was back on that stuff and he needed to take care of it. It was weird 'cause we didn't see no signs of her going off the deep end or using again before that. It all just came outta nowhere.

Caleb Bodkin

Apr 12

It's Friday night, and I'm driving to my parents' house. This has become my miserable weekly trip to the upside down version of my previous life. It's been a long week at work, and I can't wait to get to my bed.

    Winter is lingering in the Seattle area, and the weather is taking longer than usual to warm up. A couple of days ago, I heard on the news that this April is on track to be one of the coldest in Seattle over the last thirty years. Right now, it is almost nine p.m., the temperature on my dashboard reads thirty-eight degrees, and my muscles are beginning to hurt. I start to dwell on my mom's big revelation as they plan to move to San Francisco. Last year, my dad took a sabbatical for a year to cope with his loss. Luckily, his boss understands the pressures and the trauma our family is going through, especially with the media snooping around every little detail about Jake and Donna. The last thing they want is to fire the father of the victim. Unlike Brett, who was deemed a reputational hazard to his company. After all the stuff those online trolls said about him, he was painted as the villain in this scenario. People were not rooting for the Howes. Could he move cities again? I wonder what my father's plans are for San Fran. He must be somewhat excited to move back to California. I make a mental note to ask him about that when I get the chance.

Hail starts falling, and I think about how much my car value will drop after driving in this weather. Lately, I've been struggling with my sleep, so I feel drowsy, and I opt to listen to a podcast to help me stay awake. Trish has a new episode about Jake and Donna. Maybe I'll listen to that and see what she has to say.

I make it home at nine forty. The drive took longer than usual because of the bad weather. Trish's intense episode did the trick. I'm too wired right now to sleep. When I walk into the house, I see my dad sitting by himself at the dining table. He's more than halfway through the wine bottle. My heart breaks a little for him, and I decide to hang out for a while before I call it a night. Maybe we can grab breakfast tomorrow with my mom; try to have a somewhat normal Saturday morning.

I try to talk to my dad about the weather, my car, and what Trish was discussing on her latest episode, but he seems so distracted, like he's not even listening to me.

"We need to talk," Dad says after I'm done talking. His serious tone catches me by surprise.

"What about?" I say, looking confused. "Where's Mom?"

"Your mom left for San Fran two days ago. She couldn't stick around after she found out about my affair with Jessica Bartlett. I'm not going to sugarcoat the whole thing. I'd rather rip the Band-Aid as quickly as possible."

I stay silent. I don't think I quite understand what he is saying to me.

"Talk to me," he says.

"What do you want me to say? I knew things were bad, but I never thought them to be this bad! What on earth were you thinking? Like this family hasn't been through enough!" My voice is so loud I can hardly hear my thoughts racing in my own head. I take a split second to look into Dad's eyes and gauge his expression. He looks like I've slapped him across the face—so disappointed and maybe even scared, like he doesn't recognize this wild animal before him.

Maybe slapping him wouldn't be so bad right now!

"Caleb, your mom and I are adults; we have our own lives. We make our own choices just like you do, and we decided to end this marriage. Do you honestly think it has been working out fine between her and me?!" He tries to stay calm. I can see his rage bubbling under the surface, but he is trying so hard to control what he says and how he says it to me.

"Jessica fucking Bartlett! She is the most psychotic, annoying bitch I've ever met, and just when I thought I misjudged her all my life, she barges into my life and steals whatever is left of it!" I yell because I am so disappointed and disgusted. The anger building up for the last nine months is eager to come out of this prison. There's some satisfaction in unleashing all this negative energy that I've been bottling up for a while. Short-lived satisfaction, which I know I will regret later, but for now, it feels good, like scratching an itch.

"Caleb! Watch your tone! I am your father!"

"That was you, wasn't it? With that bitch the day the guy broke into the house? You lied! You said you were going outta town for business! You were just across the street with that bitch!"

"Stop right now!" Dad yells back. He has nothing to say. No defense at all.

"That's why Glenn has been weird lately! Mom said you guys don't talk like before! He fucking knew!"

"Who the hell do you think you are talking to me like this!"

I stare at him for seconds, not knowing what to say next. I clench my fists so hard to keep myself from hitting him, my nails dig into my palms, and it starts to hurt. And then I storm out of the room and run upstairs to my bed. I lock the door to my room and sit for I don't know how long, but now that I'm alone, I let my thoughts roam free, and I don't hold back on any hatred or resentment I feel toward every person who contributed to this tragedy that hit our family. I contemplate walking over to the Bartletts' house and having a word with that psycho whore!

But then I decide that I will NEVER speak to him again … Ever.

How did I go from being so privileged with a fantastic family to being completely alone in the course of months? Saying that I'm heartbroken is an understatement. It is almost unfair to choose simple words to describe my pain.

I calculate my next steps as I lie in bed, waiting for sleep to put me out of my misery, even for a short while. First things first, I'm staying in my apartment in Seattle. I don't wanna see or talk to anyone. I'm just gonna keep busy with work and stay alert for any assistance the police may need from me. I don't care what happens to anyone anymore.

We live amongst the most selfish creatures on this planet … and we are supposed to belong to this tribe and show loyalty to people around us who belong to this narcissistic breed. But if history repeats itself, then how can I show any remorse or loyalty to any other human being?

I want to know the details of what went down with Jake. I want justice.

As just as this world can be…

I will never forgive my father for shattering this family. For taking away everything I have in a second without giving it a thought.

He can fuck off for all I care.

Trish_ona_mish

Transcript of episode 522 – published on Apr 12

What's up, Mishionaries! It's Trish, and you're listening to another episode of Trish_ona_Mish. Today's show is gonna be lit because we're talking about The Jake-Donna Special! Shoutout to all my LIV, Insta, TikTok, and blog fam—thanks for tuning in. And to all the newbies, welcome! As you probably know, I've been covering the Jake Bodkin and Donna Howe murder case for the past nine months. Can you believe it's already been that long? Time really flies when you're on the grind! Some intense revelations kept popping up, and they dragged us all into a dark tunnel of surprises and details about the doomed love story between two teenagers in the suburbs of Seattle.

Just last week, we have managed to convince LIV to switch Donna's account into its Phantom status. Mishionaries went out on a limb and assumed that Donna, someone believed to have no digital activity at all, had actually subscribed to the new service by LIV we all know and are familiar with now: "Epilogue."

Turns out we were right! She does have a Phantom account, and it is active now.

We are playing the waiting game of finding out more about Donna. I've been hoping (like a lot of you) that her Phantom content is going to reveal more about her and the circumstances of her death.

What do we get instead? One story. A picture. It is unnerving, and that is me sugarcoating the whole thing. But, of course, you can find it all over the internet because the story is gone by now. Two nights ago, one of you played the right card in this game and triggered Phantom Donna to post a story. It was just a written note in white text on a black screen.

"I am here. I am here to watch. I will never leave you."

Which trigger did we accidentally use to make this story appear? I don't know! Who did she mean? What was that about? Did she expect her own death? Did she know her killer? Wait! Was she really murdered?

All these questions are baffling the whole community. I mean, honestly, I'm reading your comments, and my head hurts from all the possibilities.

The police are again going through the same process to get the material from LIV, but this time for Donna's account. After the ads, I'm going to read your questions and comments and try to think out loud with everyone here, try and make sense of it all, and maybe answer some of these questions.

And we are back! As promised, I went through many of your comments, and trust me, there are a lot! And I chose the ones with the most recurring topic, most interesting comments, or intriguing ideas. So here we go:

Question No. 1: from Flora_Yas she goes: I have confirmed news by credible sources that the police got Donna's material from LIV because

THE SOUND OF TUNING OUT

Donna's death is now ruled as a homicide. You can bet your money on this, Trish, because the police somehow confirmed that the death is a murder! Any thoughts on this? Love your podcast and your blog!

Thank you, Flora! I honestly have seen a couple of comments and messages saying the same thing, more or less, but so far, I have nothing to confirm this piece of info. And honestly, I think her material can be linked to Jake's case (she is a person of interest, after all), which is an ongoing murder investigation. It only makes sense to continue with an existing case rather than open a new one. Because Donna's death was never officially recognized as a murder investigation. But maybe you know something we don't. Or perhaps some new evidence has been uncovered? I doubt it, though. It would be very hard to hush up something this big.

Anyways, next question: this one is from Chris Garcia. He goes: without mentioning names, we need to talk about the racism that's been going on in the CrimeBC platform. As a minority myself, it's hard to read the comments section these days without getting offended or feeling like I have stepped into a toxic minefield without any warning. Honestly, Trish, maybe you can start your channel with a disclaimer alert: "warning, racism ahead!" I've seen your responses to some of these comments, but it is still very disturbing to experience such hatred in one of my favorite spaces online. Thanks for the great coverage, btw!

Chris, I am so sorry you have to go through this, especially while on my page. I can't tell you how much I've been careful with this case because there are a lot of sensitive topics we're talking about here, from mental health to women's rights, and finally, we have added race into the mix, and I swear if you follow me, you should know that I am half Irish (my middle name is Oona FGS!), half Black because you've seen me! And still I was being called out as racist for mentioning the African American suspect in the recent Bodkins home invasion! We try to remove the offensive comments and block the users who persistently attack others (because nobody talks to my Mishionaries this way!), but we can only do so much. We are all prey in this virtual jungle. And it makes me sick to my stomach reading some of these comments on my blog; seriously, people! Shoo!

I've got another one here from Tina_ops; she goes: this reeks of a big conspiracy: first, the police ignore Jake's case and treat it as an accident when clearly it's not! Then they continue to ignore the evidence and continue to ignore the media and the signs all over the internet, then LIV gives them the content created by Jake, and they keep a hush-hush on the whole thing, and finally, they find a mysterious Black man to blame it on! How convenient!

I mean, hey, it's easy to sit back and judge what someone should have done with no actual experience or understanding of the consequences. Jake's stunt was not the safest, and for the family, the police, and everyone to instantly assume that a horrible accident took place was not out of this world. We don't know what came out of the content from Jake's account yet! I'm using all my patience and waiting for the breakthrough (fingers crossed). We have to give them time, and even if there is some action to be taken, these procedures take time. It can be frustrating, but everything must run its course to be done the right way.

Let's talk about police work for a minute. You know, when it comes to their job, they're all about the facts, not opinions or theories—even if they seem totally believable. And just because something is popular or commonly believed, that doesn't make it true either. So let's all keep that in mind! Brett is a key witness, and he said he saw a Black man in the area on the day of the break-in. The police must do everything they can to get to the bottom of this.

Question number... I dunno I lost count! Damn! This question is from Boring Doe: (haha) I can't fathom why some of your followers are defending the father! I can't stand him; can you tell me if I'm being unfair? Love you and your podcast!

Love you too, Boring Dude, sorry Boring Doe! Listen, like I said, you're free to like or not like whoever you want, but I'd like to think of my followers as an open-minded, cool, awesome bunch who love everyone until proven hateable! So far yes! You're being unfair! People are bullying the guy, and we don't know much about him. The police confirmed his alibi! So what do we have against him, really ... Come on, people, give him a break! I am not defending him, but we have invaded his privacy and attacked him constantly, and guess what! He is mourning the loss of his one and only daughter without even a job to distract or support him. Honestly, if I were Brett, I'd want this to blow over ASAP!

Finally, let's end on a positive note; this last note comes from Talulah92. She says: Trish, we need to talk about Glenn Weaver, baby! He is HOTTT (she wrote it in all caps and ten Ts! Haha). Can you tell us more about him? The mystery is making him even sexier!

I hear you, sis! Glenn Weaver sits on the throne of guys and gals that rule my world! I mean, wow! Every time he gives an interview or a press conference, I watch it more than once, and not only for the new info, haha! That is one fine dude!

I don't wanna seem like a stalker, but in this case, I AM! Glenn Weaver is forty-nine years old (I know, he looks way younger!) and is single! WOOHOO! Together with his team, Weaver solved hundreds of homicide cases. It seems he is the type to focus on his career and has no time for romance ... or he is a total playboy! Not sure, but in either scenario, he is sexy AF! All I know is that I LOVE THE GUY, and WE can't get enough!

That's all for this episode. Stay tuned for the latest developments on this case and other cases and mysteries I'm covering.

Love yas!

#16 The Ghost

Off we go! Today, I started my road trip to Saskatchewan, Canada.

Google Maps says I need approximately thirty-five hours to reach a tiny town called Forget, assuming I don't make any stops. Which means it will take me about five days to get there. I plan to drive for seven to eight hours every day. The total distance is a little more than three thousand miles.

Hardley anyone knows about this town. It is pronounced For-jay, by the way. People make road trips around Canada. They mostly visit the West Coast for its stunning national parks; not many visit Saskatchewan, though. This is precisely what I need right now—complete isolation.

I've been tormented for far too long. This is my trip to redemption, and I need to make it as short as possible.

I left my house at six fifty a.m.; I had one suitcase, a carry-on, and a bag of snacks, which I got from the CVS around the corner last night. It's open 24/7. I couldn't get any sleep thinking about this journey, so I decided to make use of the wasted hours.

It's silly, but I felt so restless. I kept hearing noises. A door opening and shutting, a creak, water running, and footsteps. None of it was real; I was just caught somewhere between the real and the dream world and couldn't get any deep sleep because of my excitement. So I decided to save some time and get whatever I needed while I waited for the sun to rise. I even moved everything to my car and waited.

Finally, at six thirty a.m., I made my last cup of coffee in the kitchen and set off in my beat-up sedan.

I turned on the radio, did not like anything on. Somehow, every song that came on was associated with a sad or disturbing memory. It just tells you how fucked up my life has been so far. It ruined the mood, and I was not ready for that.

This is a good day. Good things are going to happen. My past must not follow, so I decide to turn off the radio.

I switch to a podcast called One Day at a Time. It seems fitting for the occasion, right? It makes me realize that I'm not alone, that the whole world suffers, and everyone is trying to get this fresh start. My mind drifts into a reverie of my paradise to come. I feel very lucky.

My new home is in a tiny town called Forget, where my great-grandfather migrated in the early 1900s. The population was last reported in 2016: fifty. It's just what I need. It will be easy to dodge people there—the perfect hideaway. Somewhere to disappear.

I looked up Saskatchewan before I left. It is surrounded by beautiful mountains, hills, and grasslands under an endless blue sky. I imagine my little cabin as enchanting as those small cottages in the fairy tales I used to read as a kid. I don't know whether I am going to love it or be terrified! Seriously though, it's almost too good to be true.

The guy from the podcast is talking about gambling in college. He had a side gig as a bartender at some place called the Lucky Cat (which sounds familiar, but then all gambling places try to add the word "Lucky" to their name), where he met a bookie and indeed decided to start throwing money on college basketball. I'm instantly hooked on his story because it sounds like a retelling of one of my personal experiences. "I'd estimate by the end of college I lost a total of 10k," the guy on my podcast app says. It gives me goosebumps as it sounds like an echo of something I once said. I have to stop the podcast halfway through to go to the diner and have my breakfast.

I'm sitting at the bar eating my eggs and sausages, minding my own business, but the lady at the bar won't leave me alone. She keeps asking whether I want to top up my coffee if I want any sugar, or extra napkins. To the last question, I say yes. She hands them to me, and I see the tattoo on her hand.

I freeze. A silly tattoo of a cartoon ghost. Just like the one she used to have. I remember the night she got it. We were in college, and in a moment of drunken weakness, I decided to read my mother's suicide note to her. I remember reading the line that my mother had written in her lousy English describing me as "a ghost in the background of her life." I guess she meant to say that she and my dad treated me like a ghost as if I never really was there.

After I was done reading the suicide note, she hugged me and cried. That's how she decided to get that silly ghost tattoo.

I look for the waitress, but she's already walked away and into the kitchen. I wait for her to come out, but she doesn't, and I have no time to waste, so I decide it's not worth it.

I know for sure it's not her.

She's long gone.

I need to get going to make it to my appointment with Larisa at nine thirty a.m.

I'm so nervous, and I know it's not only because I'm going to that spot where I almost lost everything. I also have that feeling of butterflies in my stomach when we meet someone we love after a very long time.

I've never been so sentimental because the world has never given me anything to be very sentimental about ... Except for Granny.

THE SOUND OF TUNING OUT

```
Transcript of the Interview with the
Defendant on 7/5
```

Jul 31

PROSECUTION EXHIBIT D PART II

Whereupon the following proceedings were had in the Seattle Police Department, Seattle, Washington, on July 5, 2025, and were transcribed from the video on July 31, 2025.

APPEARANCES:

Detective Micheal Smith (MS)

Detective Glenn Weaver (GW)

Sergeant Eric Barnes (EB)

Defendant (D)

Proceedings

GW: Why did you kill Jake? The reasons for killing Donna are obvious. But why Jake?

D: I don't know what you're talking about.

GW: He knew Donna was in danger then and maybe confronted you? Where is Donna's phone? If you cooperate, it will be a win-win situation, and everyone goes home happy.

D: If you know so much, why ask me all these questions? If you're so sure, then bring in the evidence.

GW: Where were you at 9:52 a.m. on July 11, 2024?

D: I don't remember.

GW: Does that time remind you of anything at all?

D: Not particularly, no.

GW: Because we believe this is the exact time Donna was killed.

D: How? What ... what ... What happened?

GW: Since you're not the killer, you'll be happy to know that new information has resurfaced, and we were able to confirm Donna's time of death.

D: How?

GW: If you answer my question first, I will answer yours.

D: I don't remember what I was doing at the specific time! Can you remember what you were doing last Monday at eight a.m.!

GW: I was in the shower, thinking about the time I was going to arrest you. You know what strikes me as odd? You're not my first criminal to interrogate, and they're usually caught by surprise at some point. They mess up some details and change their stories ... but you don't. You're consistent.

D: I've got nothing to hide.

GW: It's only a matter of time before we tie the loose ends together. It's in your best interest to cooperate.

D: I did not kill anyone.

GW: Maybe not on purpose. Maybe it was an accident? We can help you if you tell us the truth.

D: You've got the wrong guy.

Trish_ona_mish

Apr 22

Wow ... before you read any further, click here to watch Jake's latest story.

SPOILER ALERT! Donna makes a guest appearance!

WHAT IS GOING ON HERE?!

Because some of you are commenting that they can't view the story from their iPhones (you need to install the latest iOS update btw), here is the gist:

Jake and Donna are sitting somewhere outdoors, which looks a lot like the same woods where they found Donna's body (I'm betting it's the same favorite spot); anyways, Jake has his arm around Donna, and she puts her head on his shoulder. Jake looks at the camera and says, "So I'm dead. What do you want to tell my followers?" Donna pokes his side, and he jerks his body (so, Jake is ticklish). She takes the phone and speaks directly to the camera, "Thank you for supporting me and being there for me, although you don't really care for these videos, I know that."

In the background, Jake says, "No, I don't really."

Donna, "But you agreed to do this with me. You said this is my safe zone, a demo for the big revelation I am about to make once I die. I am grateful for meeting you because then I decided that my afterlife is going to be in Florida with you. Thanks for making these videos and making me a part of your life."

She gives the phone back to Jake. He talks to the camera, "I don't know what she's talking about, but I'm dead, so no one really cares, haha."

She nudges him, they both laugh, and the video ends.

All right, so here is my take:

1. OH MY GOD!!! THEY WERE SO CUTE TOGETHER!!

2. We know that Donna was the real reason Jake responded to the promotional email from LIV about Epilogue.

3. I don't see any hint of violence in Donna. Also, I don't know why she would kill Jake! They were planning on going to Florida.

4. I know I know what you're thinking! We all saw the CCTV footage from when she was working at the grocery store in her hometown when she attacked one of her colleagues. I've read all the comments. Yes, I agree Donna was not as stable as she looked in the videos.

CONCLUSION: I blame her father for not taking her mental health seriously! I mean, there's a chance here that she hurt herself and others!

I HEARD A RUMOUR, THOUGH! Unconfirmed but BIG!

If (and that's a ginormous IF) it is true, it could point toward a new lead:

Sources say that Apple is now involved in the investigation. Something about a new account. Is it the killer's account? I also heard unofficial news saying that the account belonged to Jake. Was our favorite rock star involved in something shady?

#17 The Ghost

I make it to the insurance company's office at eight forty-five a.m. It is a tiny old building, maybe smaller than my own house. I wonder how many clients they have and how easy it is to do marketing in the middle of nowhere.

I try the door, but it's locked. no one seems to be in yet. I go back to the parking lot, light up a cigarette, and wait in my car. A few minutes later, an old lady parks right next to me; she steps out of her car and waves me into the building.

Weird … how does she know who I was?

I follow her in.

I wait in the lobby alone. I hear the sound of the air conditioner rumbling in the background and what sounds like water boiling. Larisa walks in with two cups of tea. Regular black tea. She moves slowly in her floral cardigan and black pants. She is of a petite build with short, wavy white hair. She has her reading glasses hanging around her neck.

"There is nothing more refreshing than tea in the morning," she says.

"Thank you, but I don't want any. I've just had coffee," I say.

She ignores what I say, adds two cubes of sugar to my cup, stirs it, and smiles at me while handing it over.

I am not offended. Her disregard for my request seems more like a loving act of a grandma when she force-feeds her grandchildren something she cooked, or something she believes is good for them. For some reason, old people always assume you are too shy to ask for something to eat.

Then she moves to sit at her desk, carrying her cup. She lights up her screen, puts her purse on the desk, places one cube of sugar between her teeth, and sips it. My grandma used to do that. I smile to myself.

"Thank you for meeting with me today. You know, you remind me of my grandmother a lot; she used to do the same thing."

"What? Sell insurance policies?" she says while smiling and looking at the file in front of her.

"No." My smile widens, and a chuckle escapes through my words. "The way you drink your tea. Are you from Russia originally?"

"I am Russian. Never anything else."

We talk about my move and how I should cancel any ties or commitments in preparation for my departure. All the while, she's smiling and nodding. No objections, no trying to sell me more of their services, nothing like that. I tell her about my problems here (no details, of course), financial problems, family drama, a modified version of the truth. She listens, sympathizes, and supports my decision. "It sounds like this town is no good for you."

Larisa is my parting gift from New Jersey, where I had spent my miserable years. She is the sweetest person I have ever met, and I am grateful for her.

After what seems like fifteen minutes, I realize I've been talking to Larisa for over an hour. I can't believe it!

"Thank you so much for your time and help, Larisa. I have to get going to make my daily driving goal." And I suddenly realize that I might have revealed way too much in the process of being sentimental toward this total stranger—an unjustified sentiment.

But then, who's gonna ask Larisa about me?

THE SOUND OF TUNING OUT

I stand up and straighten my shirt, and before turning away, I smile and look up to shake her hand and say my final goodbye. But Larisa's face seems so grim all of a sudden. She looks so concerned and sad; her skin too heavy for her face, sagging so low, as if it is melting off her bones. She frowns and points to the window. Her frown creases the skin between her eyebrows, and it looks like those waves I used to make in the sand on the rare occasions when my mother took me to the beach. I follow the direction of her finger, and I see a bird sitting on the windowsill.

"Go," she says. "Chase it away. Now!"

"Excuse me?" I say with an obvious shock in my tone.

"Get that awful bird away from my window." I stay put, stunned. She walks closer to me. "Your nana did not tell you this is bad luck?" She yells, "Go! And take your bad luck with you!"

I don't say anything back. I simply walk away. When I get in my car, I see that the bird has flown away, and Larisa is staring right at me from the window. What a creep!

I drive away as fast as possible, trying not to think about those last minutes of our meeting. I remember Nana saying that a bird flying into a window is a bad omen.

When I think about it, even my nana was a bit creepy at times, which is why old fairy tales fascinate and scare me.

What just happened? It is ridiculous and ... a little funny.

When I get on the highway, I start laughing hysterically.

Text Exchange Between Jake and Donna

May 24, 00:53 a.m.

DH: Thank you for the gift. You don't know how much it means to me

JB: Happy 4 month anniversary

JB: I was afraid you might think I'm imposing on your life like that, but I want you to stay healthy and keep track of your sleep. Also, we can use it to create your big debut in the social media world

DH: You're not imposing. You're all I have

DH: Maybe I should fake my own death and get a new ID in Florida! Haha

JB: So dramatic as always

DH: :D

JB: Check these videos out and help me choose one to add to my Epilogue

DH: I like this one! It has way more depth to it

JB: ok

DH: You can keep the other one for my next entry. I'll allow it this time. It's not cheating. It's called being prepared

JB: oh, thanks, mighty you

Caleb Bodkin
Apr 27

The police are searching for something in the woods. I don't find this out from Dad, Glenn, or even my mom. This knowledge comes to me through Google Alerts.

Glenn won't tell me what is going on. I can't believe he's punishing me for what Dad did. Does he really think I support Dad's cheating on my mom with Jessica Bartlett?!

When I call him, he is very reticent and formal. He does offer me one piece of info, though, which makes me hold back all the insults I'm about to shower him with.

"Caleb, we are onto something big here. Please let us do our job for everyone's sake. For Jake's sake."

He doesn't tell me anything else.

What the hell is going on?

Trish_ona_mish

May 6

Somebody broke the code; the trigger for the increased activity on Donna's account is #myblueoblivion

Effing duh!!! It is the one line in Donna's LIV account bio!! How did I miss that!!!

It's also causing Jake's account to post more stories related to Donna and their relationship. This new story by Jake is seriously baffling. It's a piece that seems to belong to another puzzle. It makes me doubt everything! Have we all been looking at the picture upside down?

The story shows Donna standing in a wooded area, as we have seen in almost every story by Donna or involving her. She looks disheveled and sad. Not her cute, sweet usual self as we see her with Jake. She goes:

"If you're watching this, that means I'm dead; this is a confession about what happened almost ten years ago. I decided today to take matters into my own hands because he is coming for me. I saw the documents ... I—"

She stops and drops the phone, and now the frame shows the sky and the top of some trees, but we can still hear her talking to someone.

"What are you doing?" a male voice says to Donna. He sounds familiar.

"Nothing. What do you want?" she says.

"I want my phone," he says to her.

"How did you find me?"

"I tracked my own device, you idiot. What the hell is wrong with you? Haven't you used a phone before?" He sounds angryyyyy as hellll! There is no trace of teasing or friendliness in his tone. The guy is serious!

"I'm sorry. Here, take it."

She picks it up and gives it to the guy, and we hear a lot of shuffling around. It sounds like she's running away. The camera moves quickly, showing nothing but a series of shaky, blurry, disorienting footage.

"Wait," the guy says as the recording shows the blurred surroundings of the trees, the sky, and the ground. The guy checks his phone, and before he switches off the recording, we can see who he is.

It's Jake.

Seriously WTF!

Somebody explain this to me! Why is Donna's video on Jake's account? Why did she steal his phone? Was that a prank? Did she do this to piss him off? And wait! Just hold on a minute! What the hell happened ten years ago?!

My head is about to explode!

I'm getting a drink; I will read your comments and then go live on my LIV because I cannot type fast enough!

See yas later!

#18 The Ghost

After the shock and the laughter wore off from my meeting with Larisa, I go back to my podcast.

"I maxed out my credit card … I've always made sure I have enough money so that my family won't be suspicious … I had no cash … cutting people out of my life because I want to avoid confrontation, explanations, social obligations…"

Everything sounds so familiar. It's like listening to a soundtrack of my life.

"I must move on, and I must face my enemy," the guy says.

I decide to make a little detour and commit to the steps of my treatment all the way.

I wonder if it was even still there. For a moment, I think it must have gone out of business and closed down because I can't find it. But then I see a little red rooftop in the distance, and I'm freefalling into the arms of its gravitational pull.

The feeling of nostalgia is surreal. I stay in my car, taking in the moment. Mourning a life I lost and a series of dreams doomed from the beginning. And the credit goes to this sickness I had and to this place where I nurtured this habit.

Going in was a bad idea, but I did it anyway. I'm homesick.

THE SOUND OF TUNING OUT

Damn! I didn't know I was this sentimental! I have never been this emotional, not even about more important things.

I decide to check my spot.

How is it possible that everything still looks the same after all these years, down to the smell of beer, old wood, smoke, the humidity due to little ventilation, the music in the background, and the sound of the news on the small TV above the bar? The state of Chicago is celebrating its incredible triumph of winning the World Series. It's eleven in the morning, so only a couple of truck drivers are having their coffee at this early hour. One guy looks up from his phone when I enter the room and then goes right back to it as if I'm a fly or a ghost. The dullest-looking, uninteresting person that is me.

Good, I think to myself, the last thing you wanna be when you're on the run is memorable.

I can't wait to go to my seat. It feels like meeting your long lost love with whom you can't live for the rest of your life. A forbidden type of love. Before I start to make my way toward my guilty pleasure, I get interrupted.

"Can I help you?"

I turn around. It's just the waiter. An older guy, shabby looking, unshaven, he is wearing a hat.

"I was just checking to see the machine in the back."

"I'm sorry, you can't go there."

"Oh..."

"Why do you wanna go there anyways?" He is silent for a second, then he continues, "Bad day, huh?"

And then I see it. I can't believe I hadn't seen it before the second I laid my eyes on him. This is him! The one and only Mr. Smith! Of course, he doesn't recognize me. And the realization hits me. That's why I've seen him every day. He works here, maybe even owns this place. I don't think that he's a gambler. The more I think about it, the more it seems like he was genuinely concerned about my future. Maybe he has a child my age ... I am disgusted with myself. I hit a guy old enough to be my father and probably tried to play the role better than my own. This is the way I repaid him. I am so ashamed of myself.

Mr. Smith is looking at me quizzically. Does he recognize me? I have changed quite a lot, haven't I?

His gaze burns a hole through my head, and I have a headache.

"Can I get a cup of coffee?"

Without saying a word, he goes to the back to get it.

I sit down on the first chair I see, which happens to have a view of the corridor leading up to the toilets in the back. Only one door, unisex. I put my head in my hands, trying to massage the pain away.

When I look up, I see a woman staring at me. Her hair is dripping wet, as if she has just stepped out of the shower. While she stands there staring at me, sizing me up, I tear my gaze away from her, wondering where my coffee is. I decide that I have already wasted enough time and that the coffee is not worth the wait. I'll make another pit stop where I can also buy some cigarettes. I head out. I unlock my car and am about to enter when I see the woman opening the door and following me. She is all laughs, and I can't decide if she looks hot or disturbing.

Hot, I decide.

"What an awful guy!" she tells me, with a smile.

"Pardon me?"

"The guy who owns this joint," she says, almost yelling as she walks closer.

"You know him?" I ask her.

"Nahhh, but I know his kind." She giggles. "I practically showered in his filthy bathroom. I've been on the road for a long while."

"Where are you headed?" I ask her.

"North, you?"
"Same direction "
"Can I come with?"
"I don't know ... I am in a rush."

She looks familiar. I don't know where I've seen her before, maybe here? Was she a regular?

Mr. Smith bursts out, running toward us. We both get into the car like two teenagers in trouble. All the while, the woman is laughing. I start the car and rev out of sight and out of his way.

"What was that all about?" I ask her as I look in my rearview mirror.

She is still smiling. I think I can do worse ... she seems like a fun-loving travel companion, and I can do without listening to bad music or gambling podcasts.

"Let's just say that he's gonna be thankful for the location of his shabby place next time he needs to use the toilet."

"Why though?" I say.

"He's in the middle of nowhere. He can go behind any tree," she says impatiently as if to explain her joke to a three-year-old child.

"I mean, why break his toilet?"

She doesn't say anything for a while.

"He reminds me of my father," she says finally.

And just like that, I am on her side.

I understand.

Caleb Bodkin
May 20

A part of me is satisfied because, as it turns out, my brother was the same bubbly, caring, cool guy I've always loved and trusted. He never strayed away from the path to his dreams. He was planning on pursuing a career in the area where he excelled all his young life. If anything, I'm impressed by the level of maturity he showed in avoiding a life of fame and spotlight. It's a shame I can't tell him how proud I am of him because he chose to help someone as he pursued his goals. And then he fell in love with her because also, as it turns out, she was beautiful and talented. The series of unfortunate events that defined her childhood and teen years, while overwhelmingly sad, did help shape her mature personality and sculpt a muse to inspire her writing.

And I was right. The idea of Epilogue was not attractive to Jake. He must have ignored the promo email in his inbox. But Donna was the reason he created these videos. They made videos together, and she chose the ones that went into his account. It was their little secret; no wonder Donna wanted to keep her thoughts and fears hidden, now that we know what she was talking about in the video. Glenn told us that most of Jake's videos weren't even originally recorded for Epilogue or his Phantom account; they were just memories of covers, special moments, etc. The new content was mostly about Donna. I now realize how my brother got into this whole afterlife posts thing. It was fun to do with someone he loved, and although he wasn't serious about it, he wanted to enjoy the moment with her, like when we used to play GTA or COD. Jake was never really obsessed with video games like I was. He just wanted to hang out with me. Jake and I spent a lot of time customizing characters, building cities, looking for cheat codes, and looking up walkthroughs. I believe our little research projects every time we couldn't solve a puzzle or finish off a boss influenced his choice of having his own YouTube channel as he got older. Jake enjoyed watching me play and loved the backstories of these games. He wouldn't even fight me over the controllers.

It will be very hard to abandon my past because it's packed with beautiful memories of us, the whole family. I can't go back to that street. It's tainted with shattering heartbreaks one after the other. All three houses on our cul-de-sac are abandoned now, with a "For Sale" board planted on the front lawn.

The last time I was at our house, as I was packing the last of my memories and things I cared about into one suitcase, I couldn't wait to leave the house. I was sad and scared. An overwhelming feeling of loneliness roamed the whole house like a ghost shadowing my every move. On my way out of Red Hills, I parked my car and went into the woods for a quick walk, and I regret it now because ever since that day, I've been having recurring nightmares.

I'm waiting for the next steps as we all watch the bad guy go down. It's not as satisfying as I thought it would be. I don't feel any better about the loss of my brother.

He's gone.

I do feel vindicated, but I must start a new chapter and a new life.

I'm not excited. It's gonna be exhausting.

#19 The Ghost

My new travel partner and I decide to part ways right before the border. I don't tell her where I'm going, and although she tries to find out, I manage to dodge every question about my destination or full plan. She refuses to share her name, and I do the same.

For the first two hours, we drive in silence. Everything is a joke to her. I'm pretty sure she's high on something. So after we drive away from crazy Mr. Smith, I stop at the first rest area and ask to check her pockets to make sure she has nothing illegal on her. I can do with some fun along the ride, but I don't need any more trouble with the law.

Surprisingly, she agrees to my search. She must be so desperate, and I get this panicky feeling that she must be in some deep shit.

I shrug it off, and we continue. I don't ask about her past because I don't want her to return the favor.

She tells me about a hiking trail somewhere around here that leads to a waterfall where she loves to go swimming. Then she plays some music. It's not my favorite; it's too heavy. A tormented girl, too sad at times, too weird at others. She is singing about someone stealing her pearl and leaving her an empty shell, traveling in the tranquil blue seas and whatnot. I think I've heard it before; someone used to play it a lot. Was it a roommate? An ex-girlfriend? I'm not sure.

We stop to refuel; she offers to pay, and I take it.

THE SOUND OF TUNING OUT

I get a few snacks and some iced tea for the road.

"Have we met before?" I ask her.

She breaks into laughter and heads to the toilets without even answering me. I don't know what to make of that.

We drive and drive until I can't go anymore.

It's nighttime. And I am tired and bored of the roads. So we stop at a motel for the night. It's not a well-known chain. But it'll do. I just wanna rest for a few hours.

I'm happy with my progress. I've driven for hours today.

We book one room. Luckily, it has two beds. I'm not planning on complicating this arrangement even more. As I lie awake thinking about my plan and my day, I realize that dragging her with me was a big mistake, and I decide to leave without her in the morning.

I toss and turn, trying to get some sleep. The darkness of the night casts a chilling gloom over everything. She sure is odd. The smile on her face grows irritating rather than refreshing. I don't know why; I can't explain it.

Also, she snores ... very loudly ... how unattractive. It's probably because she's been high all day.

I replay my day in my head, and her glassy gaze keeps popping into my memories. I can only characterize it as emptiness.

Is that pain I see, or is she just blank?

Also, the way she walks, like she is about to stumble over, which she did a few times today and then started laughing hysterically. I can't travel with someone like her; she is a liability! What was I thinking? She might steal something, get into a fight, or worse, use drugs. On another note, the green highlights in her hair are very distinctive. I don't want anything to grab people's attention.

This is not good. I need to sleep. I plan on driving all day tomorrow. I don't wanna fall asleep behind the wheel.

She is snorting now like a pig, breathing heavily steadily and exhaling snorts in between. I turn to face her bed to see if she is okay.

When I turn, I see her stretched on the floor between the two beds like a starfish. She is staring at the ceiling, laughing and laughing. She can hardly breathe.

"What the...? Are you okay?"

"Oh, yes..." she manages to say between her uncontrollable jolts of laughter.

At first, it doesn't seem like she can hear me. She curves her body, clutching her stomach like she's in pain. But then I realized that she was using that move to gain momentum and stand on her feet in one swift motion. She then turns to face me and laughs even harder.

Her skin is too pale. Her hair is too dark, with occasional flashes of green reflected by random lights from the street and surfaces in the room. Her eyes shine in the dark like a big predatory cat. She is too skinny ... if she stayed still, she could easily pass for a mannequin. The glimmer in her eyes does not hide the emptiness, but rather exaggerates it.

"What's up with you? What are you on?" I say.

She lunges at me and starts tickling me.

"Knock it off!" I wrestle her away, which surprisingly takes some effort, maybe because I'm exhausted, but she's showing real resistance. She is stronger than she looks.

I push her violently, harder than I intended. She drops to the floor, still laughing, and leans on the night table to gain balance. Her long, dark, greenish hair covers her face, and it is almost a relief that I can't see her grin anymore. She comes at me again.

"I am warning you. If you don't stop, I will throw you out of the room," I yell.

She stops, changes direction, goes into the bathroom, and turns on the water faucet. I'm not even curious about her intentions. I grab my bag and run to my car in my boxers and tee.

And I drive away.

No more weird shit.

Just drive.

Trish_ona_mish

May 20

I have three tattoos, each symbolizing one case that has impacted my life choices so far. I have previously shared with my Mishionaries pictures of two of them. One tattoo is of a half-opened copy of The Odyssey, because that specific book was the main reason I checked the stills of the security cam and helped lead the police to the killer in the Silverstone murder investigation. It was the only indicative that showed the inconsistency in the video. In the middle of all the usual clutter in the frame, a book stood out. At first, I didn't notice the inconsistency, but then I realized its position had been subtly shifted between different timestamps, a minor detail that should've been impossible unless someone had tampered with the scene. That small inconsistency was the clue we needed. It didn't just place the killer at the crime scene—it proved they had manipulated the video to cover their tracks. Of course, the stills did not reveal which book was opened and abruptly shut, but I made a point later to go to the library and check the exact same title. I know it's the same as the one in the footage because the librarian confirmed to me that they never change the spots for the classics. Also, I used the images to match the color, the dimensions, and all the details.

The second tattoo says "OLD NAVY." Yes, as in the store, with the same font and everything. It is hidden under my left breast. Close to my heart. It relates to the very first case that influenced my curiosity and led me through this path down the rabbit hole of the criminal investigation world. While not nearly as famous as the other two cases, the unsolved case of Clara Cantave's disappearance rocked the community where she lived with her single mother. She disappeared on July 18, 2013. She was only eleven. When I look at pictures of her, I travel back in time to our playdates and silly games in my room. She was last seen wearing a yellow T-shirt with the words "OLD NAVY" written across it. We bought that shirt together at the mall after my mom took us for ice cream, and Clara made a huge mess. That was only a few days before she went missing. The case remains unsolved.

My new tattoo is of a crashing wave. I asked for it to be on the left side of my ribcage. It's been a while since I've been touched by a case like this one. We have all seen Donna's last story, where she revealed who the real killer is. The police finally made an arrest. And I never thought I would say this, but it's devastating.

#20 The Ghost

I loved her ... no matter what the results may indicate, I know I loved her...

But what can I say? My sickness got the best of me.

When I lost her, I eventually lost that safety net, and I went right back to square one.

THE SOUND OF TUNING OUT

PART SEVEN

Excerpts from The Bitch in the Room: The Power of Authenticity in a Conformist World

By

Molly Martinez

Prologue

Nov 6

I've never been a fan of cold weather, nor am I an early bird. I like my beauty sleep way too much. It was exceptionally hard for me to get up early, be ready, and leave by seven thirty a.m. So you can imagine how horrible my mood was on the morning of November 6, 2025.

I sat in the jury assembly room with one hundred and fifty or so others. Nothing happened for quite a while. My mind drifted, and I started to think about the rest of my week. For the next forty minutes (in my head), I confronted Kyle about his evasive demeanor when I mentioned spending Christmas with my sister and her husband. I overdramatize the situation since it is all happening in my head, which has been hurting me all morning. I also talked to him about taking two days off after the Christmas holidays to make it worth our while to travel all the way to New York City.

While waiting, I started thinking of the exaggerated excuses I would present to the judge to request a waiver.

"Don't be that person who talks up a project deadline that will be missed without them or how many important clients rely on their presence every day. That gets zero fucks given," my friend told me the night before over the phone when I asked his opinion on the best techniques to use to be excused. He's been called for a civil trial before. Something minor; I don't even remember what it was.

People have this misconception about running your own business, which is that you choose when to work and how much to do. False! There is flexibility since you don't have to show up at the office and impress your boss, but that also means that your work spills over the twenty-four hours of the day, leaving you with no personal time at all. So that's why I wanted to get out of this commitment. I have too much at stake.

Also, I don't like to have this much control over someone's life and future.

After listening to the speech by a superior court judge, I sat back and started reading my book, which was a present from Kyle last Thanksgiving. It was a cozy mystery. It was so good that I felt it was such a waste to read it in this ugly room. I should have been in my favorite chair with the fluffy pillows and a cup of ginger lemon green tea in my hand.

They started by calling out number fifty. My number was 2089. It was going to be a long day! Next, I filled out a long personal questionnaire about my criminal history, whether I knew anyone in law enforcement or lawyers, and my views on guns, gangs, etc.

The judge began giving instructions. The entire room shifted and exchanged looks and murmurs once we found out which case we had been called into.

The Jake/Donna Case was one of the most talked about topics in the last year or so. Not just in the US but all over the world! I swore I'd seen teenagers in India doing the "Dean Challenge" on TikTok, replicating Jake's death scene while playing the same song, or sometimes, different songs; I even saw one version involving a dog and a skateboard!

The judge listed out the details of the charges and allowed the defendant to give the pleas by charge. In this case, there were multiple charges brought against him—first-degree murder, second-degree murder, obstruction of justice, manipulating evidence, breaking and entering, and more. The net result was he pleaded not guilty to all the charges; therefore, we were heading to a trial. Then, the names of the victim(s) and witnesses from both sides were read out loud so that anyone with personal knowledge of individuals on that list or the accused could bring it up to the judge when they were called in. The witness list was eight cops and nineteen civilians, including the accused.

I went into this meeting thinking of ways to abandon this case at once. But when I found out that the case I was going to be reviewing was one of the highest profile cases in the nation for a long time, I couldn't lie, I almost immediately changed my mind.

I remembered speaking to Kyle about this the night before. I specifically told him that I had no intention of going through with this jury duty, and he went something like, "What if it was Courtney and Kurt?" We both laughed at the ridiculous idea, and I said, "Well ... I can't say no to fame, fortune, and a potential book deal."

It was real then ... this was the biggest case of the decade. It was not only the mysterious circumstances, the plot twists, and the continuous feed from the Ghost LIV account or Phantom, whatever they call it; it was also the involvement of the Silicon Valley companies in the matter that brought people from all walks of life to the same circle to discuss the same topic from different angles.

I paid closer attention because my involvement was no longer a burden I wanted to get rid of. They called us in groups of twenty for a jury of twelve plus four alternates. This trial was expected to last between two to four weeks. Some looks of pain and objection were exchanged amongst those in attendance.

Holy shit! Four weeks! That was a lot of time to be away from work! Could I still pull it off?

THE SOUND OF TUNING OUT

After almost two and a half hours, they picked the next wave of potential jurors, and this time, I was selected. Then, they took us to the courtroom.

One court officer led us to the courtroom down the hall. Once we were all filed in, two rows of ten, I looked around the room. The ten jurors already selected were sitting in the jury box. The suspect was sitting nearest to us.

I'd seen him many times on the news, mostly in pictures. It would be very easy to overlook him in any setting. His bland looks made him almost invisible in any room. But you couldn't blame me for staring; It was like watching a lion behind bars at a zoo, from the safety of your seat, where you wouldn't mind a commotion or something exciting happening for the added thrill.

But he was sitting in his chair, quiet, occasionally looking around; he was obviously avoiding eye contact with anyone but his attorney.

The questioning of potential jurors by both the prosecution and the defense is called Voir Dire, which translates to "speak the truth." It definitely took longer than it should have, as people took the chance to talk over their outlooks on the law and their experiences. I hate it when people do that. I mean, honestly, I don't care.

When they got to me, they asked if I had any experience with mental health issues—no; if I had any stocks in LIV Inc.—no; if I followed Jake's channel—again, no; how many times I watched his material—occasionally when someone sent it my way, about three times in total; if I was a fan of metal music—God no!; and if I could be impartial—yes.

I was picked.

I repeated the oath after the court clerk.

I had to consider the issues faithfully, according to the evidence.

There was no room for prejudice or random opinions.

This was not social media. This was reality. The change was too drastic. I felt so overwhelmed. There was no repeating, skipping, or playing at double speed, no zooming in or out, and no instant mark to leave to indicate your approval or lack of it.

Everything was happening in real-time, and everything counted.

One

For as long as I can remember, I've been interested in true crime media, documentaries, TV shows, podcasts, etc.

That said, I never wanted to experience this process for myself. I enjoyed watching it on my TV and was content with that. In general, I am a very serious person. I do not take any task lightly. That's why I didn't want to be a part of this jury. But once I knew it was the most famous case in America, I was happy I got selected. I couldn't resist.

"You know you can't have prior opinions before accepting this duty. Meaning you need to forget all of these theories you were having before seeing the evidence for yourself," Kyle said to me when we were having dinner that night in his apartment with his roommate Joe and his girlfriend, Tania, who couldn't stop freaking out about the whole situation and made it seem like we were two teens excited to go to a boy-band.

"Here is the catch, though ... we are going to get sequestered," I told Kyle.

"For how long?" Tania asked.

"What is that?" Joe asked.

"When the jury gets isolated, so their judgment won't be tampered with or biased because of the media coverage. They usually do it for high-profile cases like this one," Tania said.

"Well, I'm gonna be sequestered for two weeks at least."

"Sequestered where?" Joe asked.

"A hotel in Seattle," I answered.

"But what about work?" Kyle said.

"I'm taking time off. I'm going to leave Samantha in charge while I'm gone. That will cost me extra pay to compensate for her extra hours."

Samantha is my second-in-command and web developer. I don't know what I would do without her. She's only twenty-six, but sometimes I feel like she is more responsible than I am.

"When do you go?" Kyle asked.

"The judge gave us two days," I said.

My friends and family managed to put together a quick going away party for me. I was about to go away for at least two weeks. Locked up at some hotel with eleven strangers and police enforcement. I was going to have limited and monitored communication with the outside world, including family.

Jury members were not allowed to talk about the case with anyone, but what if your case was the Jake and Donna murder trial, the one everyone in the country was talking about? The name of the hotel where we were staying was supposed to be confidential, but our accommodation was pretty much an open secret since day one.

We stayed at a luxury hotel in Downtown Seattle with a fitness center, spa, and lap pool. It was elegant, relatively new, and close to the courthouse. We stayed in standard rooms on the sixth floor. The rooms had TVs and phones, but we weren't allowed to use them—ever. The elevator never stopped on our floor. If any jurors wanted to leave the hotel, we had to take the service elevator with a guard.

"This won't be a walk in the park," the judge told us. "We will all do our best to make this as acceptable and as comfortable as possible."

THE SOUND OF TUNING OUT

The media extravaganza surrounding the trial had gotten out of control, especially with the influence of online communities; this can be said about many things around us these days and is not typically a testament to the importance of the topic to the average person's life. Rather, it is a valid example of herd behavior prompted by social media. It felt like the whole world depended on us to make this decision.

High-profile cases had the juries sequestered decades ago when media consisted of only newspapers, TV, and magazines. Back then, the news of major events took time to travel across the country, and some news in the East never made it to the West, let alone the rest of the world. Today, the entire world knows who Jake is! He's more famous than his idols. Everyone is on LIV, and everyone wants a real thriller to follow. People are not satisfied with fiction anymore. They want real drama. Followers and even casual social media users have opinions on all matters involving this case, let alone the traditional media sources and TV channels.

We were told that we were permitted to receive our phones once per day to check voicemails and make calls in the presence of a deputy.

Deputies were required to screen, monitor, and log all television, internet use, reading materials, mail, and phone calls to ensure we were not exposed to any opinions, information, or news about the trial or the criminal justice system.

So, on January 4, I walked into the hotel room with nothing but my books, my diary, and my thoughts.

I watched a pre-approved comedy from the early 2000s but fell asleep halfway through.

Two

Once sworn onto a jury, you have to always sit in the same place in the jury box.

When we first arrived at the courthouse, we were led to the room by a police officer. I walked into the room, went to my spot, and kept repeating, Keep an open mind.

I am a very opinionated person, but I have to admit that growing up with my stepmother helped me over the years to become more flexible and accepting of differences.

Rosa is more like a sister than a mother. She has always maintained her young spirit. Also, Rosa is only fifteen years older than me. So many people questioned her judgment when she decided to marry a guy who was almost twenty years her senior. Everyone judged her for marrying a somewhat wealthy older guy, including her own family. Only my father and I knew her true intentions and how good she was to us. I am so grateful for her.

I imagined Rosa sitting next to me, and I tried to replicate her reactions to what was happening around me. I often do that at work in particular situations when I know that staying positive and neutral seems to be a challenge.

THE SOUND OF TUNING OUT

Laura Beeson was the leading prosecution lawyer. She started her statement by explaining her responsibility and accountability to the public. She then went on about the procedural steps and what she planned to achieve and prove to us, the jurors.

Laura was very confident, eloquent, and stern. I felt overwhelmed and a little intimidated.

I reached for my phone to look her up on LinkedIn, to gain a tiny bit of satisfaction that I'd got her figured out and that my initial judgment was correct. I quickly remembered that my phone had been confiscated once my hand touched my empty pocket. It had happened a lot in the past two days, and I realized how attached I was to my phone.

I saw the ring on her hand and assumed she had children, too. I pictured her staying up all night, or probably, every night for the past months working on this case, studying and reviewing the material, going through every detail to present all of her hard work to me ... in the most convenient manner, to persuade me that she was right in sending this man behind bars for the rest of his life.

I mean who am I? I've been working my ass off to promote my so-called "brand" for the past seven years, at least. Seven years of my life! That's almost twenty percent of my time on this earth!

At first, I thought having an eco-friendly brand for synthetic leather products was a great idea. Sustainability is a huge issue these days, and I am a firm believer in the cause. But where did that get me? I have invested time and money and haven't made my big breakthrough yet. I'm thirty-four, for god's sake!

I'm bored just talking about myself. Average looks, which I compensate for with my expensive and out-of-my-budget taste in fashion; average life, average everything. I spend most of my nights watching adaptations of my favorite crime thrillers. I don't even know where my relationship with Kyle is going.

Laura didn't know all that, though. Instead, she saw a polished-looking, professional, thirty-something-year-old who looked too confident for her own good.

She started displaying her powerful statement by telling her version of what we already knew. Jake was killed; at first, everyone thought it was an accident, but then the video from his Phantom account showed that he had been attacked before his death. They showed us the bloodied video of the teen jumping to his death. She read the medical report explaining how Jake could still perform the signature move by running on a wall of fake speakers and amplifiers, even after being hit on the head multiple times with a weapon. It was very graphic. I winced but tried not to react. Then, she moved on to pictures of Jake's funeral, where we could see the defendant.

She described the brother's medical condition, how threatened he must have felt when the defendant walked into their garage, and the possibility of him threatening the life of a young man with a disability at his own home in broad daylight.

She then started to talk about the defendant, his history, lifestyle, family, gambling problems, and other mental issues. Prior to that day, I had no information about his background, family, or any of these details. So I listened closely to his story. He was born and raised in New Jersey. His dad came from Canada in the fifties and started a small business. After a while, he had to sell it and began doing odd jobs in the neighborhood. His father was a sleazy jerk. His mom was an alcoholic. He struggled with addiction as a teenager. His mom killed herself when he was fifteen, and then he lived with his father and his new girlfriend for a few months. After that, the "other" woman left his father because it turns out she wasn't the only other woman in his life. Shocking! Things took a turn for the worse when his dad got into a terrible car accident while drunk driving. He lost his right foot. From then on, he stayed home

24/7, drinking, yelling, and making things even more difficult for his son. He drank himself to death eventually. It was not suicide. His body just couldn't take his lifestyle habits anymore. He was eighteen when his father died.

Shortly after, he met a beautiful girl. She made him believe in himself, pushed him to further his education, and unlock his potential, which he did. He went to a community college for two years, then followed his girlfriend to Rutgers, where he got a bachelor's degree in business administration. They married not long after that.

As he was watching his team win the Chicago White Sox win the World Series in October of 2005, his wife gave birth to a beautiful baby girl with stunning blue eyes.

They named her Donna.

Three

Last night, I did not sleep well. I've always been afraid of the dark and never really liked sleeping alone, even as an adult. I don't believe in ghosts or anything supernatural, but I still get creeped out. I know it doesn't make sense, but it is how I am. It was justifiable, though, particularly after hearing and seeing the gory details of the crime the day before.

We saw pictures of the bloody scene where Jake had died, followed by the footage that led to his death, the images of Donna's corpse, and the medical analysis proposing strangulation as a possible cause of death. However, the official cause of death is undetermined to this day.

It had all left me uneasy.

I couldn't help it. Once alone in the hotel room, I was back to thinking the scariest thoughts. My brain recalled a compilation of horror movies I'd watched over the years and used it to prank me like an annoying roommate.

I woke up with a splitting headache and a bad case of nausea. I didn't speak to anyone all day; just listened and tried to focus on the subject.

The defense lawyer began presenting Mr. Howe as a victim of society, painting a picture of a good, hard-working man who, despite being brought up in an unhealthy environment, made the best out of it. He met a nice girl. He got a good education, a good job, and a good family life. His only crime was spoiling his daughter and giving her the illusion that she was entitled to perfection. His addiction was the side effect of his rough beginnings at his family home in Jersey.

Mr. Caddell moved on to the trauma that Brett had suffered from losing his wife and dealing with the aftermath of raising a child alone. And how these challenges are multiplied by one hundred when dealing with a teenager who lost her mother early in her life, how she couldn't cope with the loss, and how he struggled financially and emotionally to keep up with her demands. How ungrateful his daughter turned out to be.

Mr. Caddell is a stocky man with excellent credentials and a history of successful cases. I remember Dave, one of my business associates who was obsessed with the case, telling me once that Brett had a strong chance of getting away with murder because of his lawyer.

Yes, the public opinion I had heard all around me was that Brett was most likely guilty.

How could he afford him? I wish I had paid more attention to Dave that day and gotten over myself. I had always ignored him because I thought he had a thing for me, and I never did, so I'd always try to cut our conversations short.

I looked at the other jurors, trying to study their expressionless faces. Was there a training I missed? Why was no one reacting to any of the horrible details we were seeing?

The defense's argument was as follows:

Brett had indeed been an addict all his adult life, and he'd done some shameful things because of that, in and out of relapses and continuously losing and wasting income. So, he was not necessarily the citizen of the year, but he was not a killer either.

He was also a dedicated father who never remarried, never even dated, and paid for therapies and rehab stays for his troublemaker of a daughter.

He joined support groups to be creative with solutions when dealing with his issues with Donna. He was a respectable employee, a responsible neighbor, and an excellent community member. He gave back through occasional volunteer work through his organization or the parenting group he was a member of. He suffered undeserved punishment by ending his career in finance early, people invading his privacy, and he had to endure nasty actions by the online and the Red Hills Ridge communities. This led to a spike in his blood pressure and other health issues. (Proof included doctor appointments, test results, and copies of hefty bills paid.)

However, Mr. Caddell primarily focused on emphasizing that there was no direct link between Brett and the crime scene.

Everything was assumed to create a villain to solve the case at the expense of this miserable soul.

The defense attorney kept emphasizing that the police department had no physical evidence linking Brett to the attack on the victims. No murder weapon was recovered after all.

Mr. Caddell suggested that the Seattle Police Department had made Brett Howe's guilt a foregone conclusion. During his opening remarks, he described the police as unfamiliar with a serious crime investigation,

"The police had overlooked the possibility that Donna and Jake's deaths resulted from drug abuse. That Donna had left a suicide note in her room before running away. Or ... the two deaths were not linked at all!"

He stressed that the evidence and the crime scene were mishandled from day one, that the family destroyed any evidence that could have cleared Brett, and that anyone could have been a suspect in this case.

"We have one crime investigated three months after the fact, and another after six months. All DNA evidence, or any solid link to potential suspects for that matter, was either tampered with, overlooked, or destroyed by then, including the coroner's reports which have been inconclusive in Donna's case, so really, how strong is the evidence?"

The defense lawyer showed us the abuse aimed at Brett on social media, how he was fired from his job, forced out of social media, his career was over, and with his debts and financial liabilities, he was forced to get the cash from the insurance policy.

The defense took the time to describe Jason Howe, Brett's father, as abusive. Caddell spoke about Jason's girlfriend, drinking problems, and complete disregard for his wife and kid. His wife, who barely spoke English, was alone in this country, foreign to the culture and world surrounding her. She couldn't even communicate properly with her son.

So, was he trying to justify Jason's infidelity? Besides, all that shows the reason behind bad parenting, but it is not an excuse for it.

Earlier, I thought the evidence was too overwhelming to dismiss as circumstantial. But I couldn't deny that Caddell had rearranged the thoughts in my head, and I was no longer sure of Brett's involvement. He left me wanting to know more.

I felt like a pendulum ball swaying according to the force from one side to the other and sitting still once there was no power to nudge me toward a direction. I was confident that Brett had something to do with the murders because the story created a reasonable chain of events, causes, and results for each step, so the whole story made sense.

When I returned to my room that night, I was left with the conclusion that if the story made sense, it wasn't necessarily true.

The prosecution's story presented solid grounds to study him as a suspect. But I had to find a direct line between the suspect and both victims. I had my doubts and prejudices toward Brett before I was a part of the jury, but at that point, my opinion mattered, and all the evidence and facts were part of the process. I had to start on a clean slate and think of this case as a completely foreign object. I needed to identify every angle and face every fact with a neutral perspective.

I heard Rosa's voice in my head going, "You know nothing about him. He is a blank canvas. Keep an open mind."

As Mr. Caddell spoke, I remember looking at Brett without thinking about the circumstances that put us in the same room. He was an average guy, your neighbor, your friend, your colleague, your client. He could be anyone, honestly.

The victims were innocent kids with questionable life choices, dark pasts, and crazy lifestyles, and I wonder how unfair this world was to these two. I thought about my fifteen-year-old niece, whom I love so much. I shuddered at the thought of something terrible happening to her. I love her so much it makes me not wanna have kids of my own because of how intense my love is for her.

I thought about grabbing a cup of tea, but even the smell of it made me dizzy. Instead, I just washed up and went to bed.

"Tomorrow is gonna be a long day," I heard one of the other jurors saying.

Four

My nausea was getting worse. It seemed impossible to stay focused and go through the whole thing while keeping a low profile. I was in a horrible mood. Usually when I feel this way I become very impatient with those around me. So, I tried to avoid talking to anyone because talking to people alone is not the only way to agitate me. On such bad mornings the simplest things drive me mad. For example, this lady sitting next to me keeps shifting in her seat and every time she does she lets out a loud breath. The guy in front of me keeps fidgeting with his hair and when I took a closer look I noticed that he has some sort of condition in his scalp. Red pimples all over his head underneath his thinning hair. I know I am not supposed to but, I can't help it. People's lack of self maintenance annoys me and therefore I judge them for it.

After I sat down in the courtroom, I try to distract myself so I scan the room quickly to see if I recognize anyone from the news. Trish_ona_mish was there, I follow her, and I listen to her podcast while running errands all the time. I resisted the urge to wave or smile at her.

The prosecution started by calling in a representative from the coroner's office. He testified that there was inconclusive evidence as to the specific way in which Donna had died. Suffocation could not be ruled out as a possible cause of death. She could have suffered a milder blunt-force trauma to the head that may have rendered her unconscious. Samples taken from Donna's liver and muscles revealed the absence of drugs or alcohol.

The prosecution presented their evidence:

- A toll ticket that proved Brett had left the conference. The ticket was timed at 8:42 a.m., giving him enough time to get to the spot where Donna died and back into the conference. This ticket was uncovered months later when Brett was unable to renew his car registration due to an unpaid toll penalty. He had missed the toll payment. The notices by the collection company had been sent to the wrong address, so the fees kept piling up, and he couldn't renew his car registration.

- Web sleuths managed to find Donna's LIV account; when they stumbled upon it, the account had only thirty-eight followers, one of whom was Jake. (Wow! These people need to get a life!) Messages between Donna and Jake on that account indicated that Jake was fixing some settings on an Apple Watch that belonged to Donna. The messages also revealed that Jake had bought the watch as a gift for Donna because he wanted her to get healthier and focus on sleeping better. Then, they tracked it to its last known location using Donna's Apple account associated with the same email used for her LIV account. The last known location was in the woods, a few yards from where her body was found. This meant that she was killed somewhere else and dragged to the spot where they later found her. Donna's phone was never recovered, though. The police traced that Apple Watch to a store in Seattle through the serial number and confirmed the buyer as Jake. Glenn Weaver made a smart move by not telling anyone, including the families, about this major breakthrough. Only two other members of the investigation team knew about the watch. I was impressed by how discrete everything went down, especially since the police had to get a court order to Apple to provide the credentials associated with Donna's account.

- The watch's activity and heart rate measurements revealed that an attack had occurred at 9:35 a.m. and that she had "almost certainly" died by 9:52 a.m. But then Donna's watch shows that she walked twenty-four steps after her death, which proves someone had moved her body, probably to cover some tracks or evidence. All this does is prove that Donna was, in fact, murdered and did not commit suicide. Sadly, it does not reveal the way she died.

The info about Donna's Apple Watch was kept confidential for a very long time, so there was no leakage to the media until today. I looked at Brett's face as they presented it. Before he started crying to the point where they gave the whole court a fifteen-minute break, I saw surprise, and just for a split second, I saw something else: panic?

- Brett's call log showed a call at the same time as the break-in, which aligned with Caleb's statement.

- The phone records showed Donna and Jake's exchange and that someone was texting from Donna's phone after her death.

- The photo evidence: Brett posted a picture of himself at 8:03 a.m. to his Facebook at the conference. It was definitely out of character, and no other post was made after that.

- The camera footage from the hotel where the conference was held indicated that he left around eight thirty a.m.

Had he been planning on killing his daughter for so long? It was hard to believe that this plain guy before me was a monster.

Mrs. Beeson started to present the evidence for Brett's motive:

- His gambling diaries

- His bank statements showing his financial troubles

- The first payment he got in the year 2015 was around $300K

- The second payment he got last April was around $800K

Then Laura Beeson moved to the details the police uncovered as they investigated Donna's digital footprint. Donna's LIV account was called "Sullen_Girl05" after a song; according to Laura Beeson, it was her mother's favorite. I did understand that this was an attempt by the prosecution to emotionally hook the jury to their narrative, an added spice to the recipe. Still, it worked on me because I am a sucker for these little sentimental details. In this account, she posted samples of her writing, short poems about her suffering, and about the "boogeyman who knocks on her door every night, and no one can hear his roars but her." The prosecution interpreted the boogeyman as her father, who was scripting a scenario of her accidental death just like he did with her mother years before. The motive? Insurance money!

- How did the prosecution come to this conclusion? One of Donna's Phans triggered a story that went viral. The story detailed an alleged murder. Meanwhile, based on Donna's connection to Jake's murder investigation, the police got a warrant for her Phantom stories and sifted through them for any evidence. She didn't have many, so they quickly found the one that mattered. Besides the eerie stuff that look like they came from a horror movie (some of which were already triggered by the followers), she had one story where she detailed the events of the day when her mother died.

They played the video. It showed Donna sitting in a room. I assumed it was her bedroom. She was sitting on her bed with a bookcase behind her. Donna began to describe some disturbing details:

She was looking straight at the camera. Her eyes were the most beautiful shade of blue. It felt like she was looking through me.

"I don't know who is going to see this. I don't know if this will make any difference or if the right people will give it the attention it deserves." She looked down as if to avoid our gaze.

"I never really spoke about that before, so please pay attention. This is the heaviest weight that I had to carry ever since I was ten. I've never even told Angela." [Her doctor.]

She looked up and stared for a few long seconds before speaking again. Donna was beautiful; although she needed serious maintenance work, she was naturally beautiful. I couldn't help but think of all the possibilities if I could give her a proper makeover. That being said, she had that creepy vibe going on, which could be attractive and mysterious to some.

She began to speak again, "I was too afraid. And I didn't quite understand what happened at the time. The more I played it in my head, the more I understood what had actually happened. It was terrifying... Not just what happened (takes a deep breath), just thinking about the fragility of our bodies as I lie in the backseat right behind him.

"I woke up briefly in the car. Everything was upside down, my side was hurting a lot, and my head felt too heavy. I wanted to throw up, and it was hard to breathe. I shut my eyes and hoped to wake up in a different world ... in my real world.

"I remember hearing a movement before I could see it. In the passenger seat, my dad shifted and removed his seatbelt. I could only see my unconscious mom in the driver's seat.

"I almost called out to him, but my voice wouldn't come out. Then I saw his bloodied hands reach out. He removed my mother's seatbelt. (a soft sob) As he did so, her arm moved, and that cartoon ghost tattoo on her wrist was visible. For a second, I got distracted by a memory of me making fun of her once.

"Hopefully, one night in your adult life, you'll have enough fun and end up with a mistake like that.' I didn't know what she meant back then." Donna let out a sad chuckle mixed with tears and then continued, "He touched her neck, looking for a pulse, I think. When he found it, he covered her mouth and nose. And just like that, Mom was gone." Donna cried some more,

"I kept quiet for so long. At first, I didn't know what I saw. It's like my heart understood what my mind didn't, and it kept nagging and nagging that something was wrong, that what I saw meant something. But I kept asking, why? Why would he kill her? Until I found out about his gambling problems. All these bills piling up, collection companies' letters, sometimes we barely had enough for food." She sniffed, wiped her face with the back of her hand, and then said:

"Dad, I saw what you did. I know now why you killed her. Now it looks like you're coming for me. I saw that you took out a policy on me."

She looked defeated, sad, and weak.

"No one can do anything now. It is too late. I guess that's why you cremated Mom, although my aunt did not want to. You just burned the evidence."

She sighed and closed her eyes. She looked like she was meditating. Then she said:

"If you are watching this, spoiler alert." She moved her hand to her mouth, making the gesture as if she was about to whisper a secret to the whole courtroom.

"I'm dead!"

The video ended there. The courtroom was silent except for a sound of tapping. I followed the sound and found my eyes resting on Brett, tapping away with a pen on the desk and looking nervous and angry.

He was not aware of me looking at him.

He looked lost in his own head.

Five

Last night, when I got to my room, I was so exhausted and nauseous. I didn't even call anyone; I didn't eat dinner. I just headed to my room and fell asleep with my clothes on.

I woke up at three a.m., still in my white shirt and gray slacks. The lights and TV were on. I ran to the bathroom to throw up some disgusting yellow bile and realized then that my stomach was empty since I had nothing to eat all day yesterday except for cream of wheat for breakfast. I was starving and very dehydrated. I opened the snack bar in my room and went for a bag of chips. Thankfully, they had salt and vinegar, my favorite flavor. I didn't recognize the brand, but I went for it anyway. For some reason, it made me even more nauseous, so I tossed it in the trash. My appetite was being unpredictable; I thought maybe because I had changed scenes and routines.

I brushed my teeth, chugged an entire bottle of water, changed into my PJs, and hopped back into bed. When I woke up again at seven a.m., I was feeling better... Refreshed. After all, I had slept for almost ten hours.

That day, the prosecution was supposed to call their witnesses. A pretty Asian lady took the stand. Dr. Angela Zheng treated Donna Howe for a while. Their relationship developed beyond the professional standard; she was her confidant and best friend. She testified that Donna hated her father and blamed him for her mother's death but never told her she had seen him kill her mother, as mentioned in the video.

She talked about Donna's love for Jake and the relationship they had.

AZ: I was not Donna's psychologist during the last three years. After moving to Seattle, I became her friend. We stayed in touch, and she kept calling me. I loved Donna like a daughter. She was a good girl in an awful situation and a very unhealthy environment.

Attorney: How long have you known Donna Howe?

AZ: Since her mother died about nine years ago.

Attorney: All right. Now Donna was in touch with you while also seeing another therapist in the Seattle area; did she ever tell you why?

AZ: Well, she did that to give her father the satisfaction and the illusion of his control over her. She wanted him to believe that she was making the progress he wanted and that she was happy. He did not know about her other plans.

Attorney: Is this based on your assessment, or did Donna tell you that specifically?

AZ: Donna did. She was planning on running away and never coming back. She had just turned eighteen and was free to go anywhere, and that was her plan. Donna wanted to return to Florida, where she grew up and where her most cherished memories of her mother took place. She hated the weather in Seattle. She loved the sun's heat on her skin and dreamt of living close to the beach. She also wanted to be closer to her mother. And closer to me.

Attorney: Was she planning on running away alone?

AZ: No. Jake Bodkin was planning to study sound engineering in Florida as well. They had plans to go there together. He wasn't going to run away. He was planning on attending some program at Full Sail University in Florida. She was going to explore her options, but she had plans to study creative writing and poetry.

Attorney: Can you describe the relationship between Donna and Jake based on your conversations with Donna?

AZ: From what Donna told me, he had a very likable, cheerful personality. He was a genuine guy from a good family and a beautiful home. She often fantasized about having a similar situation where she had hectic holiday gatherings and crazy bickering with siblings and cousins. She once told me that Jake was the only source of comfort in her life because while he cared for the people around him deeply, his way of handling stressful situations was inspiring to her. How he joked about sensitive topics without offending her made her feel like she belonged.

(Mrs. Bodkin was sobbing, and the father covered his face as he did the same. It was heartbreaking)

Attorney: Were they in love?

AZ: Donna never said that she was in love with Jake. At least she never mentioned it to me, but she most certainly adored him and valued their friendship. Yet Jake did tell Donna that he was in love with her.

Attorney: What were your impressions of Mr. Howe?

AZ: I think Brett Howe could use some professional help, or maybe he's already getting it. It seems like he is overwhelmed by specific traumas in his life. Before Donna's death, he'd always been paranoid. While I understand that parents cope differently with raising a troubled child or traumatic experiences such as losing his wife in a car crash, I don't believe Donna was his number one priority as he makes it out to be.

Attorney: How many times did you come in contact with him?

AZ: Not as much as I would have liked to do. Typically, with cases like Donna, I do more frequent meetings with the parents, provide reports and actions required, and follow up with them. In therapy, kids learn by doing. I need to work with the whole family when the patient is young. For older kids and teens, we discuss feelings and problems, try to share ideas and understand their strengths and weaknesses. I need to organize meetings with the child and parent together or with the child alone. It depends on the child's age. I also have to meet with the parents to give them homework so that they can tackle the problems and improve the child's behavior at home.

In total, I met Brett Howe fewer than ten times over five years. That's nothing.

Attorney: Can you talk to us about Donna's state of mind, stability, and mental problems in the days or months leading up to her death?

AZ: I did think that it was a good idea for Brett and Donna to start over somewhere new. I remember Donna being so disappointed when I told her I agreed with Brett. She wasn't talking to me for the first three months or so after they moved to Washington. Donna wouldn't return my calls or emails until she was fed up with the bullying at her school in Red Hills. One night, she called me crying, almost out of breath. I remember we spoke on the phone for two hours that night. So, what I am trying to say is that Donna was like a foggy day ... but she started to clear up and show her true self the more she hung out with Jake. Toward the end, our conversations were much more pleasant. More positive, with an undertone of hope.

Attorney: Did Donna discuss her LIV account with you?

AZ:, Donna talked to me about this a lot! She loved the idea. She had an obsession with closures because she never got any from her mother's death. So when Jake told her about the new feature, she created that LIV account.

Attorney: could you please clarify? Are you saying that it was Jake Bodkin who told Donna about the feature, Epilogue, offered by LIV?

AZ: I know that everyone thinks it was the other way around, that he signed up because of her influence, and yes as I recall Donna told me that the idea did not appeal to Jake. But prior to speaking to Jake Donna had no social media accounts and only found out about the promotional email from LIV about their new feature through Jake. She liked the idea, and I believe she pushed him toward it.

Another prosecution witness, Sarah Blackwell, was called. She testified that Donna passed by the grocery store where they both had worked two years before Donna's death. She wanted to grab a few snacks before heading to the trail, where she died later that day. Sarah said that Donna's demeanor was lively. "Did not look like she was gonna kill herself, if that's what you mean," she said.

Sarah described Donna's relationship with her father as unhealthy. She spoke of Brett as a disturbed psychopath who played the victim after killing his own daughter.

"You do know that Donna tried to tell you guys about her father's issues?" She looked directly at the detectives and officers in the audience as she said that, and as she rolled her eyes, she looked back at the attorney and continued, "But like, she got ignored over and over again ... first when she was just a little kid, then as a messed-up teenager, and now they're callin' her a crazy lady."

Attorney: What did Donna tell you about her relationship with her father?

SB: She said Brett didn't do much to help with her messed-up mind. Instead, he made it worse, kept givin' her drugs and uppin' the doses and stuff. He is the reason why she was an addict!

But then Caddell questioned Sarah about the one time Donna had attacked her while she was working at her family's convenience store. It stopped me in my tracks when they showed a picture of Sarah at a party a couple of days after the incident with a large blue bruise on her cheek and a purple one on her neck. Then, they showed CCTV footage of the incident. That looked a bit too intense.

I kept remembering the looks on their faces, Jake's family and friends. And it broke my heart that Donna had no one but the doctor, Sarah, and her aunt, Nicole, to speak in her favor. The closest connection to her world here sat in the accused seat. How lonely must she have been?

More witnesses were called in; the most intriguing by far was the King County Medical Examiner, to testify that Jake was hit on the head for the purpose of killing him, but then his body responded differently to the trauma. I'd never heard of such an incident before, but he provided examples of past cases with similar outcomes. Some guy in New York attacked his parents; one of them woke up briefly and, like Jake, exhibited zombielike behavior before succumbing to his wounds and dying.

Laura Beeson wanted to show us a fragile girl with an abusive, controlling, twisted father. On the other hand, Caddell brought into the light the rebellious teenager who added to the pressures of life and addiction and made her father snap by relapsing. Through his questions to the witnesses, he painted a picture of a troublemaker, a drug addict who was rehabilitated on multiple occasions with a hefty price, wrecked her father's car and almost hit someone while driving under the influence, and acted like a rich brat when her father was struggling to make ends meet. She lived to punish her father for surviving the accident and made sure he paid for it.

To me, Caddell's story (while good) was not very convincing. It failed to make me sympathize with Brett, and it certainly did not take my mind off the idea that Brett had possibly killed someone—more than once.

It also seemed too suspicious to me that he was the only source of solid info about Donna. He had a very close grip on what went in and out of her life. This was weird, even for a troubled teenager. I was curious about Donna and Brett's relationship before her mother's demise. I agreed with Sarah that a troubled teenager's credibility against her father would be questionable unless something drastic happened ... like her death.

Before dinner, I called my sister. She told me that she came down with the flu, so we didn't speak for long, only five minutes or so.

They organized a movie night for the jury members. The movies were donated by court staff. Everyone was down in a common room that only jurors and court staff could access. They were watching some Western classic. I think it was a Clint Eastwood movie. I don't know, but I didn't stay to find out.

I went back to my room. I fell asleep while reading a memoir graphic novel I'd meant to read for over a year.

I love those.

Six

All the jury members were fully aware that we were not allowed to discuss the case with anyone, including amongst ourselves, until the deliberation process began. As instructed by the judge, we had to keep our perspectives and opinions to ourselves until it was time to deliver the verdict.

Mita, the Zumba instructor who seemed to have missed the memo, talked to anyone about anything. I mean, I'd heard her discuss some details with Ben before; he was another juror who (I thought) had a crush on her. After breakfast, she approached me in the ladies room in the hotel lobby.

"So, what did you think?" Mita said.

"About?"

"It is such a sad story," she said.

"It is," I said to her while washing my hands and drying them without making eye contact. I opted for the hand dryer, hoping the loud noise would kill the conversation.

It didn't work. Mita waited until I was done and started again. She was taking her sweet time washing her hands. Nobody is that thorough when they wash their hands. I knew this was a blatant attempt at keeping the conversation going.

"Yeah, I know, but don't you feel bad for Brett? He reminds me of my uncle struggling to provide for his brat daughter who thinks the world owes her something because she lost her mother."

"I don't know about that. We must consider solid evidence before us, not our interpretations of facts or personal experiences. I suggest you do the same," I told her as I straightened my shirt and opened the door to leave.

She avoided me after this encounter. I might have sounded like a bitch, but I could not fake any pleasant attitude. I was in a terrible mood for some reason and couldn't be bothered with her or anyone else.

I was also homesick. I wanted to curl up in my favorite chair and binge-watch my favorite shows while going through my social media feed, swiping through the digital version of my existence, one section at a time. I wanted to check my calendar for my daily tasks and then mindlessly check my Instagram feed to feel good and bad about my life: a motivation to achieve or a trigger for a mild case of depression.

The prosecution called Nicole Lazenby to the witness stand. She is Anastasia Howe's sister. She testified that Brett and Anastasia were in love for the first three years of their marriage, but then things went downhill. She said that "Annie" had helped him to overcome his sickness, but then he kept on relapsing, and that caused severe problems between the couple. Donna was never involved, but she was too young anyway. And then, a key revelation without proof, Nicole said that Anastasia had wanted to leave Brett before the accident.

Nicole also said that she was not suspicious about her sister's death. It never occurred to her that such a thing could be planned when your kid is in the car with you. Also, Brett was not in good shape after the accident, which concealed any guilt.

THE SOUND OF TUNING OUT

Nicole never knew about the insurance policy. When Laura asked her if she thought Brett was capable of murdering someone for the money, she said it was a possibility.

Next, the prosecution called in Charles Butler, an insurance specialist. He looked so nervous. I could tell because he kept fidgeting with his thick glasses, wedding ring, and the glass of water in front of him. He is a middle-aged, stocky guy. I think the last time he went shopping was last decade. The financial responsibilities associated with raising a family in Seattle and the mediocre lifestyle he was leading were the probable reasons for that.

LB: Were you handling the insurance policy by the defendant?

CB: Yes.

LB: When did he complete the policy for the victim?

CB: 2022.

LB: Two years before the victim's demise. Then, the victim was still a minor. Donna was only seventeen. How does that work?

CB: Buying life insurance for a child is quick and easy compared with buying a policy for an adult. All you have to do is fill out the electronic application form, but the child won't have to go through a medical exam typically required for adults. Then, you have to wait while the underwriting is done online.

LB: How much was the amount of the policy?

CB: $800,000.

LB: Was this the first time the defendant received money from your company?

CB: Yes.

LB: Does he have any other life insurance policies?

CB: No.

LB: When was the amount paid out to him?

CB: In April of this year, once Ms. Howe's death was confirmed.

LB: Can you tell us more about the policy terms?

CB: The policy covering the victim also included a "double indemnity" clause, which provided a payout of twice the policy amount in the event death was caused by an accident. "Slip and fall" accidents are considered eligible.

LB: What is "accidental death" under your terms and conditions?

CB: Death must be caused by an unexpected event, such as a slip and fall, traffic crash, or accidental overdose on prescribed meds.

LB: Ms. Howe's body was found in December last year. Why did it take so long to pay the money? What procedures are mostly time-consuming?

CB: Paperwork, the process of verifying details and circumstances of the death, the investigations to confirm the cause of death. If the policyholder commits suicide within two years of the policy term, the beneficiary will not get the payment. However, our company provides suicide coverage from the third year onwards, subject to terms and conditions. We had to wait for the toxicology report to prove that she had no drugs in her system. Life insurance companies need to protect themselves as well. Someone could buy a policy to commit suicide so that the next of kin receive the payment. If the insured person commits suicide within the first two years after getting the insurance policy, the death benefit will not be paid out to the policy's beneficiaries. This is what we call a suicide clause.

LB: So, to reiterate here, finding Donna's body is the starting point of getting paid the insurance policy on her life, right?

CB: Yes, ma'am.

We headed to the common room for refreshments and coffee when we were done. I ate some crackers and headed back to my room. After that day's questioning and statements, I jotted down the main ideas.

The coroner's report said that she had no substance traces in her system, and they suspected strangulation or trauma to the head ... but the official cause of death was undetermined.

If Brett did kill Donna to claim the insurance money, he would want her body found as soon as possible. He persistently organized the search parties because he didn't want to be the one to find Donna. He didn't want any reason for the police to suspect him. It didn't matter who killed her (murder or suicide) because the two-year suicide clause had passed by then. And as far as anyone was concerned, Brett had a solid alibi for Donna's time of death.

Unless the police caught the killer, there was no way to find out exactly how Donna died after all that time. Also, the more Donna was linked to Jake's death, the more likely the police would be up Brett's business. Finding her body was a solution to most of Brett's problems.

My mood had been crappy all day. I barely spoke to the other jurors and was cranky when I talked to my boyfriend. We almost had a fight in front of the deputy. He looked so uncomfortable, and it was all in all awkward.

"It is not easy being sequestered," he said as we walked out of the room where we received our calls. "But hopefully, things will be finalized as scheduled."

Which meant we had one more week to go ... with any luck.

Seven

It was only ten a.m., but I was already exhausted. I am never lazy. I am always out and about running errands and checking off items on my to-do lists. This fatigue felt like an anchor pulling me downward to places I never wanna go. I felt so depressed and anxious because I was helpless.

At that point, I started to regret my decision to be on the panel of jurors. I needed to see a doctor about this stomach issue, maybe run some tests, and find out what was wrong with me.

The prosecution called a witness, pulling me out of the dark, painful space I had created for myself in my head. Jose Gomez is the insurance company representative handling Brett's account back in Florida. He testified that the insurance policy covered some of Donna's therapeutic residential program costs. He also confirmed the amount paid to Brett after Anastasia died in the car accident.

The next witness was an ex-counselor at the wilderness program where Donna spent ninety days. He said that the program cost close to nothing and had a bad reputation for mishandling the patients, neglecting them, and, in some incidents, even abusing them.

Next witness: Jessica Bartlett, the neighbor who found Jake. I didn't find her attractive per se; she looked like a garden salad if it were a woman, healthy but not appetizing.

THE SOUND OF TUNING OUT

The prosecution asked her to describe the scene, the horror, the relationship with the family, and the disruption it had on her own family.

Then came Caddell with an appetite for destruction: his questions served to highlight the mishandling of the crime scene by the police, how the family and neighbors (including Jessica) moved the speakers that fell on Jake in a failed attempt at saving his life, how they moved his body, how they allowed people into the crime scene before the arrival of the police. It was a mess indeed.

But then it got personal.

Caddell: Jessica, or do you prefer Mrs. Bartlett?

I remember thinking it was weird calling her "Jessica" like that. They never use first names at the court...

JB: I actually go by McLynn now.

Caddell: Oh, I am sorry. May I ask why?

JB: I just finalized my divorce papers a month ago.

Caddell: I'm sorry to hear that. Now, let's go back to our case, shall we? Have you always been close with the Bodkins?

JB: We've been next-door neighbors for six years, since we moved to the Red Hills area.

Caddell: Thank you for this information, Ms. McLynn, but that was not my question. Were you close with the Bodkins during Jake's life? Were there any playdates, visits, dinners, or game nights?

JB: No.

Caddell: Are you still friends with Diane Bodkin?

JB: No.

Caddell: Are you living with Frank Bodkin?

There was an objection as this information was not deemed necessary or relevant to the case. But Caddell said that he was getting to the point. The judge allowed the questioning to continue.

JB: Yes.

As the questioning continued, I realized the point Caddell was trying to make here. Jessica got closer to the family after Jake's death. The friendship with the Bodkins spiraled out of control, leading to an affair between Frank Bodkin and Jessica Bartlett. Both are divorced now. The Bodkins sold their home, the mother lives in San Fran, and the father lives in Seattle with his girlfriend.

Caddell brought this up to show that the other team was not perfect, either. Yes, Brett was a problem gambler with many flaws, but so were Frank Bodkin and Jessica Bartlett. He wanted to show that his opponents' credibility and moral compass were also debatable. The defense brought new information to light: Frank lied to his wife and Caleb about his whereabouts the day someone broke into their house. He had been with Jessica at her house when Caleb came looking for help.

"Yes, we were having an affair at that time, and we are not proud of that, but this has nothing to do with the intruder … this doesn't change anything," Jessica said.

I agreed with her. As much as I disapproved of their infidelity, I thought Caddell wanted to distract us from the main topic here by showing the dark side of the family and the community.

The following two witnesses were kids from Donna's class (one from Washington and another from Florida). They testified that Donna was bullied, mainly for her withdrawn character and appearance.

The kid from Florida (Angus) said that she came to school in worn-out rags, and her reputation as an addict and a patient of mental illness preceded her, making her an easy target. According to Caddell, the school did not do much to protect Donna's medical history, which was supposed to be confidential.

Caddell summarized the everyday life of a student at Red Hills High. "A toxic environment infested with bullies with no limitations and no consequences for their actions."

THE SOUND OF TUNING OUT

He asked the kids all the right questions, and they easily handed him over all the answers he was fishing for. They talked about the bullying that Donna suffered, with proof from social media platforms, some of the things the kids wrote on Brett's house and FB wall. Moreover, a kid killed himself a few years ago due to cyberbullying (his name was Hunter something—I am really bad with names).

"Who's to say that Jake was not one of those bullies who played with Donna's feelings and exposed her insecurities, bringing the worst out of this poor, damaged soul?" Caddell said.

Diane Bodkin buried her face in her hands and cried. Her ex-husband shook his head and looked at something on the ground. It didn't look like he was looking at something in particular. I think he was hiding his anger at the claims.

"Who can predict what someone so unstable can do to those who hurt them when provoked?" Caddell continued.

My take on that: Although Brett's job paid well, he lived a minimalist lifestyle; he had a very old car and kept all the money to himself to indulge in gambling. This was selfish parenting while creating the illusion that he was caring and dedicated to his daughter only, secluding her from everyone so as not to be found out.

The defense argument sounded more like making excuses rather than bringing out facts.

I was not biased, but I was not convinced of Brett's innocence yet, though he was still not guilty beyond a reasonable doubt.

Eight

The hotel we stayed at was excellent, but something was still not right. My stomach was getting worse. When I woke up on January 11, I went straight to the toilet. I threw up and still felt like shit. I didn't have anything for breakfast, so by two p.m., when we were dismissed for a break, I was starving and had to go to the vending machine for something with sugar; otherwise I would have collapsed.

The hotel provided breakfast, dinner, and a snack. Lunch came from "Order," a café on the second floor of the courthouse, and Franko's Pizza. The night before, our dinner was grilled salmon with asparagus, a favorite of mine on a typical day, but the sight of it made my stomach go into knots, let alone the smell.

A doctor came at seven p.m. to see me; he checked my fever because I felt like I was burning up throughout the day. He suspected a viral infection, so he scheduled an appointment for me to run some blood tests. The court proceedings took a one-day break until they decided whether I could be dismissed as a juror, depending on my health situation.

Aside from my digestive system drama, I found the drama at the courthouse today very eye-opening.

They called Glenn Weaver to testify. Boy, was he handsome, not too tall, maybe six feet, which was perfect and even too tall for a five foot two girl like me. I could safely guess that the guy worked out frequently. He looked like he put enough effort into his looks but not too much to the point where you might question where his priorities lie. He didn't look obsessed with himself, is what I am trying to say. His reputation for being cocky added rather than took away from his charm. But not for me, I am a thirty-four-year-old struggling entrepreneur with enough career and family drama. I wanted a relationship to make my days easier rather than complicate my evenings. Maybe that's why I never opened up to the idea of marriage. Some romance scenarios are only good on the screen or on paper like a cocky, handsome guy might be attractive in a movie, but in reality, if my boyfriend shows me any signs of overconfidence, it is just not going to work out. Because if he has legit reasons to be overly confident, it will make me insecure about myself, and if he has no reason to be so, then I am going to dump that delusional asshole.

That's why I love Kyle. His moderate success feels like a safety net and a leash to bring me back to reality rather than put me down every time I dream big. Also, his hippie-like personality calms me down and shows me the things that matter most, which are usually the ones we take for granted.

Anyways, Glenn is hot, and that's that. Back to the more important thing about Glenn, which was his statement, not the brand of his perfect charcoal suit. Glenn went over the analysis of the material provided by LIV from the Epilogue content recorded by Donna and Jake:

"Our analysis of the videos took into account multiple factors: date and time of the video, location, content/topics discussed, change in behaviors from the first recorded video to the latest ones, and external info such as Donna and Jake's chats, CCTV recordings, witness statements, phone records, receipts and other materials that are part of this investigation and that help to tie the story together. Although the location was enabled in Jake's videos, that was not the same in Donna's case. We could still pinpoint the spot due to the view and the surroundings.

"I am going to walk you through all the evidence we found in the videos and the way our team analyzed every detail to arrive at this conclusion.:

"On January 2, 2024, Donna and Jake were at a local coffee shop called Roasted. Located at 2268 Hills Ave, Red Hills Ridge, WA 98065, United States. This was a coincidence, not an arranged meeting because we have no reason to believe that Donna and Jake had any relationship before the said date. The school records show that the two were attending Red Hills High at the same time during the fall semester in 2022, but according to witness statements, the two had no interaction or any relationship during that time. Donna was a year older than Jake, and she attended the same high school for only one semester. According to the evidence previously presented, she dropped out because of a bullying incident.

"We believe that Donna stole Jake's phone to record a LIV story and post it to his account because she wanted to leverage the number of followers Jake had at the time (around three thousand followers). She was planning on killing herself and leaving a suicide note, which contained one of her favorite poems, and was found by her father in her bedroom. She wanted to record a video to explain the details of her personal trauma, her mother's death, and what she saw the day her mother died. Donna wanted to make sure that so many people saw her message and resolved to steal Jacob Bodkin's iPhone to post her video on his account for his followers. Jacob used the 'Find My' app on his Apple Watch to track his lost phone once he realized that his phone was missing. He followed Donna into the woods, where she was recording the video. He asked her why she had taken his phone, she freaked out, gave him the phone and ran away. The text exchange between Jacob and Donna on later dates indicated that the two grew closer after this incident, developing feelings for one another. He talked to her about social media and this new service that uses a database of preapproved content to send messages to your loved ones after you die, Epilogue by LIV. Jacob convinced Donna to 'postpone' her suicide until she created a LIV account so she could do it the GEN Z way. 'At least die young the right way.'

"'Not because you made a great argument but because you were so casual about it, and your upbeat style felt like the kind of cool breeze that does not exist in the hell where I was living.' Those were Donna's exact words. It looked like they enjoyed each other's company.

"Jake got Donna an Apple Watch to have her own LIV account and record these videos. They planned to expose Brett Howe and his crimes after Jake graduated and moved to Florida with Donna, where they both planned to attend Full Sail University. The messages showed how concerned Donna was that her father would find out about this plan and kill them both.

"When Donna found the documents containing the details of the life insurance policy her father had taken out on her, she wanted to kill herself and expose him. Had she gone ahead with her initial plan, Brett would have failed to claim any amount because it was only January, and the term for the suicide clause had not been completed yet. According to prosecution lawyers, she wanted to kill herself for that purpose specifically.

"Brett was counting down until July to stage Donna's suicide after the term of the suicide clause concluded, two years since he signed the agreement in 2022.

"Jacob and Donna texted/talked daily. Some pictures and witness statements proved that they met frequently.

"He signed up and promised to make a video every time she did.

"'My content switched from saying goodbye to my life to saying goodbye to my trauma and the cause of it, which is my father. I am not going to die. I will leave him behind and start a new life somewhere I love, where I belong, close to my mother,' she told Jake on one occasion.

"'These videos are not a tribute to anything. They are confessions and reminders for my future self to guide me back to this path if I stray away.' This is a quote from one of Jacob and Donna's conversations."

A lot of the attendants at the court got emotional, especially Jake's family and friends. It was heartbreaking. With every statement, Glenn gave evidence from the chats or witness statements taken during the investigation phase.

"This is a beautiful story, Mr. Weaver. I do appreciate the time and effort taken to corroborate every claim except for the one that truly matters to this case. It is the one that Donna Howe continuously made about Brett Howe killing Anastasia Howe in 2015. And your team's claim about Brett killing his daughter and next-door neighbor. It is a well-written attempt at a motive at best, but it proves nothing, your honor." Caddell ended his interrogation and comments with that.

I went to my room to lie down, relax, and think about my blood tests. After an hour or so, I decided to call Rosa. Hearing her voice, I instantly felt better. I was so thankful for her existence in my life.

"I have been extremely emotional these few days. I don't know whether it is the case, or the loneliness, or the stress, but I have never cried this easily," I told Rosa.

"Stress has always been a reason for your UC flare-ups. There is nothing new here and no reason to worry too much." She told me. "Relax ... I am sure it's nothing."

I decided to believe her. She's always right. It was probably nothing.

Nine

The examination room was bare and somewhat depressing. The doctor sat across from me as I anxiously fidgeted in my seat. The air was heavy with anticipation and uncertainty. The doctor smiled kindly and reassuringly as he glanced at the bloodwork results.

"Congrats Molly, you're pregnant."

Week Six...

I could not believe it...

When I told Rosa the news, I had to be on speaker. This was a requirement to ensure that the jurors adhered to the rules. All conversations were monitored to eliminate any outside influence. That was one of the hardest parts about being sequestered because I'm not one for talking around a lot of people.

Officer Harris might as well have been my BFF at this point. He knew everything worth knowing about my life. I looked in his direction in search of disapproval for being so irresponsible and acting like a dumb teenager when I spoke to Rosa.

"I don't know what Kyle's reaction is going to be..."

"Hmmm, are we alone, or is our friend listening?" Rosa asked.

"We are not alone, of course."

"Wow ... this guy knows everything about you, you know that. Maybe he can tell Kyle? Haha!" Rosa said.

The deputy didn't say anything, but I thought I saw a hint of a smile on his face.

"I'm sorry, Officer. I promise we'll behave," I told him.

"I'm terrified..." I continued.

"I know. You only joke about the stuff that truly scares you." I didn't say anything back. Instead, I focused on holding back tears.

"You have to discuss it with Kyle and see what you both wanna do next. Although I know the answer."

"Yeah?" I manage while trying to suppress a crack in my voice.

"It doesn't matter what I think. I am here for you."

I didn't say anything. Officer Harris frowned, though.

"When are you going to tell him?"

"Probably when this is all over," I answered.

"Are they gonna dismiss you?" Rosa asked.

The officer looked at me and shook his head as I was about to cross the boundaries of approved conversation material.

"I'm sorry. Rosa, I'll call you tomorrow, please don't tell anyone. Not even Dad."

"I'm with you, whatever you decide to do."

I don't know why, but when we hung up, I cried, and I cried, and I cried ... Officer Harris could not leave the room. He got me a glass of water and tissues.

"If you don't feel like you're up for it, you can be dismissed. Just say so. You have a strong out-of-jail card," he said.

"Honestly, I am desperate to stay away from my life right now," I told him.

I didn't wanna face Kyle, work, friends, or anybody.

THE SOUND OF TUNING OUT

This was a blessing in disguise. I was falling deeper in love with this situation every day.

They ordered pizza (garlic ughhh), and the court staff gathered games to lend to occupy us. We played Monopoly for two hours. It was a nice change. I played with Tony (twenty-eight, from Boston, who worked in the registration office at a university, had a girlfriend, and one dog) and Ben (forty-two, married for six years with two kids, ages eleven and thirteen, unemployed was working in financial services, he was arrested in college previously—DUI—never served on a jury). I couldn't hide my judgmental expression when he told me he was married. I mean, it was so obvious in the way he flirted with Zen-Mita. Barf.

After that, I went to my room and ordered a frozen yogurt. I watched two episodes of a sitcom, and before I knew it, I was already drifting into the dream world, and I slept peacefully.

Weird.

Ten

The next stranger to find out about my pregnancy was a sixty-something judge who had no time or patience for my story.

"Can you continue with the trial, miss?" the judge asked me.

"Yes, I can."

Yes please … keep me hidden in the safety of this isolated haven away from everyone I know…

I continued, "Yes, sir, I am capable physically and emotionally. The doctor said that the baby and I are healthy."

So weird saying that…

"Then that's settled. Thanks for your transparency, and please keep us informed in case of an emergency. The trial is scheduled to conclude in a week's time, so it won't be much longer now."

When I left the room, Mita gave me a look. She was dying to know what I'd been up to; in fact, the members of the jury were all curious about my meeting with the judge. Since we had been sequestered and kept away from the media and real life outside, we were more interested in our limited surroundings. I knew all eleven jurors' names, jobs, marital status, their children's names, and hobbies. That was a big social intake in one week.

"Are you staying with us?" Amanda asked. She was one of the senior jurors and often took on a maternal role.

"Yes, I was just updating the judge about my lab results. Everything seems fine. It was just a stomach bug."

"I hope it's not infectious." She raised her eyebrows and looked at me like I had something to be blamed for.

"No, don't worry."

Once her facial muscles relaxed, she decided we were friends again. She told me about her daughter's nineteenth birthday and how it was hard to restrict her conversation with her daughter to fit into the boundaries set by the authorities. Her daughter, Sophia, was obsessed with the case and kept asking her about any updates, so the last time she spoke with Sophia, the deputy had to end the call abruptly to make a point.

I left the breakfast room and headed back up to my room to relax and clear my head before heading to the courtroom. I suspected Amanda calmed everyone's doubts once I left the room.

We were in the courtroom a bit later than usual that day. It was eleven thirty a.m., and they were about to call the next witness on the list.

Forensic psychologist Christopher Palmer assessed the mental state of Brett Howe. He testified that Brett's behavior was consistent with a diagnosis of psychopathy or sociopathy, two similar though not identical disorders characterized by pathological deception, scamming and defrauding others, and lack of conscience or remorse.

And then the most anticipated witness: Caleb Bodkin.

He looked younger in real life. I remember seeing him once in a press conference and in one of Jake's stories, which flooded the internet in the early days of Epilogue's launch. It didn't look like he'd recovered much. He looked so unsure of himself. This case had been dragging on for over a year and the traces of trauma on his face did not fade with time. Instead, agonizing developments and twists in this heartbreaking story kept on intensifying his suffering. His sunken eyes spoke of long sleepless nights. The acne, slumped shoulders, and overall look of defeat made me feel guilty, as though we were collectively abusing this young man by forcing him to do something against his will for our satisfaction. As he took the stand, I couldn't help but wonder about the family's day-to-day life post this tragedy. With all the media attention, it was not easy, indeed.

He talked about his brother. When he found out about his death, the day (presumably) Brett broke into the Bodkins' house in search of something we still don't know.

The way Brett tried to throw off the police by saying he'd seen a Black man in the neighborhood.

"Why do you think Mr. Howe described the intruder as black?" Laura asked Caleb.

"I think he wanted to make sure that no one would suspect him," Caleb said.

Then, he described how Brett came over multiple times to drink with his father and not only played victim but also a friend.

He talked to us about the devastating effect this crime had on him personally, his family, and even his job. Although his boss had been very understanding of his situation, the case kept him distracted at a critical time in his career. As a new hire in an extremely competitive market, he wanted to be defined by his value to the organization, not by his personal life. He talked about his medical condition and how the stress had caused his body to shut down many times, which was both life-threatening at times and humiliating.

Finally, he spoke about his parents' relationship, which was damaged to the point of no return.

"Brett killed us all; his greed and criminal nature preyed on the goodness of the people around him, starting with his daughter, who suffered a great deal during our high school years. Believe me, I know, the kids called her Donna Darko..." He was in tears now, barely catching his breath. "We want justice; we want to make an example of this psychopath, and maybe then I can try and move on..." A couple of times, his gaze caught mine, and I tried so hard to fight those tears. It might have been the pregnancy hormones, but I felt like crying throughout the whole proceedings.

Eleven

I decided to wait until after the verdict to deal with the issue of my pregnancy. The countdown was nearing its end, and I needed to focus on the task at hand.

The defense called new witnesses, another doctor who treated Donna in Seattle and another two specialists from the rehab facility where she stayed for six months before meeting Jake; they all confirmed Donna's suicidal state. This was evidenced by a suicide attempt three years before her death. Her shrink testified that she suffered from acute depression and that the methods to address this issue were in line with the medical recommendations.

"People's responses to treatments are different. Simple as that," he said.

Then Laura Beeson brought up an interesting piece of information. She took an excerpt from an entry by Brett Howe on the Online Support Group: Parents of Troubled Teens. The entry was dated September 4, 2023. Brett Howe wrote, "The police spoke to Donna's therapist. He said that Donna did not have any suicidal tendencies."

"Well, I never said those words exactly. Brett may have misinterpreted my words. This is a natural reaction during extremely stressful times, a trick our minds might play on us, creating an illusion of hope. He must have been so worried that day," the doctor continued.

I had expected that the defense would use the troubled teen card. We all knew Donna was not the perfect girl, and we knew that she was using, but how could we connect that to the idea of her being responsible for Jake's death? And why? I didn't see the point of doing this and wasting our time…

I wrote all the details because I knew I would need them later when I had to vote. I knew that we had access to all pieces of evidence, but I needed something to remind me of my own perspective and the impact the evidence left on me the first time I encountered it.

It was essential to keep those emotions and views in check and on record because others would replace them over time. I had to contribute to the innocence or guilt of a man, so every piece counted.

Next, they called Kaitlyn Armstrong, one of Brett's coworkers from his previous job.

Caddell: Mrs. Armstrong, are you still working for Woodward Investment Group?

KA: No, sir.

Caddell: What was your position at Woodward Investments?

KA: I was an HR manager.

Caddell: Did you work there while Mr. Howe was an employee?

KA: Yes

Caddell: How was Mr. Howe's performance during the years you worked there?

KA: Brett was disciplined, intelligent, and hardworking. He never broke company policy, and his overall evaluation always exceeded expectations.

Caddell: When did he leave Woodward Investments?

KA: I believe he was let go in March 2024.

Caddell: He was fired, right?

KA: Yes

Caddell: I'm sorry, am I missing something here, Ms. Armstrong? Didn't you just say that Mr. Howe was an excellent employee?

KA: He was "laid off," not fired, due to organizational and team restructuring. The executive management was trying to reduce expenses and realign objectives. This happens quite often in the business world during financially challenging situations. However, this was not one of them.

Caddell: And why not?

KA: Because this restructuring involved laying off only one employee, Mr. Howe. In reality, the buzz in the media was the reason for his dismissal.

Next, the defense called Donna's therapist in Seattle, Roman Hahn. He described Donna as a psychotic teen, out of control, and basically damaged beyond repair. But then Laura grilled him with questions about the details of Donna's diagnosis and his efforts in working with Brett to help Donna. I was trying my best to be objective and ignore any bias I had in me against Brett or the defense team. However, Dr. Hahn did not look or sound as confident and professional as Dr. Zheng. His terminology, demeanor, and whole accusatory tone while speaking of the relationship between Donna and Dr. Angela. He kept attacking another professional in the same field, which is a big no-no in my books. You don't shine by attacking others.

As I said, the drama in the courthouse was not as intense that day. It was just the same thing being said over and over again by different people and in different situations.

The next day, we were supposed to hear from Brett himself.

I admit, it was hard to sleep that night with all the anticipation.

Twelve

Brett was tall, with hooded eyes, thin lips, a bulging belly, and glasses. Fifty percent of his hair was gray, or on the way to being gray, starting to bald in the middle. He didn't strike me as a dangerous man capable of double murder or triple possibly. I worked with men like him all the time. I passed them by on the street every day. If I hadn't known any better, I'd even mistake him for one of my dad's friends. Although he was much younger than my dad, he did look older than his age.

He didn't look at the jury, didn't look at anyone, and tried to keep a neutral face. When his attorney asked about the note and the bracelet, he cried.

Caddell: How old was Donna when you took the insurance policy?

BH: Sixteen.

Caddell: Why did you take the insurance policy on Donna's life?

BH: I was advised to do so by a friend. It guarantees insurability. It guaranteed that Donna would have coverage even if she developed a health condition later in life. This would have also allowed her to buy more coverage in the future without having to go through a medical exam. Considering her medical history and lifestyle, I was looking out for her.

Caddell: How is that?

BH: Well, after the accident, she was in a coma for about a week. The doctors were very worried and kept a close watch on her for almost six months to ensure that no permanent damage was caused due to the impact. I was thinking that I would be locking in insurability if Donna had a change in health. I mean, what if she suffered serious complications later on in life? So this sounded like a good way to guarantee her coverage over the years. It started like that, but then I saw the change in her behavior, the drastic change in character. Donna became fearless. It seemed like she wanted to punish herself for surviving the accident, and she wanted to follow her mom wherever she was. She strongly believed in the afterlife.

Laura rolled her eyes and shook her head at this.

Brett continued, "It allows you to lock in a low rate."

Then, it was Laura's turn to question Brett,

LB: Who is the beneficiary in your daughter's life insurance policy?

BH: I am.

LB: Solely?

BH: Yes.

LB: You said the rates will increase with each year of life, but you will be paying premiums over a longer period of time. Right?

BH: Still, the amount paid will be lower because the rates for a child are pretty low. The $38 monthly premium for $100,000 coverage at age zero payable to age one hundred will add up to almost $35,000 less over one hundred years than the $96 monthly premium for a thirty-year-old paid over seventy years.

LB: I see, Mr. Howe. Do you have life insurance on yourself?

She was getting frustrated.

BH: No.

LB: Huh, it seems weird to me because that would be very helpful for Donna should anything bad happen to you, especially when she has no other family members to turn to.

Brett said nothing and looked at Caddell.

LB: How much was the insurance amount you received on April 26 last year?

BH: Eight hundred thousand dollars.

LB: What did you do with that money?

BH: I paid off some of the liabilities I had.

LB: How much did you receive for the insurance policy on Anastasia Howe?

He stopped to remember or pretended to remember "300K."

LB: Why did you have a policy on your wife and not yourself?

BH: I didn't think of it at the time.

LB: How did she die?

BH: Car accident.

LB: Were you driving?

BH: No.

LB: What do you have to say about the video from Donna's LIV account?

BH: It breaks my heart that those were the last thoughts she had of me.

His voice broke, and his facial features scattered all over his face to indicate that he was crying, he pressed his index and thumb into his eye sockets but I saw no tears and I failed to sympathize. "It is not true, of course. Police and medics' reports confirm what I say. My daughter was confused and suffered mental instability all her life," he continued.

LB: Has she ever confronted you with these ideas or imaginary events, as you called them earlier?

BH: No.

LB: Never?

Laura emphasized the surprise in her tone.

BH: No.

LB: When did you take the insurance policy on Anastasia?

Brett cleared his throat. "I don't remember."

LB: I'll tell you because I did my homework too. It was forty-five days before her death.

She continued immediately.

LB: Question: in 1996, you had a similar experience, my research tells me.

BH: I don't recall.

His expression shifted. It no longer showed sadness.

LB: You had a 1991 Honda Accord that was lost in a fire, right?

BH: Yes.

LB: Did you collect any insurance money?

BH: I'm not sure. That was a long time ago.

LB: How much was the insurance payout?

BH: Like I said, I don't know.

As he said that, I saw his face without any layers of fake emotions to hide the true ones. He didn't look boring anymore. I saw a sinister expression on his face. But not for long.

LB: It was five thousand dollars, Mr. Howe. What happened to your father's home in New Jersey?

BH: We lost it in the nineties.

LB: 1998, right?

She didn't wait for an answer. "Another fire. How much did you collect this time?"

BH: A little over one hundred thousand dollars.

LB: So between the payouts from the car fire, house fire, and the deaths of your wife and daughter, you have collected nearly $1.1 million over the course of twenty-five years.

She paused for five seconds before continuing.

LB: On July 13, 2024, at 11:53 a.m., you withdrew twenty-nine thousand dollars from your bank account. Then again, on July 14, 2024, you deposited it back. Why?

BH: I was sad and nervous about Donna's disappearance, so I had a strong impulse to gamble away my fears. But I had a change of heart.

LB: So you didn't take the money because you were planning to flee?

BH: No.

LB: But you found out about Jake's then-accidental death from the papers the next morning, so you felt like you could return?

BH: No.

Caddell: Objection.

Laura continued, "That's why you stayed at a motel that Sunday close to the Canadian borders."

"No, that night I slept at home."

The CCTV footage from the motel did not show his face. The person Laura referred to as Brett was wearing a hat, and he paid with cash and signed with a fake name. So this was not solid. However, it made sense.

Brett ended with a few statements that stuck in my head.

"I love my daughter. I would never hurt her."

"I didn't know Jacob all that well. Why would I kill him?"

"Donna was troubled and couldn't live with the survivor's guilt. That's why she wanted to punish the both of us."

"I know I am sick. I need help." Referring to his gambling problems.

The next day, Jan 16, both sides delivered their closing statements.

By then, I had already made my mind up after listening to all the witnesses. Those final comments would not change much, but I was adamant about keeping an open mind.

Thirteen

When I think about my time as a juror, I miss it. I miss those relaxing evenings, not worrying about my cellphone ringing or messages or emails coming through, not worrying about my existing or potential clients and how to make them happy.

The evenings were my favorite part of this experience.

As the day when we had to leave the court and the sequestered life was approaching, I was getting more nervous about facing the reality of my situation, like telling my boyfriend about the baby and deciding what to do about it.

"Do you think he's going to propose?" Rosa asked on the speakerphone. I looked at Officer Harris; he was not as good as the jury at keeping his face expressionless. He almost rolled his eyes at the question, which made me even more nervous. I hated sounding needy. I didn't want anything to make me look any less independent.

Serving as a juror changed my perspective. And I can't help but believe that it had been placed in my path to help me see my life through a new lens and perhaps find a new frame that sat the structure and accented its beauty and meaning.

There were days when so much was taken out of me, I literally had to come to the hotel room, which was my home for two weeks, and zone out. I thought about the case constantly and went over every fact, piece of evidence, and testimony I heard that day.

I got to know eleven strangers in a very intimate setting. Every night when we settled in the hotel, it felt like we were on vacation. It somehow reminded me of the time I went to the Bahamas with my sister for three days, and it rained constantly. At first, we thought it was a bummer, but then we got to make the most out of the amenities at the Atlantis. Seeing the same faces multiple times throughout our stay at Starbucks in the morning as we were getting our coffees or at the comedy club or the movie theater at the resort bore many similarities to this experience, believe it or not.

As a jury member, I spent almost two weeks eating meals and talking about families, jobs, and pets because we couldn't talk about the case until it was time to deliberate. We formed a genuine bond because we shared a big responsibility toward the victims, their families, the community, and the future of our country.

When my time as a juror came to an end, it was bittersweet. It wasn't easy or fun, but I put in time and effort. Before heading back to my reality, I needed to see this through and make sure that justice was served.

I went in with the right attitude, took it seriously, learned something from it, and appreciated the opportunity to perform my civic duty while keeping in mind that people's lives and futures were on the line.

The most important moment of our trial was only hours away.

We were about to take our seats in the jury box for the thirteenth day.

"Members of the jury," said our judge. "Every so often, there are unknown facts, but we've heard all the witnesses and now must evaluate the facts, their credibility, and whether you think they make sense."

"The prosecution must prove the defendant's guilt beyond a reasonable doubt," he reminded us. "It is your duty to return the final decisions."

The friendly usher led us out of the courtroom, down a corridor, and into a deliberation room. In the middle of the room was a big rectangular table, fifteen chairs, and a window looking out onto the street.

Ben started, "Do we want to start with a vote and work our way back?"

Myron: "I think we should discuss the evidence and our take on the statements, then we can take a vote."

"Who shall lead the deliberations? You know, to keep the order in check," Andy asked.

"Sophie," three different voices went at the same time. Sophie looked around, raised her eyebrows, and smiled like she appreciated the trust we had collectively put in her, but at the same time, it was obvious she expected it.

I agreed. We all loved Sophie. She was a retired admin assistant in her sixties, sweet, wise, calm, and always friendly. She would have made a very successful talk show host; she knew how to carry a conversation better than anyone. She used to work in the admin office at the University of Chicago before retiring in Washington.

We started our discussion. It went on for almost seven hours. We needed a unanimous vote for the verdict, and we had eleven in agreement.

Only one thought Brett was guilty, and that was me…

I couldn't believe it. I thought the evidence was overwhelming. But apparently, they all agreed that yes, he lied about his whereabouts, but nothing put a weapon in his hand and placed him where Donna and Jake were killed at the time of the murders.

In her closing arguments, Laura Beeson wanted to emphasize the importance of the CCTV recording at the hotel where the finance conference took place and which Brett was attending. It showed him leaving the hotel at eight thirty a.m. and returning at eleven forty-five. The prosecution stated that he left, killed Donna, went back up to his room, cleaned himself, and returned to the conference room. He was wearing a black suit and a white shirt, an easy-to-replace-without-noticing kind of outfit.

Laura Beeson argued that this showed premeditation because he booked the room two weeks before the incident. The Finance Conference finished at five p.m., and the next day, the session started at nine a.m. and ended again at five p.m., so Brett had enough time to go back home since the drive would have taken between thirty to forty-five minutes, depending on traffic. Why book a room unless he wanted to establish an alibi and clean himself after the murder?

She said his urgency in repaying his debts made him organize these search parties, not his genuine concern for Donna's well-being because the insurance company would not pay the amount unless the death was confirmed.

It all fell into place and made perfect sense. But it seemed that I was the only one who saw things this way.

And no one chose to listen to Donna's version of the events in 2015.

"Surely I'm not going to put someone behind bars for the rest of their lives just because a ten-year-old thinks she saw something, keeping in mind her serious head injury during the accident," Ben said.

"Fine. Let's disregard everything that 'poor crazy little girl' said," I mocked, fully aware of how obnoxious I sounded as I ignored the raised eyebrows and side looks from everyone. "What about his pathetic excuse for leaving that crucial finance conference he paid, what, one hundred and fifty bucks to attend, plus the cost of a hotel room? And he left mid-session? Right around the same time Donna died?"

"But he said that he left the conference to get his laptop, which he had forgotten at home that day," Maura said. "It's more believable that he stepped out to get his laptop rather than kill his daughter and come back."

"Yes, someone killed Donna, but there is no solid evidence that it was Brett. That's all that smart watch activity is telling us. My money is on a drug deal gone south," Jim said.

"I know we're not supposed to judge the character of the victims, but her LIV posts are weeeirdddd! It tells me she was not right in the head," Mita says.

What? She sounded like a talented kid to me! How could I be so off!

"She even tried to attack her friend at the store. She had a violent side for sure," Mita continues.

"To me, Brett is a psychopath who shows no remorse for his actions and used social media platforms to promote a certain image as a victim, a concerned parent, even posing in crimebc.com forums with multiple user IDs to defend himself," I said. "He's using his dull looks, uninteresting lifestyle, and boring personality to his advantage to position himself among the masses."

Nobody answered, and I saw Mita and Ben exchange a look as if to say, "What the hell is she on about?" I felt like I was in a study group, and everyone was trying to explain the not-so-complicated math equation to the dumb member.

"He even continued to message Donna when he knew she was dead. He was determined to throw everybody off!"

Finally, Ben said, "The only thing that holds weight here is the trail of insurance policies he had compiled over the years. But again ... with no weapon, no confession, and not enough physical evidence, I can't just assume that he killed his daughter and the neighbor's kid."

I got so agitated. I knew it was unprofessional on my part, but I kind of raised my voice when I spoke next.

"He abused society's trust in him, committing insurance fraud. He was a disappointment as a father; he exposed his daughter to an unhealthy way of living by isolating her from everyone and then to unconventional ways of treatment and subjecting her body to constant medical substances throughout her adolescence. A time when she is most tender emotionally, physically, and mentally, let alone when diagnosed with PTSD."

No one made eye contact with me. They disagreed and didn't want to fight with the arrogant bitch who was all talk and no substance, so into her looks and covered with luxury brands, her opinion carried no weight. I tried one last time, "Try to keep an open mind ... for the weak."

In reality, the world is a very harsh place for those who represent a fraction of the masses.

No one wanted to listen to a troubled young girl as if her mental issues made her words unintelligible. I was discussing my doubts and the evidence before me, not trying to convince others of Brett's guilt but looking for the answers in their reasoning.

I couldn't find their arguments convincing.

The deliberations lasted for three days.

On the third day as I left the meeting room, I passed Mita on my way out. I extended my hand to shake hers, she reluctantly reciprocated the gesture and huffed a sarcastic "Thank you."

I overheard someone say, I think it was Ben, "well, there's always one of those, ha"

They all shook hands but nobody wanted to shake mine, they were angry at me. Sophie wouldn't even look in my direction.

Nobody else seemed to think that Brett was guilty.

Fine. I have my insecurities, and I have my flaws, but being a pushover is not one of them. Never. That's how my dad raised me and my sister and that's how Rose made sure I faced my predicaments. That's why I maintained my vote. I was keeping an open mind. I was giving the court another chance to look into this case; and if the next twelve jurors think he is not guilty, well, then at least it'll be twenty three against one; and

I'll feel bad maybe about wasting everyone's time, but it won't compare to how bad I would have felt if I had caved only to find out that Brett had been actually guilty. With that in mind, I stood alone and decided to own the "Bitch" label.

I dreaded the moment we were going to tell the world our decision.

We were in the courtroom again. The judge read a statement from us the jury, in a nutshell it said, we tried, but couldn't agree and not because there was a "lack of effort" but due to "adherence to individual principles and moral convictions."

The judge looked our way thanked us and said "I'm declaring a mistrial."

I didn't want to look Caleb in the eye. I kept my focus on the judge. I tried not to look when the words came out of the judge's mouth.

But when the moment came, I did look; I couldn't help myself.

I saw the look of hurt and surprise. I heard the commotion. And I couldn't control it anymore ... I ran to the bathroom and threw up.

PART EIGHT

Caleb Bodkin
Aug 14

Dear Jake,

My therapist told me to write to you. I still see it as a desperate attempt at closure, but you know what? Why the hell not.

It's Saturday. The clock turns three p.m. It's time for another visit.

I just took Fenrir for a walk, fed him, and left. He's trying to adjust to living in the small space of my Seattle apartment.

With me, I packed my smoothie (soy milk, kiwi, and banana), my reading material, AirPods, my phone, and my wallet. I set off to the Swedish Medical Center in Seattle. It is a short fifteen-minute Uber ride. I got there, and I greeted everyone. They know me on a first-name basis by now. I've been coming here for the past four months. This time, I got them a box of donuts and a Box O'Joe from Dunkin.

"Hi, there," I said to Sandra Fischer.

"Hello, Caleb. Looking great this afternoon." Her face lit up when she saw me, as usual. I can tell she adores me. I'm like the good grandson who gets her freebies with every visit.

"Thank you, Sandra. Is he available for a visit?"

"Well, we both know he's not going anywhere, dear," she says with a warm, sympathetic smile. "I don't think it's going to be much longer now."

I froze, unsure if I was ready for this. My face must have shown the uncertainty I felt because Sandra had a worried look on her face.

"I think what you're doing is brave, and if you were my kid, I'd be very proud to have raised such a wonderful soul."

"Aww, if you keep saying that, I might start believing you."

We both laughed at my cheesy joke; I guess it was easy to impress someone from a different time.

I moved on to room 4012. It's where they keep the dying body of Brett Howe.

After the mistrial, Brett returned to jail to await the retrial scheduled for two months later. He was beaten up multiple times but eventually managed to form some sort of an alliance with one of the inmates, who helped him stockpile antidepressant pills taken from others. He eventually gathered both the pills and the nerve to go through with the suicide—an act that seemed wildly out of character for a coward like him.

On April 6, Brett attempted to kill himself, but he didn't die. Instead, he went into a coma.

Before taking those pills, he asked his lawyer to mail me a box. When I opened it, I found your lost Seahawks hat, a stack of letters titled "Message in Blood," and a cartoon ghost keychain, the same one I saw in our garage. He didn't give me details but confessed to killing you, Donna, and Anastasia (Annie).

His motive behind killing Donna and Anastasia was money. On the other hand, he killed you because you found out about Brett's intentions to kill Donna. We saw from the recording on Donna's LIV that she feared her father would kill her for the insurance money, the same way he did her mother years ago. Brett didn't know about those videos back then. So, how did he know to go after you?

I understand now that you were following Brett's posts on the online group for parents of troubled teens. On July 12, you read the post by Brett in which he said that Donna was missing. You were worried and texted Donna. Brett had her phone. Imagine his shock when he found out that you knew his dark past and his even darker plans for the future. During your confrontation in my parents' garage, Brett realized that he simply needed one last kill to completely seal this dark chapter.

"I decided to be a good person. This is a huge task for a person like me, god knows! So you know what I do when I have a big project ahead of me? I break it down into smaller, easy-to-digest bites and take each one at a time. Like an opera with multiple scenes, I am about to write the final act. In the first scene, I take the poison and wash my filthy soul away."

I gave his confession to the police. Glenn later told me that they investigated the crimes he referenced in these letters, including an incident that involved a bar owner who operated gambling machines illegally at his bar for years in Sayreville, NJ. Denis Maurer was arrested in 1989 for running illegal gambling operations. He was paralyzed in one arm and had partial vision in one of his eyes. In the interviews with the police, he talked about being attacked by a teenager one night. The teen struck Maurer on the head after an argument. The man suffered nerve damage, resulting in paralysis in his right arm. He was fifty-two when that happened and died nine years after the incident. He probably never reported the attack because he didn't want to be exposed for his illegal activities.

Before Brett sent me these letters, we were all stuck in limbo. We couldn't move on, not when things kept taking a turn for the worse. Our parents divorced, and your killer was still at large. I also felt bad for Donna. Yet, a part of me was happy because I could understand you again. It all made sense, then. You were still the caring, loving, smart, ambitious kid. Your charm made Donna open up, and you inspired her to live and make something out of her hidden talents. She was a gifted poet, by the way.

The details that were revealed during the court hearings were devastating. The whole world watched, commented, and prayed for justice, except for the twelve jurors who decided that Brett's involvement was not as clear as broad daylight.

Sorry, eleven, there was one member who made her vote based on common sense. Molly Martinez had her fifteen minutes of fame because she was the only juror who believed Brett did it. Good for her, I guess. Because of her Brett didn't walk out a free man. I plan to send her a "thank you" letter.

Dad's relationship with Jessica Bartlett helped him, I have to admit. I was so mad at him at first, but then I realized that no matter what the cause was, she made him happy. As happy as you can be when you lose your favorite son. They live in a two-bedroom apartment in Seattle now. I went to visit them once since they moved in together. Claire and Tobey talked me into trying to make amends.

Our mother moved to San Francisco; she focuses on her job and lives close to our aunt. I talk to her daily to check on her. Next week, she will meet my girlfriend for the first time. Claire is awesome. I talk to Mom about her all the time. While I do care for Claire so much, I also feel like she's a positive topic to speak to Mom about. Whenever I mention Claire, Mom changes her tone into a bright one, which I've missed so much. A tone I haven't heard since you were alive.

Everyone thinks that our mother is tough and is making the best out of this tragedy. They think about the scholarship under your name, which she gives at Full Sail for three thousand dollars. They think about her extraordinary successful record at her new job, where she exceeded expectations within the first fifteen months under the crazy circumstances she had to endure. But they don't see what happens when she is alone in her beautiful apartment. She lost her family, not just her youngest kid. She and Dad could no longer coexist, and it wasn't only because of the affair he was having. The affair was a result of that. So, I keep checking on her and hope she will find love again. But I doubt that will ever happen. Your murder has completely shattered her soul. She has no more energy to love anything new.

Your signature Seahawks hat, the one I was looking for all this time, was soaked in blood. He took it because it was stuck to the murder weapon, an axe of some sort. It had his DNA, too.

"I took it in the heat of the moment. I was too nervous, and blood was everywhere. I freaked out. I want to spare you the painful details. And I want to tell you that the blow on Jake's head was fast and pain-free, but we both know I can't tell that lie; we all saw his Phantom video.

"Yes, that lawyer was right. I was about to flee the country and go to the middle of nowhere in rural Canada. But imagine my surprise when I read the news about the 'stunt gone wrong' the next day."

The keychain was a gift from his late wife, Anastasia. It mimicked a tattoo that she had. "She got it one night in college while we were both too drunk." He had always kept it, which was why he returned to our garage months after he killed you.

So his letters just confirmed that he got away with murder ... more than once.

His doctor told me the first time I went to see him, "You never know; his brain might still be processing your voice and what you tell him. So try to speak to him, and maybe you'll find the closure you're looking for."

Two weeks ago, when I thought I saw a frown on Brett's face, Sandra told me, "We had one patient a couple of years ago who was in a coma for over a year. His mom would come every single day and talk to him. Every single day until he woke up! You never know when, but miracles do happen."

I stare at his face and keep remembering your funeral, the way he was crying. I remember thinking what a nice guy. The tears were genuine, he told me in one of his letters. "I cried because here I was attending the neighbor's kid funeral while mine was left in a ditch for the stray animals to feed on."

I visit him twice a week, and I read to him. I read his confessions. I read Donna's poetry. I play your music and Fiona Apple.

In his letters, he mentioned on numerous occasions that he has a fear of Russian folklore and fairy tales. He even had a few books at his house. I think they were a gift from his grandmother. Glenn helped me to get all of these books.

So these days, when I go to see him at the hospital, I focus on the stories that scared him the most, like the Rusalka, a malevolent nymph who was said to lure men to their watery deaths or even tickle them to death in some versions. Weird, I know.

There is a wide belief that people in a coma can still hear. Therefore, it is assumed that even while a person may not have the ability to speak, they may continue to feel pain or anguish, even if they cannot express those feelings.

Whatever is on the other side, wherever he might be, I want to reach out. I want to use his senses and whatever is left of his brain cells to weave the ghosts and monsters that shall create his hell. When I sit there and start reading those children's books to him, it might look sweet to the nurses and the doctors who pass by or the security guard on watch. They might think me an angel for caring for this outcast when he had ruined my life.

His letters contain a great deal of fucked up info about him and his family. I wonder how the jury never saw him as a criminal. How did he get away with it? The story was whole, and it all added up. But I guess ghosts exist, and he was one of them ... He committed all these crimes, and none could be traced back to him. Who could pull off something like that? Only a ghost could!

I hope that I am slowly and silently killing him.

I am hoping he is stuck somewhere dark, dying slowly and painfully.

Last week, I noticed a small sound in his breathing. It's kind of like a hoarse, wet sound. Yesterday, it was much worse and significantly louder. It sounded something between a snore and a deep gurgle. He had mini seizures or reflexes like he was choking. The nurses came in a few times, and I was asked to leave.

That's why I made an exception today, and I showed up for the third time this week.

I came to listen to the death rattle.

I stopped reading and listened in carefully. His breathing became shallow. The intervals between each intake of air into his lungs became longer and longer.

I counted. During this minute, he gasped for air only three times...

Eventually, he stopped. I saw froth around his mouth and nostrils. The nurse rushed in and asked me to leave. A doctor followed. A few moments later, the doctor announced him dead.

Finally, I was able to walk.

I try to live. Every day.

I go out with friends, work hard, and support my parents by talking and visiting.

It all feels forced and wrong.

I keep thinking that in thirty years, my face will physically change as I become older, but the memory of my brother's face will stay young. And

THE SOUND OF TUNING OUT

then I have agonizing thoughts like how my future kids won't know their one and only uncle.

Your Phantom account has shared a memory of us. A recording of one of our raids from 2015 from Destiny. I know why you shared this particular recording:

We'd been playing for a few hours, so we were all saying that we should probably call it a night as it was late, and I had a driving lesson early the following day. Before going into battle with Oryx (the toughest boss fight), we decided to stop for a quick break so some of us could get a drink, use the restroom, etc. Suddenly, one of our titans began to walk straight ahead until he eventually hit a wall. It looked like he was lagging. We tried to check with him, but there was no response, and he still showed as AFK. Then we heard him snoring through his mic. He had probably fallen asleep on his controller. After a while, his mom woke him up, yelling at him for staying up late. It was so funny.

I was tagged in that memory, which meant I could share it on my own stories on LIV, so I did. I decided to write for the first time about us. Our fun times that belong on screens or some faded side of my brain. The caption said,

"Jake, I miss you ... a lot. I sometimes race your ghost on Wreckfest. I never beat your record, so I can always play with you and see you in game..."

I didn't read any comments. It was hard to read through the blur of my vision.

#21 Floods

I've been driving for so long now ... I lost track of time.

I crossed the Canadian borders about an hour ago. Not much more is left. I can feel it rather than see it.

Home is near.

I pass countless farmlands, river valleys, grasslands, forests, and lakes. It is beautiful and serene out here. I feel so alone and at peace. The sky is full of clouds, with the sunset shade casting an orange filter on everything.

It is a lot colder than I had expected. I need to stop somewhere to grab my jacket from my luggage. The heating system is not working in this old piece of junk. I'm glad I don't have to worry about it anymore. The radio keeps going off playing that stupid podcast from the gambling support group. I disconnect my phone from the car's sound system and opt for the radio. More depressing songs by the same artist. I can't recall her name, but I am sure she was a favorite of my roommate in college, or was it a friend from work? I can't remember. I turn it off.

I stop at a crossing. No one is there, but I don't want to break any rules. This is a new beginning. I am here on a clean slate in a foreign land and want to keep it that way. I stop for a bit too long as I mentally time-travel through different stops in my miserable life. A journey of wasted money, youth, and lives ... I feel numb, unaware of my own limbs, and unable to move a muscle. Silence stretches for far too long, and I feel like I am floating beyond what I see, flying above the clouds, looking down on my home, and drifting away from this dream, just like all the other dreams and fantasies I have lived throughout the years.

A sickening thud cuts my wings and brings me down to where I am in my beat-up car. An ugly bird has hit the windshield ... It looks hurt. It is barely moving, shivering there on my hood.

I never liked birds, and I am not going to start now.

I step out of my car and toss its fragile body all the way into the endless fields.

I wipe the remainder of the bird's blood on the sides of my pants and try to open my car when I catch a subtle movement in the distance. Someone is walking in the fields. It looks like a woman; maybe she's a farmer ... I try to fix my gaze on her; she doesn't look right. Is she drunk? As I squint, trying to see what is up with her, my fear builds up, so I backtrack and drive away.

My curiosity starts to fade as her figure grows smaller in my rearview mirror.

Remember, no more weird shit. I get in my car and drive.

It's not long until I get to my beautiful tiny heap of a wreck that I plan to fix into a comfortable home.

It's getting significantly and quickly darker.

Daylight is reduced to a few streaks in the dark skies above me. The road is empty, with no lights but the reflection of my headlights on the studs on the ground. I can still see silhouettes of scattered buildings with hues of colors on the brick.

I cross a narrow road surrounded by big trees with high branches covered in thick leaves. Their dark green looks black against the faintly lit sky.

Once the trees clear out, I drive over a small bridge; beneath me is a river or a creek. And then I see it. I have reached my destination—a small brown building abandoned with not more than two or three bedrooms. I scan the building for damages and required repairs as I quickly park my car in the property's parking area.

To turn this glorified shed into a cozy, livable space, I must fix the broken windows and back door and check the sewage system and other water fixtures. Maybe I'll farm some pigs, chickens, cows ... some vegetables, even grow pretty flowers ... who knows?

One step at a time.

I walk into the house. Two bedrooms, a small living area, a kitchen, and one bathroom. It's small, but it is more than enough. I can build a secluded, lovely haven where no one can bother me.

There are three wooden chairs, a coffee table, and a small dining table in the kitchen with two more chairs. There are no curtains, and I doubt there are any electricity wirings here. As expected, this will take time and energy to fix, but I've got plenty of both.

I decide to check the bedrooms. The first room is completely empty except for a wooden frame with a picture of a family. A father, a mother, and a little girl.

I go to the next room there. At first, I see nothing but a small leather chair and a matching ottoman. The leather is torn, and the color has faded, leaving patches of ugly nothingness—a color I cannot describe except the absence of any character or flavor. If death were a color, that would be it.

And then, I hear the sound of the wall breathing, and I see her ... she could almost fade into the gray walls of this miserable room. Like a chameleon, she blends in with the surroundings, and suddenly, I realize that the whole house is that hideous color of emptiness.

"Hello there," she says. "I've been waiting for you."

"Do I know you?" I ask.

She looks familiar, but I don't know where I met her.

"You've been stalling for no reason. You should have been here a long time ago."

"Who are you?" I ask her again.

She smiles. But somehow, her expression grows darker, and her features start to fade into her melting face of gray goo. "You're wrong, you know. This is not the place for new beginnings. This is the aftermath," she says.

All her features are being forced inwards into the back of her skull, but her blue eyes remain fixed on mine.

I hear noises in the distance ... like someone is laughing, almost cackling, and what sounds like strong waves crashing onto rocks.

Weird, since the ocean is nowhere near this town.

Fear rocks my insides like an electric shock...

"Do you remember how to swim?"

I'm crying as I slowly start to recognize the girl with pale gray skin and deep blue eyes.

"Are you a ghost?" I ask her. My voice is barely audible.

"Look who's talking..." She laughs and laughs for what feels like a lifetime. "My dear ghost," she says in a voice that is not her own. She sounds like my mother, and with that, a memory so vivid comes to me. It feels like I am back in my mother's old bedroom, reading her suicide letter. Fragments of her words start coming back to me: "My dear little ghost ... I pity you ... It is hard to be invisible..."

"We don't have memories here ... we only have to travel through the path," she says.

I am aware of everything now. I remember everything. I don't really remember. It is more like I am present in the path I walked through at every second of my life, present and aware of every event, action, and emotion.

"I miss you. I'm sorry," I say as I whimper, feeling so weak and heavy.

"I'm only here to watch." She sounds angry.

I see a figure pass by the window quickly, and I hear banging on the front door. Then it swings open, and someone comes in laughing hysterically. Footsteps approach the room.

As my eyes are fixed on the door expectantly, I steal a glimpse of the girl standing by the wall. She is oddly still; her eyes are on me with an unblinking gaze.

"What are you doing here?" I ask her, and I notice that the whole room is shifting. She is melting into the wall. I can no longer see her body, only her face remains darkened with anger. Her face is being pulled away into the gray wall, which does not look like a wall anymore. It is one big wave that is about to crash over me.

"The question is, what are you doing here?" she says. She sounds like thunder, so loud and angry.

I can't see but rather feel something coming for me.

The door to the room opens. Just a crack. It shows complete darkness, and somehow the darkness is spilling into the room like a thick liquid. As it comes nearer, I start to make out a face.

I recognize fragments of it, all wet and laughing ... coming ... longing.

I see the same smile I saw when I ran away from Mr. Smith and again when I ran out of the motel room.

As it extends an arm, I see a ghost on the back of the wrist.

About the author

Shane W. O'Haire is a mystery-thriller author, and The Sound of Tuning Out is their debut novel.

Printed in Great Britain
by Amazon